The Secret Life of Anna Blanc

THE SECRET LIFE of ANNA BLANC

JENNIFER KINCHELOE

SEVENTH STREET BOOKS®
AN IMPRINT OF PROMETHEUS BOOKS
59 JOHN GLENN DRIVE • AMHERST, NY 14228
www.seventhstreetbooks.com

Published 2015 by Seventh Street Books®, an imprint of Prometheus Books

Cover design by Nicole Sommer-Lecht
Cover image © David et Myrtille / Trevillion Images

This is a work of fiction. Characters, organizations, products, locales, and events portrayed in this novel either are products of my imagination or are used fictitiously. I took some liberties for the sake of the story. Some books and songs were released a year or two later than 1907, when the novel takes place. For example, the book *The Circular Staircase* and the song *Harvest Moon* were not published until 1908. Emma Summers and the Boyle Heights Rape Fiend were real people, but the details of their lives have been changed for the sake of this story. The character of Anna Blanc bears some resemblance to Fanny Bixby, one of California's richest young women, who became a police matron in Long Beach in 1907. However, this resemblance is purely coincidental. I learned about Fanny Bixby after I wrote the book. The novel was actually inspired by police matron Alice Stebbins Wells, who in 1910 became the first woman police officer in Los Angeles. She was nothing like Anna Blanc.

Inquiries should be addressed to
Seventh Street Books
59 John Glenn Drive
Amherst, New York 14228
VOICE: 716–691–0133
FAX: 716–691–0137
WWW.SEVENTHSTREETBOOKS.COM

19 18 17 16 15   5 4 3 2 1

Library of Congress Cataloging-in-Publication Data Pending

ISBN 978-1-63388-080-1 (pbk)
ISBN 978-1-63388-081-8 (ebook)

Printed in the United States of America

For Jonathan, Samara, and Seamus,
who mean more to me than the entire Western canon.
And for my mother, Sandy, who told me I could do anything.

Chapter 1

Los Angeles, 1907

Anna Blanc wore a six-inch hairpiece made from the tresses of a yak. She had crowned the abundant puffs and curls with the largest ostrich feather hat in Los Angeles. The look was dramatic, the latest from Vionnet at the House of Doucet, and a terrible choice when running for a train. She sprinted along the moonlit tracks, her big hair bun bouncing, her feathers shaking, her satin gown trailing an undignified sprig of rosemary snagged from the bush where she'd been hiding. Above her, the majestic dome of La Grande Station rose from the expanse of dust and steel, menacing her like some giant guardian of propriety. As she flew past a palm tree, her veil caught on a frond and tore, revealing an eye, a nose, a cheek. "Biscuits!" she swore.

It had occurred to Anna that she should wait to board the train until the last possible moment, so it would be harder for any pursuer to drag her back off. But, just as the last passengers were stepping on board the late-night train, and Louis Taylor was waving frantically from a car window, two men had approached from the tracks carrying a tin bathtub. One was very thin. One was a cop. This gave Anna pause. She had always admired policemen and wanted to be one, but not this one. His face was scarred, like he had been mauled by a dog. More importantly, he might have come to hunt Anna but had gotten hung up by whatever was in the tub, in which case she needed to stay in the bushes.

As they passed closer to Anna, beneath a sputtering gaslight, she rose on tiptoes, peeking through the leaves of a hibiscus bush, and saw a large, lumpy sack oozing in the tub. It looked violent and disgusting and made her feel ill. It could be a deer, but she thought not. No one called the police when a train hit an animal. It had to be a corpse, likely a woman or a child, because the lumps were too small to be a man . . . unless parts were missing. She resented the sickening lumps for turning her stomach on this most special of all nights.

By the time the policeman had left, the train was rolling. Anna popped from the bush. She charged through the warm December night in glamorous shoes, her taffeta petticoats thrashing down the rails. She felt the rumble of the locomotive in her pounding pulse. It belched black smoke, filling her panting, petal lips with grit, showering her with dirty ash.

Louis hung from the door of the car, bareheaded, reaching for her as she sprinted, his eyes bulging, his tongue tip pasted to the corner of his mouth, his striped, silk necktie flapping in the wind. She grabbed his hand and leapt, losing one François Pinet shoe.

Louis leaned against the oak paneled wall, sweating, heart pounding, and exhaled deeply, as if he'd been holding his breath. He grabbed a perfect Homburg hat from the luggage rack and flipped it on. "So much for a quiet departure. There wasn't a person at the station who didn't see you board."

Anna collapsed against the wall next to him, her mind racing with dangerous possibilities. "He might find out I was on the train, but he won't know where I got off." Even as she said it, she didn't believe it. She half believed that there was nowhere beyond the reach of her father, the man who restricted her freedoms, down to the very books she read. She felt a quivering panic in her chest, and wetness spread under her arms. She looked down at her shoeless foot and made a little sound of distress.

Louis took her arm and cooed, "Don't fret, darling. Your father can't stop us from marrying, you know. It's the twentieth century, and he isn't in France anymore. This is Los Angeles."

She looked up, dread clouding her grey eyes. "You have no idea what he can do."

Louis raised one eyebrow, which, together with his spanking fine mustache, looked very debonair. "Darling, once the deed is done, it's done."

The car insides were cozy, like a nice hotel, with polished wood, vaulted ceilings, and emerald velvet seats. Anna scanned the faces on her getaway train. To her relief, she recognized no one among the traveling suits and black derbies. She barely recognized Louis, whom she'd spoken to only twice, though they'd attended the same balls and exchanged a dozen mushy letters. They'd kept their affair entirely secret.

Anna's father set a high price on her beauty, and would just as soon keep her as an ornament, like a prized Ming Vase, as relinquish her to another man. He'd driven away every suitor who had shown up on his doorstep with violets and honorable intentions. This being widely known, Louis had taken a different approach. He'd delivered his passionate declarations through Anna's friend Clara, while studiously ignoring Anna in public and never coming to call.

Anna limped on one heeled shoe as Louis urged her down the aisle to an empty row at the back of the car. He walked so closely behind her that when she swayed with the train she fell against him. He had a man smell, humid and spicy, like her father's Bay Rum aftershave.

"Someone was hit by the train," she said. "That's why the train was late."

Louis shook his head. "Yes, I know. Let's not speak of it. I mean, it's not a nice topic for a lady." He raised his eyebrows hopefully. "Unless you want to."

"No. It's just . . . it's hard to get hit by a train unless you try."

He nodded soberly.

Anna would have said a prayer for the deceased, but there was no point. All suicides went to hell. Plus, suicide by train was bad manners, as someone else had to clean it up. A considerate person would take too much laudanum or something, and die in their bed, or drown at sea, so as not to inconvenience other people. She opened her mouth to say so, but Louis clapped his hands over her eyes. "Don't look."

Anna smiled indulgently. "Why not?"

"Because *my* darling is a lady."

This seemed like a bad reason for anything. Anna peeled his fingers off her eyes too late. The train was passing through a gully, and all she could see was darkness and scrub. She looked inquisitively at Louis.

He whispered, "Alameda Street. You know. The women, um, shall we say, wave at the train."

Anna took her seat, scrunching her forehead, knowing there must be more to the story. It was long past midnight. Louis slid in closer than was strictly proper, turned his face to hers, and raised his eyebrows. Their legs touched through nine blessed layers of fabric. Anna blushed. A girl was supposed to object and scoot away, but she didn't. She found she didn't mind at all. His thigh was curiously hard and warm beneath his wool trousers. What she wanted to do was touch it.

"I haven't had a single moment alone with you, and I intend to make up for it." He gazed into her eyes as if checking to see if they were green or gray or blue, and whispered, "Take off your glove."

Anna glanced up the aisle of the near-empty car and saw nothing but the backs of heads. She quickly peeled off her glove. He took her hand, hid it beneath the fold of his coat, and began to draw figure eights on her naked palm with one slow finger, sending shivers from her wrists to her lips, and to other parts.

"When the lights go out, I'm going to kiss you," he said. Anna felt like she was still sprinting for the train.

A heavy *bump, bump* made the lovers start. Anna's eyes cut to an old woman, who hobbled down the aisle, dragging a monogrammed Louis Vuitton case as cracked as her powdered face. Her dress had layers and layers of horrid black pleats and was so long out of fashion she could have worn it to Lincoln's funeral. The old lady parked herself one row in front of Anna and Louis in the otherwise empty back of the train. She turned around and stared at them from under wiry gray eyebrows. Sour old lady breath floated over the seat. Louis glared back at her. She clucked in disapproval and turned to face forward. In a few minutes, her head nodded and she began to snore, snorting in, whistling out.

Anna giggled at this a little maniacally, fueled by the excitement of running away, of holding his hand. She had never touched Louis before—or any man except her father. Not without a glove. She felt dizzy, almost drunk, sitting next to him, fingers entwined and caressing, and she had not foreseen it. As eager as she was to marry Louis, it had never been because of love. She chose him because he was well regarded, dressed well—a real Beau Brummell—and was clever enough to circumvent her possessive father. People said lots of nice things about Louis in spite of his poverty—how presentable he was, how sympathetic and well mannered, and how that rumor about his mother, which had traveled clear across the Atlantic, couldn't possibly be true.

Despite Clara's romanticizing the affair, Anna had accepted his proposal not so she could have a life with him in particular, but so she could have a different life. She'd never confess this to Clara, who loved her own husband to distraction—almost as much as she loved Anna. Good, complicit Clara, who had smuggled Anna's trunks out of the house and had them sent to Louis's apartment in Glendale.

Being with Louis now, it occurred to Anna that she didn't not-love him. And it was rather thrilling to be holding his hand, alone on a rough velvet seat, at night, in the back of a vibrating train.

When the lights finally went out, he kissed her in the dark, one soft brush of lips on lips. With dreamy, heavy eyes, he cooed, "You are the dandiest girl on earth."

Anna sighed and held her face up for another, but he placed two fingers on her puckered lips and smiled. "No more kisses," he whispered. "I'm afraid I'd cause a scandal."

Anna flushed. He'd already caused a scandal by stealing her away, and, if no one were looking, she didn't see why he shouldn't kiss her again and for longer. Instead, he removed her hat, plucking out hatpins one by one, and coaxed her cheek down onto his itchy, tweeded shoulder. Her enormous, yak-hair bun crushed against his face, but he didn't seem to mind.

"Now, go to sleep." His voice was silky and low. "I don't want you tired when I kiss you tomorrow night."

Anna bit her lip. He was even more handsome than she had thought before, like a hero in a book. His hands were so lovely caressing hers. She couldn't possibly sleep with him so near. She might never sleep again. She might actually be in love with him. Anna said a silent, sheepish prayer of thanks to Saint Valentine of Rome, patron saint of lovers, and promised to go to confession for deceiving her father and running off with a Protestant.

The train rattled through fragrant lemon groves, cool air whistling through a slightly opened window. Anna awoke to the pungent perfume, with her face pressed onto Louis's chest, one hand in his lap. His head was thrown back, mouth slightly open, his thin mustache quivering with each exhalation. She reluctantly withdrew her hand, straightened up, and, to her horror, found drool on his shirt where her mouth had been. After dabbing a trail of spit from her cheek, she adjusted her towering, lopsided hair in a hand mirror and shook him awake. He opened his eyes with a yawning, "Good morning, darling," and a crooked smile that said, "We just spent the night together." Anna matched it with one of her own.

The train made a grinding, screeching sound as it pulled into the station at Riverside. Louis gathered up his coat. "This, my queen, is the beginning of a dream come true. We're young. We have money. We finally have control of our lives."

Anna smiled, but reserved her exhilaration for when the deed was done. Louis reached out to touch her cheek. He recalled his hand as the old woman one seat up turned her eyes on him. "In my day," she said in a guttural Russian accent, "people didn't make love on trains."

Louis smirked. "In your day, madam, there were no trains."

Anna's eyes widened. She pressed her lips to prevent them from smiling, an act that she could not condone. The old woman harrumphed and looked at her old leather case. She looked at Louis, then to her bag, and back again. It was a gesture of command. Louis brushed past the old woman as if she were not there.

"In my day, gentlemen helped ladies with their bags!" the old woman called after him.

For the first time, Anna noticed the monogrammed letters on the woman's case—TLS. She smiled and bobbed. "Good day, Mrs. Smucker." Anna picked up the bag and carried it to the platform.

It was cool in the desert, though the morning sun made the bare, stony mountains golden. Anna hurried to catch up with Louis. He stood beneath a stand of fruited date palms, smoking a cigarette, waiting as a porter brought their trunks. He exhaled a stream of smoke. "Nasty old thing."

Anna rubbed her arms beneath her satin wrap. "Shhh, Louis. She's not some laundress. Her son's the mayor of Los Angeles."

"You know her?"

"Not by sight, but I know Mayor Smucker has a home in Riverside. His daughter Tasha, who was in my class, is named after her paternal grandmother. Tasha is a Russian name—like Natasha in *War and Peace*. This woman rolls her *r*s like a Russian. I know the mayor's mother has a very hard time keeping servants . . ."

Louis gave Anna a sideways smile. "Clara warned me about this."

Anna's words tumbled out with increasing speed. "The mayor's housekeeper calls our housekeeper every few weeks in search of new staff for his mother. It's sort of a joke among the servants. Even a bad-tempered person can keep staff if she pays them well, so let's suppose that she does not pay them well. She certainly has the money. So, let's say she's a miser. This woman's bag is worn past respectability, but it's a Louis Vuitton and cost a bundle. Her dress, too, was expensive, last century. This suggests either a change in fortune, or that its owner does not care to spend the money to replace it. I favor the latter explanation as her bag is monogrammed TS—Tasha Smucker." Anna took a deep breath. "Which has no ring to it, whatsoever. I could never marry a man named Smucker."

Louis grinned and hailed a cab. "Then I'm lucky I'm not named Smucker."

The cab driver motored Anna and Louis through streets lined with feathered palms to the Mission Inn. The hotel catered to the East Coast rich, who came in droves to winter in sunshine and to see about their lucrative citrus groves. Louis chose it not only because it was fashionable, but because it had a chapel. It reminded Anna of a Spanish castle, with its wrought iron railings and gardens of purple bougainvillea. It dripped with bells. Anna stared up at the dozens of campañas adorning every arch, tower, and alcove beneath the red tile roof and wondered if they would ring for her when she was pronounced Mrs. Louis Taylor.

The couple passed through towering oak doors into the grand lobby. They strolled arm in arm, Anna hobbling on one shoe, ostrich feathers bobbing, her coat sooty, her satin frock looking slept in, her big hair tipping south. A fourteen-foot Christmas tree scented the room, adorned with baubles and tiny candles, waiting to be lit. There were bowls of oranges, red poinsettias, and elegant guests reading newspapers in leather chairs.

Louis sauntered up to a marble counter, wearing Anna like a badge of honor. "Mr. and Mrs. Louis Taylor. We have the honeymoon suite."

The clerk took in the couple with one broad stroke. He frowned his disapproval. "Welcome, Mr. . . . I'm sorry."

"Taylor," Louis said.

The clerk found the name on a list and handed Louis a pen to sign the register. "I see you've reserved the chapel, Mr. and *Mrs.* Taylor."

Somewhere in the lobby behind them, two men began a conversation. Anna heard snippets.

". . . California has her grip on me . . . I bought citrus farms . . ."

"Riverside's a world away from Boston . . ."

". . . my home's being built in Los Angeles."

"Following the oil? The oil money? You and everybody else. We're finding our place in the world. First city with electric lights. The streetcars are the best in the nation. Telephone system, too . . ."

". . . I'm just here for the weather and the fruit . . ."

Anna didn't care at all about their conversation or why so many people were coming to Los Angeles, making her city spread out like spilled lemonade. She was giggling at Louis who, reluctant to let go of her, was trying to sign the register with his left hand, having first nearly overturned the inkpot. He finished with an exaggerated flourish, grinning at his almost-wife. She hadn't realized he was so charming.

The clerk turned his back to Louis and picked up a telephone. Louis cleared his throat, "I'm on my honeymoon, sir, and I'd rather not spend it in the lobby, if you know what I mean."

Without turning, the clerk raised one heavy hand, indicating that Louis should wait.

"If you would just provide us with the key . . ." Louis said.

The clerk frowned and hung up the phone. "I'll be very happy to provide you a key, sir, once you've paid."

Louis looked to Anna. She had told him they could have the bill sent to her father.

"You want us to pay in advance? We never pay in advance," Anna said. It was true. The Blancs always had a tab.

"Forgive me," the clerk said. "I'm not acquainted with the Mr. Louis Taylors of—where did you say you were from?"

"You have nerve!" Louis said, though the clerk's suspicions were entirely founded.

"Are you familiar with the Blancs of Los Angeles? You can send the bill to Christopher Blanc. He's my father," Anna said.

The clerk replied evenly, "Shall I call Mr. Blanc—just to tell him you've arrived safely?"

"No!" Anna's exclamation echoed off the tile and faded into an uncomfortable silence. The clerk pressed his priggish lips.

A man's smooth voice came from behind her. "I can vouch for them. This charming lady *is* Anna Blanc, and I'm sure her father is good for it."

The clerk's demeanor turned like a well-trained horse on a five-cent piece. He handed Louis the key and bowed to the disheveled couple. "I'm sorry, sir."

Anna untwined her arm from Louis's, her face as cool and white as the marble counter. She'd rather sleep in the desert than be helped by an ersatz friend who would give them away, accidentally or otherwise. She turned to face the threat and sized the man up the way a lady should—that is, without seeming to. He was well bred, barely noticing her shoeless foot and the toes sticking out of her stocking. His accent said East Coast. He must be important, to be shown such deference by the desk clerk. He was not a politician or a businessman. He didn't have the doughy look of a man who worked long hours. He must simply be very rich. His clothes were perfect, his dark curls slicked back. He was toweringly tall and handsome. She searched her memory for his person and came up blank.

"It's Miss . . . Mrs. . . . Taylor. You are . . . You know my father. Of course. He introduced us at . . ." She extended her hand and waited for him to fill in the blanks.

He smiled at her with the sweetness of a boy on the brink of adolescence, though he had to be thirty. "Edgar Wright." He took her hand and then extended his hand to Louis. "Of course I know your father. Everyone does." He smiled some more. "And don't worry that you don't remember me. We've never met. I saw your picture in the paper at your coming out. Was it two years ago? Of course you'd be married by now."

Anna spoke with the barest tinge of bitterness. "You would think so."

Mr. Wright studied her face with too much interest. "You're even more beautiful in person."

Louis stepped closer to Anna. "I appreciate your good word. Now, if you would excuse us, we're on our honeymoon." He slipped his arm through hers in a gesture of possession.

Mr. Wright bowed impeccably. "Congratulations. I won't keep you."

"You won't be seeing my father soon? Or speaking to him?" Anna asked.

"Unfortunately not," Mr. Wright said.

She smiled her relief. "Well then. Goodbye Mr. Wright. And, thank you."

Louis jingled the keys in his pocket. "Goodbye Mr. Wright." He squeezed her arm. "Darling, you should rest. Let me take you to our room."

Anna immediately forgot Mr. Wright and thought of what might happen in that room. Her stomach flipped like she was on a swing.

Louis led her off to a white staircase that wound around and around, up to love.

At the door to their suite, Louis felt for his watch. "Oh boy. I didn't realize the train would be so late. We're due in the chapel in . . ." He checked the time and winced. "Ten minutes. I'll just pop down to postpone."

Anna held his arm. "No, don't!"

Louis looked surprised. "We can do it later, Anna. Don't you want to change?"

"Yes, but . . . Let's do everything right now. Everything."

To Anna, fashion was a sacrament. It was a testimony to her eagerness that she dressed with no attendant and presented herself for her wedding with a crease in her veil, no powder, her *robe nuptiale* half-buttoned in back, and only one shoe. She pinched her cheeks mercilessly to give them color and tucked a sixpence into her slipper for luck. The coin was a token from her English mother, who was presently rolling in her grave.

The priest waited at the gilded altar under a domed ceiling painted like the sky. Two hotel maids in white caps and bib aprons stood as silent witnesses. The room smelled like incense and lemon oil. Louis and Anna processed down the aisle, Clara's borrowed lace train flowing behind. For a brief moment, Anna's feet revolted and she dragged on Louis like an anchor. She felt dizzy and had to lean against a wooden pew. Why was this so difficult? In her head she knew she was doing the right thing. Any future would be better than spinsterhood under her father's roof, and she might have just fallen in love with Louis. She looked to the stained glass saints for guidance, then back at the door. The clock was ticking.

Louis put soft lips to her ear. "Don't be anxious, my queen. I'll be gentle."

"Me, too." She thought of cigarettes, lively dances, mystery books, brandy, and love—all the things her father denied her. She thought of Louis's hands on the train. She squared her shoulders and willed her feet to move.

The priest began the rite in English. Anna groaned. Here was one more thing she'd have to bring to the confessional. "You promised you'd pretend to be Catholic and get a Catholic priest," she whispered.

"I tried. The Catholic man wouldn't do an elopement."

"You could have said we were orphans."

"We'd be very rich orphans. I don't know what you're so bothered about. People question your loyalties when you're Roman, you know."

Anna sighed. She'd rather be free and in need of absolution than postpone and get caught. "But now we'll have to do it all over again."

Louis shrugged.

During the vows, Anna kept looking over her shoulder. She promised to love with sincerity, crossed her fingers when she vowed to obey, and said "I do" before the priest had finished his sentence. Louis slid a band onto her finger—a ring purchased on her father's credit. His chaste, ceremonial kiss tasted sweet, like freedom, and Anna laughed at nothing in particular. She paid the priest and Louis led her back to their room to the peals of a thousand bells.

In their suite, a bottle of Cuvée Femme waited, chilling in a bucket of ice with a note from Mr. Wright: "All my best wishes for a blessed union."

"How kind." Anna dropped the note on the floor. She was thinking about Louis's hands and wondering what exactly was involved in consummation. She smoothed her wedding gown and perched on a chaise.

Louis poured the champagne and raised his glass. "To you, my queen."

After two glasses, Anna's head was rushing. Louis was studying her, watching her bring the glass to her lips, watching her sip the amber liquid, watching her drain the glass. She felt scrumptiously self-conscious. He ran his fingers through his crispy, brilliantined hair. "Sunset seems a millennium away."

"Why don't you ravish me now?"

His eyebrow arched up. "It's 10 a.m."

Anna shrugged. "Not in China."

"I see." He lunged for her, toppling her onto the chaise. Her glass smashed upon the floor. A thousand bells rang in Anna's head, and she knew for certain that she was *very* much in love with him.

The door burst open with a *bang*. The desk clerk stood on the threshold with his priggish arms folded, flanked by two breathless police officers.

That marked the end of Anna's golden reputation and her marriage to Louis Taylor.

Chapter 2

Anna's room resembled her—dramatic, tasteful, but just barely. The carpets were plush and pink. Flowery paper from the orient climbed the walls, hand-painted with colorful birds. An imperious Louis XV bed draped itself in stiff, white velvet and the windows wore crepe curtains from France. Anna kindled a fire in the marble hearth, never mind it was seventy-two degrees outside. It was Tuesday, and on Wednesday Mrs. Morales would have the floors polished. Someone would be under her bed with a mop. She tossed another log onto the fire.

Raising the shade, she opened the window to cool the room. The outside scent of hot chaparral gave way to the wintry smell of chimney smoke. She could see Catalina Island. A hummingbird with opalescent green wings sucked at the feeder outside. Confused by the smoke, it whirled in circles before flying off.

Anna struggled out of her frock and flopped onto the bed in her chemise and two-piece drawers, sticky with the heat. She reached for a stack of books that sat near a glue pot on the marble nightstand—*Etiquette for Young Ladies*, *Little Lord Fauntleroy*, and other boring titles. She picked up a paring knife, stolen from Cook. She unsheathed the knife and placed the tip to a book spine; then, with a voracious rip, she disemboweled it. Slitting through binding threads, separating signatures from the cover, she tossed the paper onto the flames and repeated the process until the pages from every book were burning and the stiff fabric covers sat in a pile beside her.

When she had finished, she slid on her belly under the bed, emerging with dust on her corset and several more books—forbidden books by Doyle and Poe, books about crime, banned by her father specifically because she found them interesting. Books the housekeeper should not find under her bed in the morning.

She slaughtered *The Curse Upon Mitre Square*—a salacious description of the hunt for Jack the Ripper—this time burning the cover and keeping the pages. She stabbed *The Murders in the Rue Morgue* through the spine. The sharpened knife slipped, slicing her index finger. Blood dripped onto the floor.

"Biscuits!" She held her dripping finger over an empty book cover, staunching the wound with her petticoats. The blood bloomed into a red hibiscus flower on the cloth and the cut began to sting. After a moment, she pulled away the bloody wad to observe the injury—an inch-long gash.

"Hmm." She pinched it until it gaped like a mouth and released it. She did it again. How curious she looked on the inside. There was a knock at the door. Anna froze.

An efficient female voice, with a thick Mexican accent, rang from the corridor. "Miss Blanc, may I come in?"

"One moment." Anna grabbed a silk coverlet and tossed it over book parts, knocking the glue pot. It rolled into the blood on the floor. She struggled into her gown one-handed, an attempt to cover the red stain on her petticoats. She unlocked the door, pressed her unbuttoned back up against the wall, and posed as if it were the natural thing to do. "Come in."

The door opened to reveal the unyielding countenance of Mrs. Morales. Short, broad, and board straight, she came from an old Los Angeles family. She had run the Blanc household with a cool dignity since Anna was a baby. In a backhanded way, she'd run Anna.

Surprisingly, Mrs. Morales said nothing about the paste, the blood, the disordered coverlet, or Anna's strange posture, although she did sniff briefly at the fire. "A Mr. Wright called this afternoon while you were out."

Anna looked blank. "Who?"

"Mr. Wright. He says you know him." Mrs. Morales handed her a calling card. Anna took it and shook her head.

The housekeeper's face was neutral. "He said he's come from Boston and was sorry he didn't get to see you."

Anna lifted her chin. "He must have the wrong house. I don't know him, and I've done nothing wrong." She darted a hopeful glance at Mrs. Morales. "You didn't tell father, did you?"

"He left your father a note."

"Well, that was a misstep. He'll never get to see me now. Next time, just tell him yes, I will marry him, whoever he is, and to meet me in the garden at midnight. Otherwise, I'm going to be an even older old maid. But, I don't suppose you care."

"Miss Anna, I have other news."

Anna was impatient for the woman to leave. "What?"

"Louis Taylor eloped."

After a moment of silence, Anna said, "Oh." She wrapped her arms around herself. It was only January. The ink on the annulment papers still dripped. "With whom?"

"It's not important. Good night, Miss Blanc." She proffered no sympathy. Her condolence came in the form of ignoring the blood, the glue, the fire, and the strange posture—all clear evidence that Anna was up to something. As she left and closed the door, Anna wondered if Mrs. Morales loved her.

She threw a chair.

Chapter 3

In an upscale millinery shop in downtown Venice Beach, amidst a sea of plumes in every hue, Anna tried on a shimmering peacock-feather headdress. She admired herself in a table mirror from several different angles. She was a vision and she knew it.

Anna's chaperone tried on a scratchy, straw hat adorned with multicolored feathers. She cocked her head, and then cocked the hat. She looked like a macaw. Her name was Miss Cooper. She had the slack-faced look of a mental patient. Anna resented her very existence. No other girls her age had chaperones unless they were courting, which Anna was not. Few men courted annulled girls, and all of them feared her father.

Anna plucked off the headdress and handed it to a sales woman. "Add it to my tab, please." She began pinning her own chapeau back into place.

"I most certainly would, Miss Blanc, but . . . your father hasn't paid for the five hats you bought in December." The sales woman smiled apologetically.

Anna's eyes widened and she flushed crimson. No one ever refused a Blanc credit. "Well then," Anna said. She put on an air of carelessness and spun around, passing two rich ladies, who were staring, and clipped toward the door. In her beaded clutch, where money should be, there was nothing but a few calling cards, her keys, and a handful of stolen Lucky Strikes.

The shop lady followed obsequiously. "Why don't I save it in the back for you? Then you can straighten all this out and come back tomorrow."

Anna lifted her chin. "No, never mind. I don't like it." Bells tinkled as she swung out the door, through the stone arches onto Windward Avenue. Miss Cooper replaced the straw hat and scampered after Anna.

Outside the shop, the air was tangy with ocean smells, dust, and steaming horse manure. The street swarmed with people baking under hats and parasols or seeking the cool shade of the colonnade. Like Anna, they had fled the even hotter city and taken the train to spend a day at the beach.

A rumble of distant voices hummed under the crashing of waves and the regular noise of the crowd. Cops in black leather helmets loitered, sweating in wool uniforms. Anna ignored it all, knocking on her forehead like it was a door and she wanted in *now*. Her new lack of credit foreboded bad things. Why was she in the doghouse this time and, more importantly, what had given her away? Had Mrs. Morales found Anna's contraband books?

Anna peered at Miss Cooper, hoping for a clue. "Father didn't say I couldn't buy clothes. It wasn't part of my sentence. He must be angry at something new."

The chaperone, who knew little about anything, shrugged and fanned herself with a limp handkerchief that stuck to itself in two places.

Anna no longer felt like swimming, bowling, or being rowed in a gondola through the Venice canals. Even the musclemen had lost their appeal. "Let's go." She strode toward the Pacific Electric red cars that would take her back to Bunker Hill.

The crowd's noise was distilling into a singsong of female voices. "A ballot for the Lady! For the Home and for the Baby!" Anna turned to look. Hundreds of women came marching around the corner from the boardwalk carrying banners that demanded, "Votes for Women." They wore dull, dark skirts and a variety of hats, none of them nice. It put Anna's own clothing crisis in perspective. Her countenance brightened. "Jupiter!"

Bells tinkled as people emerged from shops to gawk. A woman in a tricorn hat and knee britches handed out pamphlets as she marched. "No taxation without representation!" Anna took one. The tract featured Paul Revere riding his steed. He had bosoms.

"I think the suffragettes are wonderful, even if they are poorly dressed," Anna said.

Miss Cooper blew her nose on the handkerchief before mopping her head with it.

Anna continued. "I don't know why I've never supported them. No one I know goes to meetings, but why shouldn't I? Besides that father wouldn't allow it. I should be able to vote. Don't you think so?"

Miss Cooper scrunched up her face, trying to think and failing. "I'm . . . not sure."

Anna assessed the scene with wide, interested eyes. Under the shade of a candy-striped awning, swirled iron chairs clustered around little tables. Anna gestured toward them. "Dear Miss Cooper, it's so very hot. Why don't you rest here and have a Coca Cola while I follow the march? I'll meet you back here as soon as . . ."

Miss Cooper scowled. "Do you think I'm a fool?"

Anna did, but thought it impolite to say so.

She wanted to join the parade. "Goodness me! Look over there!" Anna pointed past Miss Cooper's shoulder. The chaperone turned. Anna lifted her skirts and bolted, flying down the sidewalk, quickly putting distance between herself and Miss Cooper. She disappeared among the sweating bodies of pedestrians. Miss Cooper blundered after her. "Miss Blanc!"

Unfortunately, Anna's progress was hindered by her good breeding. The sidewalk buzzed with pedestrians that she couldn't very well shove aside. She greeted each one before darting around them. "Hello. Good day. Excuse me." Miss Cooper, faced with the possibility of losing Anna and thus her position, had no compunction about shoving people out of her way like a fullback at the Rose Bowl. At a furious waddle, the dumpling was actually gaining on Anna, which was humiliating and disheartening in the extreme.

Anna had all but lost hope when, having reached a particularly impassible clump of old ladies, someone yanked her against a store front and hid her with a sign that declared, "We Demand Amendment!" Miss Cooper barreled past, through the babbling biddies and on down the street toward the beach.

"Is that your mother?" asked her savior, a girl with a smile that was half sympathy and half smirk. She was young, one of the masses, but pretty in a practical way. Twin boys hung off her skirts and, like most children, were whining and making gaseous smells. One pinched his sibling, who in turn, clobbered him with a lunch pail.

Anna extricated herself from behind the splintery wooden sign. "I'd rather not talk about it, thank you."

She turned to go back the way she came, when the woman asked, "Are you marching? Because I could use a hand here."

Anna looked at the girl with the ungainly sign and grimaced at the urchins. It was a shocking request, given the social distance between them, and Anna aspired to be so impudent. She smiled uncertainly and lifted one end of the sign. "All right."

"You might want to take that hat off. It shouts your name. And by the way, I'm Mrs. Eve McBride."

"Oh, yes. You're right. I'm Miss Anna Blanc." Anna inclined her head and nodded. She removed her hat, praying she would not freckle, and pinned it against the sign with one hand. They joined the marchers in the dusty street.

A red-haired man in a boater's hat darted in front of them and snapped their photograph. He had a long, curly mustache and a pockmarked face. "Dilly of a picture! You beauties are going to make the front page!'" He jogged along backward.

"I decline to be on your front page. Ask someone else," Anna said curtly, swishing in step.

"It isn't up to you, Cinderella." He grinned. "I can see the headlines. Rags and riches."

Eve rolled her eyes.

Anna bit her lip. This was very bad. She had thought that if she returned by dinner, her father would never know she'd joined the march. Miss Cooper certainly wouldn't tell. But if her transgression were plastered across the front page, she'd be in the soup.

Anna's eyebrows came together, forming little wings. "Please! If you run that photograph, I'll be disowned. Thrown out into the streets."

The photographer tossed back his head and laughed. "We wouldn't want that, pretty thing." He trod backward through fresh road apples, changing out his film. "I'll tell you what. I won't submit that picture if you'll wink at me. In fact, I'll send you the picture as a memento so you won't forget me." He winked and attempted a rakish smile, but only looked ridiculous.

Anna raised one eyebrow. "And if I don't wink at you?"

"Then I'll be heartbroken and you'll be famous. You have my word. Here, give me your card."

Anna dug in her purse for a calling card and, frowning, extended it to him pinched between two fingers. He had to tug it out of her hand.

He read it and grinned, camera tucked neatly under his arm. "That a girl, Miss Blanc. Pretend you like me as much as I like you."

Anna scowled. "I don't even know your name!"

"Tilly. Bill Tilly."

"Enchanté," she said flatly. She winked and was blinded by a flash from the man's second camera. Her eyes widened in disbelief. She sucked in breath. "You, you, you rat! You, you cad! You cad rat!"

Tilly chortled. "You're a dandy girl, Miss Blanc. Votes for women!" He shook his fist in the air and disappeared into the crowd.

Eve slapped her thigh. "I could've told you he would do that."

"Then why didn't you?"

She laughed. "Don't be mad, sister. Have a sense of humor."

Anna found nothing funny in the situation but consoled herself that her cause was noble and her hole could not get any deeper—not without breaking through to China. Her father had already taken her allowance and her credit and shackled her with Miss Cooper. Though there were endless ways to be naughty, he was fast running out of punishments.

The march concluded in a grassy plaza at the midway where an all-woman brass band oom-pah-pahed from a grandstand draped with red, white, and blue bunting. A rollercoaster rattled on its tracks, and vendors sold sugary puffs of fairy floss—the good, cherry pink kind that melted on the tongue. Glistening musclemen lifted barbells along the board-walk, turning their backs to their admirers so they could watch the ladies playing instruments. Beachgoers were being drawn by the music, abandoning plans to catch the next train back to Los Angeles. Soon the plaza was thick with people. A woman in spectacles took the podium and the music stopped. She lifted her hands. Her voice carried like that of a Baptist preacher. "This government is not a democracy . . ."

Many in the crowd—men and even some women—pulled sour faces or sniggered and heckled. Eve and Anna held up their heads and clapped feverishly at all the right times. As the oration progressed, the crowd along the shore-side of the midway began to simmer. Anna turned to look. Someone was throwing overripe vegetables. She saw a tomato hit "Paul Revere" in the face. "Jupiter!" Anna said, as unhappy policemen began migrating toward the conflict.

Eve tugged Anna's sleeve. "Let's go." Anna wanted to stay for the fight, as she was good at lobbing tomatoes, but she liked Eve and let herself be led away.

Anna checked her watch. "It's five o'clock. I'm amenable to capture. Miss Cooper has my money for the train." She plopped on her plumed hat and pinned it into place. "Do you know, marching today was the most important thing I've ever done? What could be more meaningful than championing the cause of women? After all, I am one, and I've been sorely abused."

Eve smirked. "Hah! Tell me how you've been sorely abused."

"Besides not getting to vote? There's involuntary old maidenhood for one, an inconstant husband, an embarrassing chaperone, a revoked allowance, hat-shop bills that remain unpaid. I'd like to give a speech about it."

Eve grinned. "Your passion is inspirational."

"From now on, whenever I can, I will make statements." With a wicked smile, Anna reached into her clutch and pulled out two Lucky Strikes.

Eve raised one scandalized eyebrow and laughed. "I guess so!" Anna offered her a cigarette. Eve took it. "Thanks. I'll smoke it later."

"Chicken," Anna accused. She lit up and pumped her lips, blowing an impressive series of smoke rings.

Anna became aware of a shadow alongside hers. She turned around, glowering, expecting Miss Cooper, or perhaps the hateful photographer.

It was an officer of the law.

Chapter 4

The Venice police station was a multistory brick building with arched windows, a flag, and a certain modest grandeur. Anna approached on the arm of a limping man, whose face was as pretty and red as a monkey's bottom—Officer Carmine.

Anna shouldn't have talked back. But he had snatched the cigarette right out of her fingers and accused her of public indecency when no part of her was indecent—except maybe some parts, in which case all women were indecent. Anna huffed to herself. And isn't that why she'd been arrested, because she had female parts? That and because she had kicked him in the shin.

A police mount tied to a post shook its wiry mane and whinnied. Anna reached out to stroke its shiny coat, but Officer Carmine tugged her away. Anna scowled. "The chief of police won't be happy you arrested me." Carmine scowled back.

As they passed through the station doors, Anna couldn't help but feel exhilarated. She had never been inside a police station, and her books said virtually nothing about them. She imagined criminals with close, beady eyes and large, sloping foreheads housed in rusty jail cells, and detectives with guns strapped in holsters, pacing paths in the tile.

Trailing behind, Eve was less exhilarated. She walked through the doors with the stoicism of Wendy Bird tied to Captain Hook's mast, two little Lost Boys at her side. If Eve was Wendy Darling, Anna was Alice in Wonderland, marveling as she stepped into a fantastical new world. It was the dingiest place she had ever seen, and she adored it. The air was smoky from an endless chain of cigarettes smoldering in ashtrays. Lights hung from wires above old desks. Their glow mixed with sunbeams to illuminate the haze. The light barely reached the line of cells along the side, so that she could not see the back wall. They looked like caverns calling out for exploration.

There were indeed prisoners—some with beady eyes and some without, including seven boisterous suffragettes from the food fight. The women rattled the bars of their cage, singing, "Boys will be boys, and boys have had their day; Boy-mischief and boy-carelessness and noise . . ." Anna recognized Paul Revere, who had given her the pamphlet and had bravely taken a tomato in the kisser.

Eve's escort, an Officer Glade, had a twinkle in his eye. He grabbed Anna by the elbow and guided both women toward a clerk behind a counter that shone from the oily touch of a thousand criminal hands. Officer Glade nodded toward Anna and grinned. "Watch out. She's a hellcat." He parodied Officer Carmine's swagger. "Women don't smoke on my beat." His voice went high in an imitation of Anna. "But Officer, I am smoking on your beat." He threw back his head and laughed. Eve bristled.

Anna and Eve gave their names to the clerk and Glade herded his captives into a cell with the other suffragettes, who by now were beginning to smell like a compost pile. The door locked with a clink. Anna wanted to inspect every part of her prison cell—the obscenities carved in the walls, the suspicious brown stains on the cement floor, the splintery hard benches—but the cell was crowded with criminal ladies slimed with garden waste, and Anna didn't want to risk touching them. She stayed close to Eve, who looked mad. The twins took turns clanking on the cell bars with a clamshell. Anna gazed longingly through the bars at a man in plainclothes who she imagined was a detective but was probably a clerk. "I've always wanted to see the inside of a police station."

"What do you know? Dreams do come true," Eve said.

Her tone was snarky. Anna chose to overlook it, as she'd just gotten Eve's children arrested. "No, they don't."

Eve cocked her head, as if curious that this privileged girl could be so disillusioned. "What's your dream, then?"

"I'd like to trap criminals, like the spinster in *The Circular Staircase*, but it's probably against the law, because of my female parts."

Eve crinkled her forehead.

Anna continued. "So, since that's impossible, I'd like to get married. And that's also impossible . . . unless my father eats bad fish or something."

"You know, marriage is not as blissful as people make it out to be."

"In my experience that's positively true, but there's not much else, is there?"

"You could be a school teacher," Eve said.

Anna didn't like children. Her greatest fear was that her prayers would get crossed with some other Catholic's. Anna would get pregnant without even asking, and some other woman would get a motorcycle or permission to play flag football. Anna never prayed if there was a married lady anywhere near her in the pews.

Anna puckered her face. "I suppose I could become a nun."

Eve smirked. "I work at a police station."

Anna's gray eyes widened. She blinked her feathered lashes. "That's taffy! Women can't work in police stations. It's indecent." She wanted very much to believe they could.

"Mostly I do social work, care for any women prisoners, interview female victims or suspects that are real sensitive, things like that. Central Station's a lot bigger than this station, so there's plenty to do."

Anna's eyes glazed dreamily. "You are so . . ." Her voice cracked. "Fortunate."

Eve rubbed her temple as if she had a headache. "If you were married and had more sense . . ."

"Is that the requirement—to be married?"

"One of them. You're supposed to have experience working with the poor. Me, I knew somebody. Otherwise, I wouldn't have had a prayer. There aren't many positions."

Anna shook her head vigorously, as if to shake the thought right out. "I shouldn't entertain the idea. I'm not at liberty to apply. But, do you think the captain would give me a tour of the station?"

"Of course not. You're a prisoner."

At the back of the cell, two old vegetables held up a curtain for

Paul Revere, who was peeing into a potty. Anna crossed her legs. "I have to go, but I'd burst before peeing in the cell. Do think there's a privy in the back?"

"Yep, but it's not for you."

Anna scanned the station. Next to a windowed office, she saw a door that led to the back of the building.

A clerk strode up to the cell and straightened his tie. He addressed Eve through the bars. "Mrs. McBride, who do we call to collect your children? Can your husband care for them until your legal issues are resolved?"

"My husband's dead." Eve pressed her lips together. "At least he better be."

Carmine slunk up to the cell and positioned himself before Anna. He cleared his throat and recited. "I'm very sorry, Miss Blanc. It was all my fault. Why don't you wait in the captain's office while we call your father." He gritted his teeth and grimaced. The captain watched, frowning from the station floor. It seemed that Carmine was in as much trouble as she was.

Anna flashed a victory smile at Eve, but Eve didn't notice. She had her back turned to Anna and was speaking to the clerk in whispers. "We have no living relations."

Anna's smile dimmed. She spoke to Eve's shoulder. "Thank you for saving me."

Eve turned and looked blankly at Anna, then turned back to the clerk. The cell creaked open and Anna took her freedom. Surely someone would come for Eve.

Carmine locked the door with one of the keys from a large brass ring. "Please follow me, Miss Blanc."

As she glided across the main room, Anna smiled sweetly. "May I have a tour of the station, Officer?"

Carmine's nostrils flared, but he didn't speak. He ushered Anna into the captain's office, left without a *bon voyage*, and forced the door closed behind him. It stuck on the frame and slammed into place with a whack.

While a guided tour of the station was not possible at that time, a self-guided tour of the captain's office seemed a satisfying alternative. Anna rifled through the papers on the desktop, which proved to be dull and bureaucratic—a petition signed by dozens of officers protesting wool uniforms in summer; a grocery list in a woman's hand—*manteca, bistec, tomate*; and an anonymous note about who had stolen a certain goat. Anna rattled each drawer in turn, finding them all to be locked. She tried to pick the locks with her hat-pin, but the tip broke off.

She flipped through books on a shelf behind the desk and found a police procedural manual. Turning her back to the door and undoing her blouse, she sucked in her stomach and squeezed it down her corset. She stuffed two more small law enforcement books down her bodice and draped her shawl around the bulges.

Anna heard squabbling on the station floor. She cracked open the door and stuck out her head in time to see Paul Revere pitch the potty at Carmine. A tense hush fell over the station. Tinkle trickled down his uniform. The faces of prisoners and staff alike shone with silent glee at the dripping man who couldn't believe just how bad his day had become.

Glade laughed into the silence—a booming, "Ho, ho, ho."

To Anna, the potty fight was a coup. She slipped out of the captain's office and through an adjacent door. She would take her own tour, perhaps find the bathroom, and be back in the office before her father came to bail her out. He wasn't due home from his trip until tonight. It could be morning before he collected her; at least she hoped so. She preferred to delay what would certainly be a fierce overreaction.

She found herself in a corridor with several doors and no indication where any of them led. There was a horrible sewage stench, which didn't bode well for the toilet. She heard the captain's voice, sharp in the main room of the station, making reference to her whereabouts and how being covered in piss was not an excuse for letting a prisoner wander away, and he had a mind to put Anna back in the cell and Carmine with her. Angry boots stomped toward the door, no doubt attached to Carmine.

Anna rattled a doorknob, hoping for a place to hide. It was locked. She hustled down the corridor to the next door. To her relief, the handle gave. Stepping through, she edged it closed, just as the door to the corridor opened and Carmine shouted, "Miss Blanc?" His voice trembled.

The room reeked worse than the hall. It was white walled with a cold cement floor and a curtain that divided the chamber. Behind the curtain, a light cast shadows onto the cloth—shadows of a man and a woman and a lump on a slab. Anna covered her mouth with a perfumed handkerchief and tried not to gag. The man's shadow was long and overly thin, made more so by the angle of the light. He pulled a sheet away from the lump—a lump shaped like a body. Anna perked up. A body in a police morgue could mean just one thing . . .

Murder.

The door flung open with a bang, smacking Anna in the face and sandwiching her against the wall. She swallowed a scream and held still. Carmine stuck in his red face and looked about like a child in a game of hide and seek who thought his playmates were cheating. He grunted at the stench, as if he himself didn't smell like an outhouse. Satisfied that Anna was not present, he removed himself, leaving a lingering scent of urine. Anna breathed in little shallow pants of fetid air, trying to catch her breath without making a sound or losing her peanut butter sandwich. She felt a warm trickle on her brow. Reaching up, she smeared a streak of blood across her forehead. She paid no mind to the wound. Her attention was focused on the drama playing out before her.

"Well, can you identify her?" asked the thin man.

"Are you sure it's a she?" the woman said.

"I realize the body's in bad condition. She was in the water a long time."

Anna chewed her handkerchief. The woman leaned over the slab. She had the silhouette of a matron, busty, thick-wasted, with a large feathered hat. What appeared to be a dead fox swung from her neck like a pendulum in the space between her bosom and the lump. She slung it back over her shoulder. "It's one of Monique's girls. Rose something. See the tattoo? There's no love lost between me and Monique, but I don't like seeing innocent girls murdered in cold blood, even if it is the competition."

"It was a suicide."

"Suicide my ass!"

Anna brought one hand to her mouth in a silent, airless gasp. In a flash of black taffeta, feathers, and dyed red hair, the woman flung the curtain aside, coming face to face with the fugitive as the drape swung back into place. Caught and not knowing what else to do, Anna hit the floor like a dropped confection, feigning a swoon. The woman considered her only a moment, and stepped over her body and out the door, leaving a heavy trail of rose perfume.

Anna played possum in case the thin man should come out from behind the curtain. She lay with her cheek pressed to the cold cement floor, and alternated between marveling at the woman's gall and wondering how one could tell if a decomposed corpse had been murdered. She heard a door open and shut. A gust of air made the curtain swell. The thin man had left through a different door. Anna sat up and listened.

Out on the station floor, she heard the woman's bland voice. "There's a debutante passed out in the morgue."

Anna heard shouting and a rush of feet. She dropped back onto the tile, closing her eyes. She was glad that even minor head wounds bleed rivers. Her face contorted in pain, only partly an act, as the stolen books were jabbing into her belly.

Officers swarmed into the room like agitated bees.

"My God, she's hurt." A man with an upper-class, East Coast accent kneeled beside her and took up her limp hand. "Give her air!" He lightly touched her bloody brow, where a small purple lump was growing. "Captain, you will answer for this!"

Anna stirred, tossing her head and offering up a dramatic, "No, no." She blinked her eyes open and looked around as if bewildered. Then she truly was bewildered. The person holding her hand was not an officer, but a dark-eyed young man with an excellent tailor. She blushed. She knew his face. He had sent champagne to her room on her ill-fated honeymoon at the Mission Inn.

The man was Edgar Wright. Anna primly pulled the hem of her skirt down to cover up a stockinged shin.

Mr. Wright put her hand to his lips. "Thank God. Thank God."

Chapter 5

Anna leaned on Mr. Wright's arm as she pretend-limped down the steps of the station to his Cadillac limousine. It was shiny and ocean blue. Her luck had definitely turned. She could tell that he liked her, but that embarrassing business with Louis Taylor hung in the air. Since being tainted by the scandal, she'd had few suitors for her father to chase away.

Mr. Wright helped her into the passenger seat and walked around front to crank up the car. Anna quickly fished in her bodice for the three books that were ramming her ribs like rhinoceroses. She wrapped them in her shawl just in time to flash Mr. Wright a gorgeous smile as he slipped into the driver's seat.

He smiled back. "Now that we're alone, Miss Blanc—it is *Miss Blanc*, isn't it?" He raised his eyebrows. "I heard you weren't married."

"Yes! I mean . . ." She blushed a deep, deep crimson. "It's Miss." Anna didn't elaborate, though he seemed to be waiting for an explanation.

When he saw that none was forthcoming, he cleared his throat. "Now that we're alone, won't you tell me what really happened today?"

Anna's eyes searched the ceiling for the right thing to say. As a rule, the truth would never do. She trod uncertainly. "It's the strangest thing." She stared out the window into dark strawberry fields, looking for suggestions. "The last I remember . . . I was trying on hats with my . . . um . . . cousin." She tapped her lips. "And then . . . I found myself on the floor looking up at you, Mr. Wright." She beamed at him. "Thank you for coming to my rescue. Although, I must say, I don't know why it was you."

He stared past the dashboard, watching the road and smiling. "It was just good luck. Mine, I mean. I called at your house. I'm trying to interest your father in a business deal. Mrs. Morales said he would be back in town today. And I wanted to see you, of course."

Realization lit Anna's face. "Oh, it was you who called before. In January."

Mr. Wright frowned. "Yes. I had hoped you would remember me."

"Oh, I do. Of course I do." She twisted a curl on the nape of her neck and smiled.

"So, I was waiting for your father when the parlor maid—Miss Lupita?—got the call from the police. The poor girl panicked. Mrs. Morales was out, so Miss Lupita asked me for advice."

"She didn't!" Anna hated indiscreet servants. They were holes in the dike that would have to be plugged.

He grinned. "I couldn't very well just leave you in jail."

Anna sparkled up at him. "Then, I am forever in your debt, Mr. Wright."

"I assure you, Miss Blanc, it was my pleasure."

Anna settled into the buttery seat and sighed, happy that it took a long time to drive from Venice Beach to Los Angeles, though Los Angeles kept reaching its fingers further toward the sea. She stole glances at Mr. Wright, at his large, smooth hands on the wheel, and thought how lovely it would be to be a different girl—to be golden again, with a shining reputation and a different father.

The world outside the window was dark but for distant pinpoints, which looked like fallen stars on the land. In the headlights, the road abruptly petered out into an open field. Edgar brought his big, blue car to a lurching stop so they didn't end up in the weeds. There had been nothing along the road for a while—no buildings, no farms, just flat, unclaimed land. Edgar gave Anna a sheepish grin. "I'm afraid we've been on a road to nowhere."

She gave him an incredulous smile. "But why would anyone build a road to nowhere? It seems a lot of work for nothing."

"They're all over the outskirts. Development companies lobby to have them built, roads going nowhere, waiting to be roads to somewhere. I suppose they represent hope. I'm sorry to inconvenience you, Miss Blanc."

"I'm in no hurry to see my father, Mr. Wright. I'm inclined to take another road to nowhere."

Edgar laughed and turned the car around. He retraced his way half a mile back to a fork in the road and rejoined the main highway. They drove past new houses and stores and schools for new people coming to California for new lives. But Anna didn't have a new life. She was like one of the roads branching out from the city, forged in the hope of purpose but left empty, going nowhere.

It was late when they drove past the little funicular railway known as Angel's Flight, which ran to the top of Bunker Hill near the drive of the Blanc estate. The streets were clean and wide, sprinkled with palm trees and grand houses with the best views of the city. Up ahead, Anna saw the rooftop under which she would soon be upbraided, and tied her shawl tight around her bundle of books. "You should drop me off on the street. Father will be more upset at finding me alone in the company of a man than at my having been arrested, although he'll hate that too."

"Not a chance. I just found you unconscious and bloody on the floor. I'm not abandoning you on the street in the middle of the night. Anyway, it could work in your favor." He raised his eyebrows. "A father's more likely to show mercy if there's a witness."

As Anna and Mr. Wright ascended the marble steps of her home, passing under tall, white columns, Miss Cooper descended, nose to heaven, suitcase in hand. She didn't return Anna's pleasantries. If Miss Cooper had ever felt the least affection for her charge, it was certainly gone now. Anna assumed the parlor maid would also appear with her own suitcase at any moment.

They found Christopher Blanc in his Louis XV parlor smoking two cigarettes at once, California's second-largest fault line running down between his eyebrows. He addressed the twelve-foot ceiling, his French accent rattling like an earthquake, starting out soft but gaining power until it shook the chandelier. "*Oh lá lá*. My daughter has a police record! *Mon seul enfant!*"

Anna smiled casually, as if she had just returned from a tea party—her habitual way of speaking to the impending eruption that was her father. "Welcome home, Father."

His jaws ground against one another like two tectonic plates. "*Mon Dieu*."

Mr. Wright spoke in a soothing voice. "Mr. Blanc, your daughter's innocent. It was all just a terrible mistake. The officer accepted full responsibility. It was just a case of being in the wrong place at the wrong time. And look, she's been hurt." He lightly touched the skin above Anna's wound, which, when cleaned up, was a disappointment. It looked to be little more than a scratch.

Mr. Blanc's eyebrows drew together in concern, and his hands fell limp at his sides. The earthquake was over. He looked at Edgar. "What happened to her?"

Anna smiled a little too sweetly. "You might ask me, Father. I was actually there."

Mr. Blanc grunted. "Never mind. What happened?"

She blinked and bit her lip. "I don't really know. I was shopping with Miss Cooper, this I remember." She glanced from side to side. "Suddenly we were surrounded by marching suffragettes. Hundreds of them! A lady handed me a pamphlet . . . and then everything went black."

"There was a scuffle at the march. She must have been struck. When I arrived at the station, she was unconscious," Mr. Wright said.

Anna touched her forehead. "I was a political prisoner—an accidental one. You can't actually think I would smoke?"

Anna rooted furiously in her beaded purse for the suffrage pamphlet, which she planned to produce as evidence in her defense. As she withdrew the pamphlet with the lady Paul Revere, a Lucky Strike fell from her bag and bounced, spilling little bits of tobacco onto the

Spanish tile. She winced and braced herself for the aftershock. Mr. Blanc's face went from vermillion to lily.

Mr. Wright stifled a smile. "I had better be going. Mr. Blanc, perhaps we can talk in the morning? Miss Blanc, don't hesitate to call me anytime you get arrested."

"I will, Mr. Wright." She smiled as if her father wasn't there.

"*Oh, mon Dieu*!" Mr. Blanc said.

Mr. Wright winked at Anna as he headed out the door.

Chapter 6

At eight o'clock, it was already hot. Mr. Blanc and Anna breakfasted on the terrace, eating salted kippers and sour crème and studiously ignoring each other. The cold fish smelled like the ocean. Catalina Island floated on the horizon. The only conversation came from a parrot hanging in a cage: "*Merde*."

Mr. Blanc hadn't spoken to Anna for a week—not since the *LA Times* had displayed her picture on the front page in the company of an undesirable, promoting a cause he didn't believe in, and making eyes at the photographer. He stormed over to the *Los Angeles Times* building, swearing up and down that the girl winking from the cover was not his daughter and if they didn't fire the photographer and print a retraction, they would be sued for libel. And so they did, but to no avail. That wink, preserved for posterity, tarnished her reputation, which had already been downgraded from golden to silver. Anna was now bronze at best. Her bridal value was going down, down, down. Mr. Blanc put Mrs. Morales on Anna duty and forbade her to leave the house until a new and better chaperone could be hired.

Before being fired, Tilly had had the audacity to call on Anna, and while she didn't receive him he did leave her the photograph as promised—the one depicting Anna and Eve holding the large suffrage sign and smiling. Anna loved it, and kept it with the contraband books and other treasures under her bed.

Anna admired Eve and envied her for getting to work at a police station so close to detectives. Anna had always wanted to be a detective, but she never could because she was a woman. She couldn't even marry a detective. It would be beneath her.

While Anna ruminated thus, Mr. Blanc read the business section of the *Los Angeles Herald* because it was not the *Los Angeles Times.* He growled and shook his head as if he didn't believe a word of it. Anna picked up the stolen police procedural, which hid under the cover of *The Little Princess.* They both put fork to mouth without taking eye from page. He ground the salty kippers between his teeth. She took delicate bites.

Suddenly, he put down the *Herald* and spoke. "Anna, Edgar Wright has asked permission to court you. I gave it." Anna choked on a slippery kipper, shocked that he'd given his blessing. She would have been less surprised if he'd told her that he was the Antichrist, or that he'd taken up underwater ballet. He continued. "He's wealthy and interested in banking. I see the possibility of an alliance. How do you feel?"

The "how do you feel" part was more shocking still. "I didn't know you cared how I felt," Anna said coolly, though her mind raced with possibilities.

Mr. Blanc grunted. "He seems to take your foolishness in stride, but don't test him. Now that you've sullied your reputation, he may be your only chance at an exceptionally rich man."

"You're the one who drives off good matches."

"Hah! No one as good as Edgar Wright."

"Well, it's very unlikely I could get into trouble when I'm under house arrest!"

He ground his kipper between clenched teeth. "You're just like your mother!"

They were interrupted by Mrs. Morales, who strode through the patio doors and cleared her throat for a pronouncement. "The new chaperone has arrived. I thought you'd like to have her start as soon as possible so that I can return to my duties."

Anna found her enthusiasm insulting. Mr. Blanc assented and Mrs. Morales soon returned with a wiry, freckled woman of about forty who wore the ugliest frock Anna had ever seen. It was the color and texture of masticated kipper and had sweat stains under the arms. The chaperone glowed like a Sunday school teacher.

"May I present the Widow Crisp? Widow Crisp, this is Mr. Blanc, and Miss Anna Blanc, your charge," Mrs. Morales said.

Mr. Blanc stood, looked the Widow Crisp up and down, and seemed satisfied. He spoke like a general addressing his men. "I assume Mrs. Morales has briefed you."

"She has," said the Widow Crisp.

"Good. Anna's last chaperone wasn't vigilant. I hope you won't make the same mistake."

The Widow Crisp leveled her gaze at Anna. "I assure you, Mr. Blanc, I won't let her out of my sight." In those prim, thinly lashed eyes, Anna detected a threat.

Chapter 7

Anna lay still on a settee in the parlor, wearing a green satin evening gown, her arms crossed like Sarah Bernhardt sleeping in a coffin, preparing for a tragic role. Edgar was supposed to take her to see the great actress in *La Vierge d'Avila* that night and had never showed. The play had ended an hour ago. If it hadn't been about a nun, and likely preachy and boring, Anna would be angry. The grandfather clock gonged midnight.

Unlike Anna, her father was enjoying Mr. Wright's constant attention. No doubt they were together now, working late at the bank. She wanted Mr. Wright to steal her away from her father, not cozy up to him like a doting son. But she could hardly complain. His approach was succeeding. Mr. Wright was hanging on like a rodeo cowboy.

Having a suitor didn't make Anna's life any more interesting in the here and now. Mr. Wright was either at the bank or wooing investors at fancy dinners to which ladies were not invited. When they were together, they were never alone. Anna's movements were still restricted. She spent most of her time bored and away from other human beings, unless one considered the Widow Crisp a human being, which Anna did not.

Anna plucked up the *Herald*, which lay folded on the table, and glanced over an article on children forced to slave in dangerous factories. The newsprint rubbed off on her fingers, making them feel dirty. She had almost dropped the paper when she noticed an ad from Arrow promoting their shirt collars, something every woman in America looked forward to. The advertisement featured a strong, square-jawed man, debonair and unsmiling, in a crisp white collar, shirt, and black tuxedo. He was the reason that women read the *Herald*. He was the Arrow Collar Man.

Anna let her eyes peruse his illustrated body. Just below his waist, the advertisement ended and there was another—an ad for the White Cross Vibrator. A young woman, pink-cheeked and glowing, cradled a metal contraption and beamed. It looked like a gun. Anna read, "You will tingle with the force of your own awakened power, and all the keen relish and powers of youth will throb within you. Rich, red blood will be sent coursing through your veins and you will realize thoroughly the joy of living. Your self-respect, even, will increase one hundred-fold." Anna clipped the ad.

The next ad had no pictures. "Wanted by the Los Angeles Police Department—an assistant matron of irreproachable character to handle police issues pertaining to women and children. Fifty dollars per month." This advertisement made her heart thump even louder than the Arrow Collar Man. Surely being an assistant matron would awaken her powers, make her feel joyful, and increase her self-respect. It could be as healthful as owning a vibrator.

In the foyer, the front door hit the doorstop. Anna tore the matron ad from the paper and crinkled it into her pocket. Mr. Blanc stomped into the parlor followed by Mr. Wright, who at least had the decency to look sheepish. Anna stood and threw down the paper. "It's after midnight! You were supposed to take me to see Sarah Bernhardt! And this after you worked all day Sunday! I may as well not have a beau!"

She thrust the ad for the White Cross Vibrator into her father's hands. "Daddy, I want this."

He grunted. "Ask Mr. Wright. He owns the factory."

Mr. Wright took Anna's limp hand and kissed it. "Miss Blanc, I'll give you anything you want."

Anna snatched back her hand. "I wanted a night at the theater."

Mr. Wright gave her a rueful smile. "I'm sorry we missed the play, and I will make it up to you, but it couldn't be helped. There's a bit of a crisis at the bank."

Mr. Blanc wandered over to a decanter and poured brandy into two sparkly crystal glasses. He handed one to Mr. Wright. "The bank comes first. She knows that."

"I could help at the bank," Anna said. "I have nothing else to do."

Mr. Wright smiled. "You overestimate me, Miss Blanc. If you were in the building, I'd get nothing done."

Anna didn't know if she should be flattered or insulted, and so couldn't decide what to say. Mr. Blanc's brow rippled with a frown. "Make yourself useful, Anna. Do charity work. Women find that satisfying."

Anna rolled her eyes. "I'm not knitting blankets for orphans."

She glanced at Mr. Wright, whose brows had lifted in mild shock.

She sighed. "I might try something else."

Mr. Blanc nodded. "Very acceptable. Ask the sisters at the Orphans' Asylum tomorrow." He punctuated the statement with a grunt that indicated the subject was closed.

Chapter 8

The next morning was Saturday. The Santa Ana winds came up, blowing hard from the east, licking up the last drops of moisture and charging the air with electricity. The hot winds infused the city with a restlessness that could not be sated. Horses bolted, teenage girls ran away from home, and ordinarily peaceful men started bar fights or struck their wives. Anna loved the winds, which came every year, though they made her hair wild. They mirrored her insides.

By seven a.m., Anna had changed clothes six times, tried four different positions on the settee, and was pacing the parlor like a caged leopard. She needed employment or she would simply go mad. She pulled out the advertisement for the assistant police matron position and stared at it. Mr. Wright would never allow it. It wasn't decent. The Widow Crisp would never allow it. It went without saying that her father would never allow it. Even if the Widow Crisp and Mr. Wright allowed it, which they would not, if Mr. Wright married her she would have to quit so she could carry out her wifely duties. If she worked secretly as an assistant matron and Mr. Wright found out, he might get mad and find a different sweetheart. If Mr. Wright found a different sweetheart, she would be trapped in her father's house and would simply have to kill herself. Anna crumpled the advertisement and tossed it in the trash.

By eight o'clock, Anna had driven her bumblebee yellow Rolls Royce convertible to the Orphans' Asylum and was dragging herself up the path. Her skirts whipped in the wind. The Widow Crisp dogged her every step. The majestic stone building shone in the sun like fool's gold, an empty promise. In the garden, three barefoot urchins took turns throwing a knife into the rotting carcass of a dog.

Anna went straight toward the Headmistress's cottage, hoping to avoid the children. It was ivy covered and storybook charming. Window boxes brimmed with geraniums that danced the turkey trot in the wind. It was green and pink and could almost be made of candy. A witch could live inside. In fact, one did.

Anna knocked on the cottage door. A nun in a long black robe and convoluted wimple opened the door. She was old, smelled like mothballs, and had a hairy mole that almost blocked one nostril. She greeted Anna with pursed lips and a knowing smile that made her mole quiver. "Miss Blanc, do come in. I am Sister Hildegard, Headmistress. We do welcome your patronage, no matter what is said."

This remark stunned Anna and she frowned. To have such a reputation without any of the fun of deserving it. The injustice was galling. Insults always took Anna off guard, especially those proffered with a smile. They confused her, and she could never think of anything smart to say. The Widow Crisp smirked. Anna followed the nun into the parlor and tried to relax her brow so as not to cause wrinkles. Anna's speechlessness seemed to please the sister, who offered her a chair and a cup of tea as black and bitter as sin.

The room was adorned with an excess of doilies. Afghans in drab colors were draped over chairs and settees. Anna watched the Widow Crisp slip two doilies into her sleeve.

Sister Hildegard set down her cup. "We most desperately need blankets. Do you knit?"

Anna was beginning to doubt that volunteer work was for her, when there was a rhythmic rapping at the door. The nun hobbled to the door and answered it. Something like glee lit her face. She stepped aside so the woman could enter. "Miss Blanc, I think you know *Mrs. Louis Taylor*, our volunteer coordinator."

A young woman sashayed through the door, showing Anna her expansive, glistening gums and gray teeth. Anna's eyes popped. She did know her, though she knew her as Miss Enid Curlew. Miss Curlew was a soulless viper of a girl, very rich, and no friend to Anna. Once, she'd told the whole second-grade that Anna hadn't worn drawers. During assembly, she'd tripped Anna on purpose and Anna fell. Anna's skirts flew up, and all the girls looked to see if the rumor was true. It was.

Miss Curlew, Louis Taylor's new bride, smiled wickedly at Anna. "I know it's early in the day for a visit, but I suppose it isn't early in China, is it, Miss Blanc?"

Anna's mind sizzled away, scorched with humiliation. Her pale lips struggled to form words. "Yes. I realized I. Yes. It's very . . ."

Without finishing her tragically unwitty sentence, Anna fled. She shoved past the horrid hag, out the door, onto the porch, and collided with the one man in the world she wanted most to avoid—the man with dreamy hands, the breaker of her heart, the man who was for sale, the indiscreet beast who had told Enid Curlew about Anna's eagerness to be ravished—Louis Taylor.

It was the first time she'd seen him since the Mission Inn atrocity. For a moment, they were frozen there, close enough to kiss. She could smell his spicy cologne. Anna's lower lip trembled. He grasped her arms and gazed at her with lovelorn eyes, as if he'd been the one betrayed. "Anna. We have to talk."

Mrs. Curlew-Taylor emerged from the cottage and smashed Louis on the head with the teapot. "You filthy dog!"

It broke the spell and the teapot.

Oolong dripped from his brilliantine onto his shoulders and tiny porcelain shards stuck to his hair and shirt. Mrs. Curlew-Taylor folded her skinny arms. "Why ever did I marry you?" She clobbered Anna with a victory sneer that shattered her like the teapot, clearly taking pleasure in rejecting a man that had rejected Anna.

Anna came to her senses, dodged around the unhappy couple, and bolted down the path. The Widow Crisp burst through the door, knocking Mrs. Curlew-Taylor into the geraniums. The Widow hiked up her skirts and sprinted after Anna in a brand new pair of men's sneakers. She overtook Anna, grabbed her by the arm and leaned into her face. The old raven's expression was so chilling, it made Anna wonder where Mrs. Morales had found her new chaperone and whether she had skipped the agency and gotten recommendations from a street gang.

The Widow's Sunday school voice was heavy with the threat of tribulation. "I'm not an empty-headed hen who can be dodged and ditched, Miss Blanc."

Anna tried to wriggle free. "I was his wife!"

The Widow Crisp clung like a vise. She grasped Anna tightly by the elbow and walked her to the front of the yellow car. "I don't care about your tragic love affair. I'll not lose my bread and butter on your account!"

Anna set the crank, and the Widow Crisp steered her to the door, pushed her behind the wheel, and slid in beside her. Anna needed no encouragement. As fast as cars were, there was no car in the world that could get Anna away from the Orphans' Asylum fast enough. Her heart was pounding, her breathing shallow. The future played in her mind: an endless series of afternoons spent knitting in parlors, suffering humiliations at the hands of women like Mrs. Curlew-Taylor, and, if she were lucky, evenings spent shooing flies off dried-out turkeys and melting gelatin molds while the man she might someday love missed dinner. And, if she weren't lucky, there would be no love, no marriage, only waiting in the custody of a chaperone that looked like a saint, but most probably had a rap sheet and criminal connections. She accelerated.

The wind shook Anna's yellow convertible and bombarded it with leaves and city dust as it careened down West First Street. A palm frond blew across her windshield. She drove much too fast considering the wind, and the fact that she shared the road with a cable car, a donkey cart, and a crowd of women that spilled out from the doors of Central Station, the headquarters of the LAPD. As she steered around them, a police matron stepped out of the station in a crisp white uniform and shouted something authoritative, motioning for the women to form a line. They did. Anna fixed her eyes on the matron in the rearview mirror, hoping it was Eve, and almost hit a yellow dog. The Widow Crisp clung to the dashboard, her knuckles pinched white.

It wasn't Eve but some other hardworking, working class, lucky, lucky woman. Anna pulled over and tried to collect herself. She pounded on the iron steering wheel with her fist. She bit her lip much harder than usual, taking off a layer of skin. She needed to clear her mind, which was feeling more and more like a hopeless and dangerous place, a hotbed for insurrection. The wind was egging her on, whipping her hair.

She closed her eyes and tried to extract herself from the moment, to focus on the things she had to look forward to: knitting, marrying, shooing, waiting. Anna would choose death over this future if she had any chance of being reincarnated as a police matron, but Catholics didn't believe in reincarnation, and even if it were true God and Anna did not always see eye to eye. She would probably come back as something lower down the chain, like a shimmering moth or an opalescent beetle.

Anna knew she should approach the problem practically. She could lie to the people at the police station and get a job as an assistant matron under a false name. She could then lie to Mr. Wright and her father as to her whereabouts. They were far too busy to miss her anyway, at least for a few weeks. She could lie to the Widow Crisp . . .

This is where her plan fell down. She was shackled to a chaperone who was not weak, not stupid, and not on her side. She wilted, flattening her forehead on the steering wheel.

The Widow Crisp gave a mocking grunt. "You're a fool, with all your sentimentality. Mr. Taylor's handsome, if you like the preening type. But he's lazy and broke. Though he is better than you in one sense; he knows how bread is buttered."

It occurred to Anna that this wholesome-looking woman also knew how bread was buttered, and that they were about the same frock size. "Dear Widow Crisp. You've suggested that your zeal for my protection isn't driven entirely by concern for my welfare, that you are worried about the security of your position. If your primary concerns are financial . . ." Anna let the word hang in the air.

"You haven't got a penny, Miss Blanc."

"But I am well decorated. I have ice." Anna took off her ruby necklace and dangled it in the air between herself and the Widow Crisp.

The stone was large and luminous, surrounded by diamonds. Anna had no idea how much it had cost. She watched to see if the raven could be lured by the shiny trinket.

The Widow Crisp took it up, felt the weight of it, examining the stones. Anna grabbed it back. "They're not paste. Perhaps we can find an arrangement that suits us both?"

"Maybe."

"I want to spend two weeks alone, to do whatever I like, no questions asked. And . . ." Anna looked distastefully at the Widow's mousy frock and chewed on her lower lip. It was badly cut and coarsely sewn from a material that looked more like corrugated cardboard than any fabric with which Anna was familiar. She pinched the Widow's sleeve to see if it was as stiff as it looked. It grated on her fingers. She curled her upper lip.

The Widow snatched her arm away. "And what?"

Anna inhaled, closed her eyes, and puckered her face with all her might. She steeled herself to exhale the horrid words. "I . . . want your clothes." Anna braced herself on the steering wheel as if recovering from some great exertion.

"Hah!" the raven cawed. "These clothes were tailor made. I want your ring too."

The Widow pointed to a rose gold band on Anna's finger. It was set with a large round emerald, surrounded with tiny seed pearls. Anna hesitated because its beauty was rare. "Then I want six weeks, and you'll need to knit blankets for the Orphans' Asylum. If you tell anyone, I'll say you stole these."

The Widow peeled back her lips in a malicious smile. "You speak my language, Miss Blanc."

Anna dropped the jewels into her hand.

In the dappled light under the canopy of an avocado tree, Anna stripped off a gown of Irish lace and stood for a moment letting the warm wind caress her. She would prefer to stay naked on a day that promised to be hot enough to kill livestock. She stood ten rows deep into the orchard, and all around her were waving branches, smudge pots, and fallen fruit.

She handed her dress to the Widow Crisp, who stood naked and thin, her own rough frock in a pile at her feet. Anna picked it up. It smelled of acrid sweat and medicine; it smelled like the Widow Crisp. It was damp under the arms. As Anna slipped into it, the rough fabric scratching her skin, she thought there could be no better disguise in the world; the frock was so far from anything Anna would ever wear. It was more than a breach in taste. It was a capital crime.

Her fingers deftly fastened the buttons that ran up to her chin. It mostly fit, but it strained across her bust and would need to be altered. She thought it couldn't matter for one day. No decent person would be looking at Anna's bust and certainly no officer of the law. "If you burst my buttons, you'll pay for it," the Widow Crisp said.

Anna ignored the comment and padded on bare feet through the orchard, crunching in leaves that sailed up into the wind, avoiding sticks, failing to avoid a moldy avocado that squished between her toes. Her own lilac-colored shoes waited safely in the car. She put them on. Their elegant silver buckles glowed at the bottom of her monstrous frock, but the skirts would mostly cover them. She set the crank and hopped behind the wheel.

The Widow Crisp emerged from the orchard like a pig in pearls, wearing Anna's Irish lace, smelling of Ambre Antique perfume. The gown caught in the wind and waved goodbye to Anna like a flag. She peeled off, leaving her chaperone cursing at the side of the road, her pretty dress sagging at the Widow's bust line.

If there had been a mirror, if Anna could have seen herself, she would have lost her nerve. As there was no mirror, and her mind was muddled by the wind, she parked her yellow convertible several blocks from the station and stepped out in the heinous, sandpaper frock. Her hair was still done up with a perky feather clip, which topped her ensemble like a peacock on a dunghill. She passed the fruit seller in the sombrero, and the limping dog, and came to the long line of ladies that snaked around the sidewalk.

The Central police station was grander and busier than the one in which Anna had been incarcerated—built of heavy, gray granite blocks, with multiple stories to accommodate a receiving hospital above, quarters for the surgeon, larger stables, and a bigger flag. Parked out front, there were several police wagons hitched to white horses, a dozen bicycles, and one shiny gas-powered police car with a gold star. Anna brushed past the women, climbed the stone steps, and peeked through the glass of the double doors. The station bustled with victims and suspects reflecting the flavor of the city—Mexicans, French, Russians, Jews, Chinese, Englishmen. With a deep breath, the wild wind caressing her face, Anna summoned all her nerve and pushed open the door.

The matron Anna had seen earlier was arguing with the captain, violently shaking her head. He looked seasoned and wore his authority comfortably, but she projected a fierce moral authority that left them closely matched.

"It was wrong!" the matron said.

The captain rumbled back in a Scottish brogue. "We have a reputation to uphold, Matron Clemens. It's as simple as that!"

"Have it your way, Captain Wells, but don't expect me to do the hiring!" She folded her arms, immovable as God.

Anna stepped closer. "Excuse me. I'm here to apply for the assistant matron position."

The matron turned on her and growled. "Wait in line like everybody else!" She gave the captain a glare that would have incinerated a lesser man and stomped off to her desk.

The captain threw up his arms. "Jesus, Mary, and Joseph!" He stepped around Anna and swung out the front door. It slammed behind him. Not knowing what else to do, Anna followed.

On the front steps, both Anna and the captain surveyed the line with desperation. It hadn't occurred to Anna that this army of women might be here to apply for one assistant matron position. She would now be last in a queue that ended somewhere around the block. Unsure whether to join the line or ask the Widow Crisp for her jewelry back, she began to slump down the stairs just as a uniformed officer came sauntering up, giving each lady the head to toe. She backed up against the rail to let him pass. He was slick, though unshaven. His eyes lingered appreciatively on Anna's bust. Anna felt both attracted and repulsed, but her heartbeat quickened when she read his badge. "Detective Wolf."

The captain lit up when he saw the detective. "Morning Wolf. What have you?"

"Nothing," Wolf said.

"I'm not surprised." The captain scratched his head. "It's hard to bait a rape fiend with a woman that ugly."

Despite a year of finishing school, Anna's mouth hung open, and her chin almost grazed her nubby dress.

Wolf said, "Especially if she passes out drunk in the middle of your operation. I had to go relieve myself. When I came back, she was on the ground. I couldn't get her up. In the end, I dragged her to the side of the road and covered her with leaves so no one would find her and uh . . ." Wolf noticed that Anna was listening. He lowered his voice. "Get a big surprise."

Anna gasped, shocked that an officer would treat a woman thus, and began to question whether she knew anything at all about the world. The captain stifled a smile. "Where's our bird now?"

Wolf shrugged and sauntered toward the door. "Probably still at the side of the road."

The captain raised a finger. "Hold on a minute. I need a favor. I'd like you to do the hiring for the assistant matron's position. Matron Clemens is . . . out of sorts."

Wolf turned on his heels and raised an eyebrow. "Again? I thought that was a monthly thing." He flashed a blinding smile. "I'll do it with pleasure."

"You're beef to the heels, you are," the captain said. Slapping Wolf on the back, he slipped into the station.

Wolf took to his task with enthusiasm. He scanned the line for candidates who presented well and who might act grateful later. The first twenty-five women, those with the foresight to come early, those who might actually make efficient, sensible matrons, appeared to Wolf to be sober minded—no fun at all. He glanced down the line, passing up several women in their forties, and two pretty girls with tightly wound buns who looked tightly wound.

Then, his eyes settled on Anna, backed up against the rail, her bosoms all but bursting from a frock that shouted, "Grateful!"

CHAPTER 9

In a bare interrogation room, Wolf considered Anna across a table. She faced him with an overeager smile.

"What's your name?" he asked, leaning back in his chair, clipboard at the ready. She looked perplexed, as if this were a hard question. He raised his eyebrows and waited. "Holmes," she said after a moment. "Anna Holmes."

It occurred to Wolf that a stupid matron would be worse than an ugly matron, and he may as well pack it in now. But she was the sweetest little candidate he had ever seen. He enunciated clearly, as if she were foreign or mentally deficient. "It is *Mrs.* Holmes, isn't it? We don't hire unmarried women, and you're not wearing a wedding ring."

"That's right. I mean my ring is . . . being fixed." Anna felt the place where a ring would be.

He gave her a wide, encouraging smile at this prompt response. She sat up straighter, her gorgeous chest rising.

"And your husband doesn't mind if you do this kind of work?" He addressed this question to her heaving chest, as if the gaps between buttons were lips that could speak.

"No. He's overseas with the . . . with the . . . He's overseas." Under the table, Anna gripped her purse so hard that the tiny beads made imprints on her fingers.

He nodded, drawing two round bosoms in his notebook. "How many grades have you completed in school?"

"Twelve." She twisted the chain on her purse, straining the links until they pinched her finger. "Plus finishing school."

"Good. Do you have any experience working with troubled women and children?" He raised his eyebrows hopefully.

"Yes. Through my work with the Orphans' Asylum."

He leaned forward. "So you're comfortable working in, ah, the saltier parts of town?"

"Yes, I like salt." Anna laughed.

He chuckled with her. "And you can type?"

"Yes," she said. "But, I'd really like to do detective work, like you."

He shook his head in wonder. He liked this silly girl. "There are no women detectives, Mrs. Holmes, pulp novels aside. How many words per minute?"

She hesitated. "Three hundred."

Wolf suppressed a grin and imagined her naked. "Do you speak any Spanish?" he asked.

Her mouth curved in a tentative smile. "Yes. A little. My Latin and French are better."

"Please, say something in Spanish, Mrs. Holmes."

"Los-An-ge-les."

Wolf licked his lips. She was perfectly ridiculous, strange, and mouth-watering. He had to do the hard thing, the responsible thing, no matter how good she was to look at, how amusing she would be around the station, or how grateful she might prove to be in the stables behind the station while her husband, if she even had one, was overseas. He sighed and stood, straightening his uniform. "Well, I think we're done here."

Anna's face fell ten stories as if she realized the significance of his words. Wolf fell with her. She seemed desperate. She'd be grateful. She was scrumptious beneath that ugly dress, and he could tell that she wanted it so badly. He racked his brain for any reason to hire this girl, a reason he could justify to Matron Clemens.

"Thank you, Detective Wolf," she said, her voice unsteady. She kicked the table by accident as she stood. She dropped her purse onto the floor and bent to pick it up, the scratchy fabric of her dress straining against her little behind.

Wolf sincerely regretted disappointing her. He was disappointed. She might be a bad liar, but she had nerve, and she was a luscious little peach. "Thank you for coming in, Mrs. Holmes," he said. She caught her trembling, rosebud lip between her teeth and extended her hand. He shook it. It was as soft as petals. She let him hold it a moment too long, and took a deep, sad, quivering breath. A button popped off the front of her frock, revealing an oval of creamy white, and before he could stop his mouth it said, "You're hired."

Sweat beaded on Wolf's brow as he led Anna among the desks to meet the man in charge. His lips stretched in a tense smile, his skin a little paler than before he had hired Anna. "Captain Wells, may I present Mrs. Anna Holmes, our lovely new assistant matron. She types, speaks Spanish, but most importantly, she's nervy. I say that's a vital quality for a matron who will be venturing into unsavory territory."

Unlike Wolf, the captain looked Anna straight in the eye. "Nice to meet you, Mrs. Holmes."

"Likewise," Anna said with the hint of a curtsy.

"You'll report to Matron Clemens." The captain gestured toward the woman he'd been fighting with earlier.

Matron Clemens narrowed her eyes at him. Anna bobbed her head and sent her new boss an unreciprocated smile.

The captain exhaled. "Don't mind her. She'll come around. In the meantime, if you have a question or the men offend you, you can talk to me or to Detective Wolf."

The captain smiled broadly over Anna's shoulder. "Look Wolf, here comes our lost bird. Aye, she is a little bent."

A man in his early twenties, dressed as a female, hung on the station door. He had a cleft chin, a dimpled smile, and a green complexion. Leaves stuck to his bonnet and a twig hung from his drawers, which were visible above his blonde, hairy legs as an inch of his skirt was tucked into his lowers. His blue eyes squinted against the light.

Under his breath he sang. "Shine on, shine on, harvest moon, up in the sky. I ain't had no lovin' since January, April, June, or July . . ."

Cheers and whistles rose from the station. Someone shouted. "Nice pegs, Singer!" He curtsied and rallied himself for the journey across the floor.

Wolf's conversation with Captain Wells on the stairs began to make sense to Anna. This drunken creature belonged buried in leaves at the side of the road.

Captain Wells held up a bottle and shook it. "You can do it, lad. I've got a little hangover cure here. You'll be right as rain."

Officer Singer headed toward the bottle like a hungry toddler just learning to walk. Anna stared. As he wobbled past, his big booted feet stepped on his hem and he fell, grabbing desperately at the air for support. His arms found Anna's tiny waist, and he held on tight. He grinned up at her. "Nice feather." Just inhaling his breath made Anna feel drunk. She pushed him away with all her might, sending him flat against a nearby wall. Their audience laughed.

Reaching up in horror, she felt the perky feather clip and flushed a deep rose red. She was ashamed to have accessorized so incongruently. She hurried to unclip it and stuffed it in her pocket. By the time she returned home, the feather would undoubtedly be as bent as the young police officer.

While Anna was distracted with her hair clip, Officer Singer's mouth opened and he started to gag in the style of a dog that had eaten too much grass. Before she could dodge it, he sprayed the station with whiskey and whatever he had eaten for dinner the previous night, which apparently included spinach and corn. Green, corny chunks of sick stuck on the hem of Anna's ugly frock and on one of her lilac shoes, clogging the filigree on the elegant silver buckle. Officer Singer wiped his mouth on his ruffled sleeve and, feeling the full force of his hangover, slid down the wall. "Oh, God."

Chapter 10

Anna couldn't decide if she were lucky or unlucky, whether God was rewarding her for providing blankets for the Orphans' Asylum or punishing her for corrupting the Widow Crisp. She crouched near the front counter, scrubbing her shoe so hard the lilac polish came off, leaving a regrettable brown streak that would have to be fixed. She had abandoned the ugly vomit-covered frock for a crisp new matron's uniform, which Matron Clemens had provided, though the cost would be deducted from Anna's pay.

The skirt was sensible, unflattering, and white. The blouse, which wrapped around her neck like a boa constrictor, was also white, as was the mannish necktie. It was more ugly than a nurse's uniform, but it looked nicer than anything from the Widow Crisp's trunk and gave her bosoms a little more wiggle room. Anna felt both honored and horrified to wear it.

A girl about Anna's age, with hair the color of a clementine, peeked in through the glass doors of the station, blushed her freckles into oblivion, spun around, and went clipping down the steps. Officer Wolf swept past Anna and out the door in fervent pursuit of the spy. He was grinning.

Behind the counter, a clerk minded his own business, hiding behind thick spectacles. He had ruddy, shiny skin and a mouth so tiny it could belong to a child. He hadn't even looked at Anna, though everyone agreed she was very nice to look at. She needed friends at the station and so cleared her throat to address him. "Excuse me, Mr. . . ."

"Melvin," he said in a librarian's hush.

Anna glided over. He leaned away from her. It surprised Anna, but she took a step back and found her most harmless smile. "Nice to meet you, Mr. Melvin. I'm Miss Bl . . . I mean, Assistant Matron Holmes." She bobbed. When he said nothing, she said, "I don't understand why that drunken officer is wearing a frock."

He peered up from behind his cola bottle glasses and spoke in a butterfly whisper. "It's an undercover operation, Matron Holmes. Joe Singer's trying to catch a criminal who . . ." He lowered his voice until it was barely audible. ". . . does unspeakable things."

Anna tried to imagine "unspeakable things" but was interrupted when Matron Clemens appeared, her face frozen in a professional mask of aloofness. "Matron Holmes. There's been a suicide at one of the parlor houses. Detective Wolf says you're familiar with all the cribs and parlor houses from your charity work, and that you are quite intrepid. Is that correct?" She looked hard at Anna.

"Yes, ma'am," Anna lied. A parlor house must be a teahouse. She wasn't sure what a crib was or where she could find one, but clearly it had something to do with babies.

"Good. Go down to Canary Cottage, collect the orphan, and take him to the Orphans' Asylum."

Anna blinked. Matron Clemens dropped a file and two coins into Anna's hand and glided off without further instruction.

"Yes, ma'am," Anna said to the woman's retreating backside. She opened the file and saw the names Peaches Payton and Georgie Payton typed on a document.

She turned to Mr. Melvin and spoke, one butterfly to another. "Would you kindly refresh my memory? What is a crib?"

He looked up and mouthed the words, "A low-class brothel."

Anna burst out, "She wants me to go to a brothel? Jupiter!"

Matron Clemens and Wolf looked her way. She flashed them her most competent smile, and turned back to Mr. Melvin with a look of desperation.

He spoke quietly to Anna, staring down at his necktie. "You'll have to go from time to time. They don't allow brothel girls to raise children once they're weaned. Some of the girls farm them out, but if not, the matrons have to go get them and take them to an orphanage or reform school." His words were directed at his tie. "Don't worry. You won't even see the girls. The brothels on New High Street keep their curtains drawn. There's a city ordinance to that effect."

Anna leaned closer. "I see. Where can I find them?"

Matron Clemens, unsmiling, was on her way over.

"You better go," he said.

"Thank you." Anna slipped out the door with her file and her coins. The wind had died down to a hot puff. She paused on the landing with no idea where to go, her brow wrinkled in consternation.

Joe Singer slouched at the top of the steps beneath a pepper tree, holding up the wall and smoking a cigarette. He had replaced the frock with a police uniform but hadn't removed the bonnet. He sang to himself. "I have loved lots of girls in the sweet long ago, and each one has meant heaven to me." He stopped singing and addressed her as if reading her mind. "Go left on Main, left on Commercial, right on New High Street. Look for the Esmeralda Club. Canary Cottage is the third brothel after the Esmeralda Club on your right. Three stories high. Green trim."

Anna launched herself down the stairs, taking them two at a time to get away from the reprobate faster.

"You're welcome!" he called after her.

Anna rode the trolley down Main Street, shaded by towering brownstones. It was easily six cars wide and buzzed with carts, bikes, people, horses, and Model-T Fords. She turned on Commercial, passing furniture stores, hatters, and factories. The motion of the trolley amplified her jangling nerves. Brothels were Beelzebub's parlor, vile pits where bad things were done that she didn't understand. Women were never supposed to be in them. Anna caught herself biting her nails. She rested her hands in her lap and tried to think up excuses in case anyone she knew saw her in Satan's parlor, but quickly realized it wasn't necessary. No one she knew would ever be in a brothel under any circumstances. She was venturing where no civilized person had gone before, like Marco Polo, Christopher Columbus, or Dr. Livingston. She inspired herself.

Visiting Chez Lucifer was not the only challenge of the day. She would have to get the child to the Orphans' Asylum without encountering the witch or, worse yet, Mrs. Curlew Taylor.

On New High Street, Anna pulled the trolley cord. The bell dinged and the streetcar lurched to a stop. She followed Officer Singer's directions, wandering past storefronts with bright awnings, which offered everything from dripping blocks of ice to prickly cactus paddles. As she moved down New High Street, the awnings began to sag and the vendors along the hot cement walk became fewer, replaced by saloons with signs that read, "Closed." She heard the whistle of a nearby train.

Anna walked over broken glass and into a cloud of stale beer fumes and urine stench. She stepped around a red lace garter soaking up mud in the gutter. She stepped on something and felt it crunch and roll under the sole of her shoe like sweet gherkins.

A disembodied voice howled. Anna sprang off and, to her horror, saw fingers. Her eyes followed the smashed hand to the arm of a little man sprawled behind a fraying potato sack full of empty whiskey bottles. He was nursing the smooth glass top of a bottle. Anna could see his slimy white tongue wiggling inside. He didn't seem bothered about his crushed fingers. They were the least of his injuries. His lips swelled into a bloody pucker and a plum of flesh hung under each eye. He'd been soundly trounced. All the same, he leered at Anna with surprising energy.

Anna quickened her step. She stumbled to a stop in front of two arched windows that looked like eyes. A sign in gold letters read, "The Esmeralda Club." She peered down the street, looking for brothels. She spied an empty beer mill, a vacant pool hall, a silent dance hall. The drunken officer had said that Canary Cottage was the third brothel, but Anna didn't see a single "Devil's Lair" sign, and most of the buildings looked sinful. How could she tell where the brothels began or ended? There was no one to ask this early in the morning. The reprobates were all still asleep.

A city ordinance, Mr. Melvin had said, forbade houses of ill repute to leave their curtains open. Anna proceeded until she found a building with the curtains drawn. It was a large stone edifice that rose from the street in three layers, ornate and decorated like a cake. It might have belonged to a prosperous family, had it been in a different neighborhood and had it featured sheer lace curtains at windows open to let in the breeze on this gruesomely hot day. But the windows were hung with heavy velvet drapes, pulled closed. She counted one.

Anna passed two buildings with no curtains, which she thought might be ordinary saloons. She skipped those. She passed a complex of small, grungy apartments encircling a courtyard where several pairs of drawers dried on a line. Raucous snores drifted from a window. The curtains were dark, heavy and closed. She counted two.

On down the street, a three-story building had bright green window trim and closed scarlet drapes—the third crib. It was neat, but garish, in a color combination that would offend Christmas. The proprietor, whoever she was, could clearly use a decorator. Even the wicked must have an aesthetic.

In front, a thin, angular man sat behind the reigns of a coroner's wagon hitched to a pair of shiny black horses. He looked like a mantis saying his prayers, eyes closed, mouth active. Anna stopped in her tracks. He seemed vaguely familiar, like the cousin of an acquaintance met once and forgotten. One of the horses swished its tail. She held the file up to shield her face and tiptoed past.

In a vacant lot next to the brothel a cat stalked an unseen creature in the grass. Three cats crouched in a jacaranda tree, white velvet against the rough bark and green leaves. A litter of tabby kittens swarmed over a woodpile, sharpening their claws and pouncing on prey, real or imaginary, amidst the dry weeds and feathery, fragrant anise. All across the field she could see them—spotted cats, orange cats, black cats, long hairs, and their mixed-up progeny—more cats than Anna had ever seen in one place. When Anna approached, they waved their tails and padded toward her as if expecting her to feed them. Anna knelt to pet the first several, but they were dusty and flea-bitten, and she was quickly overwhelmed. She resorted to stomping and shooing them. "Go back!" They hopped into the brothel yard or wandered off into the field.

A picket fence surrounded the brothel. A cluster of cowbells hung from the gate. Chickens clucked in a coop, and a poison green motorcycle with a sidecar dripped grease onto the grass. Red letters on a green sign spelled out, "Canary Cottage."

Somewhere behind Anna, a male voice hollered, "Detective Snow, will you please come help with this? I have an appointment!" Anna snapped her head around. The praying mantis had come to life and was standing behind the wagon, sliding out a wooden stretcher covered with a sheet that billowed in the wind. She followed the direction of his gaze. An officer stepped out from behind a tree in the cat field, shooing vultures away from something on the ground. They flapped their ratty wings into the air, the wrinkled red of their heads visible even at a distance. They circled.

"The dead don't mind if you're late, Coroner," called the officer. He stopped shooing and let the vultures settle. What the man did next shocked Anna more than anything she had seen that day. He kicked a bird so hard that it sailed upside down into the air, one black wing at an unnatural angle. A bit of meat dropped from its cracked beak. The other startled scavengers looped into the sky, only to settle back down on their dinner, which Anna guessed would soon include their wounded companion.

The horrid officer began jogging toward the wagon. Anna turned away. She felt a sickening in her stomach and crossed herself. Never had she been surrounded by such evil—suicide, debauchery, cruelty, and callousness. And on a day that was so hot, she felt licked by the flames of hell itself.

She shook the cluster of bells and prayed that someone would come out so she didn't have to go inside and face the inevitably gaudy furniture in that tasteless den of inequity.

No one came. Anna scanned the building's facade for signs of life. From the corner of her eye, she saw a blood red curtain part, revealing the hint of a pale face. Anna shifted her focus to the window and the curtain shut.

The brothel door opened and spit out a woman, taffeta rustling, fox stole swinging, her face chalked with rouge. Anna lifted her chin so high and tight it ached, and tried to channel Matron Clemens's air of authority. "Good afternoon. I am a police matron . . ." Anna's Matron Clemens impression abruptly fell away. She squeaked, "You're that woman from the morgue!"

The woman's red hair, sharp eyes, and the curve of her back under a glossy black dress made her look like a condor. She perused Anna, top to bottom, with raptor eyes lined with Kohl. "And you're the swooning debutante, who is obviously up to somethin'."

Anna took a step back and folded her arms. "I'm Assistant Matron Holmes and I'm sure I don't know what you're talking about."

"Atta girl. Always deny everything."

Anna's eyebrow shot up. Though "always deny everything" was the motto she lived by, Anna took offense at the suggestion that she was doing anything wrong, especially from a woman who devoted her life to doing wrong things.

The condor looked at her sharply, piercing through Anna's mask. "Calm down, princess. I don't mean no offense. I'm in an ill humor on account of some bastard keeps killin' our girls." She raised her voice so that the officer could hear. "And the other bastards ain't helping!" She stuck out a puffy hand. "Madam Lulu."

Anna took it gingerly and shook. "Someone is killing your girls?"

"That's what I said."

"Do you have any evidence? Because the police say both deaths were suicides and I know that if I were in Peaches' position, I would kill myself."

That wasn't exactly true. Suicide was an unpardonable sin. Anna would all but kill herself, go to confession, and hope she would later die of her injuries.

Madam Lulu guffawed. "You ever heard of a woman slittin' her own throat?"

Anna considered this in light of the detective novels she'd read. "That won't be sufficient at an inquest."

"There ain't gonna be no inquest! Now, there's a limit to what I can do given my field of employment. Can't really lean on the police." Madam Lulu stared at Anna with eyes as black as eight balls.

Anna shifted uncomfortably. "I'm sure the police know what they're doing."

"Makes it worse, don't it?"

Anna knit her brows. This woman had little confidence in the LAPD.

The madam surveyed Anna from toe to head, taking in her fine, albeit vomit-stained, shoes, her unspoiled hands, and the faint scent of her Ambre Antique perfume. Anna shifted uncomfortably.

"You're quite the princess under that ugly uniform," the madam said.

"You mistake me!" Anna sounded defensive, even to herself, and far too loud.

"I bet you know some influential people in this town. I bet you could pull some strings. Make things happen down at the station."

Anna's voice wavered. "That's absurd. I haven't any connections."

The painted bird smirked. She turned heel and waddled into the house, leaving Anna at a loss as to what to do next. She had been charged with collecting the child and wouldn't leave until she did. But Mr. Melvin had said she didn't have to enter the sin house, and by God she would not. She stared at the dwelling that was painted like Christmas and waited.

A little black girl in a maid's costume, not yet a woman, emerged from the house holding a plump boy no older than three. He was neatly turned out in short pants and a crisp blouse, with a fine embroidered collar. His scrubbed face was red and swollen from crying. The girl caressed the child. "Bye bye, punkin. We'll see ya real soon." She kissed him and leveled an accusatory stare at the matron who would carry him away. "Lulu said to tell ya that Georgie's ma was named Daisy Tombs. Her real name. In case you could find his kin. But ya mustn't tell 'em she was a parlor girl 'cause no baby needs that."

The girl held out an envelope. "She left a letter."

Anna plucked it up with interest. "A suicide note?" Before she could open it, the maid placed Georgie in her arms. Juggling the boy, her purse, and the file, Anna stuffed the paper in her pocket.

The maid said, "Will you tell Officer Singer not to be a stranger? Used to come see us three, four times a week. I guess he's busy with his police work."

Anna's mouth gaped in reply.

Georgie erupted in hopeless sobs as the maid retreated. Anna pressed the child against her breast and shushed him, swaying from hip to hip. He blubbered. She sang to him softly, but she was desperately sharp, making him wail even louder, as if to drown her out. She would have been offended had not his situation been so dire. His lot seemed as unfair as Anna's own. She was taking this boy to the Orphans' Asylum, to the wicked witch, and unless they found his kin, he was going to have to live there.

Taking a deep breath, Anna turned back to the boardwalk, clutching the blubbering child, and found herself inches away from the corpse of Peaches Payton.

Chapter 11

The body lay covered by a sheet on a stretcher borne by the coroner and one Detective Snow—the cruel man who had kicked the vulture. His cheek had a bite scar and his ear had once been torn. Anna's eyes flashed recognition. She had seen both these men before, at the train tracks, collecting the body of the suicide on the night of her elopement. She pressed herself close against the gate to put space between herself and the dead girl as the men passed by. The thin sheet that draped across the body fluttered in the wind. One tiny bare foot protruded. Anna caught a glimpse of the second foot, peeking from beneath the sheet in a shoe that was a little too large.

The coroner shifted his grip and the stretcher jolted. A gust lifted the sheet and it billowed for a moment, then cascaded to the ground leaving the corpse exposed. Georgie fell calm. "Mama." He extended his finger. Anna clapped a hand across his eyes, fumbled for the latch, and pushed through the gate into the yard as the child began to howl.

"Come back and pick up the sheet!" the coroner ordered Anna, as if she was responsible for the wind. Panic squeezed her spine, though she'd done nothing wrong. She looked back toward the house seeking arms in which to place the baby. She found none.

"Hurry up! I haven't got 'til Sunday," the coroner said.

Anna set Georgie gently on the grass and hurried over to the gate, latching it behind her, but he followed her and hung off the slats. She reentered the gate and picked Georgie up. The men groaned impatiently. She crossed the yard to the chicken coop, opened the wire door, placed him in the coop and latched it. Chickens ran about, fluttering their wings and squawking as Anna scurried back across the lawn and through the gate to the body.

An emptiness spread through her chest—a sense of failure because she hadn't protected the boy from the sight of this dead thing that had once been his mother. She felt sure that Matron Clemens would have.

Anna's eyes took in the pale girl. It was the first body she had ever seen. She felt strangely detached. Golden hair fanned out from the dead girl's head like a halo. A wreath of red carnations was clipped into it, the symbol of a love-stricken heart. Carnations were the most fragrant of any flower. Anna could smell their perfume over the metal sting of blood.

Peaches wore a white gown, and she would have been pretty but for the gaping hole across the center of her neck and the fact that her right eye was missing, probably flying overhead in the crop of some vulture. She could see the girl's insides laid bare by the feasting of the birds under her chin, and the tracks of birds on the white linen of her décolletage. There was hardly any blood. She wondered how deep the original incision was, and whether a girl could, in fact, make such a cut herself. And, if she had done it, why had she given such care to her appearance only to spoil the effect with a gash across her throat. A more thoughtful girl would have slit her wrists, having first purchased gloves for the funeral. And she would have made sure that her shoes fit.

The coroner glared at Anna, who was taking too long. Anna knelt down for the sheet. She could see Snow's rain boots, smeared with blood and feathers, and could smell his feet moldering in the rubber. Her lip curled in disgust. She gingerly picked the sheet up, spread it across the corpse, and tucked it beneath the girl's legs to prevent it from slipping off again. The men moved the stretcher before she had even finished and without any acknowledgment of her assistance. As the men progressed toward the wagon, the girl's shoe slipped from her foot and dropped onto the boardwalk, tumbling into the weeds.

Anna ran back to the chicken coop to check on Georgie. He seemed all right, though the chickens were in some distress. He chased them, barraging them with handfuls of dirt and corn, which Anna deemed just fine under the circumstances.

Feeling easier, Anna left Georgie to retrieve the shoe. She picked up a stick and poked through the weeds, finding cigarette butts, broken glass, and a four-inch piece of animal intestine dripping with a creamy goo, which she flung aside with the stick. She found a sixpence with the face of Queen Victoria, who looked rather placid given that she'd been dropped in the bushes in the worst part of town. How Anna wished the coin were American and not English. She could sorely use the money. She tossed it away. Finally, at the base of a feathery green anise bush, she spied the slipper. Anna picked it up. The fine silk of it shone in the sun, special by any measure, far too good for a bad girl. The designer had scrolled his name in gold on an inner label.

François Pinet.

It was Anna's own shoe. She was sure of it—the one that had tumbled off when she'd leapt onto the train at the station. Peaches must have found it on the tracks. Perhaps, even as Anna had worn one shoe at the Mission Inn, Peaches had worn its mate in the brothel. Anna's stomach felt queer, thinking of the dead girl's toes in her shoe, of the dead girl pretending to be a fine lady, of the dead girl taking her own life, or perhaps having it taken from her.

The slipper was too nice to leave in the dirt—so nice that Anna had kept its mate, planning to have François Pinet make her a new one. She would bring the matching shoe to the station, and the girl could wear them both at her wake—Anna's penance for letting Georgie see his mother's torn body.

She stood quickly, intending to bring the shoe to the coroner, but the wagon was already heading off in a cloud of dust. Now she would have to carry the shoe along with the child, the file, and her purse on her journey to the Orphans' Asylum. Anna tramped back to the chicken coop, where Georgie had smashed half a dozen eggs, and picked him up. He began to wail again. He kicked at Anna, reaching for the chickens. His shirt was no longer crisp and white, but covered in droppings, egg, and dirt, his face streaked with tears and dust. Anna's own clothing was irredeemably soiled for the second time that day. She shifted Georgie's weight onto one hip and he smacked her in the face with his chubby fist. Her nose burned. Next time she went to the brothels, she would demand a pram, preferably one with straps.

Anna lugged Georgie up the road toward the Esmeralda Club, crossing the street to avoid the drunken man, who now leaned against the door of the saloon. He seemed even smaller when standing. He watched her with red eyes under swollen lids. His fattened mouth crooned the words, "Miss Blanc."

Anna ran.

The toddler bounced in her arms. His corrugated wails wavered in and out with each knock and jolt. He butted her chin with his head, and she bit her tongue. Still, she didn't slow until they reached the trolley stop, and the creepy, frightening man blighted the earth somewhere far, far behind them. How did he know her? Perhaps he recognized her from the paper, like Mr. Wright. Anna made a note to look less like herself. That morning, she had swept her hair up in a glamorous knot. She put her hands on either side of her head and rubbed furiously, until she was sure that her hair looked terrible.

Anna got off the trolley at Aveneda de Las Pulgas and trudged through a copse of towering eucalyptus trees. Her arms ached from carrying the child, her purse, the file, the shoe, and her anxiety over the creepy little man. She approached the Orphans' Asylum from the woods behind, slipping from eucalyptus to eucalyptus with one hand firmly clamped over Georgie's mouth. His baby teeth pinched her fingers. That was all right. As long as he was biting her, he couldn't scream. She snuck along the side of the headmistress's cottage and peered in the window. The witch was cackling at another nun. Her mole was vibrating.

"Now, don't cry, Georgie," Anna cooed. "A lovely nun is going to care for you while I go find your family. All right?" His eyes radiated hostility and he grunted into her palm. Looking this way and that, Anna padded to the porch. When she pulled her hand from between Georgie's teeth, he threw back his head and screamed. She dropped the orphan and bounded for the woods.

Anna didn't open Peaches' note until she had collapsed onto a trolley bench and was rattling down the Aveneda. It was crumpled from being in her pocket and sealed in an envelope addressed with a single word, "Georgie." Anna used her fingernail to slit it open and read.

> Georgie,
>
> Mi sweet babee. I luv u. But I rekan a difrent muther kan raz u beter. I m so sory, babee. Pleez forgiv me. I was n a low, low, plaz.
>
> Luv,
> Muther

Anna frowned and shook her head. Peaches' spelling was tragic.

Chapter 12

Officer Joe Singer stomped the length of the counter at Central Station, scowling and running his fingers through his hair. He pivoted, paced back again, and slammed a fist onto the polished wood. *Bang.* Mr. Melvin, who sat behind the counter, jumped and withdrew into his coat like a turtle, his tiny lips snapped shut like a turtle's beak. Joe shook out his bruised hand. "Sorry."

Joe strode across the room to where Eve was cleaning out her desk with brisk, deft movements. She packed up pencils and personal things, shoving them into a leather satchel.

"How could they do this to you?" Joe demanded.

"I'm a woman," she said.

"That's no excuse!"

She smirked. She had dark circles under her eyes and her cheeks lacked their usual bloom. Joe knew Eve McBride. She acted tough, but she was suffering, and it pained him to see it. Joe's father could have fixed this situation if he'd wanted to. Easy as pie. He was chief of police. Joe had tried to call in favors, bargained and begged, and still he wouldn't do it. His father didn't care about justice. Eve had lost her job because some pampered rich girl with no sense wanted to play suffragette, and Captain Wells cared more about what kind of matron Eve appeared to be than what kind of matron she was.

He softened his voice. "What are you gonna do?"

"I don't know. Go to Denver. I have a cousin in Denver."

He tugged on his hair. "Aw Eve, I'd hate to see you leave town."

Eve looked him in the eye. "Then how 'bout I stay here and you marry me."

The words hung in silence. Joe's eyebrows lifted and froze there. He loved Eve. He did. Like a sister. Well, not like a sister. They'd spent too much time in the boathouse unsupervised as kids. But that was then, and this came out of the blue.

Eve broke into a wide grin, slapped her knee, and laughed. Joe chuckled with her nervously. "That ship sailed when you refused me in the eighth grade."

She quickly picked up the heavy satchel and let the momentum turn her toward the exit, her smile melting into a straight line. "Thanks for getting me out."

"I tried to do more, Eve. You know I tried, but it's like arguing with God. The crazy thing is, my pop likes you." Joe reached for her satchel. "Let me get that. I'll walk you to the trolley."

Eve's grip on her bag tightened. "It's all right. I've got it handled, and you've got work to do." She deftly took her burden toward the door.

He walked fast to keep a step ahead of her. "I can loan you money."

"No thanks. Got some."

Joe opened the door and held it as Eve strode through. "If I hear of any openings, I'll come over. Let me know what you're gonna do, all right?"

Eve kept on going as if she were already somewhere else. He swore under his breath.

Anna was tripping up the steps of the station when Eve stomped past on her way down. "Eve!" Anna called. But Eve didn't look around. Anna would almost say she walked faster. Perhaps Eve didn't recognize her in a filthy matron's uniform sticky with egg. She wouldn't expect to find Anna at Central Station. If she had heard about the new assistant matron, it would be a Mrs. Holmes and not a Miss Blanc. Anna resisted the urge to follow Eve, since Matron Clemens was surely wondering what had taken her so long.

Anna wouldn't let this accidental snub put a damper on her happy mood. She would see Eve again soon. Heaven was smiling upon Anna. She had accomplished her mission, delivering Georgie out of the frying pan and into the fire. She did this despite obstacles that Matron Clemens and Officer Wolf could never appreciate.

Anna entered the station with her head held high. She glided to the desk where Mr. Melvin worked, eyes fixed on his typing. She leaned over and whispered in his ear, fairly beaming. "I did it. I went to the cribs. It was like you said. Thank you."

Without looking up, he whispered, "You're welcome." Captain Wells approached Mr. Melvin's desk and engaged him in conversation.

Anna stepped back and collided with Wolf. She swung around. "Pardon me, Detective."

Wolf stared bemusedly at her soiled chest, which was smeared with egg, chicken droppings, and dirt. "Matron Holmes, how was your visit to the cribs?" He seemed to be holding his breath.

"Very fine, thank you."

"I mean, did you get the orphan to the Orphans' Asylum? You look as if you've been in an egg fight."

Anna colored a little. "The boy was playing in a chicken coop and I had to carry him all the way. Don't the police own a pram?"

Wolf grinned and shook his head. "I'm sorry, Matron Holmes. The police pram is out for repairs."

"You're making fun of me."

"Now why would I do that? I'm proud of you." He patted her on the shoulder and let his hand graze down her back.

"I've brought the dead woman's shoe. It fell into the weeds when they were carrying her on the stretcher." Anna handed him the shoe. "I . . . dropped the other in . . . in a pond. I'll go swimming and bring it tomorrow."

"Thank you." Wolf's finger grazed Anna's pinky as he pressed it back into her hands. "But, why don't you be in charge of the shoe?"

"It's very curious," Anna said, turning it over in her hand. "This shoe is size three. I saw her feet and they couldn't have been larger than a one."

"That is a mystery, Matron Holmes." He was grinning again.

"Oh, and here is the suicide note. What do I do with it?" She pulled it from her pocket and tried to hand it to him.

He waved it away. "Send it to the family, if she has one."

Snow came from across the room, pushed past Anna, and thrust a sheet of paper in the general direction of Captain Wells. Four lines were written on it in an ugly hand. "Here's my report on that whore who killed herself—Peaches Payton."

"That's a parlor girl name if I ever heard one," Wolf said.

Snow showed his stained teeth. "Doesn't matter if it's not her real name. No one's lookin' for her."

Anna leaned over, trying to read the report. "Her name is Daisy Tombs."

Wolf grinned with pride. "Very good, Matron Holmes."

Anna smiled. "Don't you think it's odd that a girl would slit her own throat? Wouldn't she throw herself off a cliff or into a river or something?"

"You've been reading too many romantic novels, Matron Holmes," Wolf said.

"Madam Lulu said other brothel girls have died, too. We could have another Jack the Ripper—a New High Street . . ." Anna searched for the words. "A New High Street Suicide Faker."

The men grinned. Anna turned serious eyes on Captain Wells. "Captain, I think someone should investigate."

Captain Wells raised his eyebrows at Anna and turned to look at Snow. "What do you have to say about it, Detective Snow?"

Snow made a scoffing sound. "We did investigate. The coroner says it's a suicide."

"I trust my men, Matron Holmes," Captain Wells said. "Now excuse me." He trudged toward his office.

Snow turned on Anna. "You think I don't know my job?"

Wolf sighed. He had to nip the conflict in the bud before his pretty hireling made another enemy. "I'm sure she doesn't mean that, do you honeybun?"

"Well, it didn't look like a suicide to me," Anna said.

Wolf gave Snow a taut smile and steered Anna off into a corner. "Matron Holmes, there are about twenty murders every year in LA, and fifty suicides, each and every one of them investigated by the coroner. He's been working for the county for five years. That makes about 100 murdered bodies and 250 suicides that our coroner's investigated. He doesn't think there's a New High Street Suicide Faker. How many deaths have you investigated?"

"None." Anna glanced at the vomit stain on her shoe.

Wolf squeezed her shoulder. "Try to remember that, honeybun."

Anna returned to her desk and stuck the crumpled suicide note into her purse.

Chapter 13

Anna stepped out of the station in her eggy uniform, splattered with chicken dung, and absorbed the hurly-burly of the city. She felt powerful, joyful, and esteemed herself greatly. Next time the LAPD advertised for a matron position, she would recommend that they borrow the language from the vibrator ad.

She inhaled deeply, tingling with the force of her awakened power, and immediately regretted it. But even the garbage stench of the city in summer could not squelch her good mood. She had spent the day working with the LAPD and ventured into the underworld where no one from her set had ever gone before. She'd interviewed a madam who was a potential witness in a murder investigation and discussed the case with the detective in charge. Granted, he was hostile toward her, and perhaps it was just a suicide. But she'd put in her two cents, and the whole affair was much more exciting than anything else she had ever done, including eloping with Louis Taylor, which previously had been the highlight of her short life, whether she admitted it or not.

The cherry on top would be when Eve returned to work. Eve was smart, pretty, world-wise, and a real suffragette. They were sisters, having shared something singular, and now they would work with detectives together. Anna felt sure that Eve would never give her secret identity away.

Matron Clemens strode crisply onto the landing. Anna straightened up. "Good evening, Matron Clemens, are you off for the day?"

"I'm on my way to the jail to interview a woman arrested in connection with a train robbery. I'll sit with her tonight because I don't quite trust the jailer."

Anna smiled. "Oh. How nice." She meant it. She couldn't think of anything she'd rather do than spend time with a jailbird, penetrating the criminal mind.

"Matron Holmes, you *will* wash your uniform tonight."

"Yes, ma'am. Of course."

As Matron Clemens went on her way, Anna made a mental list of things that would make her life perfect: her own prisoner; Mr. Wright and her father's permission to be a matron and to sleep overnight in the jail; matron uniforms designed by Vionnet at the House of Doucet; and a joint assignment with Eve McBride to solve a murder.

Anna brightened. Matron Clemens would know about Eve. Anna clipped after her, catching up at the bottom step. "Do you know when Matron McBride will return to the station?"

Matron Clemens eyebrows descended in a wary frown. "You're acquainted with Matron McBride?"

"Only slightly, but I like her very much."

"She left her position."

Anna blinked. "But she couldn't have."

"I assure you. She did."

Anna felt limp, like a rubber balloon that someone had untied, letting out all of the joy. "But, why?"

"She had her reasons. I'm not sure that Mrs. McBride would appreciate me discussing her private business."

Lines formed on Anna's brow. "Do you know how I can reach her?"

"I do not. But you could ask Officer Singer."

Anna's frown deepened. "Thank you, I will."

The older woman cleared her throat. "While I have you, there is something Officer Wolf may not have mentioned. Matrons are held to the highest standard of conduct. Even the hint of impropriety will not be tolerated. Do you understand?"

"Of course."

"Good night, Matron Holmes." Matron Clemens clipped down the sidewalk and made a sharp right, heading toward the jail.

Anna slumped against the marble railing, absently running her hand along its smooth surface, dusting it of leaves. She couldn't imagine anyone ever quitting the station. Being an assistant police matron was the very pinnacle of her own experience. Surely, Eve shared this sentiment. Eve had said nothing about quitting when they were in the hoosegow together. Why would she leave? Had she suddenly gotten sick or married?

She achieved nothing by speculating. Anna would simply have to find Eve and ask her. That meant talking to Officer Singer. His very name made her queasy, especially after Matron Clemens's lecture. He had presented himself at work so drunk that he wobbled, yet the captain winked at his misconduct. If Anna had the barest whiff of medicinal Rip Van Winkle on her breath, she would be dismissed. Not Officer Singer, in his ugly nineteenth-century bonnet. Coming to work pie-eyed and petrificated wasn't the limit to his wickedness, either. He frequented brothels. His manners were bad. He had vomited on her shoe without offering to buy her a new one or even helping to wipe it off. Officer Singer was a disgrace to the LAPD. She reeled at the injustice of this goose and gander double standard.

As Anna reeled, Captain Wells shuffled down the stairs. Anna, severely flummoxed, fell in step. "Excuse me, Captain Wells."

He smiled and answered in his rolling Scottish brogue. "What is it, Matron Holmes?"

His use of her pseudonym made her hesitate. She was no longer Anna Blanc, a woman with connections, but Assistant Matron Holmes, a woman under his command. Still, hadn't he told her to come to him if any of the men offended her? Wasn't she offended now? More importantly, wasn't she right? Anna straightened her posture and plunged ahead. "I know you're concerned about our conduct and the image of the LAPD."

"That's right, and don't you forget it."

Her words rippled with indignation. "But you said nothing when that officer arrived at work so drunk he couldn't walk!"

"Ah, yes." He tilted his head back, thoughtfully. "You'll have to excuse Officer Singer. Last night, he faced the darkest side of human nature, and he did it in a frock."

While Anna was speaking with Captain Wells, Joe Singer himself came ambling down the sidewalk, easy as you please, his helmet dipped low on his brow. He hummed "Sweet Adeline."

He heard his name and stopped humming. Anna continued, oblivious to his presence. "Well, speaking of the darker side—can you explain to me why he's so often at the brothels—and not on police business!"

Captain Wells said, "I don't have to explain anything to you, Matron Holmes, and it would be good if you could remember it. But, I think you're mistaken. If Officer Singer went anywhere near the brothels, his father would have him arrested. The chief's very particular when it comes to his son."

Officer Singer picked that moment to pass, sauntering by with a knowing smirk. He tipped his hat to Captain Wells. "Evening Uncle. Evening Matron ... what's your name?" He didn't stay to hear the answer.

Captain Wells called after him. "Don't be late tonight. Your aunt's made enchiladas." Officer Singer waved without turning around. The captain bowed his head. "Good evening, Matron Holmes." He stepped off the curb, and crossed the street, pressing his lips together in an attempt to hide his smile.

Anna's ears blazed hot. She watched Officer Singer swagger down the sidewalk. His carefree humming bloomed into a happy song as he turned the corner. The lyrics no doubt touted all the women he had loved. She charged down the street, humiliated, chaffing at both the injustice and the bad timing.

Anna's elegant yellow car ornamented the sidewalk on Second Street. She stomped up in her horrible hair and dirty mannish uniform. She set the crank and slid onto the pristine seat, leaving a streak of chicken poo.

Chapter 14

Anna drove with the top down so she could feel the mischievous air, which was rising again, hot from the east.

"You selfish girl!" cawed the Widow Crisp, who was wearing her own ugly dress again. Anna had cleaned most of Officer Singer's vomit off the hem. The Widow scowled. "You've soiled my frock, almost killed me in the car, and now you're smothering me with dust. I! Hate! Wind!"

Anna happily ignored her. She pulled into the drive and saw Mr. Wright's ocean blue Cadillac parked in front. Her heart raced. "Jupiter."

She had long since given up expecting Mr. Wright or Mr. Blanc in the evenings. If she had, she would have spent more time primping in the orchard. The men invariably started work early and worked until after she was in bed. Previously, this had vexed her. If she never saw Mr. Wright, how could she encourage his attentions? But now she had welcomed it as providential. It would make her matron work possible.

Anna plucked up a half-knitted blanket, skillfully wrought by the Widow Crisp, and sashayed into the house. The Widow followed like a shadow.

Mr. Wright waited in the parlor, dressed for dinner. He stood and greeted Anna with a boyish grin. "Hello, darling. Hello, Widow Crisp."

Anna smiled back. "I didn't expect you."

"I missed you." He took her hand and kissed it. "Aren't you glad to see me?"

Anna glowed. "Yes." He looked wonderful, and she remembered how much she did miss him, or the idea of him, or the promise of what being with him could be like—like being on the train. He was everything she wanted, outside of police work. She held up the afghan and beamed. "I'm knitting for the Orphans' Asylum."

That evening, after Anna had freshened herself and changed into a stunning Nile-green evening gown, the Widow Crisp joined Anna and Mr. Wright for a romantic dinner. Afterward, she followed them into the conservatory and sniggered while Anna played piano badly. Then, she followed them into the parlor for cards, where she took Anna's last cent, drank glass after glass of the Blanc's best sherry, and flirted with Mr. Wright until his face turned red.

Anna knew she had to get rid of the Widow Crisp, or she might snap and beat her with a candlestick. Then she remembered how much the Widow hated the east winds. Anna smiled brightly. "Mr. Wright, would you take me for a stroll around the grounds?"

He looked out the window at the chaos in the garden and smiled bemusedly. "It's the perfect night. I'll have to hold you tight so you don't blow away." He offered Anna his arm. "Shall we?"

The Widow frowned.

The grounds of the Blanc estate were peppered with jacaranda, evergreens, oaks, and palms, all shaking their manes, their leaves falling like summer sleet. Anna's skirts whipped around her body, and gusts of eucalyptus pollen made Mr. Wright sneeze. He clutched his hat to his head. The Widow Crisp was unshakable, despite her hatred of the winds. She stood on the terrace, her bun come undone, her hair alive like a medusa, her glittering eyes glued to the couple.

Anna raised her voice to be heard. "Do you think I'm cuckoo to want to walk tonight?"

"No. This is very romantic—the wind blowing the stars into new constellations, you, me . . ." The corner of his mouth quirked. "The

Widow Crisp." Saying so, Mr. Wright pulled Anna behind a tree and out of the chaperone's sight. They were near a large rose bush that was shaking off its petals.

Anna laughed over the rush of the wind. Stray locks of her hair flew like bull whips. "They're sure I'm going to run away and join the circus."

He raised his eyebrows. "Well, are you?"

"I'm considering it."

"Then, can I come with you?"

Anna raised a finger to her lips as if thinking. "That depends. What are your talents?"

He leaned up against the tree and sheltered her with his body, standing very close. "I can throw knives."

Anna encouraged him with a smile. "Not at me. I won't wear sequins."

Mr. Wright shook his head. "Never at you."

"Don't you want to know my talents?" They were grinning at each other.

"What are your talents?" he asked.

"Lion taming."

"Lion taming is the most important quality that I look for in a wife." Mr. Wright snapped off a rose, which had but three tenacious petals, and dropped to one knee. "Tame me, Miss Blanc? Please? Just to be clear, I'm proposing." He gave her the balding rose and held his breath.

It was the moment for which Anna had been waiting; the moment she thought would never come again. She stood on the threshold of freedom and, dare she hope, love? "You'll marry me no matter what happens? Even if my father says no and cuts me out of his will and offers you heaps of money to leave me?"

Mr. Wright frowned. "Of course."

"Then, yes." She took the rose and smiled. She felt hope, relief, and a tinge of grief for something she couldn't name. Her eyes wandered to Mr. Wright's large, soft hands, which disappeared into his coat as he stood.

"You better have this, then." He produced a ring. Anna hurriedly stripped off her glove. He took her hand, and slid it onto her finger. Anna's eyes sparkled like the diamonds. The piece was generous and uncommon, like something made in another world by elves—or a really good French jeweler.

"Do you like it, Anna?"

"I adore it . . . Edgar." She closed her hand around it, knowing that wearing his ring would make her golden again in the eyes of the world.

He leaned in close, his hair flyaway with static electricity. The wind carried away his warmth and his scent. She lifted her chin and closed her eyes for his kiss.

Before their lips came together, their mouths but a whisper apart, the Widow Crisp rounded the tree. Edgar pulled back. Her timing was preternatural, her expression prim and disapproving. Anna silently cursed the Widow. It was a hostile act. She knew the mangy crow had done it on purpose. The Widow wouldn't care if they cavorted naked, but she would care if Anna had the briefest moment of bliss.

Edgar smiled tightly at the Widow Crisp, murmuring to Anna from the side of his mouth. "Sorry darling. I'm not much good at making love with an audience."

Anna sighed. "I had hoped she would blow away."

That night, Anna smuggled an iron from the laundry into her room, hidden in a shawl, and slid it under the bed. She lit a fire in the carved stone hearth. Butterflies fluttered in her insides. Tomorrow, Edgar would ask her father for her hand. And her father would say . . . what? And then what?

Anna pulled her egg-encrusted matron's uniform from a carpetbag. She wet the stiff fabric in a tub of cold water and scrubbed at the hard egg yolk and chalky chicken dung with soap and her father's boar bristle toothbrush. Her own silk night robe stuck to her lingerie, damp from splashes. She stripped off the lacey garment and hung it near the fire to dry, side by side with the newly cleaned uniform. She would continue to go to the station. Once she knew she was really, truly engaged, then she would quit.

Anna climbed into bed and squirmed herself warm under the covers. She needed beauty sleep, especially if her father said no, but fear of not sleeping kept her awake. She felt fidgety, overexcited from a day that was more eventful than the whole rest of her life put together. She rang for the maid to bring her sleep syrup and, when it arrived, slurped two spoonfuls of the bitter liquid.

As Anna drifted off in a barbital haze, the little beaten man lay in the gutter and called her name from a dream: "Anna. Anna."

"*Sacré bleu*! It's always something, Anna," Mr. Blanc said, as if it were her fault. The mountains in the east were glowing pink and a mist hid Catalina Island. Anna wore yesterday's frock, which she had plucked from the floor and donned quickly, her legs bare and chilled underneath. She took big steps in the dewy grass to keep up with her father, and almost trod on a dead gopher—a half-eaten one. Two brown teeth poked from its stiff mouth, its fur clumped in wet, bloody tufts.

Mr. Blanc halted in the middle of the lawn. Her full name, *Anna Virginie Blanc*, was cut into the turf in big dirt letters. They splayed across the lawn, edged with hairy roots and halves of worms, and sprinkled with a white powder. Anna put her hand on his thick arm and squeezed. A Mexican gardener approached with a wheelbarrow full of sod. He looked gravely at Anna. "*Buenos días, Señorita.*" He knelt and began scraping the powder out of the letters with a trowel. Anna shivered and pressed her lips.

"Who did this?" Mr. Blanc demanded. "Do you know, Anna?"

Anna shook her head and hugged herself.

"Never mind. I've called the police."

Anna's heavily lashed eyes widened and she spun about to leave. The last thing she needed was to be interviewed by Wolf. Her father grabbed her arm. "You're not going anywhere alone."

"I never do," Anna said in a singsong. She started to sweat.

"And, you're going to stay with the Breedloves. Will they have you?"

"Of course." Anna craned her neck to watch for police cars in the drive, and noticed the gardener's dog lying on the asphalt.

Mr. Blanc slapped his forehead and turned to the gardener. "It's herbicide, isn't it?"

The gardener took a pinch and rubbed the grains between his fingertips. He lifted it to his tongue.

"Don't!" Anna said. "Unless you want to end up like the gopher. And, I regret, your dog." The gardener dropped his hand and immediately began whistling for his dog.

Anna heard hoof beats and a mounted cop trotted onto the drive. He dismounted and knelt by the dead animal. Anna twisted free of her father and grimaced. "I'm going to go greet the nice officer." She loped off, veering toward the rear of the house, and disappeared.

"Anna!" her father shouted.

A weapon is a good idea when one does police work, or when a man uses arsenic as an herbicide when writing one's name on the lawn, or when one may have to render an officer unconscious in order to escape unseen. Anna clipped up the servant's stairs to retrieve Cook's paring knife from under her bed. She scooped up her silver hairbrush, too. The hairbrush could be used for bonking, and she was good with the blade, having eviscerated dozens of books. She supposed she could eviscerate other things, too. She would have to practice.

Anna whetted the knife until it was keen edged and popped it into her favorite beaded purse, a Frederick Worth original. The knife slit a hole through the silk and fell onto the floor, sticking in the hardwood like a dagger. It made a twanging sound. A shower of opalescent beads tinkled and bounced in all directions, pelting her feet. Her purse was gutted. "Biscuits!"

Anna's eyes shot to the clock. She was terribly late. The maid knocked at the door. Anna lunged to lock it. "Go away!"

"The officer wants to interview you."

"Tell him I'm naked," she said, and kicked herself. "Or something!" She heard the maid shuffle down the hall, sniggering.

Anna went to the fireplace and fingered her uniform. It was slightly damp and looked like it had been wadded into a ball, which it had been. Next time, she wouldn't wad. She stirred the remnants of last night's fire, retrieved the iron from under the bed and placed it on the coals. She spit on it periodically, until, finally, it sizzled.

Anna picked it up with a towel and ran it up and down the damp skirt leaving little streaks of soot. She congratulated herself. The iron worked. She let the iron linger on the more resistant wrinkly spots. Acrid smoke began wafting from the skirt. When she lifted the iron, a scorched triangle of cotton came with it. "Biscuits!" Anna hurled the charred skirt onto the floor.

The maid knocked. "Miss Anna. The officer is waiting."

"Tell him I'm coming!"

Anna kicked the uniform under her bed. When the hall was quiet, she slipped out the door in yesterday's dress. She took the servant's stairs to the Widow's room, and in a moment they were sneaking out a window with a tin of kippers and running for Clara's house.

Chapter 15

On Monday morning, Anna parked off the road behind a Coca-Cola billboard thirteen blocks from the station and walked, having dropped the Widow at her sister's rat-infested bungalow. Multistory buildings blocked the morning sun. She was out of sorts because she hadn't seen her father or Edgar and hadn't heard a word from either about the engagement. Over a day had passed and her ring finger remained bare. Surely Edgar would visit her at Clara's house and tell her tonight. The engagement would no longer be secret and she could wear his lovely ring.

Anna climbed the steps of the station in the hateful greenish, yellowish, brownish frock that strained across her bust. She clutched a leather carrying bag in russet red. It was so hideous only the Widow Crisp would wear it—unless one was being stalked and had to carry a very sharp paring knife, and one did not want to gut another silk purse. She imagined it could match with some things, like burlap, or moth-eaten dog fur, or a matron's uniform. But it could carry a whiskey bottle, four crime books, and the picture of Anna and Eve from the march, all of which would be safer at the station. She had also brought the shoe.

When Anna swung through the doors, Joe Singer was already there in his dress, having just returned from another sting operation. This time, he wasn't drunk. He leaned against the counter singing "Pretty Maiden" from *Floradora* with an elderly woman. Joe sang the girl's part. "They flirt with girls too freely and it's not the same girl twice."

Anna had to walk past them to get to her desk. The old woman leaned in close to Officer Singer and in a loud, old lady whisper said, "Is that your new assistant matron, Officer Singer? She's very pretty, and you don't have a sweetheart."

"Beauty, Mrs. Macklehainey, is only skin deep." He gave the old girl his full masculine attention. Mrs. Macklehainey smiled appreciatively and batted her lashes. She turned to Anna. "Hello. I'm Joe's neighbor. He's helping me find my dog."

Anna nodded politely and looked at Officer Singer. "I wasn't trying to get you in trouble on Saturday. I was simply pointing out . . ."

He interrupted her. "You couldn't get me in trouble, Assistant Matron Holmes."

Mrs. Macklehainey looked from one to the other and smiled. "Oh, my. Sparks a fly."

Anna huffed away.

Wolf spotted Anna and immediately crossed the floor to greet her. He smelled like cigarette smoke. "That's a lovely dress, Matron Holmes, but where's your uniform?" His eyes darted from her bust to her face and back again.

"I destroyed it." She frowned. "I suppose I should buy another."

"Yes, you should." He lowered his voice. "Do me a favor and keep Matron Clemens and the boys happy, as I was kind enough to hire you."

Anna looked surprised. "I think I've done well so far."

"Sure. Sure. Maybe we could talk about that a little later in private. Maybe in the stables at lunch time?" He laid a light, warm hand on her shoulder.

Anna smiled uncertainly and crossed over to the desk Matron Clemens had assigned her on Anna's first day. Dusty file boxes surrounded the desk like an invading army. Anna sneezed. Matron Clemens approached. "Good Morning, Matron Holmes. Where's your uniform?"

"I, um, gave it to a beggar woman. . . . She was desperate. With . . . children. May I have another?" Anna smiled brightly.

"Matron Holmes, you've worked here one day, and you're already six dollars in arrears."

"I'll earn it back. I promise." Anna tried to inspire confidence by looking serious.

"That's all very well, but I've already given you my spare. You'll have to sew a new one. And soon."

Anna blanched.

Matron Clemens glanced at the mound of dusty boxes. "In the meantime, I'd like you to go through these files and separate out the juveniles who are now adults. Then, I'd like you to integrate them with the adult files. If a file contains information on siblings or multiple children, I'd like you to type copies of the report and assure that each child has their own copy in their own file. If there are three siblings, there should be three complete files. If there are four siblings, four files. Do you understand?"

"Yes, Ma'am."

When her mentor departed, Anna bit her lip. On one hand, she couldn't wait to read real criminal records. On the other hand, she couldn't type. Anna looked over at Mr. Melvin, who typed brilliantly. His fingers blurred like a pinwheel in the east winds. Anna padded over and quietly positioned herself behind him. Every one of his fingers punched keys. Every finger knew where to strike. Anna studied their movement and position. She watched him roll in a new sheet of paper and return the carriage. His typing was wondrous. She knew she could never do it.

Anna glanced up and saw Matron Clemens watching her as if she suspected Anna of a crime—like impersonating someone who could type. The woman stood and glided toward her. Anna's lips formed an O, and her mind turned to porridge. "Mr. Melvin, I . . . Um. Mr. Melvin . . ."

Mr. Melvin spoke quietly and without turning. "Matron Holmes, extra ink ribbons are on the bottom shelf. And, I agree. A limber pinky makes all the difference."

Matron Clemens made a "Hmm" sound and went back to her seat. Anna clipped to her desk and rolled paper into her Remington. She tried to catch Mr. Melvin's eye so she could mouth a thank you, but he didn't look up. Anna hit keys until letters fell like hailstones onto the paper. She typed faster than Mr. Melvin, but in no particular order. When the page was full, Anna pulled it out and hid it in a file. She would do the real typing tonight with no one looking.

Anna flipped through the files. They each bore the name of a juvenile, their birthday, names of parents, along with reports about their transgressions, sentences, and/or actions taken on their behalf.

She lit with epiphany. If Peaches Payton had a juvenile record, Anna could find Georgie's relatives and save him from the witch. She quickly searched under Daisy Tombs, the name the little black maid had given her. Anna found the file and flung it open, skimming the entries.

December 25, 1897.

Daisy Tombs, age nine, and brother Amos, age two, were orphaned when their parents, Betsy and Joshua Tombs, drowned in a flash flood when walking along the Los Angeles River. Matron Clemens left them in the care of their uncle, Chip Jones. . . .

The entry provided an address and other details. Anna beamed. This was easy as pie. Anna would find Chip Jones and notify him of Daisy's death. He would take Georgie.

May 8, 1900.

Daisy Tombs stol kantelop frum a growsire . . .

Anna chuckled. It was complete gibberish, but she thought it might say that Daisy Tombs had stolen cantaloupe from a grocery store. The typist copied the mangled report just as the illiterate officer had written it, correcting only the child's name. Whoever had typed it had a sense of humor, or was trying to make a point.

Anna moved on to the next entry.

June 1, 1900.

Daisy Tombs was found at a dance hall wearing too much makeup.

Matron Clemens washed her face and took her home, where she found Chip Jones passed out drunk on the floor.

July 3, 1900.

Daisy Tombs and Carry Morgan had their virtue stolen by M. M. Martinez, proprietor of the Esmeralda Club, and six other unknown men, after they were given drugged champagne. . . . A jury convicted Martinez after the girls testified in court. . . . The girls were sent to Whittier Reform Academy because their families did not know what to do with them. . . .

Anna set down the file. Was it a wonder that tender girls fell into sin when preyed upon by devils like Martinez? No one would marry them. Testifying in court virtually advertised their disgrace. What else could Daisy have done? Become a scullery maid? Anna wouldn't have hired her. Girls like Daisy had best go stay with relatives in a distant town.

What about M. M. Martinez? Had he been hanged? She found his record. No. He'd been fined $100 dollars. Then, the cad had struck again. He'd drugged one Sarah Smith, age sixteen.

Anna made note of his address. His house was on a better street, not far from her own. If she could find the time, she'd burn it down.

Anna found the file on Carry Morgan, and another entry caught her eye.

February 18, 1907

Madam Chantilly Stone fild a misin purson report for Kitty Blake a.k.a. Carry Morgan wuz gon frum Yanke Doodl on Febrary 14th, were she hored.

Anna tapped her teeth with her thumb. Daisy Tombs committed suicide and Carry Morgan disappeared. Both worked in brothels.

Matron Clemens clipped up to the desk. "Matron Holmes. I don't suppose you'd be inclined to do a good deed?"

"Anything." Anna smiled obsequiously. Wolf had admonished her to make friends.

Matron Clemens dropped two coins on her desk. "Good. Peaches Payton will be buried today at four o'clock. Madam Lulu requested that the boy be there to say goodbye. They've helped raise him. I think it's all right if you stay with him."

Anna beamed. She could give Peaches her shoes.

Snow passed by and heehawed like an ass. "In this heat, she'll be a sight, And a smell."

Anna made a sound of disgust.

He grunted. "They should have buried her on Sunday."

"Sunday? When all the priests are busy with their flocks? That's ridiculous. Who would say the mass? I'm sure Madam Lulu gave her a proper wake, despite all those vile men who would be showing up at the door. She seemed to care about the girl."

Snow gave her a deadly look and lumbered off. Matron Clemens raised an eyebrow. Was it a reprimand for impudence toward a detective or a begrudging sign of approval? Afraid to find out, Anna nodded to the matron and scampered off.

It was easy to drop a child on a doorstep and run. Abducting a child was tricky. Unfortunately, Anna needed the Widow Crisp. She found the Widow in the sister's bungalow, her eyes bloodshot, and her breath antiseptic. A gorgeous wool afghan tumbled down her lap. She knitted like Helmut Melvin typed. The Widow agreed to collect Georgie, in any manner she chose, in exchange for a pair of Anna's pale blue, quilted satin boudoir slippers with two-inch Louis heels.

By the time Anna arrived at Canary Cottage with the boy, the mourners were already processing down the street behind a glass hearse drawn by a dappled mare. The coffin shook in rhythm with the horse. So much for the shoes. Anna set them down on the gate.

Madam Lulu led the cavalcade in a shiny black gown and a wide-brimmed hat in which nested half a dozen brightly colored birds. Her cheeks were rouged cherry red, as red as her puffy, kohl-lined eyes, and the same dead fox swung from her neck. She waddled on the arm of an old black man in a dapper suit and derby. Behind them, the brothel girls processed in party dresses dyed black. They were, to a girl, lovely. Some appeared younger than Anna, some older, none over twenty-five. Two of the girls held babies. These were Lulu's girls, the girls who were dying, who the madam believed were being murdered. Anna wanted to stare at them, to gaze into their solemn eyes and know what manner of creatures they were, that they would choose to live in a brothel, when surely they could work in a factory or be nuns. She tripped, trying to walk and watch them with Georgie in her arms. One girl, who was perhaps sixteen, stared at Anna. When Anna looked, the girl glanced down and smiled. Anna fell in step behind the mourning prostitutes.

When the little black maid saw Georgie, she ran over and took him, squeezing him and kissing his plump lips. "My Georgie." She turned to Anna. "Miss, won't you go back and wait in the parlor? There's lemonade."

Anna thanked her, but preferred not to sit alone in Satan's parlor, which was likely as tasteless as the Christmas colored exterior. Though she could have waited at the gate, Anna followed the procession up a hill covered in bright orange poppies to the potter's field—the burial place for suicides and the other damned who could not rest in sacred ground.

Not knowing anyone else, Anna crept over and stood by Madam Lulu. The woman squinted. "What the hell are you doing here?" If Lulu had attended charm school, she'd surely been expelled.

"I . . . don't know," Anna whispered.

"Why doesn't that surprise me?"

After a moment of bowed heads and silence, Anna crossed herself and said generously, "I hope Miss Payton had time to confess her sins before she died."

"What sins would those be?"

Anna looked confused. "Why, her life of sin, of course."

"Feeding your baby's not a sin. You know what sin is, princess? It's when you turn your back on injustice."

The implicit accusation stung Anna, and she flushed with anger. How was she turning her back on injustice? She'd asked the detectives and the captain to investigate Peaches' death, and they'd called it a suicide. For all Anna knew, Peaches had killed herself, leaving Georgie alone by choice. She left Madam Lulu and skulked back to the street to wait.

When the burial was over, Anna carried a stoic Georgie to the scrawny arms of the Widow Crisp.

Chapter 16

On Tuesday, Anna slunk downstairs to the Breedlove's breakfast room like a woman in mourning. Purple moons hung under her eyes. Monday had passed without a word from Edgar or her father. She had suffered three full days. It could mean only one thing—Edgar wouldn't marry her. He had fled without a word, just like Louis Taylor.

While the Widow Crisp still snored upstairs, Anna ate her breakfast kippers with Clara and Clara's husband of one year—Theo Breedlove. He was young, with soulful eyes, and seemed very serious, until he smiled. Anna liked him. His library was her main window to the outside world, and he pretended not to notice when Anna pinched a bottle of his sour mash bourbon. He was an aspiring writer and, occasionally, the *Herald* printed his pieces on medicine, foreign policy, ping-pong, Arctic exploration, child rearing, the harmonica, and any number of other topics.

On Sunday night, Clara had reassured Anna, petting her and cooing that Edgar loved her, whether Anna's father gave his blessing or not. On Monday, she told Anna that she ought to pack a bag, because Edgar would arrive any moment to sweep her away for a secret wedding and honeymoon in Paris. But Clara and Theo didn't mention Edgar at all during Tuesday's breakfast. They didn't hold hands under the table, as they usually did, or comment on her haggard appearance.

Anna loved them for it. They were the dandiest friends in the world, but staying with them had a downside. They paid attention to Anna.

Clara forced a smile. "What shall we do after breakfast, dearest? Flag football?"

Theo nodded his head vigorously. "Yes. We'll conscript the servants. And I was thinking that later I'd like to buy a motorcycle. I've been meaning to. Anna, you could try it out. Clara can sit on back, and I'll . . . Well, we'll have to get a side car."

Clara clapped her hands. "We'll drive to the tailor's and Anna can design matching motoring ensembles for the three of us."

Theo choked, and orange juice sprayed out of his nose. Anna just stared at her plate. "No. I'm going to early mass today. In fact, I think I'll go to early mass every day."

Theo and Clara exchanged a concerned look. Clara giggled. "Someone has to do it."

"I have a lot of penance to do," Anna said.

Theo grinned. "We know."

Anna bit the head off a kipper and chewed. "And then, I'm going to spend the day doing charity work."

"Now, don't get carried away," Theo said. "You wouldn't look good in a habit." Anna paled. Clara kicked him under the table.

Anna knew she would have to tell Clara and Theo soon—if not the truth, at least some palatable facsimile to explain her absences during the day and her typing at night. The thought made her stomach cramp. Clara would never condone anything that put Anna's future wedded bliss in jeopardy. As sparkling and light as Clara usually was, her disapproval would be proportionately leaden. Anna didn't think she could bear it. Not now. Clara was her one support—the only person in the world who Anna felt really truly loved her.

Theo puffed out his chest, stretched his arms toward the ceiling, and began flipping through the *Herald*. "My article on Sigmund Freud should have come out today." He searched page by page and did a double take in the society section. His eyebrow arched up and he slid the paper over to his wife, pointing at an article. He bit down on a smile.

Clara's merry mouth popped open. "Anna." She handed her the paper. "Best wishes." She leaned over and kissed Anna's cheek.

When Anna arrived at work that morning, her lips flipped between smiles and frowns like a jump rope. She was happy to be engaged. Of course she was. And irate to have found out about it in the newspaper. She had yet to hear from either Edgar or her father.

In revenge, Anna didn't quit her job, despite her betrothal. Why should she when they treated her thus? Besides, she had just given the Widow Crisp her prized stamp collection in exchange for sewing a new matron's uniform. Anna could still work at the station, as long as Edgar and her father were paying her no attention whatsoever. When she got married, then she would quit.

The station bustled. The tomato pickers were on strike, protesting low wages, and two-dozen had been arrested for . . . something. Anna wasn't sure. No one noticed her, except Mr. Melvin, who acknowledged Anna by looking the other way. She plopped down at her desk and began to review files on girls who were still girls, and girls who were now women. She made a pile of documents she would need to smuggle back to Clara's in her ugly russet carrying bag to copy at night. Periodically, she typed a load of gibberish on her typewriter.

Anna decided to keep a separate record of her own. Madam Lulu claimed that brothel girls were being murdered. The detective and the coroner didn't agree. But if Anna was going to be accused of turning her back on injustice, she wanted the facts. For example, how many girls were dead? She would note the names of girls who were both associated with brothels and who had suffered untimely ends within the last five years.

Prostitution wasn't illegal in LA, but girls were sometimes arrested for vagrancy if they wandered out of the brothels to lure men from the street. Also, the police might raid cribs and parlor houses for other ordinance violations. Most brothel girls had been hauled into the station at one time or another. This she had gleaned from Mr. Melvin.

Anna heard the click of boots on tile and glanced up. Matron Clemens was approaching with a broom. Afraid she wanted Anna to sweep, Anna sprung up from her seat, and slipped into the kitchen.

When Anna left work, she saw the creepy little man. He stood on the steps of the station holding a fistful of drooping yellow dandelions.

Anna could see his shoes and skinny ankles below too-small trousers, which was doubly shocking as he wore no socks. His bruises had faded to yellow, but he had a new gash over his left eye and it dripped with pus. "Miss Blanc," he said. "Oh, Miss Blanc."

Anna's insides wound tight. With the bruises gone, and the swelling abated, she knew him. He had been the groundskeeper at the tennis club, fired months ago for cutting a spy hole in the ladies' dressing room. When they'd caught him, they'd walloped him with the shovel he'd been using to plant geraniums.

A groundskeeper knew how to kill grass.

Anna backed up against the wall and prayed to Saint Dymphna, patron saint of the crazy, that no one would come through the station doors and hear the little man say her name. It would expose her, and the news would certainly get back to her father.

"Miss Blanc," he moaned. He came toward her with his arms sticking out, grizzly bear style. Apparently, Saint Dymphna had left her post. Anna could not cry for help, not with him using her real name. She wished she'd been allowed to box or study wrestling instead of ballet. He was an arm's length away, his wormy lips puckered for a kiss. She lifted her leg in a *grand battement* and connected with his groin. He tumbled backward down the stairs like a boulder. Anna rushed forward to see. The little man lay still on the sidewalk at the bottom of the steps, eyes closed, his wormy lips curved into a smile.

She was considering his crumpled form and where she might relocate the body when the station door opened and Matron Clemens strode crisply onto the landing. Anna straightened up, slowed her breathing, and assumed a casual pose, as if there was no half-dead man at the bottom of the steps. "Have a good evening, Matron Clemens."

Matron Clemens glanced down at the crumpled pervert. "Douglas Doogan! Away with you or I'll have you locked in a cell all by yourself."

He began to crawl away. Anna's heart rose in thanksgiving. She apologized to Saint Dymphna.

"Good evening, Matron Holmes," Matron Clemens said. She clipped down the stairs with her skirt swishing, as if crumpled perverts were as common as pigeon droppings.

Chapter 17

When Anna and the Widow Crisp arrived at the Breedloves' that night, there was no message from Edgar. She grabbed her chaperone and marched back out the door wearing her engagement ring. Douglas Doogan or no, she was going home. She found her father sitting at the dining table with his paper, his eyes puffy and red. In front of him, a spoon soaked in a bowl of purple wine and tapioca soup. Anna glared at him. "Where's Edgar?"

"I put him on a train to San Diego. Didn't you get his telegram?" He paused and looked sheepish. "Oh. It's in the foyer."

Edgar *had* written to her. Anna blinked a tear from her lashes and strode out into the hall. Her father summoned her back with a shout. "Anna!"

When she reentered the dining room, her father frowned. "You're not supposed to be here. It's not safe." He patted the table. "Sit down."

Anna lowered herself onto a chair. Cook appeared and set a bowl in front of her. Mr. Blanc leaned forward. "Anna, you are going to be married."

She tossed her head. "I know. I saw the announcement."

"How do you feel?"

"Deeply insulted." She frowned. "And pleased."

"*Bon*." He smiled. "I'll miss you—your beauty, your *excitation*. But now you'll be Edgar's *excitation*." He chuckled, opened his paper, and disappeared into the print.

Her father had allowed her to suffer for three full days not knowing her fate. And now, he had nothing to say but "*bon*?" Anna clenched her teeth. "Is that all?"

Mr. Blanc lowered the paper. "It had to happen, Anna, but you've done well." He smiled. He looked past Anna's shoulder and spoke to someone behind her. "We'll need a guard at the engagement ball."

Anna swiveled. Mrs. Morales stood in the doorway, smiling like a fairy godmother. "And when will that be?" She didn't look surprised by the news. Of course not. She had probably put the notice in the paper.

"Edgar will be back Saturday morning," he said. "Saturday night. Eight o'clock. *D'accord*?"

Now Anna was puzzled. Her father seemed awfully eager to make the engagement public. Was he afraid that Edgar would back out?

Mrs. Morales had seemed delighted for Anna a moment ago, or at least pleased that Anna would be leaving the house. Now she looked like she'd been sucking on lemons. She had three and a half days to plan a ball. Mrs. Morales cleared her throat. "Miss Anna, if we start now, and Cook, your attendant, and the parlor maids help us, we can work through the night and have the invitations written by morning, if we don't run out of stationery. I'll ask the butler to hire couriers. The gardener and the stable boy can help. I'll go downtown to engage musicians, valets, and a caterer. You find a florist and . . ."

"I can't help you with the ball," Anna said. "I have obligations at the Orphans' Asylum." She did want to help with the ball, at least the decoration parts, but she had no spare time. "It should be a color-themed ball, though, like they have in New York, with colored food, colored dishes, colored clothes . . . Pink would be nice. We'll have pink cream soup with marrow balls."

"*Bon*," Mr. Blanc said.

Mrs. Morales glared.

Anna slid out of her chair. "I have to go back to Clara's now. For my safety. *Bonsoir*." Anna kissed her father's cheek, smiled at Mrs. Morales's lowered lids, and made her exit.

Anna didn't return to Clara's. She went banging on the door of her dressmaker's residence—a tiny apartment above the shop. Anna would not leave the gown to Mrs. Morales, no matter how many juvenile records she had to type. She brought a picture for the seamstress to copy—a Parisian gown two years ahead of what women were wearing in LA. She had clipped it from *La Mode Illustrée*, a French magazine that a cousin sent from Paris each month. The gown's décolletage swept low in the front. The bodice fit tight and the shoulders were bare. If her father had seen it, he would have squelched the design immediately. Anna gave the Widow Crisp a tortoiseshell shoehorn in exchange for her silence.

As the dressmaker made the irrevocable cut in the fabric, Anna prayed a silent prayer to Saint Anne, patron saint of seamstresses, that her father would be too busy at the ball to notice her décolletage. Surely Saint Anne could appreciate a Parisian neckline.

It was eleven before Anna finished with the dressmaker and returned to the Breedloves. Happily, they were already in bed. She trudged into Theo's study, her arms piled high with files, and dumped them on his desk next to a Remington typewriter. They spilled across the ink blotter.

Anna helped herself to one of Theo's Rudolf Valentino cigars and crawled into his man-sized leather chair, sitting on her feet for height. She selected a report to copy. With a cigar smoldering between her teeth, she picked out the keys, one finger at a time.

The next morning, Anna left before Clara and Theo awoke, scribbling a note about guilt and purgatory. When she arrived at the station, boxes of police records were waiting for her. Anna reviewed all juvenile files up through the letter C. Besides Daisy Tombs and Carry Morgan, the broken blossoms from the Esmeralda Club, she found no other girls who had worked in a brothel and who had disappeared or committed suicide between January 1902 and July 1907. There was one girl, a

June Baker, whose body was found in a field with a needle stuck in her arm. The coroner called it an accidental overdose. It was a ridiculous place to administer medical treatment and highly suspicious. M. M. Martinez had slipped drugs into girls' drinks for nefarious purposes. A killer could give an unwilling girl too much medicine. Anna decided to include girls who had overdosed on morphine, cocaine, or other medicines. Her total rose from two to three.

Every day that week, Anna waded through files. By Saturday afternoon, Anna was halfway through the alphabet. She'd read one hundred files, containing references to some three hundred juveniles. Though she had a good system, she'd only processed nine. Unless magic typing elves appeared, Anna's pace was not likely to improve.

Her count of dead or missing brothel girls had risen to seven. In and of itself, this figure meant nothing. A certain number of brothel girls would likely run away or die from suicide or even drugs. The fact that brothel girls were dying didn't prove that someone was killing them, as Madam Lulu claimed. Still, Anna planned to keep counting, because it made her feel like a detective. It was as close to a murder investigation as she would ever get.

The illiterate officer had investigated most of the petty thefts and all of the deaths and disappearances among brothel girls. Though his incident reports were short, they were hard to read, making the work slow. She preferred to read reports by other officers, because they provided interesting details.

She learned a tremendous lot about the world—about children injured or killed in factories, kids with bruises and snapped bones, girls ruined, boys who supported their hungry siblings as pool sharks or thieves, and people doing shameful things she didn't understand.

Chapter 18

Anna sat before a toilet table, wrapped in a robe, still damp from the bath. She tilted her head and purred as Clara brushed her hair until it shone, her scalp tingling. She needed to relax after sprinting from the station to her changing orchard, to the rat-infested bungalow, to Clara's house. Anna Blanc's engagement ball was no excuse for Matron Holmes to leave work early.

Clara waited on Anna like a devoted lady's maid, as both their personal attendants had been recruited to help with the ball. She tied back Anna's locks and cupped Anna's pale, tired face, examining her complexion in the mirror. "Hm." With an arch look, she produced a pot of Princess Pat rouge.

Anna squealed. "Devil's paint!" She laid hold of it, unscrewing the top and sniffing the coral-colored cream. "Are you going to make me look like an actress?"

Clara's musical voice soothed Anna's nerves. "Better than an actress."

Anna presented her pouty lips, and Clara brushed on the rouge ever so lightly. It tasted like wax. Anna's father would rage if he knew. Matron Clemens would make her wash her face.

"See. Now you won't have to be biting your lips all evening to refresh them. Just don't kiss Edgar. It will leave a mark, and you'll be found out." They giggled.

Clara rubbed glycerin on Anna's arms and chest and whitened them with chalk dust, darkening her brows and lashes with walnut stain, piling her hair up on a Tournure frame. She helped Anna dress.

Clara oohed and sighed and led Anna to the full length mirror, running her hands down Anna's bare arms. "You are a perfect vision of loveliness."

"I do try." Anna's hair towered, her silhouette made even higher by the plumes in her headdress. The gown swept low at the décolletage and swelled over her breasts. She turned to see the drape of her gown from behind, her tiny waist, a train pooling at her feet. She was, in a word, incandescent, like a Gibson girl dressed by Vionnet at the House of Doucet.

There was a knock on the door and Theo's voice. "You're very, very late. You've missed the receiving line."

Anna glided into the ballroom, followed by Clara, followed by Theo, and they were promptly announced. Anna beamed. Everything was pink. The flowers were blush, the tablecloths grapefruit, the napkins carnation. The food was puce and cerise and coral. Most of the women, those who could arrange it, wore gowns in raspberry, salmon, melon, or mauve, and the men wore rose boutonnieres. Anna herself wore green, as she wanted to stand out.

It was a glittering affair, attended by all the important people. Half of the guests were strangers to Anna, some of them vulgar, all of them rich and invited at the discretion of Mr. Blanc for business purposes. Anna was busy fulfilling her obligation to dance with every jowly gentleman on her card. She barely saw Edgar, as he was similarly busy shaking hands with business associates and dancing with their dowdy wives.

A man from her card dragged Anna to the floor for a waltz, lumbering largely, in triple time. Anna bore his painfully exaggerated moves, trying not to make a face. Clara giggled at her from the arms of a man who had managed to secure pink tails on short notice. Anna sighed in relief when the musicians finally took a break and Edgar stole to her side. He dabbed his brow with a handkerchief. "This is torture."

She gave him a teasing smile. "Don't you like balls?"

"Not when they are in my honor."

"Surely you like dancing with all those women?"

He took her arm. "I like dancing with you."

Anna harrumphed. "How could you possibly know? You've never danced with me."

"I'd like to change that."

"Good luck." Anna glowered over at her father, who was sidling up to a woman. She raised her eyebrows. "Who's that lady?" The woman stood smoking a cigarette by a potted orange tree. She wore a pale yellow gown, painted with roses, in a style Anna had never seen. She was old, maybe forty-five, slender, and not wearing a corset.

"Now, she's a story." Edgar lowered his voice. "Her name is Emma Summers. She's a piano teacher, and one of the wealthiest, most powerful people in the state."

"Taffy!" Anna smiled.

"It's true. They call her the Oil Queen of California. She invested in oil wells, early on. Needless to say, she no longer gives lessons. She's selling 50,000 barrels of crude oil per month. She hires the men, buys the equipment, and is supervising the whole operation."

Anna was intrigued. "Will you introduce me?"

Emma Summers was walking away when Mr. Blanc summoned Edgar with his eyes.

"Ah. Excuse me, darling. I'll only be a minute." Edgar joined Anna's father by the orange tree where they whispered conspiratorially, sober and unsmiling.

Clara glided to Anna's side towing a pink satin train and a glass of blush champagne. Anna watched the men. "I really think the two of *them* should marry. They're always together."

"They have business, dearest. It's not our world." Clara took Anna's hand and held it.

"Women can do business. Emma Summers does business and has been very successful."

Clara looked at Anna quizzically. "Emma who?"

As the musicians reassembled and began playing a waltz, something dreadful happened. Louis Taylor appeared at Anna's elbow looking tentative. "Good evening, Anna. Will you honor me with your hand for a waltz?" He mooned at her with aching eyes, like a wronged but devoted lover. For once in her life, Anna wished that Mrs. Curlew-Taylor were there.

Clara spoke with all the venom of a rattlesnake cupcake. "Who let you in?"

He coughed and pulled an invitation from his pocket. "I was invited, and I believe this is my dance."

Anna dropped her eyes to her card, and there, written in English, was the name, Louis Taylor. She paled. Not only had her father invited the faithless peacock, he expected her to dance with him. Mrs. Curlew-Taylor must have a lot of money for Anna's father to do something so cruel and so desperate. Anna turned to Clara, eyes full of despair. "Edgar couldn't possibly have agreed to this."

As Clara was shaking her head, Theo Breedlove grabbed Anna from behind and twirled her onto the dance floor. He waltzed like a prince. "You looked like you needed to be rescued."

"Can't you take him out back and beat him?"

"Isn't that Enid Curlew's job? From what I hear, she's good at it."

"Yes, but where is she?"

"Maybe she doesn't like his company." They glanced over to where Louis stood and saw Clara winding up for a violent sneeze. On the exhale, she dumped pink champagne on the crotch of Louis's trousers. He stood frozen as it dripped down his legs like a toddler's accident. Theo grinned. "She's a darling, my wife."

A smile returned to Anna's lips. She blew Clara a kiss. "What would I do without her?"

Police chief Nobel Singer still had all his hair and the lean body of a younger man. He entered the ballroom grinning as if it were a parlor full of his favorite cousins. Beside him, Officer Joe Singer took in the colored room with raised eyebrows. He wore a tuxedo better than he wore a frock.

The Singers were hailed by a graying man with salmon pâté in his mustache. They sauntered over to say hello. "Evening, Mayor," the chief said, and made a gesture of dabbing his mouth.

The mayor quickly reached for a pink cloth napkin and smeared the salmon pâté. "Ah. Thank you." He slapped Joe on the back. "Didn't expect to see you here, my boy."

The chief donned a serious expression. "A man's been bothering the Blanc girl. I told Christopher I'd bring Joe along to handle him if he shows up. We've been walking the grounds."

"Is he a threat?" the mayor asked.

"Maybe not." The chief laid a hand on his son's shoulder. "But I view it as another opportunity for Joe to see how business is done."

Joe's smile dimmed. He knew how their business was done. The mayor tugged on one handle of his mustache and smiled. "Well, that's one way to get your son an invitation. How are things down at the station?"

"Hunky dory," the chief said.

Joe laughed. "Don't you believe it. He's not around much since you made him chief. You'd do better asking him about his golf game."

The mayor chortled. "I know all about his golf game. I'm his golf partner."

As the men laughed, Anna waltzed by in the masterful arms of Theo, whirling in tight circles, her lovely shoulders bare, her lips blushing, her lashes dark with walnut stain. All three men were sucked into her vortex.

"Now there's a girl who makes me wish I were twenty years younger," the mayor said.

Joe took in this vision of a girl, this tended, unattainable, spun-sugar girl dancing like someone out of a storybook. As make-believe as she seemed, something about her was familiar, and he searched his mind for an association. He wanted to place her in rags by a hearth, like a Cinderella.

Or in a matron's uniform.

His freshly-shaven jaw dropped. It was the aloof, tattletale matron whose shoes he had sprayed with whiskey and undigested corn.

"Oh, my Lord. Is she a friend of the groom or the bride?" Joe asked.

The mayor and the chief shared an amused look. The chief licked his lips. "Joe. She *is* the bride."

Joe's large eyes popped. "That's Anna Blanc?"

His father grinned. "It could be difficult to guard a girl if you don't know who she is, Son."

The mayor slapped Joe on the back. "I'll make sure you get a proper introduction. Just don't fall in love." He hailed the man with the tray of pâté.

Chief Singer excused himself and charmed his way around the room with a grin and a glass of grapefruit punch. Joe went to work guarding Anna. He barely took his eyes off her, and only partly because he was paid to watch her. He kept asking himself why a renowned beauty, engaged to one of the richest men on the West Coast, would lie about her name and get a job at a police station. He studied her person for a clue the way he studied a dodgy witness—examining her expression, the set of her jaw, the way her eyes moved beneath those feathered lashes, her impossibly red lips, her bare shoulders . . .

He never spoke to her and maintained a discreet distance, but, for her security, he never stood more than ten feet away. Once, she caught his eye and gave him a dazzling smile. He laughed at her. She didn't recognize him. She made a dignified toss of her slighted, pretty head and went on dancing.

Periodically, Joe scanned the room for signs of the stalker. He caught Edgar Wright staring at him. Joe nodded and raised his glass, but Edgar didn't smile. Joe sipped his strawberry punch and assessed the unfriendly man. He looked like what he was—an East Coast society dude. He had style, looks, old money, and, apparently, an attitude. Joe felt sorry for him. Poor Mr. Wright was marrying Matron Holmes.

A flock of ladies, pretty ones, too, flew up to fawn over Edgar, and Joe saw his winning smile. He felt less sympathetic, and went back to watching Anna spinning around bare-shouldered with her feathers and her old money and nouveau riche partners.

When he next scanned the room, Edgar was watching him again.

This time, the man glared. Joe lifted his eyebrows, and blew out a whistle. In between handshakes, banter, and dance steps, Edgar Wright was watching Joe watch Anna.

Anna took the floor with another businessman. His hands were slippery with sweat. She was bored, had a blister, and wanted champagne. At the end of the dance, the string quartet took another break. "Can I get you something, Miss Blanc?" her damp-palmed partner asked. She declined, despite her thirst, and went to dry her hands.

Anna noticed Emma Summers leaning out an open window, a breeze ruffling her hair. The sight was doubly refreshing. Anna glided over, slipping off her hot, damp gloves, and extended her hand. "Miss Summers. I'm Anna Blanc."

Miss Summers's gloves were lamb soft, tinted butter yellow. The lady gave Anna a gracious smile. "I had a dance with your betrothed. He's charming."

"Then I'm jealous. We haven't danced together all night." Anna leaned her back against the windowsill and basked in the cooling breeze.

For a moment, the women stood in silence watching the sea of whirling color. Miss Summers took out a cigarette case and offered a stick to Anna. Anna waved it away. "No thank you. The last time I smoked, I was arrested."

"Really? Good for you." Smoke streamed from the center of Miss Summers's smile. Her tobacco smelled of cloves.

Anna's lips parted slightly and her shapely eyebrows lifted. "That isn't what my father thought."

Miss Summers chuckled. "I'm not surprised."

The woman's easy dismissal of her father's opinion encouraged Anna. She interlaced her fingers. "Miss Summers, I know this is the first time we've met, but Edgar told me about you and I wanted to say that I admire you very much."

"Thank you."

"If I may presume to say so, I think we may be kindred spirits. You see, you're out in the world of men, and I would like to be."

Miss Summers perked up. "Oh. So you're interested in business?"

"Yes. That is, I believe I should know something of the bank if it is to be mine someday."

Miss Summers pressed her lips together. "What you need to know now is that banks all over the country are failing."

Anna's eyebrows jumped. "They are? Why?"

"It's a chain reaction, my dear. There was a failed takeover. Wall Street dropped by fifty percent. Do you know the Knickerbocker Trust Company?"

"No."

"They're the third largest trust company in New York City. When they collapsed, everybody panicked. People lost confidence. They're taking their money out of the banks and burying it in the garden. And when there is a run on a bank, well, few banks have the capital it takes to survive. That's why everyone's so twitchy tonight."

For the first time, Anna looked at the faces of the men populating the ballroom. She really looked. Miss Summers was right. They did seem twitchy. Her father was among the twitchiest. Anna felt twitchy herself. "And Blanc National Bank? What about Blanc National?"

Miss Summers inhaled on her cigarette, and when she spoke her words were formed in smoke. "That's a sit-down conversation, but your father has a powerful ally now."

"Who's that?" But Anna already knew.

"Here he comes."

Edgar strolled over to the breezy window, smiling, and linked his black tuxedo-sleeved arm through Anna's. "Excuse me, Miss Summers. I'm in desperate need of my fiancée."

Anna peered into his face for a hint that the sky was falling, but she saw no sign of it. So, she glared at him. Miss Summers stepped back and flashed him a crooked smile. "Far be it from me to stand in the way of love, Mr. Wright."

Anna placed her bare hand on Miss Summers's yellow sleeve. "May I call on you? I'd like to have a sit-down conversation."

The older woman dug in her purse for a card and handed it to Anna. She smiled. "I'll be disappointed if you don't."

Edgar bowed to Miss Summers and swept Anna off toward a cluster of laughing men, who all looked the same from behind in their black tails. Both Anna and Edgar were scowling.

Anna snapped. "You let father invite Louis Taylor!"

"Of course not. I was in San Diego, remember? I knew they were doing business, but I never dreamed . . ." He rubbed one eye and then exhaled in a huff. "He left before I could throw him out. Did he wet his trousers?"

"Yes. He has a medical condition. I want you to kill my father."

"Oh, I will. Once he's walked you down the aisle. And starting right now, Louis Taylor won't be coming anywhere near you. But, Anna, you can't care about him anymore. He's nothing to you. That was seven months ago. You have me, now."

Anna composed her face. "Yes. He's just a gnat in my lemonade. Let's change the subject."

"Yes, let's. I see you met Miss Summers. She's an odd choice of companion for you."

"Oh, but she's lovely. She talked to me about banking. Edgar, banks are failing . . ."

"Yes, I know. How would you like to do some banking right now?"

"I'd adore it."

"Good. Charm Mayor Smucker. He's invested a great deal of money in your father's bank, and we'd like to hang on to it."

"All right." Anna thought she should be allowed to do more than just charm the mayor, but it was a start.

Edgar escorted her to the huddle where Mr. Blanc, the mayor, and the chief stood along with the staring man. They were eating pink gelatin pudding, molded into the shape of flowers. It jiggled when they laughed. They parted to admit the couple.

Anna glanced surreptitiously at the stranger who had been

watching her all night. She had given him her most alluring smile, almost flirtatious, and he had laughed at her. Before she could look away, he caught her eye and smirked. Anna's face flashed recognition, then horror. The staring man was Officer Singer. Her diaphragm constricted and she held her breath. She hadn't known him before, dressed in clothes appropriate to his sex.

He looked like the Arrow Collar Man. She glanced away.

The mayor extended his hand to Edgar, his mustache now frosted with tinted whipped cream. "If it isn't the man of the hour."

The chief's face stretched in an ear-to-ear smile. "Congratulations, Mr. Wright. She's a lovely girl."

"Yes, she is." Edgar directed his gaze at Joe, his eyes amused and patronizing. "Don't you think so, Officer Singer?"

Joe looked amused right back. "She is something."

"Miss Blanc, I don't believe you know my son Joe," the chief said.

Anna had no breath for words. Officer Singer was the police chief's son. She closed her eyes. "I haven't had the pleasure." She tentatively extended her hand, and glanced up at him to see what he would do.

Joe took her hand in his rough fingers and raised his eyebrows. "That's strange, because I could have sworn we've met before."

Anna forced a smile, though her insides were screaming. He dropped her hand.

"Miss Blanc, I hear you're doing charity work," the mayor said.

She blinked. "Yes. I've been . . . helping the orphans at the Orphans' Asylum. Knitting. Blankets. All day. Every day."

Joe choked on his gelatin flower.

"Well, that's most admirable," the chief said.

Edgar beamed. "I'm just glad she's occupied. With this whole bank panic, Christopher and I are working day and night."

Mr. Blanc put a hand on Edgar's neck and squeezed just a little too hard. "Merging families is easy. Business mergers take a lot of finesse. Isn't that right, Son."

Anna no longer heard the conversation around her. The vile officer had recognized her. He had not told on her, yet. He just stood there eating his flower and watching her. She very much regretted getting on his bad side. He was like a cat playing with a bird, drawing out its suffering. Soon, he'd bite off her head. She'd rather not be present at her own execution.

The music started—her means of escape. "Edgar, must we talk business? You haven't danced with me once tonight."

Edgar sighed. "I'd love to darling, but I'm not on your card."

"To the devil with her card, Edgar. Dance with the girl!" the chief said.

Edgar gave the chief a broad smile. He shot a glance at Mr. Blanc, who frowned. Edgar shrugged. "I don't want to go to jail. Excuse us, gentlemen." He led Anna to the dance floor.

Edgar whirled her almost as well as Theo. "I told you fathers are better behaved when they have an audience."

"What?"

"Your father—he didn't stop us from dancing. He would have looked like a heel."

Anna chuckled nervously. "Oh. Yes." She wondered if debauched officers were also better behaved when they had an audience. Maybe Joe Singer had better manners than to publicly shame her at her own engagement ball in her father's home. But maybe he didn't. Maybe, any moment, he would tap his champagne glass with a spoon and lead the whole room in a toast to her career with the LAPD.

Anna inhaled deeply and tried to distract herself by thinking about Edgar. He looked manly and handsome. He smelled like petunias. She tried to think about his large, well-manicured hands, which were holding her, but it was futile.

He whispered in her ear. "You were charming with the mayor. Your father should thank you. I thank you. And you look beautiful."

His appreciation warmed Anna. She murmured. "You're too kind."

He pulled back a little and looked at her shoulders. "But, I wonder. Could your gown be missing a piece?"

Something inside Anna collapsed. Her night was crumbling from every direction. Her voice fell flat. "You don't like it."

"Don't mistake me. I love it. But, I don't like the police chief's son gawking at your décolletage. He's been staring at you all night."

Anna glanced over at Joe, who was indeed watching her. "Who cares about him?"

Edgar's affect hardened. "You can't imagine what goes on in the minds of some men. I can't stand him ogling you. Every time I look over, he's staring. He doesn't even try to hide it."

Anna blinked. "Fine." She dropped her arms and stepped back. "I'll change." She swept off through the pink sea with her lower lip trembling in frustration. When she reached an empty corridor she ran. Her footsteps echoed off the marble walls.

From the conservatory, a staircase spiraled up to the second floor to her bedroom. She tapped up the iron stairs, flew into her bedroom, and tore off the low-cut, specially made, two-years-ahead-of-fashion gown. She heard a rip and didn't care. She would never be allowed to wear it again. Edgar was a prude—a jealous one. And he was important to her father's bank. And he might find out she worked at the station. She wiped a tear, smearing the walnut stain. Her fate seemed to balance precariously on the whims of a young police officer with a penchant for staring, whiskey, and whores.

She rifled through the dresses in her wardrobe and settled on a beige cotton gown with stays up the neck and sleeves to the wrist. She examined herself in the mirror. The bodice was loose, the color unflattering. Edgar should be delighted. No one would look at her now. She washed her face in the basin and fixed the smear under her eyes.

Downstairs in the conservatory someone began tinkering with the baby grand, tapping middle C. Tapping it again. Silence fell, followed by a scale and a discordant bang that exploded into a sizzling rag. The music moved so fast she couldn't listen. She could only feel it. Anna had heard this kind of music only one time before, being played from the back of a truck on the Venice Beach Midway. It was salty music, derelict, her east winds in musical form.

She left her room at the top of the stairs, forgetting her gloves, and leaned down over the banister. Joe Singer was part sitting, part standing, part dancing at the bench of her baby grand. His lips were moving and he radiated something that she coveted—unrepentant joy.

He didn't deserve to be so happy or to play so incredibly well, but there it was. God's injustice. He clearly had followed her for some evil reason and stumbled on the piano. She summoned the courage to face her enemy and descended the stairs, graceful and with her chin held high. "Officer Singer. Are you here to vomit on my piano?"

"Actually, Miss Blanc, I was asked to protect you." He stopped playing and looked at her critically. "I liked the other dress better."

Anna tossed her head. "I know. That's why I changed."

He laughed. "Oh, don't mind me. I get paid to look at you. It's nothing personal."

He began to play again, a slower song that Anna found ominous. She waited for him to try to strike some wicked bargain—his silence for a thousand dollars, her resignation from the LAPD, her firstborn son.

He spoke over the music. "Congratulations."

Anna's lips tightened. "You're supposed to congratulate the groom, not the bride. It's an insult." This was especially true in her case.

"Should I congratulate the groom? Or should I warn him that his future wife's a liar?"

"I suppose you want money, Officer Singer. Well, I haven't got any. Do you like my piano? I know you do. You can have it."

He laughed. His fingers rippled across the ivory keys in one long caress. "You can't buy me, Miss Blanc."

Anna fingered the ruffle on her gown, and searched for something to say. Finally, she made a little sound of disgust and flounced down the hall. Joe got up and sauntered after her.

When Anna arrived at the ballroom, Edgar met her at the entrance. "Where's the police chief's son? He isn't in the ballroom."

"How should I know?" Anna said, and sashayed quickly away from the door.

Edgar kept pace. "You shouldn't have left the ballroom alone." He glanced suspiciously back at the door. Joe sauntered in, following Anna. Edgar moved between them and met Joe with a strained smile. His voice was tight. "Officer, I'm afraid this lady is taken."

Joe seemed as relaxed as Edgar was tense. The corners of his mouth moved up. "Mr. Wright. I'm glad you're here. There's something I should tell you."

Edgar folded his arms, glaring. "And what is that, Officer Singer?"

Anna knew her ruin was at hand. Her eyes popped like sunflowers, her knees went weak, and, for the first time, she thought she might swoon in earnest.

"Congratulations, Mr. Wright." Joe said and slapped him on the back. "Anna, shall I have the honor?"

Joe held out his arm and, before Edgar could close his gaping mouth, Anna took it, and Joe swooped her onto the dance floor. His bare, calloused hand took her soft, bare hand, and she regretted the loss of her gloves. She had expected Joe to trample her toes, as he was a barbarian in disguise, but he danced well enough and his breath was sweet. She frowned hard. "You have some nerve addressing me by my first name, and you're not on my card."

"I'm not even a guest." Joe grinned and twirled her.

Edgar tapped Joe on the shoulder, his eyes narrowed, his mouth stretched into a thin line. "I'm cutting in."

"You're not on her card." Joe said, pulling Anna closer and turning sideways so he stood between Edgar and Anna.

Edgar put a heavy hand on Joe's shoulder and squeezed like a vise. "Get away from my fiancée."

Joe shrugged him off. "Hey!"

Edgar muscled up to Joe until they were close enough to waltz, with Anna half sandwiched in between. Anna laughed, her voice stretched unnaturally high and tight. "Darling, please don't cause a scene."

She summoned the courage to tilt her head up and look Joe in the eyes, but his attention had already drifted elsewhere. All she saw was the underside of his cleanly shaven jaw. He stood on tiptoes, squinting and craning his neck to see something over Edgar's shoulder. "Excuse me," he said absently, and dropped his arm from around Anna's waist. In a blink, he was gone, disappearing among the dancers.

Anna's head snapped toward Edgar. His eyes were angry slits. He gripped her arm, cutting off circulation, and steered her off the dance floor into a lonely corner by the window. "Why did you dance with him?"

Anna threw her arms up in her best imitation of innocent bewilderment. "Father put him on my card."

"Well, I'm taking him off! What's wrong with him?"

"Who? Father or Officer Singer?"

"Both!"

"Well, Father's a greedy, tyrannical idiot. And Officer Singer ... he's a boor, but he's only watching me because Father asked him to protect me. If you humor him, he'll go away."

Edgar's brows dipped into a deep, sharp V. "Protect you? From what?"

"Someone engraved my name into our lawn. It was just a prank. The gardener's already fixed it. It's stupid, really, but I've been staying at the Breedloves' all week."

Edgar's jaw constricted. "Who did it?"

Immediately behind them, a head hit the window with a bang. Edgar and Anna started. Joe Singer had Douglas Doogan's face squished up against the outside of the glass. Anna could see his nose hairs. "I'm not sure." She stuck her head out the adjacent window and looked at Joe with disgust. "Must you bloody him at my party?"

"Oh, I'm not going to hurt him," Joe said. "I know this fellow. He likes it."

He heaved the little, kicking man over his shoulder and strode off toward a police wagon parked in the drive.

Edgar pounded his fist on the windowsill. "This is insane! Why didn't you tell me?"

"Darling, I haven't seen you." She gave him a weak smile. "Don't let it concern you. Both of them are gone."

Mr. Blanc directed Anna to sleep in her own bed that night, as Douglas Doogan had been apprehended. But she slept very little. Every sheep she tried to count appeared wearing a bonnet and the ominous face of Officer Singer. In all her dreams she was naked in some public place, and in all her dreams he was there, pointing it out and laughing in the same scornful way he had laughed at her because she had smiled her most beguiling smile for him before she knew who he was. She crossed her fingers and wished that Officer Singer would be shanghaied in the night and would wake up on a boat to China. In case Saint Michael, patron saint of policemen, had overheard, she reluctantly wished that Officer Singer liked rice.

Anna should find out what Joe Singer *did* like. Maybe he already had a grand piano. Maybe he had a different desire. If she could find out what it was, she'd have another stab at bribing him before he squealed and ruined her life.

Chapter 19

Anna emerged from a changing tent at Venice Beach wishing lack of sleep and too much champagne were beauty treatments instead of just the opposite. She felt like a sea anemone that had been poked with a sharp stick. She had spent the entire night thinking about Officer Singer and the threat he posed to her. The beast would probably ruin her just for fun.

A long line had formed outside the changing tent, and Edgar's head already bobbed in the ocean. He waved and started for shore. Anna picked her way past piles of kelp down to the water. Ropes stretched out into the waves for ladies to cling to while standing in the sea. Women were clustered on the ropes like migrating Monarch butterflies on eucalyptus trees. Anna was too well bred to fight for a spot. She waded out into the cold brine anyway, hoping it would revive her, and was trounced by a wave. The heavy wool skirt of her swimsuit tangled around her shivering legs like the tentacles of a giant squid, and she went under.

Edgar's arms reached down from behind and lifted her up. He escorted her to shore. He was barefoot and grinning, in a red-and-white-striped bathing suit that hit above the knees and clung to his body. Anna looked, but pretended not to. On better days, she loved Venice Beach. She loved to see men in wet bathing suits. But today the midway rollercoaster was out of order, she had tar between her toes, the canals smelled like fish, and only one scrawny muscleman lifted barbells. Her swimsuit was full of sand, her wet wool stockings itched, and that wasn't the very worst of it.

Officer Singer knew her secrets.

Anna and Edgar trudged through the shifting sand to a large umbrella, followed by the Widow Crisp. Anna turned to her chaperone. "Oh no. I didn't bring an umbrella for you. You'll be as red as a lobster." She pointed to the nearest palm tree, which wasn't near at all. "Why don't you sit over there?"

Edgar bit down on a smile. The Widow Crisp stomped off to the tree some thirty feet away. Anna moved the umbrella to block the Widow's view. She took off her white slippers, dumped out the sand, and re-laced their ribbons up her legs. Edgar grinned at her. He looked good in his suit—tall, strong, and fuzzy with body hair. She wished he would go to sleep so she could really look at him. It occurred to Anna that he might be thinking the same thing about her. She threw back her head and closed her eyes so he could take a good, long look.

She wondered what Officer Singer would look like in his bathing suit. She imagined he'd look good—like the Arrow Collar Man.

Edgar said, "I'm not sure why your chaperone is worried. I'm not going to kiss you on a public beach."

Anna saw no reason he shouldn't steal a kiss if he apologized for it. She tossed her head. "We are practically strangers. I hardly recognized you last night at the ball."

"I'm sorry I haven't been around much, darling. I do believe I've been a great help to your father. It's an unusual situation with the banks. It can't last." He gave her an irresistible smile. "Do you forgive me?"

Anna lifted his hand and put it flat against her own smaller one. She turned it over and languidly traced a figure eight on the inside of his sandy palm. She glanced up to find him studying her intently. It made her feel naked, and she dropped his hand. She gnawed on her lip and dug for sand crabs. Edgar cleared his throat. "When you eloped, were you alone with Louis Taylor overnight?"

Anna's tired face grew hot. She hadn't expected this from Edgar. Not now, after their engagement was public. "I'd hardly say we were alone. We were traveling third class on a full train. My father had us apprehended shortly after we arrived. You know that. You were there!"

Edgar looked away, a shock of salty black curls tumbling over his forehead. He picked up a handful of warm sand and let it fall between his fingers. "I'm sorry darling. It's just, you seem very . . ."

Anna averted her eyes.

He sighed. "Darling, you can't blame me for being jealous under the circumstances. The thing is . . . my first wife had something of a past."

Anna stared at him blankly. "First wife?"

Edgar groaned. "I thought your father would have told you."

"Why didn't *you* tell me?" She leaned away from him, away from this bad revelation. Her own fiancé had been married and no one had bothered to tell her.

Edgar scooted to face her. "Anna, darling. It's common knowledge. It's not as if I could hide it. I eloped when I was sixteen. All of Boston knew. My father nearly killed me." He reached for her, but she batted him away.

"I'm sorry. I honestly can't believe you didn't know."

Anna hugged her knees to her chest. Though it was hot, she pulled her wrap tight around her. She wanted to cover her shins so he couldn't see them. "Is that why you don't mind that I eloped? Because you eloped, too?"

"I mind, believe me. I hate the thought that another man . . . had your heart. But I understand." He raised his hand to touch her shoulder, but let his hand drop.

"He didn't have my heart. I just wanted to get away, to have a little freedom." Anna put a salty fist to her lips. "It was wrong for father to do what he did, but he was right about Louis. He ran like a rabbit."

"So, he told Louis he'd never get a cent?"

"I suppose so. No one ever told me exactly what was said."

Edgar squinted his dark eyes. "Louis was a fool."

He looked so earnest, with his curls and bronzed cheeks; Anna thought she might forgive him. She didn't mind that he'd been married. In truth, she was glad he'd eloped. Otherwise, he might never have considered marrying her now. But he should have told her. She composed her face. "Was she beautiful?"

"Very."

Anna's face fell.

"But she had a cold heart," he said.

Anna brushed the sand off her shins. "Were you very sad when she died?"

"Oh, she didn't die. She stole my mother's jewels and ran off with a soldier. It was an enormous scandal."

"Edgar, you're divorced? I can't marry you! We're Catholic." Anna scrambled away from him as if he had some dreaded disease.

He spoke in a soothing voice. "No, darling. Not divorced. Not divorced. My father had the marriage annulled, like yours did."

Anna took a deep breath. If the Pope said it was all right, she wasn't going to quibble. She let him pull her back under the umbrella and hold her hand. She peeked up at him. "Were you heartbroken?"

"No," he said. "I was relieved."

She dug her toes down deep to where the sand was wet and cool. "I won't run off with a soldier."

"What about a besotted police officer?" Only half his handsome face was smiling.

"Really, Edgar!" She gave him a reproachful look. "Now, tell me. What else don't I know about my fiancé besides that he's jealous and very, very foolish?"

"Hm. I don't eat chicken or head cheese." He grimaced. "I'm afraid of cats."

Anna suppressed a laugh. "Afraid of cats? That's silly."

"It's not very manly, I know."

She gingerly touched the long dark hair on his bare, muscular arm. "You are the standard for manly."

"If there weren't so many people, I'd kiss you for that."

On Monday morning, Anna didn't smell the city exhaust or hear the seagulls squawking overhead. She strode to the station with one thing on her mind—silencing Officer Singer. She began to chew nervously on her lips but stopped herself. Soft lips were important, in case one was ever alone with one's fiancé.

Anna arrived as Officer Singer was hanging his helmet on a brass hook. He wore men's clothes, freshly returned from some outdoor beat, his face pink from the coolness of the morning. He looked deceptively innocent, like an ad for Pears' Soap.

Anna wrung the handle of her heinous leather bag and cast her eyes about the station. Mr. Melvin typed at his desk, minding his own business, or at least appearing to. Snow sat at a desk clear across the station. His index finger was buried in his mouth. He took it out and stuck it up his nose. Matron Clemens and Captain Wells bickered like a married couple in his windowed office. The blinds hung closed, but not nearly closed enough. Wolf was nowhere to be seen. The public seating area was empty. The patrolmen were out.

No one was paying attention to Anna. She stole to Joe's side and twinkled with artificial amity. "Good morning, Officer Singer."

His reciprocating smile was real. "Assistant Matron Holmes. Why don't you make me some coffee?"

He relished bossing her. Anna could tell. She lifted her chin. "I don't know how."

"I suppose that makes sense. What can you do besides dress up like a bird of paradise?"

"I can do a lot."

"Oh, that's right. You knit blankets for orphans." He smirked. "How did you get Matron Clemens to hire you? Not with the orphan fabrication."

"Wolf hired me."

Joe threw back his head and laughed. "That explains it." He sauntered to his desk. Anna narrowed her eyes at his backside. "I have skills!"

"Like what?"

"I can tell you don't get along with your father and you broke your bathroom mirror on Wednesday."

Joe, who was lowering himself into his chair, fell hard. He stopped smiling. Anna kicked herself. The remark was personal; she shouldn't have said it. A squeaky panic hovered in her vocal chords. Joe tapped his desk, beating out some primitive rhythm. War drums. He cleared his throat. "Is there something you want from me, or did you just come over to play detective, Sherlock?"

Anna blushed, sorely regretting that she had chosen "Holmes" as a surname, and most everything else she'd done or said in the past two weeks. She tried not to look desperate, smiled with all the sugar she could muster, and lowered her voice. "Why won't you take my piano?"

"Assistant Matron Holmes, don't you have work to do?" he asked.

"No. I mean . . ." The panicked cry was back. She closed her eyes and wrestled it into submission. She'd handled similar situations before. He was no different than Cook's son, Alvin, who, when they were eight, had seen her pop the butler's bicycle tires with an ice pick. She'd offered him marbles, but it hadn't been enough. She'd offered horehound candy. He had said no. His price was a yellow goldfish. What was Officer Singer's goldfish? Not a piano. Something else. She could take any number of things from her father and just claim that Miss Cooper had stolen them. Ruby cufflinks? A cashmere coat?

She blurted. "My father has a parrot. It's not eloquent. I mean. It swears. In French, but otherwise . . ."

Joe snorted. Anna glanced toward Mr. Melvin's desk. Empty. She scanned the station. Clear across the room, Snow handed Mr. Melvin a report. Mr. Melvin took it with the pads of thumb and pointer finger. Anna turned back to Joe and held his eyes, pleading in a whisper. "What do you want from me? I'll give you anything. I'll do anything. Anything at all. Just ask me."

Joe raised his eyebrows. "Coffee."

Anna stared at him a long moment and scowled. A horse was a goldfish. A man's diamond ring was a goldfish. Coffee was not a goldfish. Coffee was an insult. She tossed her head. "All right. I'll learn." Anna strode to the station's kitchen to try her hand at boiling water.

The tiny kitchen sweltered. A pot-belly stove shared space with a sink and table. Lunch pails crowded the shelves, large and brimming to feed the men during twelve, sometimes fifteen-hour shifts, seven days a week. Anna looked about. She spied a tin of coffee under the sink. She filled the kettle from the faucet, added a handful of coffee beans, and set it on top of the stove. She perched on a chair to watch it boil.

Some time later, Anna returned with a blister on her finger and a tin cup half filled with a light amber brew. She handed the cup to Joe.

"Thank you." His smile was pure rudeness. He swirled the cup and grimaced, walked over to a brass spittoon and dumped out the coffee. It pinged as soggy whole beans hit the brass in clumps.

Anna made a little sound of objection. Joe ignored her, sauntered over to his desk and sat. Anna trailed behind him. He glanced up. "Assistant Matron Holmes, if you keep following me around, the men are gonna think you're sweet on me. So unless there's something else . . ."

Mr. Melvin sat at his desk now, eyes trained on the ledger before him. Wolf emerged from the interview room with a lady. She was flushed. He was smiling.

Anna cleared her throat. "There is. I want to know the fate of the little man who you captured stalking . . . um . . . Anna Blanc." Anna planned to find the little man's goldfish.

"I let him go."

Anna's pretty jaw dropped. "What do you mean you let him go?"

He shrugged. "Trespassing's not a jailable offense. I could fine him, but he doesn't have any money. I could kick the tar out of him, but he'd like that."

"So you just let him go?"

The corners of his mouth twitched. "I bought him a drink first."

Anna couldn't help it. All her sugar had dissolved. She snapped. "You're some police officer, scoffing at a woman's safety and contributing to the degeneracy of a reprobate!" Across the room, Wolf turned to see his pretty hireling upbraiding an officer. He slapped a hand on his forehead.

Joe smirked at Anna. "He's harmless. His name's Douglas Doogan. We arrest him all the time. I told him to stay away from you and he will."

"Well! I wish you'd do the same!" She flounced toward her desk.

Joe laughed. "Practice what you preach!"

Anna lowered herself into her chair and covered her face with her hands. She knew she needed to be nice to Officer Singer, but everything she said to him was wrong. Mostly because he was awful.

She opened the desk drawer to stow her hulking, scrofulous bag and saw the picture of her and Eve smiling like sisters at the march, which she had framed in a swirl of silver. She wanted to display it, but the photo featured Anna Blanc, not Matron Holmes.

How could a wretch like Officer Singer be anything to Eve? They weren't sweethearts, surely. Eve was superior to Officer Singer in every way. Anna's eyes lit with an epiphany. Officer Singer must respect Eve. Maybe he even recognized and was grateful for her condescension. If he knew that Eve liked her, he might amend his opinion of Anna and come to see her as she really was—wonderful. Then he wouldn't tell Edgar or her father that she was Assistant Matron Holmes.

Anna took the picture out of the frame and gingerly tore it, removing her image from the photograph. She replaced Eve's half of the photo in the frame. She stacked criminal files into a tower and crowned it with the photograph, facing out at Joe's eye level.

When Joe sauntered back past Anna, he did an about-face. He snatched up the picture and studied it. Anna's heart jumped. She brought out her sugar smile.

Joe grunted in disgust. "You have got to be kidding me."

Anna's smile drizzled away. "What?"

"It was you with Eve at the suffrage march."

Anna balanced an imaginary book on her head, and proudly pronounced, "Mrs. McBride is a friend of mine."

Joe shook his head as if he couldn't believe her words. "You're a lollapalooza. Maybe you were friends, but I doubt she thinks so anymore."

Anna harrumphed. "What do you know?" She cut her eyes to the paper she was typing and furiously pecked at the keys. She hit return and typed some more.

"Oh, I heard the whole story. How she took your cigarette. How you provoked the policemen. How your daddy got you out of jail. Eve got thirty days. She lost her job over it."

The typewriter pinged. Joe leaned over her and narrowed his eyes. "You got her canned and then you stole her job. She's a widow with children, Assistant Matron Holmes."

Anna stared into those close, hostile, Arrow-Collar-Man eyes, utterly confused. This couldn't be true. If this were true, Anna was a rat. No, worse than a rat. She felt dizzy. She dropped her eyes and tried to keep her voice steady. "You heard wrong. Eve herself recommended that I apply for a matron position so we could work together. I didn't know she'd been dismissed."

Joe laughed darkly. "And you think you're friends? For a detective, you sure miss a lot of clues."

Without warning, he reached over and yanked the sheet of paper from her typewriter. She lunged for it too late. He saw her page of gibberish. His shoulders shook with bitter laughter.

"I'm . . . testing the ribbon," she said.

"I bet you are."

He sauntered off, smiling his contempt, leaving Anna with her hands pressed to her warm cheeks.

Chapter 20

That night, Anna jabbed her palm with a pin. She did it again, harder, and a tiny drop of penance pooled on her skin. She was a despicable friend. Jab. A bad person. Jab.

There was a knock at Anna's bedroom door. "Go away."

"Let me in," Mrs. Morales called.

Anna closed her fist over her stigmata and opened the door.

The older woman frowned. "Sister Sweetinbed is on the line for you. Take it in the corridor."

"You don't have to listen to my calls. The Widow Crisp follows me like a hound dog." Anna stepped out of the bedroom and took the cold metal receiver. She thought of all the nuns who'd punished her over the years, but could conjure no image of Sister Sweetinbed, just a vague burning sensation on her backside and the impulse to run. She braced herself for a reprimand. "Hello?"

"Hi, Princess." Madam Lulu's voice floated disembodied over the crackling line. Mrs. Morales hovered, listening.

Anna's tone was stiff and tentative. "Sister Sweetinbed, what a surprise." She rolled her eyes for Mrs. Morales's benefit. Mrs. Morales seemed to relax. It was the exact reaction she would expect from Anna upon receiving a call from a nun. She swished off.

Anna tugged on the telephone cord and tried to drag it into her bedroom, but it wouldn't stretch. "How did you find me?"

"Oh please, I read the society pages. I'm calling to remind you of your sins."

Anna cupped her palm around the receiver. "What exactly do you want me to do? I've spoken with the detectives, including the captain, and they didn't take it well."

"Talk to the police chief. He's a friend of your father's."

Anna guffawed. "What would I say? He'll tell my father."

"If you don't, more innocent girls are gonna die. So you make somethin' up. And bat your eyelashes." Madam Lulu hung up the phone.

Anna slunk to her room and threw herself onto the bed. A deep line creased her brow. She thought about dead brothel girls and about sin. She thought about Georgie and Eve.

Anna's ragged, russet carrying bag lay like a bloodstain on the Persian carpet. She reached for it and dug out the suicide note. It had wormed its way into a hole in the lining cut by the sharp blade of the paring knife. Anna ran her finger down the smooth paper.

If Peaches had been murdered by some brutal beast, the note was either a forgery or written under duress. If that were the case, there should be a clue. The message itself seemed all right, something a desperate, uneducated woman might write to her son. Out of the thirty-three words in the letter, nineteen spellings were slaughtered. She had managed to misspell "in," one of the easiest words in the English language.

Anna read the note several more times until she had memorized it. She closed her eyes and ran each word through her mind in sequence. Mi sweet babee. I luv u. But I rekan a difrent muther kan raz u beter. I m so sory, babee. Pleez forgiv me. I was n a low . . .

Anna paused at the word "low," which had been spelled correctly, and frowned in puzzlement. "Low" contained a diphthong. No one this bad at spelling would ever get it right. They would spell it phonetically, L-O, the way it sounded. Anna was sure of it. Even Lady Molly of Scotland Yard would agree. Anna hugged herself. The truth would be plain to anyone who had won her convent's spelling bee. The letter was a fake, badly written by a killer who could spell.

When Anna realized the implications, her elation leaked away, replaced by a swampy feeling in her stomach. If Madam Lulu was correct, it was a sin to stand by and do nothing while fallen girl after fallen girl was being murdered. Sins of commission were much more fun than sins of omission, and Anna needed to lower her overall tally or she would never get out of purgatory.

She winced. She would have to speak with Chief Singer and show him the note. Someone had to solve these crimes or more children would be orphaned, more girls would die.

The next day, Anna called the station using her best deathbed voice, and told Mr. Melvin she had influenza. She donned a hat piled with swirls of ribbons, fluffy poufs of tulle, and rings of roses to lend her both height and authority. She dropped off the Widow Crisp and drove to City Hall.

Anna breezed through the stone arches armed with the certainty that, as the daughter of Christopher Blanc and the fiancée of Edgar Wright, Chief Singer would have to see her.

The chief had been in office for seven months, appointed by the mayor last December. Most police chiefs barely lasted a year in Los Angeles. He was due to get shot, quit, or be fired any day now. The chief had moved out the previous year from Jefferson, Indiana, where he'd served as Marshall, bringing his debauched son along with him. Although Anna didn't know Chief Singer well, he had been to the house on several occasions and showed a polite interest in Anna. He would, at least, hear her.

The lobby was airy with tall ceilings that kept the room cool. When Anna checked in with a clerk, her voice echoed. In a moment her steps were ringing out up four flights of marble stairs and through the corridor to Chief Singer's office. Anna glided in, leaving the door ajar.

The chief was leaning back in his chair, smiling, looking casual and comfortable. His skin glowed red. He leapt to his feet when Anna entered. "Sweet surprises, it's Miss Blanc!"

"Chief Singer, you're sunburned!" she said, as it was her feminine duty to dote. She offered him her dainty gloved hand.

He took it and motioned for her to sit. "Been golfing with the mayor. Should've worn a hat." He grinned and slid back into his chair. "I can't imagine why you're here, but whatever you want, you've got it."

Anna smiled and bobbed. The father was charming, clearly more agreeable than the son. "I've come to beg your assistance."

"I'm listening." He scooted closer and leaned forward with the focus and attention of a confessor. He was handsome, and Anna blushed. "You know I've been working for the Orphans' Asylum."

He nodded. "Knitting blankets."

"Yes." Anna fingered a broach at her neck. "One of the children's mothers, a . . . brothel girl, had her throat cut."

He blew out a whistle and leaned back in his chair. "Miss Blanc, you are all surprises."

"Detective Snow is calling it a suicide, but I don't believe a woman would do such a thing."

"Soiled doves lead miserable lives."

Anna leaned forward. "Yes, but there's evidence that Detective Snow has overlooked. A suicide note. I believe it points to murder."

He nodded, looking thoughtful and serious. "Is that so?"

"I've got it right here." Anna dug in her purse for the crumpled note and handed it to him. She leaned over his desk as he read it. Her words came out in a rapid stream, tumbling over any punctuation that tried to stand in their way. "I believe it's a fake. See, look closely. Virtually all the words are misspelled—'in' spelled N, 'been' spelled B-I-N."

He wore a listening expression. Anna talked faster. "See the word 'low'? It's spelled correctly, L-O-W. It contains a diphthong! Who would misspell an easy word like 'in' and then properly spell a diphthong? The letter was obviously written by a person only pretending he can't spell!" She ran out of air and gulped a breath. "That's why I want a different officer to investigate." She sat back in her chair and waited for him to see the rightness of her logic.

Chief Singer raised his brow and ran a hand through his hair. "Well, you ought to talk to my brother-in-law down at Central Station."

"I spoke with Captain Wells."

"And?"

"He says he trusts his men."

Anna stared at him expectantly. The chief nodded again and drummed a finger on his desk. Anna tapped her fingernail and watched him think. After a brief silence he said, "The coroner examined her body?"

"Yes."

"The coroner teaches at USC."

"Yes, I know. The men respect him." Anna picked up the letter and slipped it back into her clutch. "Chief Singer, I'm sure that things are not what they seem. Other brothel girls have died mysteriously, too, and the madam thinks it's murder. More people could die. If you aren't prepared to have an officer investigate, perhaps one of the matrons can do it. They've had contact with these girls."

"You are somethin' else." He studied her face. "If it makes you feel better, Miss Blanc, I'll have someone look into it." He smacked the desk and stood. "Now go home, put it out of your mind, and give my regards to your father."

Relief washed over Anna. She had won. She stood, gave him her hand and her most brilliant smile. "Thank you. I knew you'd help."

The chief shook her hand. "By the way, when you went in to see Captain Wells, did you see my son Joe at the station?" He was grinning and seemed to anticipate some favorable remark. She felt sorry for him. He was proud of his son.

"Why, yes I did. I almost didn't know him dressed as a girl. But when he fell on me—he was a little unsteady, and threw up on my shoe—I said, 'why that's Chief Singer's son.'"

Anna immediately kicked herself. But Joe Singer made her say awful things. She held her breath for the chief's response.

He slapped his hand on his head with a resonate *thunk*. "Oh my. I'll have to talk to that boy."

Panic rose in Anna's throat. "Oh, oh no. Please don't. Please. I wouldn't want to . . . embarrass him." Or enrage him.

The chief shrugged. "If you say so, Miss Blanc."

She exhaled a laugh of relief. He was so charming and pleasant, so at her disposal. "Thank you, Chief Singer, and your son is . . . Your son is *very* . . ." She pressed her lips together. "Have a good day." She dipped and headed for the open door.

Anna considered the meeting a smashing success. She had discharged her obligation to God and Lady Justice. Chief Singer would put a new detective on the case. Officer Singer would never know that she'd told on him again. With luck, he'd get in trouble anyway. She felt so happy and relieved that when she passed through the open door, she almost twirled, but stopped short at a terrible sight. Officer Singer leaned against the wall, crooning to himself. "I wonder who's kissing her now, wonder who's teaching her how . . ."

One dimple was propped up by a smirk. "Sherlock, you annoy me. A-N-N-O-Y," he said. "The O Y—that's a diphthong."

Anna squeezed her eyes together and flounced away as fast as she could, her quick steps echoing down the marble hall.

He called after her. "How's that influenza?" He paused. "Your hat looks like a wedding cake!"

Joe sauntered into his father's office and closed the door. Chief Singer stood in the corner, polishing a hickory golf club with a soft cloth. Joe relaxed against a bookshelf. "So who's gonna look into that brothel girl's death?"

"No one. It's a suicide." Chief Singer put down the club and gave Joe a hard look. "Now Son, I don't mind if you have a dram or two on night shift, but you can't be stumbling around, throwing up on ladies."

Joe blew out a breath. "The little tattletale."

"Yes, well. Forget about it. I'd like you to come down to the California club Friday night. The mayor and I are meeting the Mexican Ambassador for dinner."

Joe's mouth tightened. "Is that an invitation or an order?"

The chief leaned back in his chair and exhaled. "If it has to be, it's an order. But why don't you put your surliness aside and come because you might learn something. Life isn't black and white, son. Sometimes you have to compromise."

Joe's mind drifted to Anna, to her gorgeous piano, and her offer to do "anything." He closed his eyes. His mind drifted to compromise.

Chapter 21

It was Sunday morning. Anna's bedroom windows were thrown open against the heat. Outside, the gardener was watering the flowerbeds, and the scent of wild mint drifted up from beneath the spigot. Anna tossed her room in search of her lilac taffeta swimsuit. Today, Edgar was calling. They were going to the beach. He had already seen her blue wool suit, and she absolutely refused to rent an ugly one at the bathhouse. It meant missing mass, but such were the sacrifices one made while courting, or how was one to ever be fruitful and multiply given one's fiancé's busy schedule?

She dug through her dresser looking for the bathing suit, tossing undermuslins, sets of drawers, and negligees all over the floor. Just as she laid hold of the elusive thing, she heard a wagon pull up outside and a man's voice singing, "I'll sing to you a romance and play on my guitar; 'Tis of a dark-eyed maiden, I worshipped from afar . . ."

Anna's breath quickened. She recognized the voice. It was the talented but wicked Officer Singer, come to destroy her. She yanked back the curtains and there he was in the drive, sauntering toward the grand front entrance of the Blanc mansion in baggy denim waist overalls. He looked like a field hand. Three other men in work clothes lounged against the wagon. One patted the horse's behind.

All of Anna's limbs lunged at once, and she tripped over herself bolting for the door, never mind that she wore a night dress and her hair was down and messy from sleep. She had to intercept Joe Singer before someone else did. Had she seen her father's car in the drive? She couldn't remember. Anna skidded down the hall in bare feet, her skin sticking to the floor, her body jiggle-jiggling without a corset, her lacey chiffon night dress billowing out. She hit the marble foyer and swung open the massive front door, just as Joe Singer reached for the knocker. He stood with his hand poised in the air. He let it drop and stuck it in his pocket. She was small in the doorframe, breathing hard, looking beyond Joe, and scanning the drive for her father's car. It was gone. She let out a little cry of relief and turned hot eyes on Joe.

Joe looked at her bare toes, her thin night dress, and her hair tumbling down in a tangle. He smiled a lopsided smile. "Is this a bad time?"

Anna glared. "I'm afraid *mon père*'s not home. You'll have to come back and destroy me another day."

"Tempting, but I'd rather borrow your piano."

She sniffed in contempt. "So you are corruptible."

"No. I'm just borrowing it. It's different. And at least I'm not a liar."

She wanted to pinch him, but instead she let him in. "You know where it is."

Anna turned and fled down the hall, through the conservatory, and up the staircase to her bedroom. By the time she'd dressed, fixed her hair, and returned, the men had muscled the piano through French doors and out into the garden. They handled it reverently, like it was an enormous egg.

Anna stood by, not speaking. When the piano was loaded in the wagon, Joe cushioned it tenderly with blankets and straw. He ran his hand along the smooth ebony finish, caressing it the way she'd seen Romeo caress Juliet on stage.

He cast Anna a glance. "I'm just borrowing it."

She tossed her head. "Borrowing. Blackmailing. It's semantics."

Joe flushed and licked his lips. The three men had already settled themselves on the front seat of the wagon. They nodded in Anna's direction. She gave them a false smile and a lackluster wave. Joe Singer stayed in back, perched on Anna's stool. He closed his eyes and began to play her baby grand, slowly at first. Anna marveled as his fingers began to accelerate. The music raced around her, and he threw his head back in that enviable joy. Clearly he'd forgotten whatever guilt he'd felt at blackmailing her.

Now that he was making love to her piano, he couldn't tell on Anna, not if he wanted to keep it. She felt suddenly light and her heart smiled. Without permission, her feet tapped to his raucous rag.

Anna's lightness was short-lived. As the horses pulled the clunking wagon into the street, flooding the neighborhood with music, an ocean blue Cadillac turned into the drive.

Anna fled inside and threw herself down on a fainting couch, accidently sitting on the cat. It hissed. She grabbed it around the belly, because petting a cat is an activity one might do on a couch. Slowing her breathing, she waited for the tinkling of the bell, and tried to subdue the squirming monster. She got a scratch on her neck for her efforts.

The maid ushered Edgar into the parlor. Anna, still wrestling the mewing cat, felt her underarms dampen. She grimaced. "Hello Darling. You're early."

Edgar turned and fled.

It seemed a strange reaction to finding Joe Singer in her driveway. She'd expected him to yell. Anna sat forward and tried to see out the door. She heard his cool voice from the hall. "Please put out the cat."

"Oh. Of course!" Anna strode across the room and shoved the cat out an open window. "She's gone." It growled as it fell.

Edgar cautiously reentered the room, his eyes stony hard, his angry flush compounded by embarrassment. "Why was the police chief's son playing piano in your driveway?"

"The police chief's son? I hardly think so." She laughed. It sounded tinny.

"It was he!"

She yawned. "Was it? Well I had nothing to do with it. I donated my piano to the Orphans' Asylum. Some grubby men came to pick it up. That's all."

Edgar studied her face, his lips as firm and straight as the horizon. Anna examined the nails on one hand. The other gripped the arm of the settee like it was the bar on a roller coaster. She glanced up cautiously. He closed his eyes and rubbed his temples, letting out a long, slow breath. "I can't go today. I have to meet your father."

Chapter 22

On Monday morning, Anna sat at her desk, going through endless dusty stacks of files, and fanning herself with a newspaper. She gave herself a paper cut. "Cock!" It was a word she'd heard about the station. Since taking a rooster's name in vain was permissible, and she liked the ring of it, she had incorporated it into her vocabulary. She stuck her finger in her mouth to suck the blood.

A few patrolmen loitered about drinking cold coffee and complaining about their hot uniforms. They began to hoot and whistle. Anna looked up. Officer Singer strolled into the station in the olive wool coat of the LAPD, holding up a large cotton frock and making it dance the hoochie coochie. "Who's going to be the bait tonight, because I ain't doing it anymore. Wolf, I bet you'd like a chance to wear ladies' clothes."

"Only if the lady's still in them," Wolf said. The men laughed like a pack of hyenas, all except Captain Wells and Mr. Melvin, whose nose was in his cup.

"You're in mixed company, Detective Wolf," warned the captain, loosening his collar.

Joe walked from grinning man to grinning man. "Washington? Sanchez? Come on now, give me a break." Each one laughed and shook his head.

The coroner stomped in. "I'm missing an autopsy book. Who has it?"

Anna slumped down in her chair.

The coroner frowned at the lack of response. "All right." He strode to a bookshelf and began to rifle through it. "I'm doing a lecture on medical jurisprudence at the college next Monday night, and if you have any pride in your work you should be there. Don't eat first. Who's going?" He turned to face the men.

Anna's hand shot up like a rocket.

Joe approached the coroner. "How about you, Doc? I'll go to your talk if you'll be the girl tonight. You get a free bottle of whiskey." Joe raised his eyebrows hopefully.

The coroner's lips scrunched in disapproval. "I'm a Baptist man. We don't drink and we don't wear frocks."

Joe swore and scanned the room. "This isn't fair! You guys have to take your turn."

Anna stood. "I'll do it."

The station fell silent for a beat, and then the hyenas began to howl.

"You can't do it, Sherlock. It's dangerous," Joe said.

"I want to do it." Anna looked to Captain Wells. "It's the exact kind of thing that I'd like to do."

"She wants to be a detective. Let her do it," Wolf said. "I'll protect her." The men seemed to find this particularly funny.

Joe's arm went slack, the dress hanging limp at his side. He appealed to Captain Wells. "She can't do it."

Captain Wells handed Joe a bottle of whiskey. "Officer Singer, you make an ugly girl. But you're the prettiest officer we have. So either be the girl or take the girl. Wolf will go with you. But I'm warning you, don't screw it up again."

Joe frowned hard.

Chapter 23

Anna sprawled across her bed studying a map of Los Angeles. The coroner's lecture on Monday night would be at USC, almost four miles across the city, and that was as the crow flies. If she took her yellow convertible, her father would see that the car was missing, initiate a manhunt, and fire the Widow Crisp. Without an allowance, Anna didn't have trolley fare. She was going to have to walk. It would take hours, and she might not make it to the lecture in time. And how safe were those streets for a woman alone at night? Anna didn't know. Before her deal with the Widow Crisp, she had rarely gone anywhere alone, and never at night. She'd like to ask Theo to escort her, but then she'd have to tell Clara. She wished she could ask Edgar, but it was out of the question.

A cuckoo stuck his head out of a miniature chalet and chirped seven times. Anna would have to solve the problem later. Nothing could spoil tonight—not danger, Douglas Doogan, Joe Singer, or the fact that a brat had seen her steal the maid's dress from a clothesline. Tonight she would live her dream. She was going to trap a criminal—a man who did unspeakable things.

Anna slipped the stolen frock over her head. It was soft and thin from too many washings, and looked every bit the servant's dress. But the maid had an excellent figure. The dress fit Anna perfectly. She rolled a silky pair of stockings up her legs, and donned her lilac-colored François Pinet shoes with the big silver buckles. There was the stain from Officer Singer's vomit, but, as he might vomit on her again, she didn't want to risk a fresh pair.

Anna climbed through her open window and onto a second story balcony, toting a knotted rope she had stolen from the barn. She tied the end of the rope around the stone railing, took a deep breath, and climbed over, lowering herself backward over the side. She landed in a prickly bougainvillea. It stung. Pierced and snagged, she snuck across the lawn and down the safe, clean streets to catch a trolley to Boyle Heights.

The streetcar was packed with people, and Anna would have had to stand, except that a gentleman gave her his seat. The man was striking: white-blonde hair, with remarkable blue eyes and an elegant gray suit. He wore a patterned scarf fastened beneath his high-style collar, a pearl and diamond stickpin, and cuff links to match. His cheeks were as rosy as Princess Pat's herself.

Anna inclined her head. "Thank you."

He grasped a canvas loop directly above Anna, and her knees brushed against his trousers. He smiled down at her. "I couldn't have you stand in those shoes."

Anna winced, thinking of the stain, and hoped he couldn't see it in the fading light. She rearranged her skirt to cover them.

"Oh, don't hide them. They're lovely. If we were in Paris, I'd say they were François Pinet."

Anna's eyes widened. Hardly any men in LA knew French designers. "They are François Pinet! I had them sent from Paris. How did you know?"

"No one makes shoes like Pinet. If you don't mind my saying so, that dress is not from Paris."

Anna blushed. "No. It definitely isn't. I had to borrow it from my friend's maid. My other frock . . ." She searched the windows of the trolley for an explanation. "Caught on fire."

"Oh my. I'm glad you weren't hurt."

"I'm burned in places you can't see," she said, and mentally kicked herself.

The *Los Angeles Times* building towered on the street ahead. He yanked the trolley cord and the bell tinkled. "Ah well. This is my stop. Adieu."

"Adieu." Anna wished that he would be escorting her tonight and not Joe Singer, because he would be much better company.

The gentleman made a gallant bow and swung off the streetcar. With a rumble, the trolley began to move. Anna gazed after the handsome man, who walked with the grace of a ballerina. He turned back and waved.

Anna disembarked at the corner of Brooklyn and Soto. Joe was waiting, dressed like a printer, down to the ink on his cuffs—no doubt his idea of a clever disguise. He was whistling and sucking on a peppermint. He held out his arm to her. "Mrs. Singer."

Anna sniffed and gingerly tested the ink on his sleeves for dryness. Satisfied it wouldn't stain the dress, she took his arm. He smelled clean, like Pears' Soap.

The sky was already black, though a full moon was rising. It illuminated a place very different from Anna's own neighborhood perched high atop Bunker Hill. There was a synagogue with a large gold star and shop signs in four different alphabets. Hardly anyone on the streets conversed in English. It was like the aftermath of Babel. There were a few people like Anna in the quarter—whites who spoke English without an accent—and there was a men's club where Jews and such people did business. The strangeness and excitement made her feel like she had drunk too much black coffee.

Anna and Joe strolled through the melting pot, stiffly, arm in arm, like a married couple who hates each other.

"I didn't think you'd go through with this, Sherlock," Joe said in his easy voice.

"I didn't think you'd be sober."

"You know, your uppity ways aren't helping your career any.

Matron Clemens doesn't like you. Snow and the coroner really don't like you. You're an embarrassment to Wolf."

Anna considered this for a moment and wiped a piece of lint from the thin, soft fabric of her dress. "I don't care."

"I'm telling you this as a favor. And nobody's looking into that suicide."

She smiled tightly. "Are you saying your father's a liar?"

He glared. "I'm sayin' we're all busy trying to catch real bad boys."

"I don't believe you."

"Do you know about the Boyle Heights Rape Fiend?"

Anna considered lying and saying that she did, but then he might not tell her and she badly wanted to know. She reluctantly shook her head.

Joe put his fist to his forehead and blew out a peppermint breath. "Geez Louise. You don't even know what you're in for. I suppose Wolf thinks that's funny. Do you know what a rape fiend is?"

Anna preferred not to appear completely ignorant, so she rolled her eyes. And she did know, sort of. Mr. Melvin said it was a man who did unspeakable things. What those things were, specifically, she wasn't clear.

"Well, if we're lucky, you'll meet one tonight," Joe said.

Quite independent of her head, Anna's arm pulled him closer. His eyes flickered with surprised amusement. He sucked his peppermint. "This one attacks couples with a knife. Ties up the man. Strips the woman naked. Has his way with her, right there in front of her husband or father or whoever it is. He's done it five times here in Boyle Heights. Before that, he was doing it in Omaha."

Anna's back went cold, like she was lying on an iceberg in her underwear. She held him even closer. Without her mind's permission, her free hand reached for his bicep until she held his strong arm with both of hers. This time, his lips celebrated with a long, luxurious smile.

"How many times have you done this sting?" she asked.

"A lot."

"And you've never seen this rape fiend?"

"Nope. But I've stumbled on the aftermath."

Anna exhaled, trying to appear cool, though the muscles of her back had hardened into rocks. She noticed she was hugging his arm, and recoiled like his bicep was a hot coal. How she wished the man who did unspeakable things was only a kidnapper or a bank robber or even a crazed murderer, and not a rape fiend. Under no circumstances did she think Officer Singer should get to see her naked.

Joe handed her a bottle. "Your whiskey."

She took a long swig and quickly tucked it in her purse. Despite her good breeding, she was not about to share. She had shoes to protect, and if anyone was to be dragged into the bushes and covered with leaves tonight, it was going to be her. She felt in her purse for the smooth handle of the paring knife. Her voice wobbled slightly, but her chin was high. "If we're stalking a maniac, why didn't they give us guns?"

Joe opened his vest and flashed a Smith and Wesson, strapped over his ribs in a new leather holster.

"Where's my gun?"

He frowned and rubbed his forehead. "Let me take you home."

"No! I'm not afraid!"

"Uh huh. Sherlock, what are you doing here?" He looked at her, eyebrows up, as if he really wanted to know.

"The same as you. I'm trapping a criminal." She stared back at him, jaw set in stubborn determination, her eyes still glinting with indignation over the gun. She may not like the man, but she wanted him to take her seriously.

He studied her for a moment, looking perplexed. His expression softened and he sighed. "All right. Just keep your eyes open. We want to make sure he's the one that's surprised. He's got a knife. I've got a gun, and Wolf is supposed to show up and provide us with backup. If you see or hear anything suspicious, pinch me." He pinched her side and she jumped. He grinned. "You'll be all right."

With that, he began to ignore her, sauntering along, still holding her arm, tipping his hat to passersby and amusing himself by singing. "By the light, of the silvery moon, I want to spoon, S-P-O-O-N . . ."

Though she could do without him spelling out diphthongs, she liked the song, and his voice was undeniably good—like someone from vaudeville. He seemed so carefree, so like a man on an evening stroll, it distracted her from the fact that their purpose that night was to get violently attacked. For the sake of authentic police work, she pretended his warm arm and lovely song belonged to someone else—someone virtuous and pleasant, who liked her. Anna's tight muscles began to melt, and she relaxed her grip on his arm. Joe stretched and clenched his hand as the blood flowed back into his fingers. She braced herself for some rough comment, but all he said was, "Come on, Sherlock. You sing the patter," and dove back into the song. "By the light . . ."

Anna couldn't carry a tune in her best Liberty of London bag, but since she didn't know that, she sang the patter. "Not the dark, but the light."

"Of the silvery moon."

"Not the sun but the moon."

"I wanna spoon."

"Not croon but spoon . . ."

After several minutes of singing and make believe, Anna pretended to be gay. She matched her step to the music and sang more boldly. He genuinely smiled at her with both dimples. He wasn't such bad company, provided he didn't vomit or speak.

They passed a red fire hydrant crowned with a straw hat that someone must be missing, and an old night-owl hack hitched to a pair of mismatched horses. Joe kicked a pinecone down the sidewalk. Then Anna kicked it, sending it skittering along the cement. They took turns walloping the spiny thing as they strolled, circling the block around the trolley stop, passing the same red hydrant five or six times, waiting for Wolf.

When Wolf finally stepped off the trolley, dressed in a dapper suit and derby, he winked at Anna like a masher and walked off in the opposite direction. Joe steered her down a side street, off into the heart of Boyle Heights. It had begun. Periodically, Anna would see Wolf leaning up against a lamp post or peering from behind a juniper bush or rhododendron, which Anna thought ridiculous given his attire. They carried on this way for two hours, strolling up and down dark side streets and weed-choked alleys until most of the people had gone in for the night.

When Joe and Anna tired of singing, they fell silent. Anna became more aware of the shadows, and how the big ones could be hiding a man. Joe kept revisiting certain sites, perhaps the very places where the crimes had occurred. She thought of Jack the Ripper, and how the officers had walked right past him that night in Mitre Square; how he had held in his hands the bloody evidence of his crime. She was thinking of the strangeness and the danger and how she was hanging on the arm of a man who went to brothels when Joe startled her with a compliment. "You're pretty brave for a socialite."

"I know."

"You know?" He smirked and shook his head as if her ungracious remark was both shocking and just what he had expected. "So, how could you tell my bathroom mirror was broken?" He casually walloped a pinecone.

Anna took her turn, kicking it with her toe, sending it hissing down the road. "Because you've missed a spot shaving every day since a certain Thursday, but before that you never missed a spot."

Joe slowed his stride, and his hand went to his jaw, feeling for stubble.

"Right side," she said. "I assumed you broke your mirror sometime after you dressed that Wednesday, but before you dressed on Thursday. You had about sixteen waking hours to break it Wednesday, but only one or two on Thursday. So, I guessed Wednesday." She held her breath, watching his face for a reaction.

His eyebrows shot up and his lips curved into an admiring half-smile. "You're right." He booted the pinecone.

Anna flushed with pleasure. She had impressed a real policeman, albeit a corrupt one. She eagerly continued. "And usually, unmarried men live with their families. Your father must have a nice house, yet you live alone. So I thought you might not get along." She looked up at him for confirmation, holding her breath again.

"How did you know I lived alone? Because no one told me that I missed a spot shaving?"

"That and your shirt tails are rarely tucked in properly."

"You spend an awful lot of time watching me, Sherlock."

Anna made a little noise of disgust. "I'm simply watching my back." She kicked the cone and it rattled down a storm drain.

Joe led Anna into the Japanese section of Boyle Heights, where the night was several shades darker. There were no sidewalks or lampposts. The few people they passed looked to Anna like giant porcelain dolls, their skin reflecting the moon. The cooking smells were strange, and a trash bin overflowed with trimmings from unfamiliar vegetables. Joe had ceased to distract Anna with songs and questions, but at least he still held her arm. She dreaded the thought of traveling similar streets alone next Monday night on her trip to the coroner's lecture at USC.

She looked up at Officer Singer. He had blackmailed her, but he was useful for walking dark streets, and he seemed in a good mood—that is, he returned her look without glaring. Maybe they could strike another deal. She blurted, "I need an escort to the coroner's lecture on Monday night."

His face was perfectly symmetrical, except for certain smiles—his "scorn Anna" smile, which squished his whole face to the left; his "amused at her expense" smile—a close-lipped quarter moon; and his "mocking Anna" smile, in which he showed more of his left pearlies than his right. His left pearlies were showing, so she braced herself.

"If you're sweet on me, Sherlock, you should ask me to the fair or something, not to an autopsy."

"It will take me forever to get there. I don't have trolley fare so I'll have to walk."

"Don't risk it. He's not even that interesting."

"You could meet me at the top of Angel's Flight. At six. I have to wait until the coast is clear to climb out the window, so I might be late." She rummaged in her purse for the whiskey bottle, and held it out to him with a hopeful and pathetic smile. "Wait for me? You could have my benzene."

Joe studied her face. "You sure go to a lot of trouble, Sherlock." He took the bottle from her hand and tucked it in his coat. "I'll take you to the coroner's lecture if you tell me why you're so dead set on catching murderers and hunting rape fiends."

"For the same reason you are."

He laughed. "I'm not. I need the money. But you don't. Aren't you risking a lot by lying to the man you love? You can't keep up this charade forever. What's he gonna say when you get caught?"

"I won't get caught."

"Really, Sherlock. Why are you working at the station?"

"Why do you sleep with prostitutes?"

He threw up his hand. "That's changing the subject, but who says I do?"

"Well, don't you?" She peered into his face to see if he would lie. How did one tell? He didn't look like he could lie.

"No." He popped a peppermint into his mouth, and didn't offer her one.

Anna raised an eyebrow. "So, you're against prostitution."

He shrugged. "I'm not for it. I'm not against it. It just is."

"That's shocking coming from an officer. Aren't you supposed to be paragons of virtue? Cleaning up society and all that?"

Joe blew out a burst of peppermint breath. "Sherlock, let me give you a little schooling in life. Prostitutes pay fines to the city. The city uses those fines toward paying the police force, including matrons. So how do you think the police view the brothels?"

Anna was silent for a moment. "I see. Their fines help pay my salary so that I can come and take away their children."

"I never thought of it that way, but I suppose that's right."

Anna was quiet for a moment. "What was Matron McBride's opinion?"

Joe's face darkened. He found another pinecone and kicked it. "I guess she wouldn't like children being raised in a brothel."

"Matron Clemens said you would give me her address."

"Nope."

"Why not?" Anna demanded.

"She moved to Denver. Left no forwarding address."

"Is she your relation?"

He squinted at her. "No. Why do you care?"

Anna looked at her silver shoe buckles. "I just . . . I never meant to get her fired."

Joe's voice dropped an octave. "I wouldn't bring that up. Not when I've got a gun."

Anna shut her mouth.

While Anna and Joe strolled, Detective Wolf had been faithfully following the contentious couple, taking short cuts to intercept them, running ahead, sneaking behind, with the utmost stealth and discretion. He urgently needed to find a privy. It was late and dark, so he crept into the back yard of a private residence, located the outhouse, and proceeded to use it. When he emerged, Joe and Anna were gone and a man with a long wiry beard was pointing a shotgun at him and shouting in Yiddish.

Meanwhile, Joe steered Anna down toward Hollenbeck Park, the most forbidding place they'd been—twenty-one acres of horticultural danger. "We're lovers now. On a rendezvous." He said it plainly, like he was ordering liver in a restaurant.

Anna scoffed. "You'd rather play lovers with a male officer than with me."

"That's the long and short of it."

"You don't think I'm pretty?"

"Oh, you're good bait. But you don't fight, except with me, and every time I turn around, you're trying to get me in trouble. Other than that, you're all right." He put his arm around her shoulders and, because she was a professional, she slipped her arm around his waist. His eyes smiled and one corner of his mouth twitched.

Some might say such an embrace was an atrocious breach of decorum. Anna reasoned that it wasn't much different than dancing, and there was no chapter in the *Youth's Educator for Home and Society* that covered one's deportment when strolling through Babel, unchaperoned, stalking a rape fiend who may be stalking you, with a man who was posing as your lover for purely official purposes. Someday, she would write such a chapter and recommend that a woman should always stalk rape fiends in the arms of a policeman. She might even go so far as to recommend Officer Singer, because he looked like the Arrow Collar Man, his arms felt nice and strong, and he would serenade you.

The air smelled like jasmine. They walked the perimeter of the park, negotiating a maze of flora that made it the perfect place for a lover's tryst or an ambush. Everywhere, there were shapes and shadows and places to hide—tall, jutting pampas grass; the twisted roots of a giant fig tree; hedges, bushes, and trellises. Anna attempted to soothe herself by picturing Officer Singer in his swimsuit, but it only made her heart beat faster. She cast a glance behind them. "I haven't seen Wolf in a while."

"I know. Do you want me to take you home?"

"Certainly not."

"We'll find a place to sit and see if he catches up. Keep your eyes open."

Anna leaned on Joe, padding on her tippy toes, so the backs of her heels didn't sink into the soft grass. When they came to a muddy gully, he tightened his hold on her and easily lifted her over.

Anna was a little drunk on this brew of danger—both from the rape fiend and, she was coming to realize, the proximity of Officer Singer. He was strong and smelled nice, even on a hot July night, and his body buzzed with an electric charge that made her tingle all over. She snuggled closer to him just to see what he would do. He cleared his throat and adjusted his trousers.

They were completely alone, more alone than she'd ever been with a man, except for those few minutes with Louis Taylor, which the Pope said didn't count. They strolled deeper into the park, arms around each other, down near the lake where the moon shimmered on the water like a pearl. It smelled of algae and cut grass. They found a bench, which Joe dragged to the edge of the lake so that the water was at their back, a natural barrier to attack. He took out his handkerchief and wiped off the dew so she could sit. Bats fluttered in the trees. Crickets and frogs sang into the silence. Joe added to the music, humming something from *Floradora*, quietly, unconsciously.

Anna found herself thinking less about the rape fiend and more about Officer Singer, her curiously dampening nether parts, and how love was such an illusion because right now she wanted desperately for him to kiss her. Joe Singer, a man other than her fiancé, who stood several rungs below her on the social ladder, who had blackmailed her and thrown up on her shoe, and who, if she kissed him, would surely abandon her and break her heart so she would never even get the chance to live with him in poverty.

And she ought to consider Edgar. He was saving her from a bronze reputation and a spinsterhood in bondage. He was helping her father's bank. He was charming, well-made, and well-dressed, and she planned to fall in love with him if she could ever get a moment of his time.

No. She knew better than to trust her nether parts. Louis Taylor had taught her that. But Officer Singer was still there, with his muscly arm wrapped around her, and he would be for most of the night. The moon shimmered, the crickets chirped, the young man smelled nice. She wished she had silver shoes like Dorothy, so she could click her heels and escape to Kansas where, she imagined, all the policemen were ugly.

She looked up at Joe, watched his lips, set in his square Arrow-Collar-Man jaw, and began to chew on her own. He looked ahead, scanning the area for a rape fiend or for Wolf, barely aware of her. She smiled at her mistake. He wouldn't kiss her. He didn't even like her, and she didn't like him. Perhaps he didn't like women. Perhaps he was one of those men who would never marry, who lived out their lives in the company of other bachelors. She let out a long, low sigh. He glanced down at her with raised eyebrows. "You all right, Sherlock?"

She nodded and cast her eyes to the lawn. These were silly thoughts to have while conducting a police sting operation. She should take his example and focus on their mission. So in the interest of authentic police work, she whispered, "Do you have much experience with lovers' trysts, because I imagine you should be making love to me. Most of the night, your conversation's been rather hostile. He could be shadowing us, listening from the bushes. He would know something was wrong. Real lovers like each other. They'd be crooning or spooning or something."

"All right." He smiled his amused half smile. "I'll make love to you, if you want me to." He looked down into her eyes with his profligate Arrow-Collar-Man peepers, and against her will she blushed. "Sherlock, you're uncommonly pretty. No. Beautiful. A man could look at you all day . . . but you know it. You're clever, but you'd be useless in the home. I doubt you could fry an egg. I trust you about as far as I could throw you, but it makes you kind of interesting."

Anna scoffed. "You're terrible at making love."

"I'm not done yet. You're a tattletale, but those tattletale lips . . . I'm guessing they're honey sweet."

He stopped. Anna made a little ironic noise. "No girl could resist that speech." In truth, she liked it very much. Her heart was sinking lower, lower, lower.

"It was heartfelt," he said.

Anna sniffed. "It's my turn to make love to you." She held his liquid eyes. "Officer Singer, you're a blackmailer. But when you're sober I don't mind you. You're musically accomplished. I could listen to you all night. You dress like a vagrant, but without your clothes you'd look very nice."

Anna stopped, realizing she had misspoken in a most unfortunate way.

"Sherlock, I'm flattered," he said, and kissed her.

Anna opened her mouth to protest—and didn't. He was minty delicious, dazzling, better than Louis Taylor—much, much better. That is to say, much, much worse. His kiss was melting, fiery, and burned with all the intensity of their situation, all the passion required to overcome it. Poor boy, rich girl, a jealous fiancé, a powerful father, a fundamental dislike of the other person, and a rape fiend lurking somewhere in the neighborhood.

When they parted lips, she was trembling. His eyes had changed from vigilant, and occasionally hostile, to deep, dark velvet. His Arrow-Collar-Man mouth curled up in a dreamy half smile. "Honey sweet," he murmured.

He was a peppermint candy she wanted to eat. A man she wanted to see in his bathing suit. A man who could ruin her. His hand slipped down to her tiny waist and her nether parts sang. Loudly.

Anna was in peril. Her heart pounded like an Indian drum. When he lifted her chin to kiss her again, she hesitated, and then did what any girl would do in her situation.

She felt for his gun.

Grabbing the revolver, Anna leapt off the bench, lifted the weapon, and pointed it at him.

"Don't you think you're overreacting? It was just a kiss!" he said. He slowly rose to his feet and raised his hands in surrender.

She badly wanted to kiss him again, so she kneed him in the groin. "Fresh!" As he crumpled to the grass holding his man parts, Anna fled.

He groaned. "Sherlock! We're supposed to be lovers! I was just trying to be convincing!"

Anna ran toward the edge of the park and hid behind a juniper bush, in shadows, beside a dripping marble fountain, her insides all a flutter, her lips still burning from his kiss. The damp earth was emerald with the tiny leaves of baby tears. In a moment, she heard Joe's feet slapping the soggy ground cover, pounding the spongy grass, charging toward the street. When she peeked out from behind the greenery, she saw him standing at the edge of the park, still bent a little at the waist. He patted down his torso. "Damn it! That was my gun."

Joe looked up and down the empty road. "Sherlock!" He picked a direction and ran. When Anna felt sure her lips were safe, she extricated herself from the juniper. She rubbed the tiny stinging welts that rose on her hands where her skin had touched the shrub. She could hear Joe calling on the next block, "Sherlock! You're being an idiot! Holmes!"

Anna walked in the opposite direction, cautiously scanning the empty streets. The storefront windows were dark. The signs, barely legible in the moonlight, were written in letters she could not decipher. Where was Wolf? Had the rape fiend gotten him?

Anna needed to get out of Boyle Heights. In the distance, she saw the *Los Angeles Herald* building, glowing like a beacon. The presses might still be working, and the trolley stopped there, at Ink Alley. If it wasn't too late, she could catch the Owl back to Angel's Flight. She lifted her skirts and ran.

Anna reached the *Los Angeles Herald* building, sweaty and out of breath. Her tapered shoes pinched her toes, and her heels had angry blisters. She slowed to a walk, stowing the gun in the pocket of her skirt. The cold metal bumped her leg as she walked.

Under the burning gas lamps, drivers slumped in wagon seats, softly snoring, reins wrapped around their fists, the horses flicking their manes. Newsboys loitered in their caps and knee pants or slept in the backs of wagons. A clock chimed once. The building's big doors opened and the night crew poured out. Newsboys roused themselves and formed a chain, hauling bundles of papers from the building to their wagons.

Anna approached a worker on the steps and addressed him. "Excuse me. Did I miss the trolley?"

"You shouldn't be out alone, Miss. There's a criminal about."

"Yes, I know."

"Take the Owl with the printers. It's the last car of the night, but it's coming soon. You miss the Owl, you'll have to walk home, and you might not ever arrive."

Anna thanked him and melted into the shadows to wait. It was the natural place for Joe to look for her, and she didn't want to be found.

Soon, the trolley rolled up, and workers from the *Herald* crowded on. Anna ran from the shadows and hopped in front. As she made her way to the back, she saw Joe on the street, striding next to the trolley, searching every face on board, looking for Anna. All the dreaminess was gone from his eyes, replaced by worry and, for the first time that night, fear.

Joe's eyes landed on Anna and flashed. His fear became anger. Anna crossed her arms and turned her back on him.

"This isn't a game, Holmes! You can't just walk off in the middle of a job because you got your feelings hurt!" he said.

Anna huffed. She knew he was right. A man would never behave thus, and she had been the one to suggest that they make pretend police love. Still, she clung to her indignation, because it seemed like the right thing to do.

"Holmes!" he shouted.

"Oh, all right!" She crossed the aisle to the back door and jumped off just as the trolley picked up speed. The landing hurt her blisters. She adjusted the straps on her lovely, brutal shoes as the tram disappeared around the corner. Anna straightened up and looked for Joe on the street. She turned full circle and didn't see him. She called his name. He didn't answer.

Around her, the night shift scattered like mercury. The wagon drivers were pulling away, newsboys perched atop the stacks of papers. The lights at the *Herald* began to go out one by one. Anna steeled herself to assess the situation. Wolf was missing. The Owl had gone, and she was going to have to walk home. Joe was gone, probably on the Owl. This was a good thing. It would be safer for Anna to do the walk alone than to do it holding Joe's arm, with her lips mere inches from his mouth.

Anna's house stood a good five miles northwest of Boyle Heights—seven if she avoided the bad neighborhoods near the red light district. If she started now, and didn't get lost, she could make it back before the servants woke up and declared her missing. Anna started hustling west.

Blocks ahead, a swarm of printers swam down the street like minnows, heading west. Two peeled off from the group and entered a brick house. When the door closed, the swarm traveled on. Several buildings up, they halted and waited as one climbed the steps to an apartment.

There was safety in swarms. Anna sped in their direction. The printers crossed the road and disappeared down a tributary. When Anna reached the intersection, they were gone. She turned in a circle and saw no one. Not even a stray dog.

The night felt ten degrees colder. Anna limped west on swelling feet, hoping to find the printers. She soothed herself by fingering Joe's gun, humming Joe's song, though from her lips, it would have been hard to recognize the tune. His gun felt heavy in her hand, but she dared not pocket it. Anna wished Joe back, even if it meant kissing him passionately in the pampas grass until morning.

After an hour, the streets began to replay themselves—the sites of previous crimes where Joe had taken her over and over. Somewhere, she'd lost west. She tried a different way, placing one blistered foot in front of the other, padding softly, staying in the shadows. The sidewalks and street lamps disappeared. A trash bin overflowed with trimmings from unfamiliar vegetables—the Japanese section.

Anna was still in Boyle Heights.

Blood pounded in Anna's ears. She turned around and hurried back the way she came. Up ahead, she saw the silhouette of the *Los Angeles Herald* building. There was the synagogue with the yellow star. There was the fire hydrant with the straw hat. And there, leaning up against a building, trimming his nails with a long, sharp knife, was Douglas Doogan. He looked up at her with red, gleaming eyes.

Anna ran. She ran like prey. The heel broke off her buckled shoe and she left it behind. She didn't stop, didn't look back, turning, running, turning again. Clumsy with fatigue, she tripped on a crack and spilled onto the pavement. She lay like a puddle on the dirty sidewalk, thoroughly and completely lost, her chest heaving, her stolen skirt torn, the heels of her hands raw and stinging.

Above her, the synagogue's gold star shone. Douglas Doogan was gone. A cigarette glowed under the awning of the men's club, which had long since closed. A man in a suit smoked in the shadows. Wolf. Her heart lifted. She scrambled to her feet. "Detective Wolf!"

The man tossed his cigarette and walked gracefully off in the opposite direction. She caught a glimpse of white-blond hair beneath his hat. It was the man from the trolley. She hurried after him, calling out, but when she reached the corner, he was nowhere to be found. Maybe it wasn't the man from the trolley.

Anna walked for another half hour before succumbing to exhaustion. She found a darkened doorway near the mouth of an alley and sat curled up like a pill bug, knees to chin, paring knife in one hand, gun in the other. She felt like a girl made out of tissue paper, crouching in the rain.

If the rape fiend or Douglas Doogan didn't find her tonight, someone would find her in the morning and bring her home to her father. He would take the gun away and lock her up in the cellar, where she would turn green and fuzzy from mold. She thought of Edgar and what he'd think of her when he learned that she'd bribed the Widow Crisp, lied to everyone, and set out to trap criminals.

With all her strength, Anna willed her eyes to stay open. Time stood as still as a truly dead possum. Or did it fly by, she didn't know. Her eyelids were soggy. Clouds drifted off toward the mountains.

A man's soft voice brought Anna to attention. "Take off your clothes. If you scream or run, I'll kill him."

Her eyes focused, but a cloud had covered the moon, and she saw no man, nothing but shadows. For a moment, she thought she was caught in a dream, that this whole night was a dream. But in the stillness, she could just discern a faint whimper.

She eased herself up quietly, clutching the gun, her mind and body moving without her, as if she'd done this before. She had fired a gun only once, a hunting rifle she had pilfered from her father and which he quickly repossessed. But she had never fired a revolver, and never at a man. She cocked the trigger and stepped out from her hiding place.

Nothing. No one. She crept forward and heard the whimpering again, coming from the alley. Somehow, her soggy tissue-paper-self began to solidify like papier-mâché around the balloon core of a piñata—the kind of piñata you have to whack hard to get the candy. She slipped to the edge of the building and peered around the corner into the dark depths. She saw nothing, heard nothing.

The scent of the night was spoiled with urine smells and the stink of garbage. Overlaid on this rank perfume, Anna smelled her own fear. Her revolver shuddered. The cloud floated away from the moon, restoring its light to the dark streets. It illuminated a scene of terror.

Halfway down the alley, a man lay in the muck, tied and gagged, his eyes bulging with frustration, his trousers wet at the groin. Against the brick wall, a woman fumbled with her corset, her dress in a heap on the ground. A second man, dressed as a printer, sleeves stained with ink, stood watching the bound man and unbuckling his belt, a long sharp knife between his teeth.

Anna watched for a moment, as if it were a play—the humiliated man, the ink-stained villain with the knife, the trembling woman, all actors performing for her class at the convent, only it was the wrong play. She stepped into the alley, lifted the gun and aimed. Her throat was hard, made of steel. She was made of steel. She shouted, "Reach for the roof!"

Joe Singer searched up every street and every alley in Boyle Heights, armed only with a rock picked up from the gutter. His trousers were ripped and his knee bled from when he had jumped off the moving trolley after he'd discovered that Anna was no longer on board. He was terrified, afraid that he would find her around the next corner hurt or that he wouldn't find her at all. She had snubbed him, tattled on him, insulted him, led him into corruption, teased him, stolen his gun, and kneed him in the balls. He didn't know what he'd do if anything happened to her.

He checked his watch. It was three a.m. He told himself it was a good sign that he hadn't found Anna stripped and bound and ravaged, because if the rape fiend had caught her, that's how she'd be. He told himself that by and by dawn would come and he would go to her mansion and find her safe in her bed, furious with him for having violated her sweet lips and worse yet, for showing up on her doorstep and compromising her double life.

He shouldn't have kissed her. If he hadn't, she'd be with him now, holding safely to his arm, singing off-key. But she had been mooning up at him, pressing against him, sending him heat, and telling him to make love to her. He had to kiss her because she wanted to be kissed and she was the most interesting girl he knew; because it was a full moon in Hollenbeck Park; because she was marrying Edgar Wright and he would never get a chance at those honeyed lips again. If it hadn't ended like this, her running off into danger, he wouldn't have taken that kiss back for anything.

In the dust ahead of him, he saw something glimmering in the road. When he got closer, he could see it was a shoe. He picked it up. It was scuffed and dusty, and the heel was missing, but he recognized it. A faint stain marred the finish from where he'd thrown up on Anna her first day at the station. His stomach tightened and he closed his eyes. It didn't bode well. She wouldn't just leave it there. She either lost it running away, or being taken away.

It wasn't just the rape fiend that he worried about. There was more than one kind of danger in LA at night. There were muggers and killers and kidnappers and all this talk about white slavery. He stuck the shoe in his empty holster in the dim hope that she would need it again, and he kept on looking.

Then, he heard a blessed sound. The sweetest of sounds. Anna Blanc was yelling, yelling at the top of her lungs. "Reach for the roof!"

Anna strode forward, gun trained on the rape fiend. He bolted. Anna ran after him. Somewhere, vaguely, she heard Joe calling her name, or sort of her name. "Sherlock!" She was too focused to acknowledge him.

It took all her concentration to keep her gun aloft and her feet slapping the pavement. She had never killed before and, apart from Miss Curlew, never really wanted to. Her plan that night was to catch the rape fiend, not to kill him, but he wasn't stopping, and it certainly wasn't her fault if he took a bullet. "Stop or I'll shoot!"

The villain saw Joe hurtling toward him down the alley with such hot fury, such terrifying menace that the fiend spun around and ran back toward Anna, gun or no gun. Her heart and mind fused. Extraneous thoughts ebbed away, muscled out of place by her solitary purpose—to shoot the rape fiend. She prepared to fire, feet planted, gun arm extended, tracking him as he ran closer, closer, remembering from somewhere that one shouldn't shoot until one saw the whites of the enemy's eyes.

She looked into his face, seeing it for the first time, locking eyes with the villain—bright blue eyes with thick dark lashes. Eyes that had smiled at her when they'd talked about shoes. Anna lost concentration. The strength left her gun arm. She shot wild and hit a coal door in the side of the alley wall. The bullet ricocheted and Joe Singer went down.

Anna charged after the rape fiend, who had fled past her toward the street. She remembered Joe and spun around, rushing past the bound man and the undressed woman.

Anna fell on her knees beside Joe, crossing herself. He was sprawled on his back, chalk white, a hole in his vest over his ribs. Panting, frantic, having shot the man she could have loved if she were stupid enough to do so, she ripped back the vest. There was a bullet hole in his leather holster, and a bullet hole in her holstered François Pinet shoe, and a bullet lodged halfway through the silver shoe buckle. She peeled back the fabric of his ink-stained shirt and found smooth male skin stretched over a muscular breast and a small, rosy nipple like her own. "You're fine. You're fine. You're perfect." She lightly touched his skin where a welt the size of Texas was growing on his ribcage and a spreading redness that would no doubt turn into a nasty bruise. Anna wondered how many of Joe Singer's ribs she'd cracked.

She looked down the alley toward where the rape fiend had made his escape. The woman sat in the muck beside the gagged and bound man who had wet himself. Anna bit her knuckle. "What do I do now?"

Joe's eyes were closed, his teeth clenched, his jaw jutting forward in what might have been pain or rage. "Shoot me in the head because I'd rather die than tell my uncle what just happened here."

Chapter 24

At three-thirty in the morning, a patrolman drove Anna back to Bunker Hill. The whole trip, he smiled, and she couldn't help but feel that, inside, he was laughing at her.

She thought about the gentleman from the trolley, how kind he had been to her, how they had talked about shoes. She had the irrational thought that the rape was an act, and the man on the trolley, *he* was the real man.

She had saved a woman's virtue tonight, but she also shot an officer in the ribs and lent her lips to the man who, though he used them well, had no business doing so. She had seen a man's bare chest—a first and a highlight of the evening. She had hunted a rape fiend and let him slip through her fingers because . . . he was handsome and she liked him.

She didn't want to think of it anymore—the humiliated man, the cowering woman who had to be treated for hysteria in the one-room receiving hospital above the station. She wouldn't be able to sleep. Anna needed a distraction. She needed a good book.

She lied about her address for the sake of discretion, and the patrolman dropped her off several blocks from her house at someone else's mansion. She refused to allow him to see her to the door. Anna limped straight to Clara's. The Breedloves had a library. Not a collection of nursery books like they had at home, but an *uncensored* library. Though Clara herself wasn't much of a reader, Theo collected every book he could get his hands on. He never seemed to miss a book after Anna borrowed and gutted it.

Anna tiptoed to Clara's front door and let herself in with the key Clara had given her when Anna had come to stay. She knew the Breedloves would be asleep in their respective bedrooms. A light glowed in the kitchen. The cook had begun to bake the morning's bread. Anna padded down the hall in the dark.

The library bookshelves ran from floor to ceiling. A ladder slid on rails from side to side. Moonlight trickled through a stained glass window and cast a red-and-blue glow. It smelled of books and furniture polish. Anna scaled the ladder in her sore bare feet and scanned the shelves, considering, but passing up, Gothic romances, a whole row of men's dime novels, and a slew of medical books on every possible topic.

Her eye settled on two by Sigmund Freud—*The Psychopathology of Everyday Life*, which seemed related to crime, and *Studies on Hysteria*, which was pertinent after her experience with the victim tonight. She took them down, slipped out a side door, and lugged them home under her arm.

Anna arrived before the sun rose and limped up the back stairs to her room, spent, but not drowsy. Her mind whirled like an eggbeater. She dumped the heavy books on her bed, selected one, and read for the remaining hour before she had to get up.

The most important thing she learned was that doctors treated hysterical women with bed rest, sensory deprivation, a diet free of Mexican food, and by massaging their nether parts until they were aroused to paroxysm. She was feeling a little hysterical herself after the excitement of the night and thought about the last cure, although one was not supposed to self-treat. She wondered what a woman should do if she found herself in an extreme situation. For example, if she were shipwrecked on a desert island with someone—say, Officer Singer—and their clothes were torn, and all they had were coconuts and one blanket, and she became very hysterical, and she had rested with her eyes closed and eaten no tamales, and she was only getting worse, and she couldn't self-treat. She wondered if it would be permissible for Officer Singer to treat her, as part of first aid. She thought about it for a long, long time.

Anna dropped off the Widow Crisp at the designated bungalow and drove to the station. She arrived slightly embarrassed, but not without her dignity. She had failed by shooting Joe and letting the criminal get away. But if a male officer was kissed by Officer Singer, and made to patrol those diseased streets alone, would he have done better? She didn't think so. She lifted her chin and strode through the station doors.

Joe was still there from the night before, trousers torn, a bullet hole in his shirt. He didn't meet her eyes. Everyone else, however, gave her their full attention. Wolf had reappeared, having just finished questioning the male victim. Matron Clemens had just left the bedside of the female victim, who was recuperating in the receiving hospital.

Mr. Melvin was clicking away, typing up Joe's preliminary report, and while he didn't seem to be paying her any attention, she knew he was. Captain Wells was there, and Snow, and the coroner. A roundsman and several patrolmen were loitering about, both the night shift and the day shift that had arrived to replace them. They should have been home or on the streets already.

Though the station was crowded, it was under a disquieting hush. She saw the men pressing their lips together, holding in laughter that was pushing to get out.

When Captain Wells saw Anna, he spoke, raising his voice so all his men could hear. "Last night, our Matron Holmes chatted with, but didn't apprehend the Boyle Heights Rape Fiend. . . . But she did manage to shoot Officer Singer in the shoe." He held up Anna's wounded François Pinet shoe with the vomit stain and a bullet lodged in the silver buckle.

The men were overcome with laughter, except for Mr. Melvin, who never showed emotion, and Joe, who found nothing about the previous night at all funny. Anna's color changed from the pasty green of the sleepless to the Princess Pat pink of the mocked.

"There is a reason they don't give guns to ladies," Wolf called above the chortles and guffaws.

Snow sneered. "I wonder why he didn't take you, Matron Holmes." She knew he said it to wound her, but the question was one she had asked herself.

Joe winced as he lowered his backside into a chair. "I guess she's not his cup of tea."

Wolf winked. "Don't worry Matron Holmes, you're my cup of tea!"

Anna's blush deepened, but she cleared her throat and raised her voice. "He won't attack single women. Don't you see? He doesn't care about the women. He wants to humiliate the men."

The laughter waned as the men puzzled over this.

Wolf strolled up to Anna and said, by way of explanation, "Matron Holmes can read minds. Can't you, honeybun? So, what am I thinking?" He leered at her and the station roared again.

Anna put a desk between herself and Wolf. She set her jaw and persisted. "He complimented my shoes . . ."

This was met with a new surge of laughter. The men doubled over, gasping for air. Anna pressed on as if under compulsion, practically shouting now to make herself heard above the din.

"He knew ladies' fashion. He could be a cobbler or a milliner—but a successful one. He wore . . ."

Captain Wells interrupted her with a voice that transcended the crowd without shouting. "That's quite enough, Matron Holmes. You have work to do."

Anna's mouth was open and ready, but something in Captain Wells's tone made her shut it. With her chin lifted, she wove her way back to her desk and sat.

She had not been congratulated on saving the woman from dishonor. She was not acknowledged for discovering clues. She was teased for being unwomanly in her career aspirations and womanly in her incompetency. She reinforced everyone's expectations of her—that she would cock things up. She made their victory even sweeter by presuming to handle a gun and shooting Officer Singer.

The officers ambled off to their duties yuck-yucking and complimenting each other's shoes, returning to beats that they had abandoned to witness Matron Holmes's ignominy.

Joe Singer fled for the door like the place was on fire. He grabbed his helmet from the rack. Captain Wells's Scottish brogue stopped him in his tracks. "Officer Singer, there's a big pile of manure that needs shoveling."

Joe turned and threw his palms up. "It wasn't my fault."

"Go! Before I ask Matron Holmes how she got your gun."

Joe tossed his helmet back on the hook. "She'll tell you anyway."

He slunk out the back door to the stables, striding right past Anna without looking at her. Her stomach flipped like an acrobat on a very high trapeze. Although he was fresh, she didn't want him to hate her. He had told her she was beautiful, clever, interesting, and honey sweet. She reminded herself that he had also said she was a conceited, useless, deceitful tattletale. She closed her eyes and tried to sort it out, but couldn't.

Joe had said that Peaches Payton's death was not being investigated. Was the father lying, or the son? She should find out for certain. Wolf would know if the investigation had been re-opened.

A girl with clementine hair loitered in the public seating area near Mr. Melvin's desk. She fluttered and mooned at Wolf, who threw her encouraging smiles from the back of the station. Anna thought she looked desperate. As Wolf sauntered past Anna's desk, she stopped him. "Detective Wolf, did Chief Singer speak to you about the diphthongs?"

He grinned. "No, honeybun. Have they been stolen?"

Anna tried again. "But, you are re-investigating Peaches Payton's death?"

Wolf's smile vanished. "I told you to drop that, Matron Holmes."

He turned and walked off toward the lovesick red-haired girl. Anna sank into her chair and ground her teeth. Chief Singer had not ordered a new investigation. No one at the station believed in the killings. Regardless of what Joe Singer or any of them thought of her abilities, at least she didn't turn her back on murdered girls. It was a sin.

Matron Clemens sidled over to Anna's desk, her worn face arranged in a professional mask, as cool and efficient as a typewriter. "Matron Holmes, how is your filing project proceeding?"

"Very well," Anna lied.

"Good. The patrolmen can't do this work. Half of them can barely read."

Matron Clemens almost smiled for the first time. Anna wondered if this was a backhanded affirmation.

The older woman put two new files down on Anna's desk. "I hope you'll be finished by the end of next week, Matron Holmes. I have other things for you to do."

Anna swallowed. In the last two weeks, she had reviewed 170 juvenile files. Two thirds contained reports naming more than one child and required her to cross-check files and, when necessary, create new files with duplicate reports. With two fingers she could duplicate three files per night on Theo's Remington, if she didn't sleep. There were one hundred juvenile files yet to be reviewed. Of one thing she was certain; she would never finish by the end of next week. She wouldn't finish by the end of next month. And Anna was grouchy, had dark circles under her eyes, and was losing her bloom. If she wanted to cultivate Edgar Wright's love, she would need to sleep at night.

Anna picked up a file from the top of her stack and opened it. Maria Rodriguez. At age nine, her father had broken her arm with a shovel. Seven years later, the girl had been fined for vagrancy outside the Bucket of Blood saloon. Later that year, she was run over by a truck.

Anna's chest felt tight. Another dead brothel girl. She rubbed her forehead with the palms of both hands. No one was investigating. She didn't have time to investigate. She needed every moment to type so she could finish her own work. Except she couldn't. Even if she did nothing but type, she still wouldn't finish the work in time. She was going to fail Matron Clemens and be fired, no matter how hard she tried.

Anna sat back in her chair and crossed her arms. If failure was inevitable, trying was illogical. Therefore, Anna wouldn't try. Why should she? She wouldn't kill herself typing, only to fail. She would spend her time doing the men's work for them. She would investigate murder.

She brought out the list of dead brothel girls, closed her eyes, and reviewed the cases in her mind. She thought about how she would commit suicide if, for example, Edgar Wright refused to marry her. First choice, she would blow out her pilot light, turn up the gas, arrange herself in her best clothes, and simply go to sleep. Opium might be nice, except people sometimes drowned in their own vomit. In a pinch, she might fall on her lover's sword like Juliet, but she would definitely not mar her neck with a big bloody gash and leave her body to be pecked apart by vultures. She wouldn't attend her own wake mutilated.

Anna knew that Peaches Payton had not committed suicide, even if Chief Singer didn't trust her evidence. There had to be another clue, something that would verify Madam Lulu's conviction that brothel girls were being murdered, so that the men would finally believe her, catch the villain, and stop the brutal killings. Otherwise, there would be more blood. She closed her eyes and concentrated.

If brothel girls were being murdered by some deranged killer, and the deaths were being disguised as suicides, etc., wouldn't there be more deaths attributed to suicides, etc., than usual? Anna may not have bodies or crime scenes to examine, but she could count.

Madam Lulu said that the murders began six months ago in January. Anna started a new list, grouping deaths and disappearances by date in six-month increments. She started five years back and worked forward.

From January 1902 up until July 1902 there were two incidents among brothel girls, one death due to drug overdose, and one girl committed suicide. From July 1902 up until January 1903, there were two deaths, both suicides, and one girl reported missing. Anna continued counting in this manner, ending with the death of Peaches Payton that July.

1907 had the highest number of incidents by far. Four girls had disappeared in the past six months, while only one went missing over the previous four and a half years. Six girls had died since January, yet only eight had died in all the other years put together.

Prior to 1907, on average, two brothel girls committed suicide or overdosed each year. Since January, the number of deaths and disappearances had increased tenfold. Anna could think of no reason that the numbers would jump so precipitously, except for murder. But Anna didn't know about prostitutes, except that they were young, pretty, and sometimes did it to feed babies. She knew that Peaches was murdered, but not about the other girls.

She looked over at Snow, who struggled to write something, his forehead wrinkled like a cabbage. He had been the investigating officer in Peaches Payton's death. If she told him about the increase in deaths, he might re-open the investigation. More likely, he would take insult, bark at her, and then tattle to Wolf.

Anna had already asked Captain Wells and Police Chief Singer to take the investigation deeper. Despite her perfectly apodictic logic, they patronized her, lied to her. Now, with the Boyle Heights debacle, her credibility had reached an all-time low.

The captain needed to hear the evidence from someone other than herself. Someone who had his ear. Someone related to him, who ate enchiladas at his house. Someone who looked like the Arrow Collar Man and who wasn't speaking to her at present.

Chapter 25

Anna found Joe Singer in the stables, a long, low building where six of the dozen or so police mounts were loitering in their stalls. There was a loft, and it had that lovely stable smell of hay, leather tack, and horses. She heard a shovel scraping on pavement and his familiar tenor. "I wonder if she's got a boy? The girl who once filled me with joy. I wonder if she ever tells him of me? I wonder who's kissing her now?"

Anna's heart beat a little faster and she wondered who Officer Singer had been kissing before last night, because it seemed like he had practiced. She wondered if it was Eve McBride.

She found him in a stall with a steaming pile of horse manure balanced on his shovel. He tossed it in a wheelbarrow and winced at the motion. She unlatched the rusty gate and pushed it open. It creaked. She put on a tentative smile. "Hello."

He ignored her. That wasn't such a bad sign. If this were to be a one-sided conversation, at least she'd have ample opportunity to make her point. She cleared her throat. "You must think this is all a game to me, that it means nothing. That I'm just going to cock things up and go back to my money and my . . ."

"I wouldn't talk so loud if I were you," he said. "I'm pretty sure Wolf is in the hay loft."

"In the hay loft?" Anna looked up and saw the hay shifting curiously above her, but no sign of Wolf. She looked to Joe for an explanation. None was forthcoming.

"Go on." He leaned on his shovel and looked impatient. He had dark circles under his eyes and his hair was damp around the edges from the heat.

She frowned. She had lost her train of thought. She cleared her throat again and whispered. "I want to capture the rape fiend just as much as you do. And I want to find out who killed Peaches Payton."

"It was a suicide." He started shoveling again, scraping the cement, heaving the manure, wincing.

"No woman slits her own throat. It's ugly and violent."

"On occasion, Sherlock, life is ugly and violent. Why don't you speak to Wolf? He's the lead detective."

"I did," she whispered. "He told me to drop it. You can't tell Wolf that I'm investigating. If he finds out, he'll probably fire me. So, you have to do it."

Joe laughed. Anna lifted her skirts and picked her way into the stall, looking for little patches of clean among the filthy. She moved closer so that she wouldn't have to speak so loud. "Listen to me. It isn't just Peaches Payton. Four brothel girls have disappeared in the past six months."

Joe stopped and scraped dung off his shoe with the edge of the shovel. "That doesn't mean anything. Girls move around, go to new brothels in other cities so they can be the new face in town. It's good business. It doesn't always make the papers."

Her brow arched up. She wondered how he knew that. She certainly had not. "That may be true, but why then had only one brothel girl been reported missing in the previous four and a half years put together?"

He looked surprised. "You went through the files and counted them?"

"I stopped at the letter S."

"So you don't really know how many girls went missing."

Anna made an impatient sound. "Not yet. But I don't believe alphabetical order has anything to do with missing prostitutes. You can't possibly think all the Fs would run away and all the Ys would stay home!"

He swiped a handkerchief across his forehead. "I hadn't thought about it at all."

"I'm asking you to! In addition to the missing girls, six brothel girls committed suicide or overdosed in the past six months."

"I'm telling you, Sherlock. That's life in the low lands. You don't know it because you live on the hill."

"I understand that brothel girls are miserable and they sometimes kill themselves, accidentally or on purpose, but that's six times the six month average over the previous four and a half years."

He raised his eyebrows. "Sherlock finished high school."

She made a sound of exasperation. "You're not taking this seriously! Just like you didn't take Douglas Doogan seriously. I saw him in Boyle Heights last night with a big, long knife. The ladies of Los Angeles thank you for your protection, Office Singer!"

Joe blinked. His face flushed ruby red. "I'll take care of Doogan, all right? How did the girls commit suicide?"

Anna's heart beat faster. He still glowered at her, but he was listening. "Every way you can think of, throwing themselves off cliffs and in front of trains, poison, hanging. Some girls cut themselves. One girl weighted herself down with rocks and went swimming."

"So, every girl died differently?"

"Since January? There were six girls and six different ways."

"Did they all leave notes?"

"Some did and some didn't. But they weren't addressed to us, so we don't have them."

Joe shrugged and spun the shovel like a top. Anna stopped it with her hand. "Maybe there's something else that can explain the suicides and disappearances, but I don't know what it would be because I don't know about brothel girls and apparently you do!"

He laughed cynically. Anna frowned. "Your father is the police chief. You could convince him to have someone else besides Snow look into it."

He shoveled another load of green manure. "I could, but I won't."

Anna snatched the shovel from his hands and the manure fell back into the stall with a splat, spattering his shoes. She glared. "Why won't you help me?"

Joe snatched the shovel back. "Because coroners know a whole lot more about murder and dead people than you do, and I'm not going to accuse ours of incompetence just because you have a hunch!"

Anna stomped her foot. "No! I don't think that's the reason. I think it's because I embarrassed you. Shot you with your own gun. Well, I'm very sorry, Officer Singer. But it takes two to do the tango and you should be sorry too!"

He threw his hands in the air. "Sorry for what?"

"Your impropriety! The real reason we didn't capture the rape fiend. If you hadn't gotten fresh . . ."

"You said you wanted to spoon!"

Anna let out a cry of indignation. "No. I said lovers would be crooning and spooning. I didn't intend . . ."

"Oh come on, Sherlock. You were batting your eyelashes so fast, I was afraid you'd fly away."

Anna's cheeks went candy apple red, a deeper shade than the whole crowd of mocking policemen could inspire. With a shriek of exasperation, she turned and stomped toward the stable door.

A pair of ladies' drawers sailed down from the hayloft and snagged on her bun, covering her face as she tried to open the gate. Anna screamed and swiped at them like they were wasps on attack. She knocked them to the ground, flung the gate open, and fled.

Joe called after her, laughing. "I'm not sorry!"

Truth be told, Anna wasn't either.

Chapter 26

That evening, Anna met with her seamstress to be fitted for the best—no, the only—formal equestrian dinner gown in Los Angeles. She and Edgar had been invited to a dinner on horseback at the Raymond Hotel. Anna straddled a sawhorse brought into her bedroom for that purpose. Its four legs, balanced on towers of concrete block, raised Anna to horse height while her seamstress swathed her in a white satin that shimmered like starlight and would be the perfect contrast against her midnight-black Arabian. When mounted, the fabric spilled and rippled almost to the ground. If Anna should ever try to walk in it, it would drag behind her like a deflated hot air balloon.

Anna held still and amused herself thinking up clever refutations that she should have said to Officer Singer that afternoon in the stables. Anna wasn't good at clever refutations. Plus, Officer Singer was right. Parts of her had wanted to kiss him. He also had a point when he said she didn't know enough about dead people. She wanted to tell him that she had read *A System of Legal Medicine*, but, as she had stolen it from the coroner, Officer Singer might put her in jail. The book had all kinds of information about dead people—stomach contents, blood spatters, and tips for identifying a body after its parts had rotted off. It discussed thumb types and measuring criminal's faces. But Anna needed to learn about mental diseases, too—diseases that might lead a sufferer to suicide or murder.

When the fitting was over, Anna read. She had severed the covers of Theo's medical books and replaced them with covers from other books that she had borrowed from his collection and dismembered. She'd taken three volumes from a series called *Systems of Medicine* and re-covered them as *A History of Egypt*, Drummond's *Spiritual Life*, and *A Guide to Child Rearing*. She pulled them out and snuggled down to read.

The texts were heavy, cumbersome to hold, with lots of jargon that she had to look up in *The Wizard of Oz*—a medical dictionary. She found little of what she sought, but liked their dusty book smell, and they had interesting pictures—pictures of people with hair covering their entire bodies, Siamese twins, and one of a naked person who had breasts and, so the text said, male parts, too. Regrettably, they were far too small for Anna to get a good look.

She flipped through a book called *Nervous and Mental Diseases*, which would surely touch on suicide. Out of curiosity, she went to the section on hysteria. It included nothing new about treatment, but various theories as to the cause.

"Behind every symptom of hysteria and the obsession neurosis is a mass of suppressed sexual desire." So wrote Sigmund Freud. Anna cried out in indignation. In addition to his other crimes, Joe Singer put her at risk of a mental disease. Whether that meant she should avoid him entirely or run into his arms, she wasn't sure—medically speaking. She said a silent prayer to Saint Dymphna, patron saint of the crazy, to save her from the insanity induced by resisting the lips of a delicious police officer.

Anna went to her dresser and picked up *A System of Legal Medicine*. She had read it thrice already and had mastered most of the information, but she still lacked practical experience. She needed a real rotten, fetid corpse to examine. She yawned and rested her cheek, just for a moment, on the open book. Her breathing slowed. She fell asleep. She dreamed of hairy Siamese twins, moldering corpses, and insanity in the arms of Joe Singer.

The next morning, Anna slumped into the station, out of sorts and heavy with disillusionment. The LAPD cops were nothing like the bright, heroic, upstanding detectives in novels. Detective Snow was incompetent, Detective Wolf was profligate, and Officer Singer was a cowardly, crooning Arrow Collar Man who recklessly sent women over the brink.

Still, whenever Officer Singer was in the station, Anna's eyes wandered over to where he was and lingered there. Whenever he returned her gaze, she looked away. She thought of friendly things to say to him, like, "Do you ever go to the beach?" but she never did.

Late that afternoon, Joe sat at his desk tallying traffic accidents. Wolf sauntered over and leaned his elbows on Joe's desk. His pomade smelled overwhelming. "I'm jealous of you, young Joe."

Joe grinned, sat back in his chair, and stretched. "Oh, why's that?"

"Mrs. Holmes is always looking at you, although I can't say I approve of her taste."

Joe's smile melted away. "Wolf, you are full to the eyebrows with horse shit."

Wolf looked over at Anna, who appeared to be doing nothing, staring at the ceiling with a pen between her lips. "She's always flashing those big blue eyes in your direction."

Joe followed Wolf's gaze to Anna. "They're not blue. They're more like . . . ocean gray."

"The ocean's blue."

"Yeah. Sometimes. But her eyes are like the ocean when it's overcast—grey. It still sparkles, you know, from sunbeams."

Wolf flashed his teeth. "Officer Singer, that's tantamount to a confession."

Joe sighed. "Look. She's a matron—a respectable girl. And she's engaged."

Wolf snapped his fingers. "I knew she was lying about the husband overseas."

"I don't have any designs on her." Joe went back to tallying accidents.

"Watch out. I'm taking that as permission." Wolf licked his hand,

and used it to slick back his gleaming, brilliantined hair. He swaggered across to Anna's desk and leaned over her shoulder, so close that his cheek grazed her hair. He wafted citrus, lavender, and rubbing alcohol. "Matron Holmes, do you know how to lubricate a typewriter?"

Anna smiled in confusion at his proximity and replied in the singsong of the unsure. "Hm. I think so."

"Why don't I show you, honeybun? Here, you scoot in close." Anna scooted her chair flush against the desk and Wolf reached his arms around her to fiddle with the carriage. "That's right." He cut his eyes to Joe and grinned. Joe glowered.

Matron Clemens approached with a file for Anna and a wordless reprimand for Wolf. He straightened up like a guilty schoolboy and race-walked back to his desk.

Matron Clemens's voice was as crisp and clean as a new box of envelopes. "There has been a report that a ten-year-old girl is living at the Poodle Dog. Do you know the place?"

"Of course," Anna lied. Mr. Melvin would tell her where it was. Or Joe. She glanced over at him. His face was peppermint red.

Matron Clemens continued. "My best hope is that she's the daughter of one of the girls. Please go down and investigate. If you find her, take her straight to Whittier and enroll her."

Anna nodded. Whittier was a reform school. By reputation, it was more of a training ground for immoral behavior than a haven of reform, but Anna would do whatever Matron Clemens said. Most of the time.

As Anna took the file from Matron Clemens's hand, Snow shuffled by on his way to the door. He held a pair of rubber boots, which were neither the fashion in Los Angeles nor appropriate for the July weather. The last time she had seen him wear rain boots they were covered in blood and feathers. He sat on a bench and slipped the boots over his shoes.

Anna thanked Matron Clemens and sashayed toward the door. She briefly lingered at Mr. Melvin's desk, leaning down as if he had called her over to show her something. "Mr. Melvin, do you have the address of the Poodle Dog?"

Mr. Melvin shrunk away from her, but consulted an address book and began to write directions on a slip of paper. Snow lumbered past them in his rubber boots, trailing the scent of toe jam and whatever horrors he'd stepped in. Mr. Melvin's tiny lip jumped.

Anna whispered, "Did someone report a body?"

He nodded his head and slid her the note.

Anna leaned down and beamed into his face. "Thank you." His little mouth turned up, ever so slightly.

There was a skip in Anna's step. This was her chance to examine a real, rotting, stinking corpse in situ and improve her detecting skills. She stepped outside and paused at the top of the stone steps, scanning the street for Snow. She spotted him waiting to board a trolley. He held his hat in one hand and was vigorously scratching his head. Anna tailed him at a distance. When he boarded a trolley, she climbed on the car's back fender. When Snow pulled the cord at Orchard Street, Anna jumped off.

Snow lumbered down the dusty street eating a red apple. He slipped between two beer mills into an avocado orchard. Anna followed stealthily. The trees were large and heavy with fruit, their branches dipping down to form caves of cool shadow. She heard his dull, gravelly voice and tiptoed toward it, stepping on soft fallen fruit to muffle the crunching of the leaves. She ducked under the canopy of a tree.

There, peering through the branches was Madam Lulu. She wore a dress the color of a tree trunk.

"What are you doing here?" Anna asked.

Madam Lulu whispered, "Didn't you say I needed evidence?"

Anna crept closer. "I'm learning, too. I've been reading about legal medicine . . ."

Madam Lulu bulged her eyes at Anna. "Shut up. You're gonna give me away."

Anna covered her mouth in a pantomime of compliance, and crouched down by the madam. She peeked through the curtain of waxy green and saw part of a death scene, the back of a girl who hung by her neck, her long black hair cascading forward, her head bowed in immeasurable sadness. She wore a diaphanous white peignoir, as glamorous and expensive as any that Anna owned, with a long ruffled train that dragged in the dirt. The sleeves of her lingerie were slightly too long, covering her fingers, giving the impression of a child playing dress-up. Anna's stomach fluttered as she angled for a better view of what appeared to be a smartly dressed, upper-class corpse. "Jupiter."

Madam Lulu wriggled her shoulders. "Stop crowding me."

Snow was hovering near the girl. He took out a knife and began to hack at the rope above her head. The body landed hard. "Boom," Snow said.

Anna smothered a gasp, and Madam Lulu sneered in disgust. The coroner called from the street some fifty yards through the trees. "Snow! Are you going to help me with the stretcher?"

Snow grunted and galumphed off through the orchard, out of sight. It was the opportunity she'd been dreaming of. Anna sprinted to the fallen body, which now lay stiffly on its back, and knelt beside it. She looked at the clouded eyes, the slightly opened mouth, the pale parted lips. The girl had once been beautiful. Now her tongue swelled like a balloon, and a trickle of dried blood ran from her nose to the corner of her mouth. How curious when a living person became a thing. Anna poked it.

In a moment, Madam Lulu squatted beside her. "One of Monique's girls. Ruby something."

Anna's eyes flashed. "She's a prostitute? Are you sure?"

Madam Lulu grunted. "I'm sure."

Lulu's words set Anna's mind racing. Would Anna soon be taking another helpless baby to the Witch? The thought made her angry. She leaned over the woman's dead face and began to speak in a rapid staccato. "Her pupils are dilated. Belladonna drops, maybe."

"Lots of the girls use them," Madam Lulu said.

Anna leaned closer and took a good solid whiff. "She's fresh. That is, she doesn't smell rotten. In fact, she smells rather sweet." Anna's eyes darted up. "Why would she smell sweet?"

Anna heard Snow and the Coroner on the street. She had, at most, a minute to investigate before the men returned with the stretcher. If they caught her, they'd tell Matron Clemens, or, worse yet, Wolf. Then, she'd lose her job.

Beneath the noose still draped around the girl's neck, there was a dark line the color of a plum, its edges bleeding out into red. Anna supposed such a mark might be expected in a hanging. But could Anna prove that she hadn't hung herself? She tried to lift the woman's arm. It resisted, as stiff as a board. "Dead at least three hours. That's when rigor mortis sets in. I read that in a book. She's warm, but so is the air." Anna's voice boiled. "It's so hot. I could better estimate time of death if it wasn't so sweltering hot."

Madam Lulu rolled her eyes. "Who cares?"

In the distance, Snow laughed.

Anna tensed. She quickly examined the girl's hands. The fingers were soft and white, the nails polished, slightly tinted—something girls in Anna's set were not allowed to do. Curiously, she wore a wedding ring. Anna tried to raise the sleeves of the peignoir to examine the arms, but quickly realized that the only way to do so was to unbutton the garment and pull them down. She didn't have time.

She paused for a minute and listened. A scraping sound. The stretcher coming out of the wagon. Anna moved to the girl's legs and quickly lifted her nightdress. She detached the stockings from blue garters exposing two slender gams, and pushed up the girl's silky eyelet drawers. The shins were light pink, but the color of them faded into white the higher Anna looked up the thighs. Her heart beat faster. She rolled the legs to one side. Both the calves and the back of the thighs were uniformly dark, livid, a distinct contrast to the front of the legs. Anna squeaked with epiphany, her heart pounding. "Dual lividity! It's textbook. She's been dead at least ten hours and she didn't die from hanging. Somebody hung her after she was dead. I could prove it in a court of law." Anna looked up, her eyes wide. "Madam Lulu, she *was* murdered! I have no doubt."

The madam gasped in mock surprise. "You're a genius!"

Anna moved on to the feet and vigorously tugged at the girl's slipper. It was tight and resisted. She used a stick to pry it off. Anna recoiled. The foot had been forced, the toes broken. Anna dropped the slipper and a sixpence fell out.

A cold thought flooded Anna's mind, and for a moment, she couldn't move. What if the very small, ill-fitting shoe had belonged to Peaches? And the shoe that had dangled from Peaches' lifeless foot, it belonged to Anna.

Anna's palms began to sweat, her fingers trembling. "Madam Lulu?" she croaked, but Lulu was gone, sprinting for the trees, hell to split, raising her skirts so her plump legs could move faster. Anna heard the coroner's voice and snapped her head around.

"The world's a better place without a whore like her tempting good men," he said.

Snow grunted. "Yeah. Fancy whores tease you, show you their legs, when they know you can't afford them. And when you're all riled up, they laugh at you."

Anna was temporarily stunned by Snow's coarseness and immorality. Madam Lulu called in a loud whisper, "Hustle your frilly britches out of there before you get caught." She disappeared beneath the canopy.

Anna put the coin in the shoe with fumbling fingers and did her best to shove it back on the foot. She pulled down the gown, leaving the garters unhitched, and fled just as Snow and the coroner emerged carrying the stretcher. Snow squinted at her departing figure and growled.

Chapter 27

Anna sped the length of the orchard and cut across a field into the street, fleeing the things she had seen and heard. People stared, and she didn't care. Her lungs burned. She ran until she couldn't, and stumbled to a stop, collapsing against a saloon window, taking quick, gulping breaths. She had to compose herself. The fact that Peaches had worn Anna's shoe must be a coincidence. Anna was, after all, not dead, and she needed to remember it. She inhaled deeply, closed her eyes, and steeled herself. She must think and be calm. Matron Clemens expected her back soon. She was already late to collect the ten-year-old girl. It would be much more difficult to investigate the brothel murders if she lost her job. Anna raced up the street to the address Mr. Melvin had given her for the Poodle Dog, as if the killer himself were pursuing her.

The Poodle Dog was the same ornate stone mansion that she had seen her first day in the brothels. A maid in a ruffled apron hung wet laundry at the side of the building. Anna hurried to the door and knocked. No answer. She knocked again. Nothing. She lingered on the doorstep, unsure of what to do. She tried the doorknob, and the door swung open. Anna poked her head in.

The receiving room was tasteful and smelled of lilac. There was a Persian rug, a fountain that made burbling sounds, a Turkish couch with a canopy, and a feathery palm plant in an urn. Anna could see into the parlor, where a real Egyptian statue stood guard over a staircase that led up to the second floor. To the bedrooms, thought Anna, and wondered what exactly went on there. The place seemed far too elegant for a brothel. It rivaled the finest hotel. She stuck her head inside and called, "Hello?"

Down the stairs came a woman in her forties, her hair in curlers, a burning cigarette in one hand and some knitting in the other. She was striking by any standard, and dripped with an intimidating arrogance. She sauntered forward to block Anna's entrance, and barked in a thick French accent, "What do you want?" She smelled of cigarettes and roses.

Anna cleared her throat and put on her best Matron Clemens imitation. "Good afternoon. I'm a police ma . . ."

"Then go to hell." The striking woman slammed the door in Anna's face.

Anna was not used to such treatment, not even from a French whore. It set her teeth on edge and she pounded on the door. She pounded and pounded, and planned to continue pounding until the insolent woman let her in, or the brothel opened for business.

Anna shouted into the wood. "You have a ten-year-old living here. I have a court order to take her to Whittier. I'll call the police."

The woman opened the door a crack and scoffed. "Whittier? The girl is better off here."

Anna couldn't agree. No matter how awful the reform school was, at least the girls weren't being murdered. She clutched her clipboard firmly. "I would have thought with all the recent deaths . . ."

The woman began to shut the door on Anna, but at that moment a Pekinese squeezed out with its fluffy ears flopping. The woman lunged for the dog, leaving the door to swing open. "Look what you've done! Noireau! Come back." She threw a glance over her shoulder and called to someone in the house, "Lucinda! Keep the matron out!" The madam dropped her cigarette and flew off after the dog, her curlers bouncing.

Anna decided to go in after the little girl herself, Lucinda or no. As she stepped over the threshold, a woman appeared at the top of the stairs and stopped. At first Anna didn't recognize her. She was groomed to perfection, her pale complexion glowing, her hair piled high in a stylish mass of waves and curls. She wore a glorious red chiffon dressing gown that flowed down and around her body like water, and a pair of red, heeled shoes. Thus adorned, one would think that Eve was the renowned beauty and Anna was the commoner in her mannish matron's uniform and plain bun. Mrs. Eve McBride, former police matron, mother of two, prostitute.

The women locked eyes. Eve's eyes had no light. They looked dewy and faintly pink. Eve took a long drag on her cigarette and blew out a smoke ring. She smiled. It was a cold, defiant smile. Anna's mouth quivered between a smile and a frown. She tried to speak but found no words.

Eve's speech was slurred. "What are you looking at?"

"Eve."

"It's Lucinda now." Eve began to descend the stairs. "And look at you. You're an assistant matron."

"You . . ." Anna squeezed her eyes shut. "Look beautiful."

Eve made a scoffing sound. "Sure I do. I've got a maid to style my hair, and Madam Monique buys my clothes. Would you like to see my new mink stole?"

"I . . ."

"I'm living high now. Live music, dancing, wine. It sure beats working at a factory." Eve laughed. "What a fool. Fifteen hours a day, four dollars a week, and the boss still wanted to sleep with me. That's not enough coin to board my twins."

"No . . ."

Eve's eyes glistened. "So don't you look at me that way, Anna Blanc."

"No."

"And don't you dare tell." She took a drag on her cigarette, her fingers shaking. She looked down at the Persian rug and composed her face. When she glanced up again, Anna saw fragility and sorrow. Eve gritted her teeth. "Don't you tell Joe Singer."

Before Anna could reply, Monique slipped in with the dog, yanked Anna by the arm and shoved her outside. She slammed the door. Anna heard the bolt slide across the lock. She stood on the doorstep, fingering her skirt, and breathing. Her legs felt weightless and weak, her belly full of lead. She had done this to Eve. She had.

Anna drifted down the steps and into the street. She wanted to run straight to Officer Singer and have him tell her that it wasn't possible, that Eve didn't work at the Poodle Dog but was safe in Denver, caring for the twins and sending him postcards. Anna wanted to cry and have him console her and forgive her because he was the only one who knew what she had done, the only one who could absolve her.

But that would be a selfish act. Eve had forbidden it. If Anna ever fell to such depths, she certainly wouldn't tell Officer Singer. That's what prostitute names were for—anonymity. Keeping Eve's secret was the least she could do. Also, Joe might shoot Anna with his gun if he ever found out that his friend?—lover?—was now whoring because of Anna.

Anna knocked at Madam Lulu's Christmas-green door, her eyes glassy with uncried tears. Lulu answered before Anna could rap twice. She cocked her head and squinted at the flustered socialite. "What?"

Anna pressed her lips together and swallowed. "I have to talk to you."

Lulu stood aside and Anna entered the brothel. The décor was as lush and vulgar as the woman herself. The room went on and on. Red carpets covered the floor, crystal chandeliers hung from the ceiling. A life-sized oil painting of a woman in a partial state of undress smiled brazenly from the wall. There was a floor for dancing and two concert grand Steinway pianos. They reminded her of Officer Singer. The room winked at her.

Balconies overlooking the grand salon encircled the two upper floors. Doors on the balconies led to bedrooms. Stairs led to balconies. It smelled of cigars.

Madam Lulu motioned for Anna to sit. Anna missed the chair and sat on a side table, half in a milk glass candy dish. It cracked. She jumped up. "You were right. Peaches' and Ruby's deaths were both murders. The other deaths are suspicious. I asked Chief Singer to look into it. He said he would, but he lied." She settled herself properly into a chair.

"Naw!" Madam Lulu looked at the two halves of the candy dish. The marshmallows were flat. She offered one to Anna.

Anna shook her head at the candy. "But I don't know why! Do you know why? Officer Snow and the coroner saw the evidence. They must know it's murder. Are they covering it up? Or are they lazy and they just don't care?"

"That or they're plain stupid."

"Maybe they killed her themselves!" Anna swiped a wrist across her brow. "But Madam Lulu, they're officers of the law! Sworn to protect us. And they aren't protecting those girls."

"Do you want a drink?" Madam Lulu stood and lumbered over to the bar. She poured two glasses of whiskey and waddled back, handing one to Anna.

Anna drained it in one tip and gasped. "I went to the Poodle Dog to pick up a ten-year-old girl and take her to Whittier. The dead girl was from the Poodle Dog, right?"

"That's right."

"The woman there wouldn't let me in."

"Who, Monique? There's a reason her house is called the Poodle Dog." Madam Lulu took Anna's glass. "That'll be fifty cents. You want another?"

Anna frowned and shook her head. She gave Madam Lulu her trolley fare. "I'll give you more later." Her voice was thick. She poked a finger through the center of a marshmallow. "While I was at the Poodle Dog, I saw a friend. I guess she works there now."

Lulu scratched her head. "What's a female friend of yours doing working at the Poodle Dog?"

Anna tried to compose her face. "Maybe I was unaware of her lewd nature, and she gave way to her baser impulses. Or, maybe . . ." Anna snorted, and her voice went high. "It's because I got her fired from her job and she's a widow with children and no family."

Tears came dripping down Anna's cheeks, and she sniffled. Madam Lulu rolled her eyes. "Get a hold of yourself! You'll get boogers on my tablecloth."

Anna snorted again, took out a handkerchief, and wiped her face. She lifted her chin and tossed her head. "I'm sorry."

"So why are you here?" Madam Lulu asked.

Anna took a deep breath. "Do brothel girls put coins in their shoes for any reason? Superstition or tradition?"

"No."

Anna nodded and closed her eyes. She blinked them open. "Do you have any other clues? Any evidence at all? I have a book. It says to notice everything, that the smallest things could be important."

"I don't know nothin' you don't know about already," Madam Lulu said.

Anna stood up and stared absently at the painting of the half-naked woman. "Then tell me about the brothels. How many of them are there?"

Madam Lulu took a cigar out of a box, picked up a cleaver and *smack*, cut the cap on the marble tabletop. She stuck the cigar in her mouth unlit. "You're asking about the whole demimonde in LA? I don't know, a hundred."

"My stars." Anna took out a notebook, leaned forward, and began to scribble.

Madam Lulu chewed on her cigar. "But those ain't all parlor houses like my place. That's counting the dollar girls in the cribs down Alameda Street. The French girls, Japanese girls, the Chinese girls, the Belgian, whatever you like. Some of them places have but one or two girls."

Anna made her pencil scribble faster. "How many girls are working as prostitutes?"

"You should ask Helmut Melvin. If they get vagged, he takes their money."

Anna looked up from her notebook. "Vagged?"

"Arrested for vagrancy. There's no law against prostitution, long as we stay in our little corner. So, on occasion, they vag the girls, fine 'em fifty dollars and let 'em go. It's how the mayor pays for his fancy boat."

Anna thought of the mayor's droopy mustache dotted with pink whipped cream and her stomach turned. "How many parlor houses are there?"

"At any given time? Maybe eight. Four years ago, they closed us down, but most of us opened up again." Madam Lulu waved her cigar hand in the air dismissively. "We get raided from time to time, depending on which way the wind is blowing, but we pop back up." Madam Lulu reached in a table drawer and pulled out a little red booklet. She handed it to Anna. "Here. Have a sporting guide. It's out of date, but it will give you an idea."

"A sporting guide?"

"Sounds better than a whoring guide."

Anna read the cover. "La Fiesta De Los Angeles Souvenir Sporting Guide?" It appeared to be created for tourists celebrating the city's fiesta. She flipped through the pages. It described the different brothels, and praised their charms with vague euphemisms. Had Anna read it out of context, she wouldn't have known what they were talking about. In fact, she still wasn't clear."

"That'll be fifty cents," Madam Lulu said. She finally lit her cigar.

Anna waved away the smoke. "Which parlor houses have lost girls? I want to know about drug overdoses, suicides, accidents, and disappearances, starting in January."

Madam Lulu flipped her eyes to the ceiling. "I've lost two, Monique's lost two, the Octoroon—they lost a girl. Madam Van lost two girls. The Yankee Doodle lost one. That's all I know."

Anna scribbled this down. "Good. Can you tell me about the parlor girls? What their lives are like. What they do. Where they go."

"Go?" Madam Lulu said. "They don't go nowhere, unless they've been arrested or they're leaving town."

"Not to buy groceries?" Anna asked.

"Delivery boys bring us everything we need."

Anna thought about the girls' pale faces. Eve's pale face. "So they never leave?"

"They aren't welcome to share the streets with the proper ladies. But we do go to the races," Madam Lulu said. "That's just in the fall."

"And our murders were in the winter, spring, and summer. If they never go out, our killer has to be a patron," Anna said. "How else would he meet his victims? I need a list of your customers."

"That's privileged information. Ain't no madam gonna give you that."

"Then I have nothing to go on!"

"I'm keepin' my eyes open. I'll let you know what I see. What does your sweetheart say?"

"Edgar doesn't know anything about this."

"No, not your fiancé. Your sweetheart. Joe Singer. The police chief's son."

Anna lifted her chin. "He's not my sweetheart. I don't even like him."

Madam Lulu raised one eyebrow. "You want to solve the crime or not?"

Anna walked all the way back to the station in the heat, arriving exhausted and late, but armed with information. She wasn't sure what Madam Lulu had been implying about Officer Singer, but she thought she'd better give him another try. She had new, irrefutable evidence. Once she showed him, he'd help her, because, in spite of the fact that he had blackmailed her, she felt he would do the right thing. Now that Eve worked at the Poodle Dog, Anna felt even more determined to catch the killer. Eve would not end up with a sixpence in her shoe. Only over Anna's dead body.

Anna decided she would need to get Officer Singer alone, away from prying eyes. Snow might have seen her at the crime scene and knew she'd asked questions about the suicide. Anna herself posed no threat to Snow. No one listened to her. They all thought she was ridiculous. But Officer Singer was the chief's son—a genuine threat. Snow was party to the murders—at the very least derelict in his duty; possibly part of a cover up; or maybe even the killer. If he found out that Officer Singer was investigating with Anna, it would put Snow on his guard and put Joe and Anna in danger. Snow must not see them conspiring.

Chapter 28

Detective Snow stormed into the station. He blew straight to Matron Clemens, who was typing a letter on LAPD stationary. "Where's Matron Holmes?"

Matron Clemens appraised him coolly. "She's taking a child to Whittier."

As Snow stomped off to his desk, Anna strode through the front doors.

"Speak of the devil." Matron Clemens raised her voice. "Matron Holmes, did you take the girl to Whittier?"

"Yes, ma'am," Anna lied. She felt anxious.

"Monique didn't give you trouble?"

"No, ma'am. She was lovely. We . . . had tea."

Matron Clemens raised an eyebrow. "I suppose it's always good to make friends. Mr. Melvin has your paycheck."

Anna smiled with all her might. When Matron Clemens turned back to her work, Anna strode straight for Joe Singer's desk and dropped a note. Without slowing down, or noticing that Snow followed her with his animal eyes, she hurried through the station and out the back door. Joe picked up the note and read it. "Meet me in the stables. Be discreet."

Joe closed his eyes and rubbed his forehead, mentally bracing himself for whatever it was that Anna had in store. He couldn't think of a single good reason to comply, but he slid out of his chair and went after her anyway.

When Joe was out of sight, Snow crossed to his desk, and picked up the note.

The stables were sunlit. Summer heat made the horsey, leathery smells even stronger. Anna selected the only stall without a horse and threw herself down onto the clean straw to wait for Joe Singer, if he came. She couldn't be sure that he would. He hadn't spoken to her since they had last met in the stables and fought. He had done one thing for her. He'd hunted Douglas Doogan down at the Bucket of Blood saloon, and, because Doogan couldn't be held, knocked him silly and put him in a citrus car on a train bound for Cincinnati. Mr. Melvin had told her so. It was a romantic gesture, and Anna did her best *not* to appreciate it. She never thanked him.

Anna stretched. The straw released a cloud of dust that floated in the sunbeams and made her nose tickle dangerously. She quickly placed a finger on her upper lip to prevent a telltale sneeze. She didn't want anyone to find her except Officer Singer. Her mind whirred, sorting the facts, finding the right words to present her evidence.

She stood up and peeked around a saddle hanging over the side of the stall. Next stall over, a black mare stomped and whinnied, glistening with sweat. She heard a squeak and saw Joe swing the stable door open and come inside. He moved down the long center walk, scanning the two-dozen stalls and looking irritated. He stepped on a fresh road apple and said some unrepeatable word, scraping off his shoe.

When he neared her stall, Anna whispered, "Officer Singer, I'm here." Their eyes met over the stall front, and his cool eyes made it clear that he had not forgiven her. Her heart beat faster. Joe opened the gate and sauntered in. He leaned on the boards and folded his arms across his chest. "What?"

Anna smiled at him. Her smile lit up the stables like a little sun. It was broad, warm, and genuine. She had asked and he had come, and she felt glad to see him standing there looking handsome and hostile, unaware that he was about to see things her way. Her warmth must have caught him off guard because he cocked his head and squinted.

Anna's eyes snapped over his shoulder. She was no longer looking at Joe, but past him, down the long center path, to where the stable door was once again swinging open. Snow lumbered inside, looking back and forth, like a snake ready to strike. Anna's smile vanished and goose bumps crawled up her arms.

"Sherlock?" Joe said.

Before he could turn to see what Anna saw, she tackled him. He landed in the straw on his backside and winced, rubbing his ribs where Anna had shot him. She crouched next to him and gave him a warning look, holding a finger to her lips. He shook his head. "You're a weird girl."

She clapped a hand across his mouth, knocking him backward. Joe lay propped on his elbows, watching her like she was a bad melodrama. He obliged her request for silence for the same reason he came to the stables in the first place—one that eluded him at the moment.

Anna held still and listened. She could hear the faint sound of boots on dirt, moving from stall to stall. She now wondered if Joe had been fool enough to leave the note on his desk, and if Snow was specifically looking for them. Anna took her hand from Joe's mouth and crawled on her hands and knees to edge the stall door shut. Her uniform dragged in the clean straw.

At any moment, Snow could check their stall. If he found them in conference, a secret conference, he would think Joe was colluding with Anna. At best, it would complicate their investigation. At worst, if Snow were guilty . . . Hadn't she read it in novels a hundred times? Murderers did away with people who knew about their crime and had the power to reveal it.

If Joe were brutally murdered at the hands of a killer, it would be his own fault for leaving Anna's note on his desk for anyone to read. Even so, she wanted to save him. She looked into his puzzled, Arrow-Collar-Man face and imagined it cold, white, and dead. She had driven Eve to a life of sin. She would not lead Joe Singer like a lamb to the slaughter. She must convince Snow that they were *not* talking.

From her last visit to the stables, Anna knew that they were used for more than just horses. "Make eyes at me," she whispered, and gazed into his eyes adoringly, like they were hat shop windows. Joe gave her a confused, cockeyed look, which would never do.

She lunged for Joe, knocking him flat into the straw, and she kissed him. She kissed him with all the intensity of their situation, and all the passion required to overcome it—their stormy history, his grudge, her guilt, his uncertain life expectancy if he didn't kiss her back, and his possible killer looming in the stables.

Joe pulled away from her, breathless and bedoozled. "You're not going to knee me in the groin again, are you?"

Anna silenced him with a kiss she'd been practicing on her pillow since that night in the park. Joe took the bait. He met her passion and raised it one.

Whether this was good or bad for Anna's mental health, she didn't know, but of all the good deeds she had done in her life, this was her favorite. Snow peeked over the planks just as Joe rolled her in the straw. They were touching head to foot and she was only six blessed layers of fabric away from his bare skin. Snow or no Snow, her nether parts celebrated.

Joe remained oblivious to Snow's presence and desperately kissed his way from her lips down her throat to the inch of her neck that was visible above her high, stiff collar. "I take it back," he whispered. "You'd be very useful in the home."

Anna felt her heart falling, falling, falling. She rubbed her silken ankle against his stockinged ankle, wrapped her arms around his back, and couldn't help but slip her fingers through a gap where his shirttails were not properly tucked in.

"You slay me, Anna," he murmured between kisses. "I mean it."

"I mean it, too." And she did. He was so tasty delicious she could die.

He kissed her mouth again, and she was kissing back with everything she had, pressing herself against him, sliding her fingers across the warm, soft skin of his back, feeling his beating heart, his hands playing along the sides of her dress. Joe was whispering endearments between kisses, and Snow was peering into the stall, and Anna was hoping that

Snow would never go away so she could be justified in spooning Joe Singer forever, or at least until five when her shift was done.

Snow grunted and lumbered off. Joe continued kissing Anna, doing things with his tongue that she had not expected but liked very much. When Snow was good and gone, she waited several minutes for the sake of caution, several more for good measure, and an extra few so she could be extra sure. Then Anna summoned all her virtue and pulled herself out from under Joe.

He raised himself up, all dreamy and dewy-eyed. She was intoxicated, suppressing a desire that would very likely send her into hysterics. But she was Catholic and a professional, and the lives of loose women depended on her. When he reached for her, she evaded him.

"What's wrong?" he asked.

Panting, she leaned up against a hay bale, her hair disarrayed, her person speckled with straw. She spoke between heaving breaths. "Snow was here, but he's gone. He followed you. He's involved in the murders. He knows I suspect him. I didn't want him to see us talking, because I suspect he'd suspect that you suspect him, too. It would put him on his guard. I kissed you so he'd think you were only seducing me."

It took Joe a moment to comprehend the meaning of this statement. His face went scarlet, his nose wrinkled, and his eyes blinked from dreamy to indignant. He fairly shouted. "He couldn't see us *talking*? You knew he was standing there? You threw yourself at me. You spooned me like . . . like a love-crazed nymph because Snow couldn't see us *talking*?"

He modestly began to tuck in his shirt, which was significantly less tucked in than when he walked into the stables twenty minutes ago.

"What was I supposed to do? You weren't discreet!" she said.

"*I* wasn't discreet?" Joe tried to stand up.

Anna pulled him back down and held onto him. "If you'd hold your horses and pay attention, you'd see that I very possibly just saved your life!"

"Oh yeah? How's that?"

"If Snow thought you actually listened to me, which you should, and you realized that the suicides were in fact murders . . . Don't you see? He could frustrate our investigation, or worse yet, kill us both to keep us quiet."

Joe threw back his head and laughed. "You think Snow is going to kill us? Over something you wanted to tell me? Well, don't keep me in suspense, Sherlock. What is it?" He stared at her, waiting, his arms crossed in front of his chest. He looked good angry, all fiery and glinting, and she almost kissed him again.

Instead, she said, "I have evidence that at least two of the dead prostitutes were murdered, and by the same man."

"Go on," he said.

"For one, they both had a sixpence in their shoe."

"Well, maybe it's good luck for brothel girls to keep a sixpence in their shoe."

"It *is* good luck. Not for brothel girls. For brides. They both wore white—one a dress that could have been a wedding gown, the second a peignoir suitable for a wedding night, and she had a gold band. It's like the English rhyme: Something old, something new, something borrowed, something blue, and a sixpence in your shoe."

"Do you have the coins?"

"No. I didn't keep them."

He stood up and brushed off his clothes. "Well, that was an oversight. Sherlock, you gotta give me something plausible, P-L-A . . ."

"I've had enough of your diphthongs!"

She was tangled in her skirts and trying to stand. She reached out a hand for his help, but he ignored it. She raised herself from the ground with all the dignity she could muster, brushing the straw from her skirt. "If you want hard evidence, come with me to the morgue. I'll prove it isn't suicide."

"How?"

"Facts. Snow found the girl hanging by her neck from a tree. But the girl didn't die from hanging. I saw the body. It had dual lividity, which means . . ."

"I know what it means."

"You do?" Anna's heart started thumping again, and she beamed at him. He sighed.

Anna led Joe through the back door of the station and down the hall to the morgue. He followed her for the same reason he had met her in the stables in the first place. She had his heart by the balls.

Anna prattled on at the speed of light, the way she always did when she talked about clues. "She'd been dead on her back for at least ten hours before he hung her. I'd say strangled, from the bruising. Clearly, he'd killed her somewhere else, because why else would he wait so long? Madam Lulu identified the girl as a prostitute working at the Poodle Dog. Her eyes were dilated. She could have used belladonna, or it could be from a drug. She smelled sweet, which perplexed me at first, but chloroform smells sweet and that fits with her enlarged pupils. He could have used the chloroform to subdue her. And her toes . . ."

Joe listened quietly, his brow still creased in a surly frown. When they arrived at the door to the morgue, Anna took a deep breath and took hold of Joe's callused hand. He slipped his fingers out of her grasp. She pursed her lips. This afternoon, she had discovered that she liked Joe Singer intensely, and she didn't want him to be angry at her. She hadn't thought he would mind so much being kissed and kissed and tumbled and kissed if it were for an important cause. *She* had bravely made the sacrifice.

Anna opened the door into a cold room divided by a white curtain. It was an important moment, a chance to convince Joe Singer that girls were being murdered and to get his help with her investigation. Perhaps he would even forgive her for misleading him into declaring his affection for her. To show her appreciation, she would never mention his embarrassing words again.

Anna approached the white curtain and hesitated, bracing herself for the gruesome sight of violent death and savoring her eminent victory. She threw back the curtain. The slab was empty.

Anna gasped. "They must have taken the body somewhere else because they knew I was suspicious."

"You have an inflated sense of self-importance." He turned toward the door.

She scooted around him and blocked it with her body. "Please. All I want is for you to ask your father to have someone different investigate."

"And accuse my fellow officers of what? Incompetence? Dereliction? Murder? I have no evidence—just your word. And from what I've seen, that isn't worth much. How do I even know you're telling the truth?"

The accusation hit Anna like a runaway milk wagon. The man she liked intensely didn't believe in her. It was likely that he never had, and that she deserved it. She was angry nonetheless. Her voice quivered. "Officer Singer, I'm sorry for wasting your time. I don't know why I thought a dirty cop like you would care about justice." She lifted her chin and flounced out the door.

She heard Joe swear and kick the brick wall.

When Joe limped back into the station, Anna was already at her desk, studiously sorting through files S through Z, counting dead or missing prostitutes. Four roundsmen and two patrolmen were loitering around her like a pack of hungry dogs. She maintained her dignity and pretended not to notice, as would any girl of breeding under the circumstances. Neither did she look up when Joe passed by, heading straight for his helmet.

Joe was intent on getting out of the station as soon as possible. Clearly, Snow had told the men what Joe had been doing in the stables with the new assistant matron, and he wanted to avoid the inevitable jibes from the other cops. He was not in the mood to watch them salivate over Anna, either. If she ever so much as winked at one of them, he didn't want to know. He would hate to have to punch a fellow officer.

His getaway attempt failed. Before he reached the front door, he was intercepted by Wolf, who wore a lascivious smile. "Heard you had something delicious for dinner."

"You heard wrong," Joe said.

Anna, who was secretly listening, flushed a deep vermilion. She hoped Joe was defending her virtue and not denying her deliciousness.

"Has Captain Wells heard any rumors about my dinner?" Joe asked. "Or Matron Clemens?"

"Certainly not. If we told Captain Wells about your dinner, she'd be taken off the menu," Wolf said. "And why would anybody do a thing like that?"

"She isn't on the menu," Joe said.

Wolf raised his eyebrows. "Seems to me you said that before."

Joe glared at Wolf. "We didn't have dinner."

"Okay. You didn't have dinner," Wolf said. "If that's your story, you might want to get the straw out of your hair."

Chapter 29

When Anna and the Widow arrived home, Anna was still light-headed from her detective work in the hay with Officer Singer that afternoon. Although she didn't feel hysterical per se, she did feel a little like a love-crazed nymph. She could fancy herself in love, if she hadn't been a girl of experience, if Louis Taylor hadn't taught her not to trust passion. Otherwise, she'd certainly be doing something silly like throwing off Edgar or climbing the steps to the hayloft.

She would have to tell Captain Wells that she could no longer be the girl in the stings to catch the Boyle Heights Rape Fiend if Officer Singer was to be her partner. In the moonlight, in a park made for spooning, with his arm around her, knowing that beneath his shirt and undershirt lay his very skin—she doubted she could concentrate enough to apprehend the villain, even with Wolf hiding in the bushes.

Anna was a woman of reason, and she had reasoned that passion with one man would be the best antidote to passion with another. After kissing Joe Singer, she couldn't give a hoot about Louis Taylor. Spooning her well-made fiancé would surely be the best medicine for her love sickness now. She would lie in wait for Edgar and catch him going in or out of her father's study after the Widow Crisp was already in bed. She would lure him into a lonely corner and encourage him to do things that would leave her breathless and have him begging her pardon. Then she could look into Joe Singer's Arrow-Collar-Man eyes and see the officer and not the lover. She might even helpfully suggest that he find a different lady to spoon with so he would see Anna as an LAPD professional and not a love-crazed nymph.

She would try not to think about Joe Singer at all.

That night Edgar never arrived, thus Anna couldn't lure him into kissing her. It was still hot. The window was open, the air heady with the same jasmine scent that had filled Hollenbeck Park. Anna lay across her satin sheets and put Joe Singer out of her mind. She put his callused hands out of her mind, his body under hers, his body over hers, his legs, his peppermint lips, how nice it would have been if Snow had stayed a little bit longer, if he had stayed a lot longer. She kissed her pillow. She adjusted her drawers. She adjusted her drawers again. She adjusted them and adjusted them and adjusted them, until finally, with a little cry of satisfaction, she was finished adjusting them.

She rolled over and stretched, her skin slipping on the silky fabric. Then she remembered that, unfathomably, Joe Singer was mad at her. Her brows knit together. She had thought that any man would happily kiss any woman under any circumstance, except for Edgar, who was shy if someone was watching. It was in man's feral nature. Weren't they always stealing kisses? Didn't women always have to be on their guard against men?

She hadn't forced him to kiss her. Anna bit her lip. On reflection, it would have required extraordinary tact for him to refuse her without creating a socially awkward situation. She did leap on top of him. Perhaps a gentleman couldn't really refuse. But while Anna had been pressing herself against him, he had volunteered amorous words—that she was petal soft and honey sweet, that he was falling for her like a stone, and what on earth were they going to do. Tender words could be protocol from some secret gentleman's rulebook, but at the time she had thought that he liked her. She bit her thumb. How mortifying if he were just being polite.

Anna fell asleep dreaming of arms and hips, and swathed knees rubbing swathed knees, and real sweet nothings on willing lips in the hay with Joe Singer.

Early the next morning, Anna's eyes flew open. She knew for certain that Snow was not the killer. How unfortunate that this revelation came now. She would have to tell Officer Singer, which might be awkward under the circumstances. But if he was to help her solve the crimes and save Eve, he would have to know everything. And that was the most important thing—solving the crimes.

Her bedroom curtains glowed orange in the dawn. She pulled them back to let in the cool morning air. Sitting in the driveway, alone in the tangerine sunrise, was her baby grand piano.

Anna gulped down her kippers. She drove eleven miles per hour to the orchard she used for changing, and dressed so quickly that she didn't notice she had put her skirt on backward. She must go to Officer Singer and apologize, perhaps even grovel, for making him kiss her in the hay and anything else he wanted her to regret. The piano declared his intentions. She knew he adored it, the way he had cradled it like an infant, the way he had played it. He must be rabid to have given it back.

She shuddered. They were no longer on equal footing. He had no obligation to keep her secrets. If he wanted to, he could squeal, tell Edgar and her father everything, and she would be yanked home and locked in a tower like Rapunzel, only without long hair, so she couldn't climb out and do police work.

Couldn't Officer Singer see that she was an asset to the department—that by turning her in, the LAPD would lose someone valuable? She was brave. He had said so. The murders were real, and she was the only one who would bring the killer to justice. Convincing him of this fact was, perhaps, her best defense. Her only defense. And she would have to do it now, before it was too late.

When she arrived at the station, Anna raced to find Ruby's file and extracted the newly typed report. As she'd expected, Mr. Melvin had typed it yesterday, letter for letter—a few illegible sentences, with the coroner's pronouncement of suicide by hanging. Anna plucked a fistful of Snow's reports from the files and looked for Joe. She found him alone in the back room pouring his morning coffee. "May I speak with you, Officer Singer?" She gave him a desperate, candy apple smile.

He didn't return it. "I'm sorry, Matron Holmes. Wolf's got the hay loft for the morning."

Anna's smile turned upside down. "You could have kept the piano."

He set his cup on the table and squinted at her. "What do you think I am?"

"Please. Take the piano back!"

He made a bitter, scoffing sound. "Are you afraid of me?"

"Should I be?" She bit her lower lip and searched his face for a clue.

His expression was cool. "*You* shot *me*, remember?"

He turned to go, but Anna grabbed his arm. "Wait. I have to tell you something." She gazed up into his large, angry, Arrow-Collar-Man eyes with an expression almost like contrition. "I'm so sorry. For everything. Really I am. You're not a dirty cop. You're . . . perfect." She smiled weakly. "And you were right. Snow didn't do it."

He peeled her fingers off his arm. "That's big of you to admit you're wrong, Sherlock."

"I'm not wrong! He's still derelict, incompetent, or a conspirator, but he didn't write the note. Look." She held the crumpled suicide note in front of his face. "The killer spelled the word 'was' correctly. But in all his reports . . ." Anna put the wad of typed papers into Joe's hand. "Snow spells 'was' W-U-Z, like you would expect from someone sounding it out. You see? Snow genuinely can't spell. The killer can." Anna struck the paper. "Snow couldn't have written 'was' correctly in the letter, much less 'low.' And I'm very smart to have figured it out."

Joe chuckled coldly and shuffled through the reports. He gave them back to Anna with a bitter smile. "What a shame. All that smooching for nothing."

Anna made a noise of objection. "Well, you're being a baby about it!" She gasped and conked herself in the forehead with the heel of her hand. Could she dig her hole any deeper?

Joe narrowed his eyes. "You're calling me a baby?"

She brushed away a tear of frustration. "I'm sorry kissing me was so awful for you, Officer Singer, but I'm the one at risk of a mental disease!"

Joe's head tilted. His eyebrows went up and drew together in confusion.

Anna stood tall and set her jaw. "No one on the force listens to me—not the men, not the captain, not your father. Well, I'm going to the coroner's lecture, and I'm going to confront him with the evidence, publically, where there are medical students and other doctors to witness it. They'll understand what I'm talking about, and they'll act. I don't care what the men think of me. I'm not going to stop until I find out who's killing these girls!"

Joe studied her desperate face. "All right, Sherlock." He turned and left the room, leaving his coffee cup.

"All right? That's all you have to say?" Anna stifled a sob. He was done with her. He was going to rat her out. She picked up his coffee cup and followed after him, in a last ditch effort to convince him that he shouldn't destroy her, that she was worth something.

LAPD officers, victims, and suspects cluttered the station floor. Joe stood near the coat rack. She held his coffee out to him and whispered, "Officer Singer. Please. I'm . . . I'm a good detective."

Joe ignored the cup and took his helmet off the hook. "Sherlock, I know." He swung out of the station and down the steps, and stayed gone for the rest of the day.

Chapter 30

It was Sunday. Anna had planned a morning walk with Edgar on the empty sea cliffs after mass. She chose the spot because there were no people, and plenty of cypress trees to hide behind, just in case. She had plied the Widow Crisp with a goodly amount of Theo's liquor the night before, and had presented her with a bottle at breakfast. Combined with the communion wine, if Anna were lucky it would be enough to knock the Widow out. Anna would cover her with eucalyptus leaves and lead Edgar off to a soft, private piece of earth where they could spoon.

But Edgar had called and said he had to work. All that Anna had to look forward to was a portrait sitting later in the day. She didn't mind having her portrait painted, and Clara was coming to help her dress, as Anna's personal assistant was ill, but posing was nowhere near as nice as spooning. It was a chance to immortalize her beauty in a Frederick Worth original gown that she had augmented with a cluster of artificial birds. Even Anna Blanc wouldn't live forever. Her body would slowly change from spring blossom to withered rose to a rotting and worm-eaten corpse. Anna tried to picture the latter state and decided that the best she could do to ameliorate the situation was to be buried in something from Vionnet at the House of Doucet.

The wedding date had been set for the following June. Edgar wanted to marry sooner, but Anna had begged to put off the date, ostensibly so she could order her gown from Paris. In truth, she wanted more time to solve the murders and perhaps even capture the Boyle Heights Rape Fiend. This forestalling was nonsensical. It frustrated her main goal in life—to marry and get out of the house posthaste. Any number of things could happen between August and June to spoil her plans—most notably that Edgar would find out she was working at the station. But she couldn't quit police work now. Not when she was so close.

Anna decided to reread *Wuthering Heights* to find out how Cathy so completely bewitched Heathcliff that he forgave her the rather large faux pas of marrying another man and, subsequently, dying. If Anna could foster such a love in Edgar, it would surely survive one minor deception, a few necessary kisses, and a job at the police station. Anna thought again about luring Edgar into a dark and lonely place and securing a love that transcended death, but she wasn't sure it would be enough. Edgar was no fool. She would have to practice.

When Clara arrived to help Anna prepare for her portrait, Anna's heart gave a little leap. She'd been neglecting Clara since she had been hired at the station, and she hadn't realized just how much she missed her. She led Clara by the hand into her bedroom and they sat on the canopy bed.

Clara smiled. "Dearest, you've been a complete stranger since the day of your engagement. What's Edgar doing with you?" She giggled like she had said something naughty.

"Nothing," Anna said, guiltily. Clara squinted at Anna, her mouth still smiling, but Anna knew there was something serious beneath the giggles. She just didn't know what. She hoped Clara's feelings weren't hurt. Anna needed to come up with some better excuses for her absences, not just the Orphans' Asylum and romantic outings that never happened. Perhaps she could feign appendicitis.

Clara pressed her lips together. "I have bad news. Auntie is dying. I have to go to Summerland tomorrow."

Anna put a palm to her chest and gasped. What a stroke of luck. She hoped the aunt would be dying all month. Then she felt guilty thinking this and tried to be sad. She was acquainted with the lady, a medium of some renown, and had visited her with Clara at the spiritualist colony in Summerland. The aunt was unfashionably old, and she annoyed Anna by delivering unsolicited messages from Anna's own dead mother, all of which started with "never" or "don't." Her beach house brimmed with restless spirits that made Clara squeak with fright.

Anna found ghosts deliciously creepy, and under ordinary circumstances she would have gone to protect Clara and fend them off, but she had to be at the station.

Anna bit her lip and searched for a comforting word. "Um . . . I suppose she'll be in touch."

Clara brightened. "I hadn't considered that."

Anna swept over to a full-length mirror. Clara, smiling again, helped her slip into the scratchy gown and began to fasten the buttons in the back. Anna sucked in her stomach, but the buttons still strained at the waist.

Clara tugged. "Hmm." The lilt in her voice contained a warning. "It's going to rip if I do them up."

Anna looked at Clara with wide eyes. "Jupiter."

Clara let go of the buttons and ran her hands through Anna's hair. She lifted a Tournure frame from the toilet table, set it carefully on Anna's head, and began twisting her hair around it. "You could wear a tighter corset, but you'd have to carry smelling salts. Can Edgar put his hands around your waist?"

Anna's hands wandered to the smallest part of her midsection. "I don't know. He's never tried. Officer Singer almost did . . ." Anna stopped and put her fist to her mouth. She hadn't meant to tell Clara about Officer Singer.

Clara fumbled the Tournure frame. It fell, yanking Anna's hair, and dangled, trapped in a tangled lock.

Maybe Anna's slip had been a good thing. Her posture was beginning to suffer from the weight of all her burdens—the untyped files, the murders, the shoe, the Boyle Heights Rape Fiend, Eve's fall, and especially Officer Singer, his knowledge of her dark secret, and the risk he posed to her sanity. Maybe it was time to heave the oppressive weight off her shoulders and onto Clara's.

Anna looked at Clara in the mirror. "I have something to confide."

Clara winced. "Oh Anna, I hope it's not a big sin."

Anna's words tiptoed from her mouth. "It's not a sin, exactly. It's more of an indiscretion. I'm working at the police station."

Clara's lips parted, but nothing came out, so Anna kept going. "I gave the Widow Crisp my ruby necklace and an emerald ring in exchange for time on my own. I've been working several weeks now as a police matron under the name of Anna Holmes."

Clara let loose a shrill giggle that hung awkwardly in the air. She busied her hands, mechanically pulling the frame free and liberating a wad of hair while Anna gritted her teeth. Clara rolled the wad between her fingers and pitched it into the wastebasket. She cleared her throat. "Who is Officer Singer?"

"He's the police chief's son. You must have seen him at the ball." Anna raised her eyebrows. "He looks like the Arrow Collar Man."

"Sweetness, I met him and he didn't look at all like the Arrow Collar Man. I wouldn't even call him handsome."

Anna wrinkled her brow. "You can't have seen him up close."

Clara's eyebrow darted up. "Obviously you have."

"As a matter of fact, he's helping me catch a rape fiend. Or, I'm helping him. We do secret operations at night, posing as lovers in the park. Not alone, of course. A different officer waits in the bushes ready to spring and, when the rapist attacks, the three of us are poised to capture him. But more importantly, I'm also hunting a murderer."

Clara spoke each word carefully, as if she couldn't believe their meaning. "He put his hands around your waist?"

"Well, one time. He was kissing me, which is more than Edgar ever does. But don't worry, I was properly outraged." She pinched her lip between her teeth. "Although I did kiss him once because a suspect was watching us. He only kissed me back to be polite. And it doesn't count. You'll see when I explain it. It was a life or death situation. At least I thought so at the time." Anna smiled, dreamy-eyed. "He said I'm a good detective."

Clara remained silent so long that Anna began to fidget. She watched Clara's tight smile in the mirror. Finally Clara spoke. "Someone saw you kissing Officer Singer?"

"No. Someone saw *Matron Holmes* kissing Officer Singer. It's different. No one knows it was me." Anna frowned. "I'm more concerned that Officer Singer will tell. He's angry with me about the kiss. But maybe he won't. I'm very important to the force." She sighed. "You really should see him up close. He has luscious peepers."

Clara's closed her eyes and shook her head. "If Edgar found out about any of this, you would lose him."

"Not if he loves me the way Heathcliff loved Cathy."

"I don't think you really want to marry Edgar."

Anna's voice rose. "I do. But there's a rape fiend on the loose. And a murderer! What would you do?"

"I'd quit my job and stop kissing the police chief's son! You're spoiling your reputation!"

"It isn't my reputation I'm spoiling! It's Matron Holmes's reputation!"

Clara took a deep breath. "Sweetness, you've completely lost your bearing." Her sunny, perennial smile had disappeared behind a cloud. "If you don't . . . control yourself, I don't know what I'll do."

Anna spun around to face her. "What do you mean you don't know what you'll do?"

"You can't just go traipsing around at night, kissing police officers, no matter how good you think your reasons are. You have to stop."

"That's easy for you to say, because you wouldn't want to do those things. But I do! And if I don't catch the killer, no one else will. Innocent harlots are going to die!"

"Rape fiends? Murderers? Harlots? You know what I think, Anna? I think your father was right to take away your allowance and shackle you to a chaperone. In fact, I think he should have hired more of them, because one is clearly not enough!"

Anna narrowed her eyes. "Take that back!"

"No. You're ruining yourself, dragging your precious innocence through the muck. And you'll take me down with you." Clara leaned against the wall. She looked faint. Tears brimmed in her eyes. "You and I have been connected our whole lives. Whatever you do reflects on me. Did you think about that?" Clara fingered the ties on her bolero gown, and her voice went low. "I don't know if I can see you anymore.

Not unless you stop this scandalous behavior. You need to quit playing police officer and police . . . lover, or I'll have to make a clean and very public break."

Tears glistened on Clara's cheeks. Anna stared at her. "You can't mean that. If you loved me enough, it wouldn't matter. And you love me enough. I know you do."

"Dearest, I love you. But I can't be party to your wild behavior. Edgar Wright is the best thing that ever happened to you. He's decent and kind and you are playing him for a fool!"

Anna's mouth quivered. "I'm not! And I resent your saying so."

"Goodbye, Anna." Clara sniffed. "Call on me when you come to your senses, unless you've destroyed yourself by then."

With that, Clara let the Tournure frame tumble to the ground and hurried to the door. Anna could hear her sobs echo as she walked down the stairs and through the marble hall.

Half an hour later, Anna sat in her gown trimmed with artificial birds, unbuttoned in the middle so that it didn't rip. The corners of her mouth tipped down. Her hair was bunched up in a common bun—the best the parlor maid could manage. She held very still as the portrait artist arranged her. He was French, with intense eyes and wore blousy paint-speckled sleeves. He silently swirled the skirts of her gown into luminous drapes and folds, touching the birds, moving their wire and feathered wings this way or that. He picked up her feet and placed them so the tips of her satin slippers peeked from under the hem. Her posed hand dropped to her side. She was feeling very alone and didn't give a hoot whether her hands were gracefully gesturing in the air or showing the world her middle finger.

He made a disgruntled sound and moved her hand back into position. He stood apart to look at her. "I can't paint a scowling bride. Relax your face."

Two lines cut between Anna's brows. "I can't; I'm unhappy."

Even as her world was expanding, it was shriveling up. Life just wasn't worth living without Clara. But she loved her work at the station and she had to stop the killer or she'd spend eternity in purgatory. The crease on her forehead deepened. She resembled her father.

The painter slapped his hands back and forth in a washing gesture. "Fine. Take back your money. I won't paint a scowling bride. It's an affront to love."

Anna knew he didn't mean it. He'd had a tantrum when he'd painted her portrait for her debut. His lip jutted out and he pouted with his eyes. They were large, blue, and long lashed, under tame dark eyebrows. They sparked a revelation and she blinked. She lowered herself down onto a velvet pouf. "If I described a man to you, could you paint him?"

He raised his groomed eyebrows. "Does Mademoiselle have a lover? That would explain your tragic face."

He seemed sympathetic to the idea, so she nodded. "I don't want to forget him. He's my . . . love . . ." She looked down at the artificial birds. "Budgie. Oh, my heart!" She melted into to a cascade of artificial tears.

Anna had hit her mark. He moved to her side and placed a large paint-stained hand on her heaving shoulder. "Oh Mademoiselle, to paint you smiling would be an affront to love."

She looked up with a long face and hound dog eyes. "Will you paint him, then? I'd be happy."

The artist's face pouted in sympathy, but he had not consented. She wept harder, but his face remained tense and tentative. Then she remembered what the Widow Crisp had taught her about how bread was buttered. "We could do my portrait another day, when my eyes aren't puffy, and you could get two commissions."

It was a bold-faced lie. She had no money to pay him. But by the time he found that out, it would be too late. His face relaxed and he caressed her cheek. "Of course I will paint him, if you will smile."

Chapter 31

When Anna arrived at the station on Monday, she had a portrait of the Boyle Heights Rape Fiend tucked under her arm, wrapped in brown paper, the paint still wet. She thought it a fair likeness. His large blue eyes and thick black lashes alone were strong identifiers. Add to that his dandyish clothes and white-blond hair. Her heart thumped with excitement. She knew she was onto something. Now it remained to convince the rest of the force, who by and large thought she was an idiot.

Joe was standing at the counter with Mr. Melvin when Anna entered. The men spun quarters on the countertop in some sort of game. Mr. Melvin was concentrating, and Joe was laughing. As she brushed past them, she felt Joe's eyes heavy on her back. When she turned to face him, he was engrossed in the game, not looking at all. She had only wished he'd been looking.

She set the painting down and picked at the knot holding the twine. Her fingernail bent backwards. "Cock!" Shaking one hand, she removed the brown paper and crumpled it into a ball.

The men began to swim over like sharks when there was blood in the water—Wolf, Snow, and a handful of patrolmen. They were far more interested in Anna now that she had been labeled a tart. Normally, this would be undesirable for a girl. At the moment, it was working in her favor.

Hummingbirds fluttered in her stomach. She stood and smoothed her skirts. Wolf smiled. "What do you know? Matron Holmes is decorating."

Anna lifted her chin ever so slightly. "It's a portrait of the Boyle

Heights Rape Fiend, as I remember him. I had it commissioned. I described the villain and the artist painted him. It's quite a good likeness."

A smirk spread among the men. She leaned the portrait up against the wall and stood back so they could see it. Wolf put his hand on Anna's shoulder. "Well, that will make a lovely gift. I'm sure he'll appreciate it." The men tittered.

Joe drifted up to see the painting. He ignored Anna but considered the portrait with interest. Wolf stepped beside him and crossed his arms. Anna's heart bounced to her throat. She watched Joe stroke his dimpled chin. He was smart. Surely he could see the brilliance of this. Or maybe he would support her for her own sake. She didn't know why she thought he might. He never had before. She felt a pang in her heart and tossed her head, remembering how he had insulted her in the stables, how he was holding her secrets over her head, putting the squeeze on her.

Snow scratched his flaky scalp. "Is that what he looks like, Joe?"

"I don't know. I only saw the back of him as I was falling on my . . ." Joe glanced at Anna and censored his language, ". . . posterior."

The men laughed again.

Anna tried to catch Joe's eye, but he looked away. She stood as straight as a soldier. "Based on his knowledge of women's fashion, I believe he's a milliner, cobbler, or dress maker. You can use this painting to canvass the shops. Show it both to customers and shop keepers. One of them will have seen him. He's handsome and very well dressed. Someone a woman would notice."

"Someone you might like to interview in the stables?" Wolf asked.

The men sniggered and a patrolman made a loud, "Hah!"

She held her head high and hoped no one noticed that her hand trembled. "You can laugh, but you're not making any progress on the case. I'll canvass the shops myself. I feel I must to do something!"

"Well, Matron Holmes," Wolf said. "You're busy with the coroner's lecture tonight, but you could go on the sting with me tomorrow night." He winked at her.

Anna pressed her lips together. "Fine. I'd like a chaperone." The men howled, all except Mr. Melvin and Joe, who was blinking at Wolf, his mouth slightly open.

Joe strode over to Captain Wells. "Let me do it. Wolf shouldn't do it."

"But Officer Singer, you don't seem able to hang onto your gun," Captain Wells said.

At that moment, Matron Clemens strode through the door. Her eyes swept the officers, who were clustered around Anna like flies on a carcass. She scattered them with one frigid glance.

When Anna arrived home, she told Mrs. Morales she didn't feel well. She went straight to her room, locked the door, and changed back into her matron's clothes. A uniform would lend her credibility. She snatched up a hat and veil and climbed out the window. If Joe Singer was not speaking to her, he surely wouldn't escort her to the coroner's lecture tonight. Without his company, it would be a long and treacherous journey. She didn't have time for dinner or anything else.

Anna began walking at five-thirty, taking Grande Avenue south. Some of the neighborhoods were poor, some inhabited by people who didn't speak English. There, the houses looked owner-built, small and precarious, surrounded by corn and tomato plants. Goats chewed on weeds in dirt yards, and there were chickens, rabbit hutches, scum ponds, and garbage smells. Nice girls were not supposed to wander about unaccompanied at night, and men shamelessly stared at her as she walked along. At least these neighborhoods didn't have rape fiends. Still, she wished Officer Singer was holding her arm and that he wasn't mad at her.

Anna shared the road with a group of grubby children trudging home from the Corum Paper Box factory. They were skinny and seemed too tired to be naughty. Anna had read in the paper that the factory work was dangerous, and that the children employed there worked six days a week for only two dollars. Even a plain mother could earn twice that working one evening in the cribs. While Anna didn't know what sinful acts Eve was doing with vile men, she knew why she was doing it.

Anna turned right on Pico, headed south again on Figueroa, and walked another forty-five minutes through a checkerboard of neighborhoods—middle class, working class, black, white. On each block, eyes followed her—the woman stranger walking alone.

To her relief, she arrived at USC safely and right on the hour. A stone held the door open, and she quickly found the operating theater. It was impressive, perfectly circular, with tall oak doors and a high domed ceiling that made her feel small. It smelled faintly like an overflowing cesspool. Two hundred men in suits populated the steep rows of seats surrounding the stage—medical students with notebooks and older men who must have been doctors. There were no women and, by the way the students stared at her, she didn't think ladies were welcome. Anna scanned the theater for her personal physician to make sure she wouldn't be recognized, but she didn't see anyone she knew. Most medical men weren't rich enough to run in her circle and, apparently, the men of Central Station didn't take pride in their work. Still, she left her veil on.

In the center of the stage, a halo of globed lights shone down upon a naked body stretched across a steel gurney with a square cloth draped over its secret man parts. The thing was bloated, bruised in places, and greenish in color, but for the scarlet lividity along the buttocks, back, and the backside of the legs. Anna's heart thumped with excitement. The coroner was poking at it with a thin, metal stick, demonstrating something to a student. She descended the steps so she could better see and decided she would wait to confront the coroner until after the lecture so she could learn something more about dead people.

She approached a bench in the second row and gingerly edged past several men to reach an empty seat directly in front of the corpse. The men stood to accommodate her. The seat was hard and warm from someone else's bottom. The air smelled like men, starched shirts, and death. Next to her sat a person about her age. He had bad skin and sported a jacket with worn cuffs. He buried his nose in an anatomy book—a medical student.

According to Theo, medical students each had a dead body of their very own. They named them and got to pull them apart and pickle their pieces and hang their skeletons on hooks in their offices. Anna felt jealous.

The coroner began his lecture, "This body was found in a house after neighbors noticed a smell. The man was last seen alive six days ago. Was it a natural death or foul play?" He flitted around the corpse's leg with his pointer as he spoke. "The petechiae of the early stages of decomposition is often mistaken for marks left by contusion . . ."

Anna wrinkled her brow. She was adrift in sea of medical men who had more books, more schooling, and more experience than she did. If a coroner—not even a student but an expert in dead bodies—could mistake decomposition for the marks of violence, what hope did she have of distinguishing between a murder and suicide? No wonder everyone ignored her, including Joe Singer.

Anna did have superior intelligence, proficiency in Latin, and the Holy Saints were on her side. She paid minute attention and found that, informed by her previous readings, she understood a good bit of the talk. And even if she wasn't a coroner, she knew that sixpence didn't grow in shoes, and that diphthongs aren't spelled phonetically.

At the end of the lecture, the coroner invited questions. Anna fiddled with her pen and remained silent, vacillating. She peered around the room, and no one raised their hand. The coroner tapped his pointer on the slab, making a clicking sound that echoed in the theater. Papers started to rustle as the students began to pack up their satchels. If Anna were to confront the coroner, she would have to do it now, before her educated witnesses got up and went home. Anna leapt to her feet and raised her hand. The coroner squinted at her and pointed with his silver stick. "Yes, young man."

Evidently, he was nearsighted. The crowd tittered. Anna cleared her throat, squared her shoulders, and lowered her voice to increase her credibility. It cracked like the voice of a teenage boy. "Recently, I examined a corpse. The pupils were dilated and the face smelled sweet. Would you suspect chloroform?"

"A distinct possibility, son. Tell me more." More tittering.

"The legs were a light purple in front, darkest near the toes, growing lighter as one moved up the body. The backside of the body was a dark purple. This coloration suggests dual lividity, that the body had been moved?"

"Good!" The coroner smiled encouragingly. "Go on."

"The body had been found hanging in a tree. I deduced that the person had been drugged with chloroform, murdered, and then hanged to hide the crime."

The doctor's eyes had narrowed, his eyebrows coming together in an angry knot. Anna forged on. "You, Doctor, deemed the death a suicide. I wondered if you could explain how a dead girl could hang herself. I'm sure you remember the case."

The rustling stopped and the room stilled. All two hundred men craned their necks to fix their eyes on Anna. She squirmed, boxed in by male thighs, backs, and knees. The coroner strode to the side of the stage, squinting at Anna. He burst the silence with a hearty cackle. "Oh, it's you Assistant Matron Holmes! I recognize your squeaky voice. To question my conclusions in this forum is unladylike. As I have heard that you are . . ." He cleared his throat. "*Not* a lady, it's unsurprising. The real question is why the LAPD has not yet fired a woman who commits immoral acts in the police stables. And since those acts are committed during your regular work hours, you are technically being paid for them. It's no wonder you are particularly concerned about the fates of prostitutes."

The auditorium was stunned into silence.

Under the veil, Anna's face flushed the color of her bartered ruby necklace, but inside, she was blank and white. Never mind her abject, public humiliation. She was getting used to that. But if the coroner knew about her tryst with Joe Singer, and he told Captain Wells, she would be fired. Shaking with dread, she lowered herself back onto the bench, sitting on the hand of the student next to her. Anna shot to her feet. He leered.

The coroner pointed to the hall. "Don't sit down, Matron Holmes. The door is that way."

Whispering began as Anna quickly squeezed past the row of medical students and doctors, too flustered to beg their pardon. The coroner took up his lecture. "The question raised by the woman is actually a helpful illustration of how the petechiae of the early stages of decomposition can be mistaken for other phenomena, such as dual lividity, by ignorant individuals acting beyond their capacity. In this case, the sweet smell on the prostitute's face came from perfume . . ."

He made this pronouncement just as Anna approached the door. The audacious lie roused her from her stupor. She spun around and called in a loud voice, "Are you suggesting that she decomposed on one side only? While hanging in a tree? That's ridiculous! Not to mention she was in the very peak of rigor! You saw her. She had no time to decompose!"

The coroner scanned the room, looking through Anna as if she were invisible. "Now, does anyone have a question?"

It was a cock shame being a woman. Being right and having the facts meant nothing if one wore frocks, even if they were very nice frocks, which her matron's uniform was not. Joe Singer wouldn't be fired for immoral behavior in the hay. He'd probably be given a medal. She marched down the hall, her petticoats flapping, her hands balled into white-knuckled fists. She wanted to smack the coroner in the head with her giant purse. She wanted to conk Joe Singer, too, because he wasn't by her side, fighting this battle. He wouldn't help her.

She had humiliated herself and would certainly lose her job, all for nothing. Then who would avenge the brothel girls and stop the killings? Not a man at the lecture believed that the coroner had covered up a murder.

She traced her way home through the dark streets, sticking to the shadows. No one spoke to her or even whistled. A terrible, angry cloud surrounded her like a shield, frightening any would-be bandits away. She walked north, jogged left, and journeyed north again, arriving at home with sore feet just shy of eleven.

Chapter 32

The next morning, Anna went straight to Wolf's desk. "Is the coroner going to tell Captain Wells that Officer Singer rolled me in the hay?" She searched his face with desperate eyes.

Wolf sat back in his chair and smiled. "Good morning, honeybun. No, I don't think the coroner's going to tell Captain Wells that Officer Singer rolled you in the hay."

"Why not? He knows. He hates me. He'd like to see me fired. He said as much."

"Because he thinks the captain's rolling you, too." Wolf cleared his throat. "It was the patrolmen's idea. They're just trying to help."

Anna heaved a sigh of relief. "Thank them for me."

"They're uh . . . hoping you'll thank them personally."

At that moment, Joe breezed through the door. When he saw Anna, he stomped over, scowling, and flung his hands in the air. "I waited for you at Angel's Flight for two hours. You and I had an appointment!"

Anna bit her knuckle and winced. "I never imagined you'd keep it. You were so angry."

Joe folded his arms. "I do what I say I'm gonna do. I don't know if you've heard of that."

"I'm sorry!" Anna threw down her hands. "I'm sorry! I'm sorry! I'm sorry! What can I do to show you that I'm sorry?"

"Matron Holmes," Wolf said. "I think Officer Singer understands that you're sorry. And I'm sure that he's sorry, too. But . . ."

Joe swore under his breath and stomped off. Wolf grinned. "But Matron Clemens is out with the grippe. And so right now you need to attend to Matron Clemens's prisoner. So why don't you go over to the jail and check on her. Make sure she's being treated well. And give her my best."

He pressed a file into Anna's hands.

The clouds hanging over Anna parted just a bit, admitting a tiny ray of sunlight. It felt like the only light she had seen in days. "I have a prisoner?"

"That's right, honeybun."

"Slick!"

The city jail was two blocks from the station, a monstrosity in hard, cold stone. In one section of the building, the city housed her convicted criminals. In another section, it kept prisoners waiting to be tried, drunks, rabble-rousers, and the like. As Anna walked from the sunshine into the prison lobby, she had a sobering thought. She would have ended up there had she smoked that fateful cigarette within the city limits of Los Angeles. Or maybe it would have been Officer Singer who had asked them to put out their lights. Eve would still be a matron instead of a prostitute. Anna would never have been a matron at all. She would never have kissed Officer Singer. She would already be married to Edgar and sleeping in his bed. She was glad that she hadn't been arrested in Los Angeles, and it made her feel guilty.

The jailer received Anna, peering out from under droopy eyelids. She consulted her file and cleared her throat. "Good morning. I'm LAPD matron Anna Holmes. I'm here to attend to prisoner Eunice Partridge and to check on her well-being."

"All right." The jailer dragged himself from his stool to an interior door. When he looked down at the jingling keys on his belt, his droopy lids all but closed. He turned a key in the lock and stood aside to let Anna through. "You'll know her. She's the only prisoner in a skirt." With that, he closed and locked the door behind her.

Anna stood alone at the end of a dim, airless corridor. It smelled foul, like the hot breath of men who had never owned a toothbrush.

The chamber pots needed to be emptied. Somewhere, someone was smoking, which made the air even thicker. There was little ventilation and no breeze through the barred windows.

A thrill shot through Anna. She let herself pause to savor the moment. She was doing the work of officers, albeit for a female criminal. She could hear motion in the cells, shifting, an occasional cough. Someone was moaning or praying. She ventured forward to where the cells began, lining the corridor on the right and on the left.

The first few were empty. Behind each set of bars languished a dingy wooden bunk and a commode. She crept forward, each footstep echoing. The rest of the cells were full of criminals. When the first man noticed her, he let out a long, low whistle that set off a chain reaction. Prisoners came to the bars, unbathed and unmannered. She greeted them with a nervous, "Good morning. I am a police matron. Ah. Hello."

Some simply stared. Others rattled the bars or reached for her. A boy too young to shave but with a very adult, very fresh look on his face patted his lap. "Over here kitten, I need some company." She veered away from him and continued down between the rows of whistling men like the queen of the Fiesta De Los Angeles parade. As she approached the end of the corridor, she smelled roses.

In the very last cell, she found her prisoner. The woman reclined on a cot, smoking a Hoffman House cigar—the source of the offending smoke. Anna should have known by the rose perfume. It wasn't just any prisoner. It was Madam Lulu. Anna stared. "Eunice Partridge?"

She sported a crimson dress with enough fabric on her flounces to clothe all the children in the Orphans' Asylum. None of it covered her cleavage. Her cheeks were painted red, her eyebrows chalked black. She wore her fox stole and the big black hat with the little pastel birds.

She raised her arms above her head and yawned. "That's me. Lulu's just my trade name. Sounds better, don't it?" She stretched it out. "Luuuuu Luuuuu."

Anna went to the bars. "What are you doing here?"

"Aw. The mayor's mad at me. The welcher wants me to loan him ten grand. He already owes me fifteen, so I said no. He can't shut me down 'cause he still wants his cut, so he has Snow arrest me on suspicion."

"Suspicion of what?"

Madam Lulu raised herself onto one elbow. "Suspicion of knowing a goldbrick when I see one."

Anna frowned. "Why do you pay the mayor?"

"So the fuckster doesn't have me raided, vag my girls, and hook me with a blind pig violation."

"And the chief of police cooperates with this?"

"You betcha."

Anna thought of Chief Singer's easy charm and Officer Singer's conflict with his father. Could that be why? Could the son be the better man?

Madam Lulu raised her eyebrows. "Speaking of Chief Singer, how's young Joe? I heard you took my advice."

Anna looked at her feet and kicked the bars with her shoe. "It didn't work. He barely speaks to me."

"Don't make me feel sorry for Edgar Wright."

Anna pursed her lips indignantly. "I only kissed him because of the case. And I'd do it again."

Madam Lulu's cherry cheek plumped up in a smirk. "And again and again."

Anna lifted her chin a full two inches and tossed her head. "Yes. I'd do a lot to solve these murders. But not you. You should have loaned the mayor the money. Now who's watching out at the brothels?"

"The girls are watching out. But you have a point. They spend a lot of time looking at the ceiling."

Madam Lulu lay back on her cot and put her black boots up against the wall, which was scratched deep with graffiti. Anna let one hand rest on the cold bars. "You told me the girls never leave the brothel, except for the races in the fall. How does the killer get them, then?"

Madam Lulu puffed away on her cigar. "I don't say they never leave. They might slip out to meet a customer on the side, avoid the rake-off."

"So the murderer is a customer."

"Maybe."

"Why don't you tell them not to meet customers on the side?"

"I do. Always have. If they see men on the side, I lose my cut."

"So, you've told them about the danger and they don't believe you? They think you made it up to protect your business interests?"

"Some do. Some don't."

Anna put her fist to her lips. "I have a theory. Ruby wore blue garters. The shoe was used, but ill fitting. You could say that they were borrowed. Something old, something new, something borrowed, something blue . . ."

"And a sixpence in her shoe." Madam Lulu said. "So what? They're brides?"

"He's Protestant."

Madam Lulu put both hands on top of her hideous hat and crinkled one side of her face. "What?"

Anna began to speak quickly. "In the Bible, there's a prophet—Hosea, Prophet of Doom. He married a harlot, Gomer, as a symbol of God's redemption. He did it to make her clean. Think of our killer as the Prophet Hosea . . ."

Madam Lulu looked dubious. "He slit Peaches' throat."

Anna pointed at Madam Lulu. "Yes! Because dead prostitutes never betray their husbands." Anna prattled on with increasing speed. "Gomer went back to prostitution after Hosea married her. He'd take her back but then she'd do it again. Over and over. Our Hosea, the killer, dispatches his brides. That way they stay redeemed."

Madam Lulu cocked her head. "And how does that make him Protestant?"

Anna paced back and forth, speaking in one long string. "The killer would have to be familiar with the minor prophets of the Old Testament—scriptures for both the Jewish and the Christian religions. But minor prophets are just that—minor; only read in the Catholic mass every three years, and then they're read in Latin. Only Protestants are allowed to read the Bible. I've only read it because I wasn't supposed to. Protestants and Jews know about Hosea. Catholics don't." Anna took a deep long breath. "Do you have many Jewish patrons?"

"None."

"He's Protestant."

"If you say so."

"So, let's apply it." Anna paced along the cell with long slow steps, swinging her legs, swishing her petticoats. "The coroner is an expert in legal medicine and Snow is a detective. They've both seen all the evidence and must know that girls are being murdered, yet they do nothing. Why?" She tripped on an uneven brick and spun to face Madam Lulu. "Is one of them the killer? I have reason to believe that Snow didn't do it. That leaves the coroner." Anna grabbed the bars. "He's a Protestant." She stared hard at Madam Lulu. "Is he a customer?"

Madam Lulu held her eyes for a long moment, as if deliberating. "No."

Anna heaved a heavy sigh. "Okay. If Snow and the coroner didn't do it, our only other suspects are your customers. This gives us another clue. Either Snow and the coroner are derelict in their duty, or the killer has influence that he's using to silence them. If you would give me a list of patrons, I could look for wealthy Protestant blackmailers or . . ."

Madam Lulu interrupted, swinging her feet around and planting them on the floor. "No way. That's against the code."

Anna blinked. "Okay. Nothing in writing. Just say their names, and I'll remember them. I have a good memory. I won't tell anyone. Please." Anna stared fiercely into Madam Lulu's eyes.

Madam Lulu shook her head so hard, the fox on her stole shook its head with her. "No! No! No! It'd be like a priest telling everybody what you said in the confessional. We don't kiss and tell. It's the way it's always been."

Anna's voice rose. "One of them is a killer!"

"Maybe. But the only way a girl finds out who goes to my brothel is if she works there."

Chapter 33

It was nine o'clock, but the streets of Boyle Heights still teamed with people enjoying the first cool night of the summer—sitting on porches, playing strange instruments, stretching their legs for pleasure. Lanterns spit on posts in the dark. Anna strolled on Wolf's arm. He reeked of citrus and lavender aftershave, his damp hair freshly cut, his face cleanly shaven. She wondered if he had preened to impress her. He wasn't the Arrow Collar Man, but he was good looking, and he certainly radiated a mannish heat. He didn't distract her as much as Joe Singer, though, which was a good thing. She had detective work to do tonight. A woman's virtue depended on it.

Joe skulked nearby, providing backup to her bait. He stalked Wolf and Anna from various hiding places, shadowing them in his denim trousers, not allowing them out of his sight. He put the best of Anna's chaperones to shame. She wished her father had hired Joe and not the Widow Crisp, though it would make changing in the orchard awkward and she would have to wear his denim trousers.

She decided that she liked his denim trousers and wouldn't mind wearing them. She loved them, really, and couldn't imagine why she had ever thought they looked repulsive. They should be the next great thing in fashion. She would suggest this to Madeline Vionnet at the House of Doucet and send her a pair. But maybe she only liked the trousers because Joe's legs were inside them, and she liked his legs intensely. Anna began to feel distracted.

They turned down a particularly dark street. Joe trailed behind them, agitated. He hissed to Anna when no passersby were near, "Watch his hands, Sherlock. He's a scoundrel."

Wolf grinned. "Now that's the pot calling the kettle black."

Joe crawled through the bushes, scrambled over a wall, and peeked from behind a night blooming jasmine. It dripped with star-flowers that smelled like Hollenbeck Park—the scent that accompanied Joe's lovemaking the night they first did police work together just over a week ago. It was pretend, police lovemaking, but Anna still liked to think about it.

Deep furrows creased Joe's forehead and his face was red. "I mean it, Sherlock. You can't trust him."

That was undoubtedly true. Still, Anna held out the tiniest hope that Joe felt jealous. She cast him a lofty, devil-may-care smile. "I'm fine. Happy as a clam." She wondered if he tasted like peppermint tonight.

Wolf grinned. "Officer Singer. Don't hover. The rape fiend doesn't attack trios." Wolf steered Anna to the other side of the street, away from Joe. "I don't know about you, but I'd like a little privacy." He rubbed her arm. Joe crossed the road after them and faded into the foliage just a few feet away. Wolf chuckled with glee, high pitched, almost a giggle.

"How long has the rape fiend been terrorizing Boyle Heights?" Anna asked.

"Going on ten months."

"So one day, he just started attacking couples? Out of the blue?"

"No, honeybun. Not out of the blue. If he's typical, he worked up to it. We think he came from Omaha. They had a series of similar attacks on couples. Right after the Omaha rapes stopped, the Boyle Heights rapes began."

"I see."

They turned down an alley that smelled like an outhouse, drowning the scent of jasmine. It jolted Anna's mind. Her thoughts shifted to sewage-smelling morgues, to the man who filled them up with brothel girls, to the men who stood back and let it happen—Snow and the coroner. She felt angry at Joe, because, indirectly, he let it happen, too.

She thought of Snow, and how peculiar it was that he couldn't spell. Detectives were of high rank in the LAPD. They were supposed to be intelligent. Could Snow be intelligent but simply poor at writing?

Anna looked up at her dapper escort who was merrily whistling. "Detective Wolf, may I ask you a question?"

Wolf leaned in close. "Ask me anything, honeybun."

"Do you think Detective Snow is bright?"

He scratched his head. "I wouldn't speak ill of a fellow officer unless I was duly persuaded. But as Officer Singer is fond of you, and he's watching me, persuasion is ill advised."

Anna raised her voice to be sure that Joe could hear. "He isn't fond of me. He doesn't even speak to me. And I'll persuade you if I want to."

She slipped her arm around Wolf's waist, just in case Officer Singer was a little bit fond of her. Wolf raised his eyebrows. A nearby bush said a dirty word. Anna felt a warm flicker in her heart at Joe's response and held Wolf even closer. "So tell me, Officer, would the police hire a stupid detective?"

Wolf looked thoughtful. "Hypothetically? There could be reasons for doing it. If his relatives are important or somebody needs a favor."

Anna's voice sizzled with indignation. "But a stupid detective couldn't solve crimes! Crimes could go on right under his nose and he might not even notice."

"So you put him on things you don't care about—stolen bicycles, sneak thievery, hobos."

"Or maybe crimes you don't want solved."

Wolf licked his upper lip. "I suppose that too, honeybun."

Anna would bet that Detective Snow was the idiot cousin of someone important. She frowned at the travesty. There were so many brilliant detectives in the world who could use a job. Like Anna.

Snow could be on the case because no one cared about brothel girls or because someone didn't want the murders solved. But that didn't explain the coroner's role. He was smart. Anna cocked her head. "Is the coroner hard working?"

Wolf smiled indulgently. "Yes, the coroner is hard working."

"Have you ever known him to give less care to a particular case—a case that no one cares about, say, if his workload became excessive?"

Wolf ran his fingers through the pomade in his freshly washed hair. "No, honeybun. I can't say that I have."

"What about Snow?"

He grinned. "You'll have to persuade me."

They were crossing in front of the men's club where Anna had seen the Boyle Heights Rape Fiend with his white-blonde hair, hurrying away from her with the grace of a ballerina. She felt that cold confusion again, that inability to reconcile beauty and evil.

Wolf shifted from foot to foot, and a pained look spread over his face. He cleared his throat. "Would you excuse me?" Anna nodded. He went over to speak with a blooming rhododendron bush. "I'm going to the men's club privy. Don't run off with my girl." The bush called Wolf a very bad name. Anna flushed with pleasure.

Wolf positively giggled. He strode into the men's club, winking back at Anna. Just inside the door, he weaved through a family of well-dressed Jews who loitered in the entryway in their long, fluffy whiskers.

Anna watched the bush from the corner of her eye, but she could see no trace of Joe Singer. She sent a little smile to the bush. The group of men drifted out of the club and stood under the awning, talking and smoking in the shadowy glow from the street lamps and lights in the window. Joe discreetly extricated himself from the rhododendrons and went to stand by Anna, positioning himself protectively between her and the fluffy whiskers. She moved close and slipped her arm through his, like the first time they did the sting together.

He shrugged her off. "Would ya stop throwing yourself at me?"

"It's my job!"

He squinted at her. "Yeah, well you go above and beyond the call of duty."

Anna's positive feelings toward Joe's denim trousers disappeared. She did what any girl would do when subjected to such an unfounded insult. She put her palms flat against his chest and shoved him.

He stepped backward, recovered, and gave her a little shove in return. His face was red. She made a sound of indignation and pushed him harder. He stumbled into the rhododendron bush and sat into poky sticks and leaves. "Hey, lay off!"

Two men under the awning had their eyes fixed on Anna. They

ignored their bearded companions, who were trying to shake hands. A gray-haired Jew spit and strode off, making angry sounds in Yiddish. Four younger men followed him speaking rapidly and gesticulating.

Joe bounced up, rubbing his backside, dusting leaves from his trousers. He strode toward her, shooting fighting words, punctuating them with a waving hand, but she didn't hear them. She stood as still as a child in a game of freeze tag. Joe looked to see what had captured her attention and dropped his hand. Her father and Edgar stood twenty feet away, frozen like they, too, were playing Anna's game. Edgar took three steps forward. Joe moved away from Anna's side. She tucked up a stray lock of hair that had been dislodged during the shoving match and gulped.

Detective Wolf sauntered out of the men's club, past Edgar and Mr. Blanc, grinning and oblivious. "Ma'am you're under arrest for assaulting an officer, though I'm sure he sorely deserved it." When Wolf saw Anna's expression, he followed her gaze to the men under the awning. Mr. Blanc was puffy with rage. The fault line in his forehead trembled. Edgar looked ill.

Wolf switched on his official persona like a light. He flashed his badge at the gentlemen, his demeanor suddenly so fatally serious and professional, Anna almost laughed in spite of her dilemma. Wolf ambled forward. "Police. May I help you gentleman?"

Edgar spoke with an authority that came from wealth and superseded a badge. "Is this lady under arrest?"

Wolf creased his brow and licked his lips. "No. Matron Holmes works for the LAPD."

Veins stood out like ropes on Mr. Blanc's temples, and the tendons on his neck were as tight as bowstrings. "That's not Matron Holmes!"

Anna raised her chin. "Father, I'm conducting a police sting operation, undercover."

Mr. Blanc's face contorted. He charged foreword and grabbed her roughly by the arm. "No, you are not!"

He squeezed. Anna screwed up her face in pain, but she didn't struggle. She was done and she knew it. Both Joe and Edgar moved toward Mr. Blanc like growling dogs. He let go. Anna rubbed her bruised arm, her eyes darting between Edgar and Joe and back again.

Joe spoke to Mr. Blanc in a soothing voice. "Now just ease off, sir. Nothing untoward is going on here. Miss Blanc is being chaperoned by two police officers."

Wolf looked at Joe, confused. "Miss Blanc?"

Now Mr. Blanc's whole body was trembling. He shook his head. "*Oh lá lá*. Anna, how could you?" He glared at Joe. "Does your father know about this?"

Joe looked him in the eye, calm and steady. "Nobody knows, sir. Detective Wolf didn't even know. Until now."

Edgar strode toward Wolf and opened his wallet. He counted out four fifty-dollar bills and handed them to the detective.

Wolf smiled and pocketed the money. "Know what?"

Edgar counted out four more bills and extended them to Joe. Joe's hands stayed at his sides, balled in tight fists, his jaw shifting in minute movements, his face twisting in a look of distain. Edgar glared back, took out four more bills and held them out to Joe. He narrowed his eyes, straining his vision as if willing Joe to submit and take the money. He left his offering hand suspended in the air. "What do you want?"

Joe made a sound of disgust. "Nothing."

Anna glided over and laid a soft hand on Edgar's arm. In a quiet voice, she said, "He won't tell." Deep down, she knew it was true. One couldn't buy Joe Singer, because even if he borrowed your piano for a little while, he never was going to tell.

Edgar looked at Anna, helpless. His voice was flat. "You know that because you know him so well you'll even stake your reputation on him."

Anna looked down at her feet. Edgar threw down the money. He turned on Joe, looming over him, and stuck an index finger in his face. "Stay away from her! You and your ridiculous colleagues!"

As Mr. Blanc yanked Anna toward Edgar's blue Cadillac, she heard Wolf speak. "Now, that wasn't necessary."

Anna pulled against her father's grip to look back at Joe, soaking up her last glimpse of him, her last glimpse of her life as Matron Anna Holmes. It was like ripping a favorite gown that could not be mended or having a bullet penetrate your François Pinet shoe. No, it was much, much worse. It was the death of a dream.

Mr. Blanc tugged her toward the curb. Behind her, she could still hear the men as they argued. Edgar was shouting. "You let her risk her life!"

Joe shouted back. "She wasn't risking her life! She was with me! Safe with me! I'd never let anything happen to her! And she can do whatever she wants!"

Wolf's voice was calm. He purred at them, trying to diffuse the situation. Anna couldn't hear what he said. She wrested herself from her father's grasp and turned around. Wolf was pulling Joe away by the arm. Joe glared at Edgar over his shoulder, his fists still clenched, his eyes bulging with ire.

She wished he would look at her, gaze at her with tragic longing, run to her and kiss her goodbye, even if he got clocked for it. When he finally met her eyes, he was grinding his teeth. His gaze quickly left hers and leveled itself on Edgar, who was shouting something. Mr. Blanc opened the door and shoved her inside.

Edgar stormed to the car and got into the driver's seat, slamming the door. He was sweating and, forgoing his handkerchief, wiped his brow on his crisp sleeve, which was nothing like Edgar. No one spoke as they drove off.

When the shiny blue car was out of sight, Joe's anger was subsumed by a sinking, a sense that he'd dropped something important and it had fallen where it could not be retrieved. Anna Holmes was dead. He didn't know what would become of Anna Blanc, but he didn't think he would see her again. He felt powerless to protect her. What if Edgar asked about Matron Holmes around the station? What if he heard the rumor that he and Anna were lovers? That they had been seen having sex in the stables behind the station? Even if Edgar loved her, even if he could forgive her secret work as a matron, no man could forgive that. Anna would be ruined.

Joe's brows drew together. "Wolf, don't tell Edgar Wright I kissed his fiancée."

"Well, last I heard, you didn't kiss Edgar Wright's fiancée," Wolf said.

"I never said that. I said we didn't have dinner."

Wolf smiled. "You know, if you aspire to be a great seducer of women, you got to learn how to lie." He saw the look in Joe's eyes and his smile waivered. "You look pathetic, like a love sick puppy." He slipped his arm through Joe's. "What do you say I dress up in ladies' clothes and you take me out on the town?"

Chapter 34

Anna sat in a velvet chair under a gilded mirror in the hall outside her father's study. She rubbed her soft hands along the fabric, letting the tiny fibers brush her palms. She kicked her shoes off and felt glad that she had blisters. She deserved them. She had failed both Edgar and Lady Justice.

Dread ate at her insides. At least Edgar didn't know the full extent of her police work. Though she longed to tell him, he wouldn't understand. Cigar smoke drifted from under the door. She faintly heard her father's plaintive, scratchy voice and the occasional angry swell of Edgar's smooth voice, but she couldn't understand their words. After an hour, the study door opened and Mr. Blanc came out.

Anna stood mute. Her father's face was furrowed, and he smelled of whiskey. He pointed his finger at her. "Watch your step, Anna. No more antics or you'll end up a spinster in my house or locked away in a convent. Either way, your beauty would be wasted!"

Anna squeezed her eyes closed and said a silent prayer to St. Agatha, patron saint of unmarried women. She begged not to be a pitiful old maid, and then kicked herself for insulting the holy spinster.

Mr. Blanc pointed violently toward his study. "Go in! He's waiting for you!"

He moved off like a freight train, billowing black smoke down the hall. "*Mon Dieu*!" She heard a crash and heard him bellow something at Cook. Anna took a deep breath and forced her feet to walk toward the room where she would face Edgar.

She entered quietly and shut the door. The room smelled of tanned hides, lemon oil, and tobacco. Edgar paced, tugging tufts of hair so that when he dropped his arms his normally perfect curls stood up like little dust devils. His jacket lay on the floor and his tie hung loose and crooked. He turned his white face to look at her. Anna stood quietly and bit her lower lip.

He made a strangled sound. "I love you. But . . ." He let the words dwindle.

"I'm a business deal!" Anna blurted before she knew what she was going to say. She would have never told the truth if she had thought about it in advance. But they were angry because she trapped criminals, which was perfectly legal, when they bartered her like a pawn, trading her like a slave, which was clearly against the law. It was something she had always known but hadn't cared to dwell upon. She wanted freedom and so had accepted it. Edgar treated her tenderly and she liked him. He was chivalrous, intelligent, funny, well dressed, and well made. She thought she could love him, once she had the opportunity.

Edgar lowered his voice so they couldn't be overheard, even as he spit out the words. "You think I need Blanc National? It's a liability. Your father is a liability. His bank is bust. I've been loaning him large sums of money, which I never expect to see again."

She blinked. "I beg your pardon? Our bank is bust?"

"Anna, I didn't court you to get a bank deal. I made a bad bank deal so I could marry you!" He groaned. "And you lie to me and treat me like the fool that I am."

Anna dropped like a lead weight onto the velvet pouf. Air hissed out of it. She had known the match was advantageous to her father, but she had always assumed it was mutual. Edgar walked to the paned window and stared out at nothing. They were finally alone, but he couldn't be more distant. He shook his head slowly, his curls swaying. "I broke up your marriage."

Anna gave him a bewildered look. "What?"

"That morning at the Mission Inn. I called your father and told him you were there with Taylor." He went back to tugging his curls.

Normally, this kind of revelation would make Anna throw chairs, but she had nothing left in her, not even the strength to raise her voice. She whispered. "Why?"

"Because he is a rotten gold digger and I wanted you for myself!"

Edgar's confession flooded her with hope. Perhaps he already loved her with a love like Heathcliff's—a love that transcended marriage to another man, or even death. A love that could forgive a transgression.

She went to him and laid her hand gently on his arm. His body heat had made his shirt-sleeve limp and his petunia scent stronger. She stroked his arm down to his hand, where a little black curl peeked from under his cuff. "Kiss me."

Edgar shook off her hand and kept staring out the window. Anna blinked. Two rejections in one evening exceeded her limit. His confession hadn't made her angry, but this did—not just that he didn't kiss her now, didn't draw her heart away from Joe Singer and seal her to himself, but that he had never kissed her. Not once. Her throat ached. "I forgive your betrayal, and you can't forgive me?"

"I don't know."

Her voice pleaded. "Edgar, if you love me, can't you try to understand? Someone is violating innocent women. The police needed a girl. They approached me because I'm smart."

He smiled cynically. "Joe Singer approached you because you're smart?"

"Yes."

He chuckled, but his eyes were flat. Anna's brows drew together. "Can't you see it made me happy? I'd always dreamed of doing detective work, like *Lady Molly of Scotland Yard*, or the spinster in the *Circular Staircase*. I'm good at it. If I'd told you the truth, you'd never have allowed it."

"That's right. I wouldn't!" He swiped a hand across his eyes and sighed. "It isn't just embarrassing, Anna, it's dangerous. You could have been killed tonight, or worse." He turned and looked her square in the eye. "Do you want to be my wife?"

She blinked. "I . . . I do, but . . ."

He spoke with a sudden violence that made her step back. "Then you will stay away from the police station! If I see Joe Singer within a hundred yards of you, I'll kill him!"

Anna raised a hand and let it fall. "He's just a policeman."

Edgar's eyes were bulging now and a vein stood out on his temple. "I will know, Anna, if you've been unfaithful."

"How dare you!" Anna moved to slap him, but he caught her wrist and twisted. She shrieked. Edgar quickly dropped her arm. He recoiled, mouth dumb and open, as if horrified at his own internal monster. Anna flew down the hall and up the stairs, her arm turning red where his hand had been. He followed, but she was faster, and propriety stopped him at the stairs. Her bedroom door slammed.

She heard him call out, "Anna, darling, I'm sorry!"

The following morning, Detective Wolf ushered the Widow Crisp from her room in the Blanc Mansion, down the cool marble steps to a paddy wagon bound for San Francisco. He had recovered all of Anna's jewelry, as well as her tortoiseshell shoehorn, silver candlesticks, a bottle of Ambre Antique perfume, and several pairs of fancy drawers. He returned the things to Mrs. Morales, except for one silky pair of Anna's drawers, which he surreptitiously tucked into his coat.

Mrs. Morales waited at the threshold, and when the Widow Crisp shuffled out the door Mrs. Morales kicked her in the bottom.

Anna stayed in bed all morning, grieving her secret life as a detective. She had tried to solve the murders and failed. She had not turned her back on injustice, but it hadn't been her responsibility to start with. She was just a silly girl.

Anna would have stayed in bed all day, but she was terribly bored. Plus, her stomach was growling. Heartbreak and desperation were no reasons not to eat, and so she slipped into a negligee appropriate for breakfast. Anna's eyes stung and her nose glowed from blowing as she dragged herself down the hall.

Coming to the top of the spiral staircase, she caught her breath and sneezed. The room looked like a florist shop. She descended into a sea of blood-red roses, some buds, some blooming. Her heart bounced around her chest like a rubber ball. Every red rose in Los Angeles adorned her conservatory. She plucked a flower and lifted it to her nose, but her nose was swollen and the fragrance faint.

She headed for the breakfast table where her father was having a slice of pork cake. He smiled. "Apparently, Mr. Wright has lost his mind."

After breakfast, Mrs. Morales and Mr. Blanc escorted Anna to confession, and from that point on Anna resolved to obey. Not that she had an opportunity to disobey, as her father dogged her every step. She was surprised he hadn't leashed her. He had installed locks to keep Anna in, and a team of chaperones were on their way. This was unnecessary. Anna had repented of her lies in the confessional that morning, though Father Depaul might say he'd heard it all before. He gave her a thousand Hail Marys as penance and ordered her to volunteer at the Orphans' Asylum.

God was quite cruel. For just as Anna was trying to be good, to forget police work and Joe Singer, she opened the morning paper and saw an advertisement for the new Arrow Shirt Suit. Her heart leapt like a suicidal goldfish. There was the Arrow Collar Man, bare-legged and standing in his Arrow shirt suit, a one-piece combination overshirt and underdrawers, brand new this year. It was rather sheer and unbuttoned up to the very curve of his bottom. While she liked this advertisement intensely, she didn't know why she had ever thought Joe Singer looked like the Arrow Collar Man. Joe Singer looked much, much better. But because she didn't have a picture of the real Joe Singer, she clipped the advertisement of the half-naked man as a memento of the man she must never see again.

Chapter 35

Detective Wolf wore linen trousers creased in front and back, a vest, double-breasted jacket, gloves, and a boater's hat. His nose twitched from too much lavender aftershave. He was credibly disguised as a gentleman, though if Anna had been there she would have insisted that he change his tie. But Anna was not there.

He swaggered into an upscale shop and lost himself in a forest of overly feathered ladies' hats. He lifted one at random and pretended to admire it. It towered more than a foot, with a basket of fruit pinned to the side, including a life-sized pomegranate, grapefruit, and two lemons. It smelled like glue. Only a man would have a neck thick enough to support it comfortably. If the LAPD ever again had an occasion to dress an officer in ladies' clothing, he would buy the hat for Joe.

Across the forest, he could hear the milliner charming a lady at the till. He snuck a glance at them in a mirror. The lady wasn't interesting. She was too thin and looked frigid. But the man had oversized blue eyes, with thick black lashes and unnaturally blonde hair. He was a dandy, a dude, in his fancy suit and ascot, the kind of man Wolf distained and women loved. He flashed his eyes at Wolf, who immediately pegged him for a deviant.

Three women in the shopping district had recognized this man in Anna's portrait and identified him as their milliner. Wolf signaled through the window to Joe, who loitered outside in denim waist overalls. Joe barely nodded and disappeared from view.

The lady at the till purchased two hats and left with two round, striped boxes stacked in her arms. Bells tinkled as the shop doors closed behind her. Wolf stepped to the door and locked it with a click. He took off his jacket and hung it over a hat rack. He removed his vest, folded his arms, and leaned up against the door.

The milliner smiled at Wolf the way the girls did when they fell for his oily charm. "I beg your pardon. Can I help you?"

Wolf sized him up. The milliner's smile began to fade. "Hey, what are you about?"

It was Wolf's turn to smile. He flashed his badge. "Arresting you."

The milliner's big eyes got bigger, and he skittered like a rabbit through a door to the back of his shop. Wolf leapt the counter in pursuit and hurled into the work space where the hats were made. It smelled like a wet dog. The fop was hiding, but Wolf could hear him moving. He weaved his way among beaver skins soaking in mercury, vats of wet wool, ovens and cutting machines, hats on forms, and a motherly old woman elbow deep in a tub of dye who screamed when she saw him. Wolf shouted, "Where did he go?" but she cowered and said nothing.

He heard a *bang* as the man threw open a back door into the alley and it slammed against the wall. Wolf snapped his fingers. "Damn it! I wanted him."

He charged to the alley door and saw the milliner lying flat on his back and Joe standing over him shaking out his hand and grinning. "He ran smack into my fist."

One of the milliner's large blue eyes was turning red, the flesh above it swelling up with blood. Wolf rolled him over. Joe wiped his bloody knuckles on the fop's fine suit and cuffed his hands behind his back. "So." He lifted the dazed dandy's face by the collar. "Were you really just trying to humiliate the men?"

Chapter 36

Anna carefully picked her way down the sidewalk, trussed up like a lady, in a fierce new corset that squeezed her organs into an unnatural figure eight. It pinched, and she couldn't fully expand her lungs, but she was doing everything she could to stay in line and be a good fiancée. She would do everything except throw out the advertisement for the Arrow shirt suit, which she planned to keep until Edgar took her in his arms and made her no longer want it.

Two chaperones flanked Anna. They looked more like men than women, with fuzzy beards on their chins that resembled bread mold. Anna could not remember their names. Tramping ahead of Anna was their leader, Miss Olga Baumgartner, so muscular Anna was sure she was a man. The three persons formed a mobile human jail cell. Mrs. Morales had not hired this trio. It had been the work of Mr. Blanc himself. Anna thought he must have gotten them from the circus, but she was too tired to be amused. Her life was racing forward without her.

She and Edgar would marry next Saturday in a quiet ceremony that would get the job done. There would be rumors about the rushed affair, speculation that Anna's gown had been cream and not white, and her status would once more be downgraded. But when there was no baby, she would be vindicated. She didn't care. She felt nothing. Not excitement, not love, not sadness. Nothing. And nothing cures nothing like shopping.

Anna had one week to finish buying her trousseau. None of the extraordinarily expensive things she had ordered from Paris would arrive in time, and Edgar was taking her on a honeymoon next Sunday. He had given Miss Baumgartner a sum of money that would more than cover anything Anna wanted. At least there were four women to carry the bags.

In the new corset, Anna had to stop every few yards to catch her breath. She paused in front of the Southern California Music Company. It occurred to her that she might buy a talking machine and some records, maybe even a recording of "By the Light of the Silvery Moon." It would be heavy, but one of the muscular ladies could carry it.

Anna glided inside to the elevator, a little light-headed from the corset and the heat. Because God was still cruel, it was not working. The talking machines were on the sixth floor and she was going to have to take the stairs. The air in the stairwell was dusty, bug legs and skin flakes spun in the sunbeams. She took a sip of dirty air and mounted the first of several hundred steps.

Four blocks away, in his little apartment, Joe missed Anna's baby grand. He liked to play when he felt blue, and since Anna got yanked off the force he had felt blue. He had written her a song, which he called "Miss Jekyll and Matron Hyde." It was in a minor key. On his sorry piano, it sounded terrible. Wolf said Anna was being held prisoner in her castle on the hill and would marry Edgar on Saturday.

Joe went to the kitchen and shook the last drops out of a bottle of Siglo XX. His ratty old upright was no match for his blue mood when he was dry, so he walked down to the Music Company, where he knew the manager's daughter, a Miss Julia Lory, would be working. She was pretty and maybe a little sweet on him. She let him borrow sheet music and play the pianos. She would have his business someday. He'd saved three hundred dollars and figured he needed two hundred more. If he gave up beer for a year, he'd have it. He could practice. Get better. Maybe even make a recording.

The pianos were sold on the bottom floor, where it was cooler than outside. He sat down at a blonde Wentworth upright and ran his fingers over the butter-smooth keys. It sounded good, but not as good as Anna's baby grand. He started in on a rag, a frantic, cheerful sequence of notes to elevate his mood. His hands moved in a blur. The piano action stood exposed and the hammers were fluttering like hummingbird wings, mirroring the movement of the keys, making quiet puffing sounds as they cut through air.

Miss Lory came over and leaned against the instrument, smiling, tapping her fingers on the hard top. Joe's hands wound down and stopped. She smiled. "I heard you from the other room. I knew it was you. No one plays like you, Mr. Singer."

He smiled back. "How much is this one?"

"Four hundred dollars." She lowered her voice. "That's your special price. Normally, it's four-fifty, but I asked Daddy if he'd give you a discount."

"Really? Thank you." He started in on "By the Light of the Silvery Moon." "Give me six more months, and you've got a deal." He moved down an octave and scooted over so she could sit. She put her hands on the keys and jumped in.

Anna heard their duet as she took the stairs slowly down from the sixth floor, one by one, pausing every fifth step to rest. The corset was taking its toll. She leaned up against the rail to listen to Joe's song about crooning and mooning and spooning. Her organs, already maximally squished, rearranged to make room for her throbbing heart.

Anna wasn't alone in the stairwell. One bearded lady hoisted a talking machine over her shoulder; sweat beaded on her upper lip. She glared at Anna, who was taking weeks to reach the first floor. Miss Baumgartner lugged four bags of records. The third guard carried nothing, guarding Anna. Anna almost asked her for a piggyback ride. Instead, she sighed and took five more steps, taking quick shallow breaths.

She reached the bottom landing only to find the elevator working again. God's cruel joke. She hobbled into the showroom and, out of curiosity, looked for the source of the music.

Her face went slack. She saw Joe Singer sitting at the piano, smiling and playing her song with a different girl—a pretty girl leaning in close to him. A girl whose fiancé hadn't threatened to kill him. He laughed at something the pretty girl said, which Anna couldn't hear over the music.

Anna's heart turned poison green and sprouted tendrils that spread through her body and wrapped around her lungs. More than ever, she felt she couldn't breathe. She didn't want Joe Singer to have a girl, even after she was married, even after she was dead. Of course, she could say nothing about it. All their spooning had been of a professional nature. He had said some sweet things, but a gentleman would in such situations. He had never pursued her, and she belonged to someone else. She had no right to the jealousy she felt. It would be wrong to upturn the piano bench or club the girl with a clarinet. Besides, that would require the removal of her corset. Anna resolved to act with dignity. She would slink away.

Joe sang in his rich tenor voice about mooning, crooning, and spooning. The piano girl sang the patter, on key, smiling at him with full pink lips and white teeth. Anna couldn't bear the sight or the sound. She ran. That is, she took the deepest breath possible in her iron maiden, and sped at a crawl toward the door, hoping to God he wouldn't see her.

But, as God is cruel, he did.

Just as she made it safely onto the hot sidewalk, passing the window, hemmed in and shielded by her burly entourage, Joe saw her through the glass. He leapt from the bench, excusing himself to Miss Lory even as he hurled himself out the door. He bellowed, "Sherlock!"

Anna didn't turn around. He caught up, dodged in front of her, and jogged backward. "Hey." He grinned. "Everyone misses you down at the station. It's boring without you." He wiped his forehead on his sleeve and flashed his dimples.

Her green heart thumped. She turned her head so she wouldn't have to see him.

He bobbed around so he could look her in the face and gave her a knee-weakening half smile. "What's wrong?" He leaned close and whispered. "Aren't you gonna try to seduce me in the line of duty?"

Anna's weak knees wobbled and she snapped her head away. "No. I've given up police work."

Miss Baumgartner hurled her girth between them and threatened Joe with an evil glare. He danced around the formidable chaperone like a boxer. "That's too bad. We captured the Boyle Heights Rape Fiend. Wolf and I got him. He was a milliner, of all things. Big blue eyes, dark lashes, blonde, blonde hair. Dressed like a dandy, looked just like your picture." He gave her a cocky grin and swaggered. "Only now he has a black eye."

Miss Baumgartner took a swat at him, but he was quicker and more agile and dodged it.

Anna's eyes flashed for a moment, but their light was soon extinguished. "Don't tell me. I don't want to know."

"What's wrong with you? We should be celebrating. You cracked the case." He smiled, warm and open as if all were forgiven, making her heart pitter-pat. She had to get away from him before she succumbed to liking him intensely.

With effort, she put on a chilly voice. "Nothing's wrong with me. I just don't need to be associating with a low class policeman."

Joe flinched like he'd been struck in the face. Then, his mouth and eyes hardened. "Forgive me, Miss Blanc. I'll make sure to stay out of your way."

He stopped dancing and turned his back on her, striding off toward the Music Company and the piano girl. Anna squeezed her face as she stopped to watch him go. He didn't look back. She wanted him to look back.

Miss Baumgartner loomed over her. "Leave him, Miss Blanc, or I'll report it."

Anna stared a moment longer at his backside. For once his shirttails were tucked in. It made her wonder if he was wearing one of the new Arrow shirt suits. She would never know, and the thought crushed her. Anna took her eyes away from Joe's denim trousers and submitted to her captors. She wondered if it would sting so much to see him after she belonged to Edgar and was initiated into the mysteries of marriage.

Anna moved down the street away from Joe like an injured bird, encaged by her entourage. She felt dizzy and realized that the corset would need to be loosened or she would faint. She paused to catch her breath. "Take me to Hamburger's. Ninth and Broadway." She laid a hand on the wall for support. "I want to rest in the dressing room."

Miss Baumgartner's gaze drifted to the department store. The Music Company stood between them and Hamburger's. She raised her eyebrows.

Anna tugged at her corset. "Please. We'll cross the street so he doesn't see us." She made a little sound of despair. "He's already inside with that piano girl."

The street was busy with carts and horses, whirring electric cars, swift hansom cabs, and Fords spewing exhaust. She waited for a gap and hobbled her way across, forging a path to avoid road apples herself and make sure her chaperones would have to step in them. Miss Baumgartner squished a big brown one and it smelled.

She walked past the Music Company on the opposite side of Broadway, never once looking, and crossed over again on Eighth Street. As she reached the middle of the road, a trolley rattled by, clanging its bells. Hanging off the back was Detective Snow. If he noticed her, he didn't show it. She watched his stupid slack face disappear down the road and narrowed her eyes. A moment later, the coroner's wagon rumbled past, kicking up dust and heading in the same direction—toward New High Street, toward the parlor houses.

Anna's stomach would have flipped if it hadn't been crushed up against her liver by whalebone. She was sure there was another death. Maybe a murder. If it were a brothel girl, there was nothing she could do to prevent Snow and the coroner from disguising it as a suicide. She had promised Edgar to stay away from police work. An army of gorilla women had been hired to help her keep that promise. And there was the added difficulty that she couldn't walk five steps in a row without resting and was very possibly going to faint.

She wished she could plead her case to Joe and ask him to follow Snow as one last favor to her. Hadn't she solved the case of the Boyle Heights Rape Fiend? Sure, she had insulted him, but he had had the nerve to play piano with a pretty girl. They were even. Anna glanced back toward the Music Company. Miss Baumgartner reached out and with two fingers pulled Anna's chin away from the store. "Look straight ahead! You will have no more dealings with that young man."

Joe hadn't actually gone back to the Music Company. He had leaned against a wall and watched Anna negotiate the street, still smarting from her words and wondering why she was walking so funny. She looked like an ironing board with legs. Was she injured? Had Edgar hurt her? He was half inclined to fight off her guards, throw her over his shoulder, and run. But she could free herself if she wanted to, and she obviously didn't want to. She was all fired up to marry Edgar Wright and she had made it very clear that she didn't want to associate with lowly Joe Singer. He spat. He should count his blessings. She'd make a terrible wife.

Joe needed to think of something else. He tried to think about Miss Lory, who would make a good wife, but his heart wasn't in it. But maybe he should buy her a present—a thank-you gift for letting him play the pianos. He couldn't stay in love with Anna forever. It was a futile endeavor. Hamburger's Department Store was a stone's throw away. He could surely find something for Julia. Maybe a fancy feather clip like Anna sometimes wore, or a hat like Anna's.

Hamburger's reigned as the largest department store west of Chicago and had more floors even than the Music Company. If women's furnishings had not been on the first level, Anna would have suffocated before reaching it. A security guard lifted his cap as she hobbled inside leaning on the hairy arm of one of her lumbering entourage. Anna's skin shone faintly blue.

Anna watched Miss Baumgartner assess the terrain. A maze of curving countertops snaked through the store—glass cases stacked with shawls, handkerchiefs, and lace collars. There were rows of racks with bathing suits—plenty of places where she might hide. And there were lots of ladies. Anna had slipped away from chaperones before. If she escaped in this crowded maze, there would be no way to recover her. No doubt Miss Baumgartner knew that. Anna watched her scan the perimeter.

There were two entrances into ladies' furnishings. Miss Baumgartner took the main door, which was the busiest. She sent one bearded chaperone to the back door and ordered the other to stay with Anna. Even if she got away in the store, as long as they kept her from slipping outside, they were poised to flush her out like a quail, and would trap her at closing time.

The chaperones could plot all they wanted. Anna didn't care what they did. She suffered from a lack of oxygen, and she had no intention of being anything but good. She feebly made her way toward the dressing rooms but stopped when she noticed a man standing at the counters with his back to her. She knew that backside.

It was Joe Singer and he was browsing in ladies' accessories, picking up feather clips in midnight, emerald, and melon, turning them around in his hands. At first, she thought he was a vision brought on by her slow suffocation, but when he started to sing to himself, and when an old lady fluttered her lashes at him, she knew he was real. He crooned, "You have vowed your affection to each one in turn, and have sworn to them all you'd be true . . ."

Anna's heart sang in harmony. His interest in ladies' accessories made her tingle, as did the opportunity it presented. If she could convince him to follow Snow to the body, and if it was a brothel girl, he would find the ill-fitting shoe, the sixpence, and any evidence of foul play. He would tell his father to investigate and they would capture the killer. Eve would be safe and Anna would truly be exculpated.

Joe faced the sparkling glass case, standing with his back to a row of heavy toile curtains that marked the individual dressing rooms. Clearly, the bearded lady hadn't seen him. Otherwise, she would be running him off like he was a stray dog. But, of course, the chaperone's eyes would be fixed on her prisoner, not on the other customers. Anna took several sips of air. She smiled sweetly at Miss Baumgartner and hobbled toward the row of curtains, dragging her feet across the smooth wooden floor.

She chose the changing room closest to Joe, gave a little wave to her keeper, and let the curtain swing shut. In the tiny, dimly lit room, Anna raced in slow motion, gasping for breath like a guppy on shore. She yanked and yanked at her cotton gown until the pearl buttons popped off, leaving nicks in the fabric and spilling across the carpet. She stripped it off, her head swimming from the effort, but she had to reach Joe before he left ladies' furnishings.

She stood on tiptoe, her nose wrinkled with exertion, and slung her dress over the curtain top. When her keeper saw the gown she would be less vigilant. Even Anna wouldn't run through a department store in her undermuslins, and the chaperone knew that Anna needed assistance to get her gown back on. If the dress was visible, Anna remained as contained as a canary in cage.

She ached to remove her corset cover and loosen the ties, but there wasn't time. She counted to five and peeked out into the show room. Miss Baumgartner had indeed turned her back and had even wandered off to peruse the Princess Pat display nearly fifteen feet away.

The stars were in alignment. Anna bent to work off her smooth leather boot. Bone stays jabbed into her belly, but she gritted her teeth and hurried at a sloth's pace. When she had unfastened the boot, she thrust her arm through the curtain and hurled the shoe at Joe. She missed the man but upset the display of feather hair clips, sending them skittering across the glass like sand pipers. The boot bounced on the counter with a *crack* and tumbled under a rack of slippery negligees. Joe spun around, his brow scrunched up in irritation, looking for the culprit. But the chaperone had glanced back toward her charge, and Anna retracted her head like a turtle. Joe saw no one, just the rippling of the curtain where Anna's face had been. He ran his finger along the rough crack in the glass and set about righting the display of feather clips.

Anna waited a moment, her lungs burning. She peeked outside. A salesgirl was applying Princess Pat above the whiskers of the chaperone. Anna thought it helped. She seized the moment to sling boot number two, her last piece of ammunition, her last hope.

Joe turned to leave just as the shoe descended from its arc and kicked him in the face, stinging his cheek. This time, he caught the projectile and looked at it—a boot as smooth and shiny as still water. The label was in French. He cursed under his breath and looked for Anna.

He saw one heavily lashed gray eye and half her bowed lips peeking from a gap between the wall and the curtain. She beckoned to him with a crooked finger. Joe shook his head slowly, his mouth set in an angry straight line. Either they were friendly or they weren't, but she couldn't have it both ways.

Anna pleaded with her one eye, her lashes blinking tears of desperation, and disappeared back inside. Joe dragged a hand across his face and glanced over to where Anna's jailer primped in front of a mirror. He sauntered over for the same reason he did anything for Anna. "What?" He stood with his back to the curtain of her dressing room. Anna pushed the curtain out, took his arm, and yanked him inside. The curtain swung shut.

They were alone in the dim, closet-like space. She was bluish pale, leaning against the wall in her lingerie—petticoats to her shins, breasts and shoulders bursting from a corset that looked painful. She raised her arms and peeled off her corset cover. Joe swallowed. "Sherlock, I thought you gave up police work."

Anna fainted.

Joe caught her limp body around the middle and wondered what to do. He had assisted fainting ladies from time to time when he was on patrol and they had swooned in a public place. He laid them down and watched over them until someone claimed them or they came to. On duty, he even carried smelling salts. But he didn't have smelling salts now, and there wasn't space enough to lay Anna on the tile without her feet sticking out. That would bring her chaperones running. The last thing he wanted was to be caught alone with Anna in a dressing room when she was in her underwear, and he didn't want to leave her because, well, he was alone with Anna in a dressing room and she was in her underwear.

He braced her up against the wall with his body and with one hand loosened the satin laces on her corset. Grasping her under the arms, he slid down onto the cool tile and gathered her into his lap so her legs wouldn't stick out through the curtain. He folded her knees over his forearm, cradling her neck in the crook of one elbow, her head thrown back in one lovely vanilla arc. It was hard to stay mad when her shins were bare but for green stockings, and she was as soft as a baby. She smelled like flowers. His lips were close to her hair. He took a long deep inhale and thought of all the ways that Anna could be useful in the home.

Anna began to stir. Her eyes fluttered open and she stared into the large dark centers of Joe's eyes. She took note of her posture and was pleased with the pose. She lay undressed in the arms of a man she liked intensely. While she was unconscious, he had been free to look at her shins, which he had never seen before. Some might argue that it was a shocking breach of decorum to allow herself to be seen thus. She would argue that she wasn't much more exposed than a girl in a bathing suit. She sighed. How she wished he wore a bathing suit.

Joe spoke in a low whisper. "Let me guess. There's a reason that you're showing me your underwear and it's life or death."

She was improving now that she had oxygen, but she didn't want to get up. "Snow and the coroner just went by. They were headed in the direction of the parlor houses. There's been another murder."

He wet his lips. "And you can't go spy on Snow, so you want me to do it."

"Yes." Her gray eyes melted into his shining blue ones. "And you should do it. I was right about the Boyle Heights Rape Fiend."

He held her gaze. "Yes, you were."

Their faces were very close, his arms holding her, her satiny bottom on his hard legs. He smelled warm and delicious. She could feel his heart beating in his chest. She thought he might be contemplating kissing her. This left her facing a dilemma. She would marry on Saturday. He was not her husband-to-be. But, it was a known fact that men were more cooperative if you let them kiss you. How much more so if you were sitting on their lap in lingerie? If she kissed him and he helped her, dozens of lives might be saved. If she didn't, and he didn't help her, many more women would die. Eve might die. She concluded that spooning Joe Singer was the moral thing to do, and she wouldn't feel guilty for liking it.

Because time was of the essence, she couldn't wait for Joe to decide. She kissed him. She kissed him again with her whole, open mouth, the way he had taught her to do. Her kiss burned with all the intensity of their situation and all the passion required to overcome it—her imminent marriage, his duet with the piano girl, the fact that she would never see him again, his certain death if Edgar were to find out, and a bearded lady just outside the dressing room.

Joe pulled back. The old, familiar hostility clouded his eyes. "Are you sure you want to associate with a lowly policeman?"

Anna would have blushed, but she was pink already. "Yes," she said. "I do. I really do." And she did. She slipped her soft, bare arms around his neck and kissed him again. He reached down and ran his hand along her silky, stockinged calf. It set off fireworks in her nether parts like it was Independence Day.

It occurred to her, as she slipped her petticoats higher, that her tactic might have backfired. Joe showed no interest in the crime scene whatsoever. Instead, he unhitched her garter, stripped off her stocking, and began kissing his way from her bare toes up her softly downed leg. She had lost interest in the crime scene herself and was making little whimpering sounds.

But this was her last chance to help solve a murder before disappearing into a world of too-tight corsets and knitting circles. He left a cool trail on her skin and she shivered. "You'll go to the crime scene?"

"Um hum." He kissed a little bit higher.

Her breath caught and she wrapped her fingers in his silky hair. "You promise?"

"Um hum."

By his own testimony, Joe always did what he said he would do. If this were true, regrettably, her mission was accomplished. She allowed him one final kiss, and one more to be sure she had secured his cooperation, and one for good measure . . .

She lost count.

She was drowning in him, being swept away in his manly deliciousness. "Stop." She whispered without conviction.

Joe stopped.

She felt a sinking disappointment. He was holding her leg in midair, his lips pressed to the inside of her knee, just below the embroidered ruffle of her French drawers. He calmly set her leg down and smoothed her three petticoats over it. He smiled his crooked, dimpled "Anna's lover" smile and it turned her insides to liquid.

Anna squeaked. "Oh, don't stop."

In a flash, he was kissing her mouth and her neck with his warm, talented lips, kissing every inch of her skin not swathed in whalebone or lace, down to the very edge of her corset. He made her skin cool and electric and her nether parts sizzle. He made the mirror steam up.

Even as she felt for his Arrow shirt suit, Anna tried a silent prayer to Mary Magdalene, patron saint of tempted women. "Holy smoke" was the best prayer she could muster as she felt his hand caress her bottom through three petticoats and a pair of two-piece drawers.

Unlike God, who was currently *not* on her side, the Magdalene could relate to Anna's situation and heard her feeble prayer. Anna felt a temporary surge of virtue, as if born up on the wings of angels. She murmured into his sweet, open mouth, "Stop."

He stopped.

Joe slowly extricated himself from her lips and the tangle of her rosy limbs. He was flushed, his hair mussed, his eyes heavy. Her breath was ragged, her lips bee-stung, and her loosened corset had started to rotate sideways.

He sat against the far wall of the dressing room, breathing. "I love you."

Anna's heart fell, spooking the angels. They flew off and her virtue evaporated. She lunged for him.

He gathered her against him and kissed her like he meant it, like he loved her, like there was no piano girl. She arched up against him like a love-crazed nymph. "Stop . . . don't stop," she said, and he didn't.

He made her more breathless than the corset. Her head was spinning. The clock was ticking. Soon the body would be gone, the evidence with it, and the murders would never be solved. But she could not stick to her resolution for more than a second. Not with his body sliding on her body, and his voltaic skin only three and a half blessed layers of fabric away from her own. Not when he was chewing through her corset, and her heart was falling, falling, falling.

She needed more than a moment of self-control. She needed reinforcements. She needed them now. And so, Anna did what any girl would do if they found themselves in a similar situation, needing to tear herself from the arms of a delicious policeman so that he could solve a crime.

She screamed. "Miss Baumgartner!"

Joe winced as her banshee cry tore through his eardrum. He stared at her for a second, incredulous and betrayed, then narrowed his eyes and dashed out of the dressing room. Anna peeked after him. He streaked past the bearded lady, using clothing racks for cover, his shirt entirely untucked, the front of his trousers popped out like an army tent. He dodged round the other mannish chaperone and left ladies' furnishings being chased by a security guard. It was to be, so she thought with a pang in her heart, her last glimpse of him—Officer Joe Singer, the man she liked even more intensely than before, and whom, if she were a more foolish girl, one tossed about by passion, she might think she loved.

Anna looked into the mirror. She was rosy everywhere. Her hair was unkempt, her corset ruined, and she had bruises on her neck that she didn't recall getting. She leaned up against the dressing room wall and burped. She giggled at the burp, and burped again. She giggled uncontrollably. Her waves of giggles swelled into unrestrained belly laughs, her belly laughs into a tidal wave of whoops and snorts. Her whole body shook. She slid down onto the floor, her bare legs splayed out into the show room, shaking, shaking. She had been pushed to her limit. She was finally there. Joe Singer had made her hysterical.

Miss Baumgartner called a doctor. When Anna had been treated and lay glowing on a fainting couch in a private room at Hamburger's, Officer Wolf came in to take her statement. Given the sensitive nature of the interview, Anna had said she would speak with no one else.

"We found her hysterical on the floor of the dressing room, ready for the giggle-giggle ward," Miss Baumgartner said. "There were bruises. Her clothing was ripped. She wasn't . . . She . . . she was in her underwear."

Anna leaned forward, her expression intense. "He was a little man." She held her palm high in the air. "In a sombrero. A hunchback. With wild red hair, a long beard and . . . a monocle."

Miss Baumgartner's square jaw tensed. "She may have hallucinated, Officer."

Another chaperone stepped up to help. "He looked to me like that man from the music store."

Anna shook her head so hard her cheeks wobbled and her comb slipped sideways. "Impossible! That man was the police chief's son. He's so handsome. I would have noticed if he were in my dressing room."

Wolf had his pen poised to take notes, but at this he set it down and smiled.

Chapter 37

While Anna was being treated for hysteria, Hamburger's security guard hunted Joe like a beagle on a fox. Joe jumped fences, hid in smelly privies, raced through yards with hostile dogs nipping at his heels. The whole time, he wondered how he would explain this to his father, should he be caught, and how much time he'd be spending with Ernest, the jailer.

When Joe lost the guard on Second Street he had sweat stains under his arms and shit on his boots. He felt humiliated. His hat was smashed, and he had the worst case of sore balls in the history of love.

He boarded a tram and eased himself onto the seat. He was finished, done with Anna Blanc's doe-eyed love-in-the-name-of-the-law. He wouldn't kiss her again for love or the law, not to catch Jack the Ripper.

At New High Street he yanked the bell cord, pulled the rim of his smashed hat down over his eyes, and flipped up his Arrow shirt collar. He stepped off the trolley and kept his head down. His tongue was dry. His temples ran with sweat. He longed for some liquid comfort, but he couldn't stop to buy a drink. If a cop saw Joe anywhere near the brothels, he would arrest him on the order of the police chief, even though Joe only went to play piano. He'd been caught twice playing Madam Lulu's baby grand—the best in the city apart from Anna's. As much as he liked the jailer, he didn't relish the idea of spending another two weeks in a cell.

Joe skulked up New High Street and down Marchessault, past Canary Cottage and the Octoroon, where the mulatto girls plied their trade. He doubled back to Commercial, sneaking past the Poodle Dog, the Municipal, and the other parlor houses. He wandered the Plaza, near where the Chinese and Italians lived, Alameda, Arcadia, and Ferguson Alley, past doped up whores in brick boxes with their vacuous, staring eyes, and the young Chinese girls in brothels with barred windows. He found no sign of any suicide or murder. Anna had sent him on a potentially disastrous wild-goose chase.

Joe returned to the safe side of town, feeling relieved. He didn't think he'd been spotted. He made a wide circle around Hamburger's and bumped into Wolf, who was sauntering down First Street.

Wolf hailed him with enthusiasm. "Hey Officer Singer, keep an eye out for a bearded, red-haired, hump-backed, monocled midget who crawled into Miss Blanc's dressing room at Hamburger's today wearing a sombrero."

Joe spit out the words. "Why would I care?"

Wolf put his arm around Joe. "Because she was very clear that it was *not* you."

Half of Joe's face contracted. "Do I look like a bearded, red-haired, hump-back . . . whatever? I don't even own a sombrero."

"You know, that's what she said. Said you're too handsome to be her assailant."

Joe raised his hands. "So?"

"She wouldn't say what he did, but he left her in absolute hysterics. Had to call the doctor. If I ever find that midget, I'm gonna shake his hand." Wolf was so pleased, Joe thought he might salute.

Joe sighed. "I'll let you know if I see him." He crossed the street, heading for a soda fountain and a cold drink.

"That's good. That's very good." Wolf called after him. "You owe me. I'm the one that's going to have to tell Edgar Wright when we can't find the bearded, red-haired, hump-back, monocled midget!"

Wolf jogged up the steps of Central Station and held the door for a young woman with fresh, pink cheeks and wet lashes. She'd come to the station to report her bicycle stolen. The little peach looked ripe for comforting but, as it was Snow's case, Wolf went to find him.

Mr. Melvin ate supper behind the counter, peeling an orange he had picked from a tree behind the station and watching little spurts of juice fly into the air. Wolf sauntered over. "Where's Snow?"

Mr. Melvin chewed and didn't look up. "He's in the morgue with the coroner. They just brought in a body."

Wolf strode down the hallway. He smelled the morgue before he reached it—a sewage smell that persisted even when unoccupied. He pushed open the door. The curtain was pulled back. Snow and the coroner maneuvered a stretcher, sliding a body onto the concrete slab. It was covered in a sheet.

Wolf grinned. "Officer Snow, there's a little lady who's come to report a stolen bicycle. But I see that you're busy, so why don't I help you out and handle it myself."

Snow wrinkled his scarred face, trying to squeeze out a thought. "You're trying to take her because she's pretty."

"No. Beauty's in the eye of the beholder, so to you she'd be ugly." While Snow decided whether this was an insult, Wolf's face turned serious for a moment. "Who you got there?"

The coroner took a pair of scissors out of a drawer. His voice was medical. "Just a lady of the night."

"We pulled her out of the lake at Echo Park." Snow looked smug, like a child flaunting a secret. "You knew her."

The coroner closed his eyes and rubbed his forehead.

Wolf frowned. "*I* knew her?"

The coroner's Adam's apple bobbed up and down. "Snow, you don't mind if he helps the lady with her bicycle."

Wolf's smile had flattened into a thin line. "Are you trying to get rid of me, doc?" He took a deep, dreadful breath and reached for the sheet.

The coroner stopped his hand. "Why don't you wait until I clean her up?"

Wolf pushed the coroner's wrist aside and peeled back the sheet, revealing an oval face. "Oh, God!" He laid a hand over his eyes.

Eve's coiled hair was wet, streaked with dark pond muck and silt, and pinned to a crushed, veiled hat that must have once been white. She smelled of the lake. Her eyes were wide open, her pupils dark olives. She looked surprised. Her cheeks, which had always been suntanned, were colorless, as if she hadn't seen the sun in weeks.

Snow grinned proudly, like a child who had guessed the punch line of a clever joke. Wolf turned on the coroner and glared. "Why are you calling her a lady of the night? You know that girl's not a prostitute."

Snow nodded knowingly. "That's Eve McBride, our former matron. I seen her in the doorway of the Poodle Dog. So I knocked and asked. She uses a different name now. Lucinda or something. That confused me at first. But it was her. She told me to keep it quiet. She didn't want Joe to know. I said I would if I could screw her. So she let me screw her. Isn't that a gas? I screwed Matron McBride and the bitch cried . . ." Snow's dull eyes looked regretful. "I would have screwed her again, too, but now she's dead."

Wolf's lip curled in disgust, then he proffered a mean smile. "I had the same tender feelings about your mother."

Snow cocked his scarred head, as if wondering how Wolf knew his mother. Wolf looked weary. He rubbed his brow. "Do a kindness and keep your word. Don't tell Joe Singer. He doesn't need to know. You too, doctor. Let him think she's happily settled in Denver."

Snow waggled his head, smiling. "I bet Joe screwed her for free the whole time she was working here. She liked him."

Wolf's mouth hardened, and he cracked his knuckles.

The coroner stepped between them. His voice sounded sharp. "The body's on the slab now, Snow. Go help the lady find her bicycle."

Snow's eyes lit at the prospect of a pretty girl. He strode purposely toward the door.

Wolf bent over Eve, brushed a lock of hair from her once-beautiful face, and gently closed her eyes. "How did she die?"

The coroner scratched on a clipboard. "She drowned in the Lake at Echo Park. Apparently, she'd been out in a swan boat alone. They found it floating empty."

Wolf stared intently at the coroner's face. "Doctor, what do you think she was doing alone on a pleasure boat if she worked at the Poodle Dog? Those girls stay in."

"I'm just a physician," the coroner said with clinical detachment. "You'll need to ask someone more familiar with the recreational habits of whores."

Wolf grabbed the sheet and rolled it all the way back. Eve's legs splayed beneath an elegant white gown of soggy tulle and lace, molded to her body. The muddy veil, wadded at one side, would have reached the floor had she been standing. One wrinkled foot lay bare. Another swelled from a shoe that was much too tight. Wolf glared at the coroner. "Even you should know that a girl doesn't go boating in a wedding dress."

A voice came from the doorway, tentative and low. "Is she a brothel girl? A suicide?"

"No." Wolf yanked the curtain closed to hide the body. The curtain rattled on its metal hooks.

Joe eyes flashed disbelief and then peered at Wolf with suspicion. He growled, "Get out of my way." Joe tried to squeeze past Wolf.

Wolf blocked him and steered him by the arm back toward the door. "It stinks, Joe. I know. But why don't you let me handle this?"

Joe sidestepped Wolf and lunged for the curtain, giving it a firm yank. It rattled to one side, revealing the dead girl. Joe stared at Eve's body, expressionless. He turned to Wolf, opened his mouth, and shut it again. He scrunched up his face as the awful truth burrowed its way, violently, into his understanding.

With one strangled sob, Joe turned to the coroner and swung.

Anna lit a fire in her bedroom hearth, though it was one of the hottest days on record. She wore nothing at all. A smoky, wintery smell cut the air. The hummingbird buzzed at the feeder again. When the smoke streamed outside the window, the bird flew in circles and smacked into the glass, leaving an oily mark in the shape of its tiny body and falling to the ground. It added to her grief. She would find the little bird later and bury it in the wisteria.

She stoked the fire and tossed her books onto the blaze, one by one. She burned detective novels hidden under covers of acceptable books. *A System of Legal Medicine* went up in flames, along with *The History of Forensic Psychology* and the police procedural that she had stolen from the Venice police station the night she and Eve had been arrested. She said goodbye to Theo's medical books, because there was no way she could return them now, since she had ripped off their covers. They took a long time to burn.

She felt tragic, like a Cinderella without a fairy godmother. But she also felt relief. She was no longer carrying a dark, heavy secret—a rock in her stomach because she might be discovered. She could never, ever stop liking Joe Singer intensely, but Edgar had forgiven her and she could love him for that alone. She also had forgiven him. Though he had betrayed her, it had been driven by love. He loved her completely, even if her passion for him was only a bud. Now all she had to do was to keep her head down. If she could behave until Saturday, she would be Edgar Wright's chatelaine. She would have love, spending money, more freedom, and the chaperones would be out of a job.

Why did she feel so sad?

Someone knocked. Anna slipped into a robe de nuit. "Come in." She went to unlock the door from the inside.

Keys jingled in the hallway and six separate bolts turned, clicked, and slid before Mrs. Morales pushed open the door. "Goodness. It's sweltering in here. Why in heaven's name do you have a fire going?"

"Because this house is full of icy hearts." Anna tilted her chin toward heaven, though God never listened.

Mrs. Morales remained impassive. "You have letters, Miss Anna." She handed Anna two envelopes and left.

The envelopes had already been opened, the letters read and censored. She wondered if there had been others that had not made it through—a love letter from Joe, perhaps, telling her to meet him at midnight so that they could run away together. It made her whole body ache.

Anna waited until Mrs. Morales had turned all six bolts before she unfolded the letters and read. The first came from Clara, saying her aunt had died and she was coming home. She asked whether Anna had come to her senses and, if so, would she join them for a Looloos game because Theo liked the pitcher. Anna scratched a quick reply accepting the engagement and sprayed it with lavender water. She didn't bother to seal the envelope. She knew it would just be steamed opened and read before it was delivered.

The second letter came from a "Mrs. Eunice Partridge." Anna's heart skipped a beat. She doubted whether corresponding with a madam was advisable for a girl whose status had only recently been restored to golden. But the letter had made it through the censors and so she read it.

> Dear Miss Blanc,
>
> Thank you for your interest in our home for wayward girls. I wish I were there to oversee the property, but I'm still enjoying the mayor's hospitality. One of the girls, a Mrs. McBride, is no longer with us. She bought a farm across the river. It's a better place.
>
> Sincerely,
>
> Mrs. Eunice Partridge.

The letter was cryptic, but the message as clear as glass. Eve was dead, presumably at the hands of the killer. Madam Lulu still languished in jail, and there was no one to look out at the brothels. Anna ripped the letter into a hundred pieces and flung it into the fire. She wished she hadn't read it. Anna had doomed Eve to the brothels. Now she was dead. Anna had failed to catch the killer when she'd had the chance. Now there was nothing she could do.

That afternoon, Anna would see no one, not even Edgar. She claimed to have a headache and wouldn't come down for dinner. She refused to take food in her room. Instead, she sat at her toilet table in a black gown, combing her hair until the brush choked with long strands and had to be cleaned.

Above the mirror, Christ hung on the cross and looked down at her with sorrowful eyes. Edgar gazed out at her from a framed photograph on the glass counter. He looked handsome, and a smile lurked under his lips, as if he had some secret. She lifted a mirrored tray that held her silver comb and brush. Underneath, the Arrow Collar Man stood bare-legged in his shirt suit, looking almost as good as Joe Singer. Beside him, Eve and Anna were taped together, holding a sign and smiling. Anna looked fancy and feathered, like a white bird of paradise. Eve wore a dark, simple frock like the other marchers. Now Anna could see that Eve had been a beauty in disguise, like Anna herself when she'd worked at the station.

She kissed Eve's image, set the picture down, and began to brush her hair again, keeping company with her image in the mirror. She looked beautiful, just like Joe said. But, like he also said, beauty was only skin deep. She wasn't a good person. She was a selfish person and a useless person who really couldn't fry an egg. Her life had no meaning. No wonder God punished her.

Why hadn't she tried to get Eve out of the brothel? She could have given her some jewelry to sell and the little money she had earned in salary after the cost of her uniforms had been deducted from her pay. She could have told Joe that Eve was in the brothel. He would have helped her. Eve would have been humiliated and angry, but at least she would be alive. She thought Joe had forgiven her for getting Eve fired—at least he seemed forgiving when he was licking her leg in the dressing room; but he could never forgive her this. Her pretend police lover, the man she missed intensely, he would despise her.

Anna couldn't bear to languish in her room. She had to make it right. She couldn't raise the dead, but she could catch Eve's killer, and she could find Eve's children and try to convince Clara to raise them, as Anna didn't much care for children. As for the consequences if Mrs. Morales discovered her missing, Anna just wouldn't think about it.

She scrambled to the door and slid the bolt, locking it from the inside, so Mrs. Morales could not get in. She rattled the window. The locksmith had nailed it shut, but the pane was big enough to accommodate her body if she could remove it. She set her talking machine to play "By the Light of the Silvery Moon" on the loudest setting, then dragged the thick satin coverlet from her bed and fastened it over the curtain rod with hat-pins, covering the window. She lifted an eighteenth-century chair and wielded it like a battering ram, smashing through the glass.

Anna rummaged through a trunk and found the veil. Holding the veil in her teeth, she wrapped towels around each hand and climbed through the broken window out onto the roof. Tucking the hem of her gown into her waistband, she shimmied down the rope and bolted for the brothels.

Anna knocked at the back door of Canary Cottage, breathing her own hot breath beneath the veil. She could smell food burning. A woman in her mid-twenties answered the door—a big girl with a chestnut bun and a gob full of chewing gum. She wore heavy makeup, curlers, and a filmy off-the-shoulder blouse. "What are you doing here?"

Anna blew out a puff of breath that rippled her veil. "Lulu said you were short a girl."

"Three girls. One's passed. One got married. One's got sores." The woman flipped up Anna's veil and let her eyes roam over Anna's body. She raised an eyebrow. "Huh. I'm Charlene. Come on in."

The door led to the kitchen. In a breakfast nook, a young girl was drinking a glass of milk. She was tiny, doll-like, with blond curls and a voice like bells. She smiled at Anna, revealing a gap between her tiny front teeth. A creamy milk mustache spread across her upper lip. Charlene shifted her weight to one voluptuous hip. "Big Cindy, we got a new girl. What's your name, honey?"

This time, Anna was ready with her alias. "Aimee Amour."

Big Cindy grinned and shook Anna's hand. "I like your name. It's a real killer."

Charlene assessed Anna from behind. "Why don't you take her upstairs and show her the ropes. She can have Peaches' bed."

To Anna's surprise, Big Cindy took Anna's hand again in her soft small one and smiled. "Come on now, Aimee." She led Anna across the expansive dance floor to the staircase that led up to the balconies. The wooden railings shone with polish. Big Cindy began to climb. "Second floor's got little rooms for entertainin', and we got a lawyer who boards there whenever his wife kicks him out." She giggled. "He likes Dolly, the piano player." Anna's fist went to her mouth.

They proceeded to the third floor where the girls lived. Big Cindy had shared a room with Peaches. It was filled with childhood relics—a rag doll, a *Child's Garden of Verses*, a little silver cup filled with baby teeth, and two twin brass beds with soft pillows stuffed with goose feathers. Big Cindy sat on the bed and tucked her feet beneath her bottom. She patted the space beside her. Anna sat on the quilt, which had every mark of being made by a grandmother.

Big Cindy picked at a hole in the quilt where the batting poked out. "Don't worry sweetie. Compared with a lot of jobs, this is duck soup." She shrugged. "The scratch is good. The rake-off's fair. For every man you entertain, Lulu gets eighteen, you get eighteen, plus more for selling drinks. But you got to pay a fine to the mayor every week. Plus some complimentary attention. You got any experience?"

Anna shook her head.

"Okay. Some of the customers, they're gonna give you chestnuts—'I love you,' 'Let's run away together,' that kind of thing. You send chestnuts right back. Got it?"

"Got it," Anna said.

Big Cindy pulled up her knees and wrapped her arms around them. "Don't believe 'em and don't loan 'em money, because they never pay you back."

Anna nodded. "All right."

Big Cindy leaned closer and whispered. "If you don't mind my saying, with your looks, you're a nut not to go to the Poodle Dog. That's where the real coin is. They charge a hundred dollars for dinner and a girl."

Anna raised her eyebrows.

Big Cindy pulled a face. "I know. I wouldn't want to live with Madam

Monique either. That's okay. You'll have a boss time here, and you're so beautiful you'll make loads of cash, more than most your customers. But save every penny. In a couple of years, you could open a store or somethin'. You don't wanna end up slaving in a factory or having to marry some goop you don't like. He'll get all your money the minute you say 'I do.'" Big Cindy tapped her teeth. "Let's see. Oh yeah. You need a story."

Anna looked puzzled. "A story?"

Big Cindy cocked her head. "You know, where you come from. You can be whoever you want to be. But I recommend you don't be who you really are."

"Who are you?" Anna asked.

Big Cindy tossed her hair and put on a bad posh accent, lifting one hand in the air as if it were dripping with jewels. "I'm a society girl who lost her fortune in the bank panic." She giggled.

Anna shifted on the quilt. "Me too."

"No, that's mine. You be an actress or somethin'."

"But what's your real story?"

"Me? It isn't interesting. My pop's dead. I got eight younger siblings and they eat like termites, so I send money home."

Anna bit her lip and frowned. Big Cindy shrugged. "Let's see. Wash him before, you after. Prevents disease."

"What about during?" Anna had no intention of having a "during," but the details would be interesting.

"We got a peep hole for training."

Anna blinked.

Madam Lulu rustled in with some bright, silky frocks and things on hangers. "Big Cindy, she's a detective undercover. She don't need to know technique."

Anna's gray eyes widened. "Madam Lulu?"

"She's with the LAPD?" Big Cindy leaned away from Anna.

Madam Lulu rolled her eyes. "God no. She's from the DDDA. The Dumb Debutante Detective Agency. You don't tell nobody, you hear? And look out for her. She doesn't have a lick of sense."

Anna threw up her hands. "How did you get out of jail?"

"I gave the mayor ten thousand dollars. Of course it were counterfeit, but he don't know that yet." Madam Lulu winked. She handed Anna the frocks. "These belonged to Peaches. She'd want you to have 'em."

Anna inspected the florid things. "You act like you were expecting me. Like you knew I would come."

Madam Lulu grunted. "I know everything."

Anna picked out a short, scarlet dress and held it up against her. It was as red as blood, made of chiffon, and hit just above the knee. The arms were sheer, the neckline cut low. It was skimpier even than her bathing suit. "Jupiter."

"Men are like bulls, red steams 'em up," Madam Lulu said. Anna wondered what a steamed-up man looked like. Then she remembered the dressing room and being tangled with Joe and how their heat had made the mirror foggy. Her heart ached.

Madam Lulu tossed Anna a long blond wig. "You'll wanna wear a disguise."

Anna shook her head. "I assure you. I won't know anyone."

"Trust me, kid," Madam Lulu said with a pointed look. "Charlene! You got that powder? Charlene's my right-hand man. She told me you were here."

Anna looked confused. "She knows me?"

Madam Lulu rolled her eyes. In a moment, Charlene appeared at the door and handed Madam Lulu a packet of white powder. Madam Lulu nodded thank you. "Princess, you need to be seen goin' upstairs with one or two customers to maintain your cover. We're gonna handpick drunk, docile ones for you." She handed the powder to Anna. "Slip a teaspoon of this in their drinks before they get you upstairs. Stall them until they black out."

"Just leave 'em on the bed," Charlene said. "They'll be out for a while."

"This is a three-minute enterprise," Madam Lulu said. "If they blink, they'll miss it. When they wake up, tell them they missed it."

Charlene smiled lasciviously. "And they were sooo good."

Madam Lulu, Big Cindy, and Charlene whooped at the joke. Anna smiled, though she wasn't sure she understood.

Chapter 38

Night enveloped the brothel like a dark window dressing. Anna paced alone in Peaches' bedroom, while ragtime music floated in from the grand salon. It reminded her of Joe Singer and made her feel breathless and desolate. She looked in the mirror and saw an entirely different girl—a blond with conspicuous Princess Pat cheeks, carmine heavy on her lips, a crown of silk flowers, and Bohemian hair that trailed down to her elbows like the curly tendrils on a grape vine. Her eyes were lined with Kohl and her knees showed under the hem of her flimsy gown. She shook her head at the spectacle. How she wished she were undercover at the Poodle Dog, where the girls had better taste.

What would her father think? What would Edgar think? She knew what they would think. What would Joe Singer think?

She took Cook's paring knife from her purse, wrapped it in burlap from a potato sack she had found in the kitchen, and fastened the makeshift sheath onto her garter. She reinforced it with a second garter. The garters made a nice tool belt, though the lace was stiff and chafed a little. She flipped on a floor lamp and spun around to look at herself from behind. When backlit, the gown was ever so sheer.

She saw the silhouette of her petticoats, plain and clear for anyone to see. Anna scrunched up her face in distress. She could not go through with it. She couldn't go out in front of all those men dressed like an actress in her underwear. Madam Lulu would simply have to find a different girl to investigate—someone more selfless, who was willing to expose herself for the good of womankind.

Anna sat on the grandmother quilt, feeling defeated, uselessly righteous, and unredeemable. She raised one leg and unhitched a frilly black garter. If this was what being a detective took, if this was what being a good person took, she didn't have it in her. She was going to get out of the brothel as soon as possible, climb back up the tree and through the broken window before anyone missed her, and hope that Joe would solve the crimes.

Madam Lulu burst in without knocking. She wore yards of cherry red taffeta. "Look at you. Your mother'd be proud."

Anna snorted miserably. Her mother would drop dead, if she hadn't been dead already.

"Then I'm proud," Madam Lulu said. "Here. I got you a little present." She handed Anna a glossy mahogany box. Anna opened it. Lying on blue velvet lining was a shiny new pistol.

"A rod!" Anna snatched it from the box and examined it. The gray steel cooled her hand. It smelled faintly of oil. She held it out straight and looked through the sight, aiming at a large stuffed bear.

Madam Lulu smacked a box of bullets down on the toilet table. "It's a Browning, semi-automatic. Have you shot before? I mean, besides shooting Joe?"

Anna pretended to shoot. "Yes. I stole my father's hunting rifle once and shot cabbages in the garden. Briefly. I was caught."

"Ya just pull the trigger. Here, hitch up your skirts and heel yourself." She tossed Anna a thigh holster.

Anna caught it, set the presents down, and threw her arms around Madam Lulu. "Thank you." She kissed her rouged cheek.

Madam Lulu flushed as florid as a fire truck. "Good god, girl, get off me." Anna dropped her arms and backed off, smiling. Madam Lulu took a bottle from the dresser and sprayed Anna in the face with a cloud of rose perfume. It went straight up Anna's nose and made her eyes water. She sneezed.

"Now go kill 'em, Princess. And don't talk prissy," Madam Lulu said.

Anna looked at her reflection in the mirror. The half-naked Bohemian blonde with the overly rosy cheeks stared out at her, looking unsure. Then she remembered Eve, smiling at the march, and how she was dead, and how a million Hail Marys could not bring her back.

Anna strapped the holster to her thigh, next to Cook's paring knife, and inserted the pistol. She slid them around to the back of her leg and practiced strolling with them. With the gun, Anna felt more like a detective. Maybe she could do this thing for Eve if she got to keep the gun.

Madam Lulu gave her a shove. "Go!"

Anna took a deep breath and passed through the door.

Anna stood on the balcony overlooking the grand salon, and stared down at a sea of hatless male heads, some bald, some covered in hair. A large black man and a young woman with an elaborate wig pounded out turkey-trot rags on the two Steinways, playing a sort of mad duet. Girls and men danced, holding each other in sweaty embraces, stepping high, flapping their arms, and swinging their legs around like the hands on a clock. Anna saw Big Cindy's blonde curls shimmy violently across the floor. A few fools ate the chicken Anna had smelled burning earlier. Everyone drank benzene. The crowd spun so dizzily, Anna felt as if she'd been drinking whiskey, too.

Charlene, her eyes as red as wine, led a soft, pink-faced man up the stairs to a room where dark and mysterious deeds were done. Her lips were curled in a hazy smile. The lascivious look in his pig eyes, and her solicitude, made Anna's stomach sick. When he tried to kiss Charlene's mouth, Charlene turned her cheek.

Anna felt guilty. She would never have to make love to an odious stranger. She would conduct her investigation and go home to her father, Edgar, and their money. Anna had an ambitious plan—to meet each and every man, compile a list of suspects for investigation, and avoid the doing of dark deeds. She would casually ask men about their lives, their religion, and when they had come to town, because Madam Lulu said the killings had started in January. If she were lucky, one of the men might ask her to meet him on the side.

Anna descended the stairs. She reached the first floor and wondered if she knew anything at all about the world. "Jupiter." A man from her parish sat on a barstool singing, "My Sweet Marie from Sunny Italy." He was terrible.

Madam Lulu came up behind Anna. "Told ya you'd need a disguise." She waltzed off into the room, greeting guests with grand gestures, her fox stole swaying to the music. No sooner had Anna clipped off the last step, than Snow came in with several patrolmen from the force. They were laughing. Anna froze, standing like the statue of a nymph, as if that would somehow make her invisible. Snow's eyes perused her. He grunted his pleasure and drifted over to the bar, proving either that her disguise was a success or that Snow was an idiot.

Anna crossed the room proffering tight, disgusted smiles. She wouldn't speak to any man of her acquaintance. She already knew something of their lives and it was too risky. She would simply add their names and information to her list. As she wandered through the dizzying crowd, someone began to wail, "Aaaaaa Naaaa!" Panic choked her. She broke for the stairs. Small arms clamped around her middle. She tried to pull free, but her feet got tangled and she fell to her to her knees. One stocking pulled and ripped. Anna covered her face with her hands and trembled. She knew the voice. It was Douglas Doogan, fresh back from his trip to Cincinnati. He could send every eye in the room her way, just by calling her name.

The large black piano player leapt from his bench and delivered a blow to Douglas Doogan's neck. He pried him off Anna and dragged him to the door, hurling him into the night. A customer lifted Anna to her feet and brushed her off, planting an unwanted, one-hundred-proof kiss on her cheek. Anna wriggled away. The crowd went on merrymaking, as if tackling Anna Blanc in a brothel happened every day.

Anna retreated to a corner, shrinking behind a plaster statue of Venus, who, oblivious to the crush, calmly admired herself in a mirror. Anna cast her eyes to the floor. Madam Lulu's cherry skirts swished into Anna's line of vision. Trembling, Anna hiccupped the words, "He recognized me. Douglas Doogan recognized me."

"Yeah, but Douglas Doogan's half dog. He didn't recognize you by sight, he sniffed you out. You look more like me than you do like you, so I wouldn't worry about it."

Anna had to agree. She didn't recognize herself.

Madam Lulu punched her arm. "Buck up. People see what they expect to see. No one expects you here. There's not another man in this room who looks at you and sees Anna Blanc. And if he did, he wouldn't believe his eyes."

It took several minutes before Anna had the courage to leave the corner and begin her task again. She moved stiffly, like a china doll, introducing herself to new faces, batting her lashes furiously. "Say, are you Catholic?" Men liked to talk about themselves, especially when they were drunk. She pretended to admire them, flattered them, and pried friendly fingers off her body. When men invited her upstairs, Anna made excuses and slipped away. She made periodic trips to the smoky, burnt-smelling kitchen to record names and facts in a notebook. No one asked to meet her on the side.

Big Cindy snuggled up to Snow at the bar, trying to get him to buy her a drink. She winked at him with pinprick pupils. Anna watched with narrowed eyes. Madam Lulu came behind Anna. "Biggy's my best B-girl. Sells more whiskey than the rest of 'em put together."

Snow bought Big Cindy a whiskey. She elbowed him in the ribs. "Now you're talkin'!" Charlene brushed by and, quick as a wink, exchanged Big Cindy's full glass for an empty one. Cindy slammed the empty shot glass on the bar. "Another!" Charlene gave the full whiskey glass to the bartender and he sold it to Snow a second time. Anna raised her eyebrows in respect.

She heard shouting and turned to see the piano player muscling another man toward the door. The man had a thin, stiff mustache. One side had bent in the wrong direction.

Anna pushed back her fake hair. "Who's that?"

Madam Lulu scoffed. "Miguel Martinez. Spanish devil."

Anna's face soured with distain. "The one who drugs young girls and ruins them? And you allow him in here?"

"Does it look like I allow him in here?"

Charlene swayed over and bumped into Anna, towing a staggering man by the shirtsleeve. She tipped his chin up with one finger. He leaned like the tower of Pisa, slobbering from the corner of his mouth.

It was Louis Taylor.

Anna pressed two fingers to her lips. "Jupiter."

Charlene winked. "Aimee Amour, this gentleman wanted to meet ya. Why don't you get him a drink?"

"Deeeelighted." Anna swished off to the bar and discreetly mixed him a drink—two parts whiskey, one part spit, and a heaping double helping of the mysterious white powder. She swirled it around, and delivered it to her former lover with a nasty smile. Louis mouthed the edge of the glass like a suckerfish and slurped it down.

He swayed. Anna helped him to the floor with a discrete shove. He collapsed unconscious.

Madam Lulu scoffed. "Weakling."

Anna knelt beside him and bent down as if to kiss his sweaty face, and left a perfect imprint of her carmine lips on his shirt collar. "A little message for Mrs. Curlew-Taylor." She wiped any invisible trace of Louis Taylor from her mouth, inadvertently smearing her rouge from her lips to her cheek.

"Didn't you marry him?" Madam Lulu asked.

Anna looked up and made a face.

"God damn it, girl. Go fix your kisser."

As there is nothing more gruesome than makeup done wrong, Anna hurriedly complied. She weaved her way through the guests and pattered up stairs. When Snow saw Anna go by, he followed her, his dull eyes glued on her swaying hips.

Anna continued past the second floor, where she heard moans and high-pitched cries, like bird calls, from behind closed doors. She jogged to her room on the third floor, where there was no one, no party, just relative quiet. The calm lulled her, and for a moment she let down her guard. She put her room key into the lock and jiggled it.

A man pushed her from behind, pinning her against the wood with his bulk. "I'd like a screw." His breath was foul with decay and whiskey. The voice and the smell were familiar. Officer Snow.

Anna's muscles turned to rock. "I ain't on duty now." She slipped her hand down, trying to reach her knife.

He pressed against her harder, trapping her arms at awkward angles. "This won't take long."

She winced. "I ain't on duty, I said."

Snow made a stupid, grunting pig sound. "Don't I know you? You sound familiar."

Anna glued her chin to her chest, letting her curls drape the sides of her face. "No. I'm new."

"Hey! Look at me when I'm talking to you." Snow stepped back so he could grip her head with two hands and tried to force it around. She resisted, keeping her nose to the door, but her jig was up. As her neck gave way to his force, she heard a twang, like the time she'd run into a flagpole.

Snow yowled. He grabbed his neck and bent over, protecting his head with his elbows. Big Cindy stood behind him with an iron poker. She yanked Anna by the arm and dragged her around the corner, down the stairs to the second level.

The girls slipped into an empty room and leaned against the wall to breathe. Anna glanced at Big Cindy and then at the poker.

"Lulu's room's got a fireplace," Big Cindy said. "You should see it. It's got a bear skin rug and a canopy bed . . ."

"Thanks."

Big Cindy grinned. She took out a linen handkerchief, spit on it, and began to wipe the wayward rouge from Anna's cheek. "Snow's gonna be mad. But we'll just say Douglas Doogan did it. He'll thank us." She giggled.

Anna looked about the room. The wallpaper had fuzzy *fleur de leis*. Drapes in toreador red hung across a window that opened over the party below.

The lights went out. A moment later, the lights went back on and the party continued. Anna walked to the window, pulled aside the curtains, and looked down. "What was that?"

"Oh, that's the mystery man." Big Cindy put on a whisper. "He likes to keep his visits secret."

"I would think they'd all like to keep their visits secret."

Big Cindy shook her head. "Naw. Most of 'em are proud to be here. Plus, the mystery man pays extra."

"Surely the girls know who he is."

"Names, na uh. We know what they feel like, you know—if he has a mustache, or if he's real skinny." Big Cindy put a hand up and poked at her curls.

"There's more than one? How many are there?" Anna realized she was sitting on the bed. She quickly leapt up, brushing off her bottom.

Big Cindy shrugged. "It's hard to keep track."

"Can I get a list of . . . physical characteristics?"

"Are you crazy? Lulu would skin me alive. She won't give up her mystery men. It ain't right. Besides . . ." Big Cindy raised her eyebrows. "They're money bags."

She scooted to the door. "I think it's safe, now." She raised her hands gracefully above her head and waltzed into the hall.

Anna followed. "Can I go with the mystery man?"

Madam Lulu loitered nearby, leaning over the rail. She smoked a cigar, a ratty green cape draped over her arm. When she saw Anna, she drawled, "I've been lookin' for you."

"Aimee wants to meet the mystery man," Big Cindy said.

Madam Lulu frowned. "No. Anyway, he's not your man."

"But how do you know?" Anna asked.

"I know." Madam Lulu handed Anna the cape. "We're going to visit Monique. Miracle of miracles. I convinced the bitch to let you in."

Big Cindy giggled. "I bet that took a lot of dog biscuits."

"Nope. The first girl killed in January worked at the Poodle Dog. She wore a white dress, blue garters, and had a sixpence in her shoe."

Chapter 39

Anna and Madam Lulu slipped down New High Street. Lulu's ratty green cape covered Anna from neck to toe, except for the moth holes. Outside a beer mill, she saw Tilly lurking with his camera, probably hoping to snap compromising photos of someone, like he had done to Anna. She shrunk into her cape.

They arrived at the back door of the Poodle Dog and knocked. Monique opened the door in a stunning *robe de soiree* with an empire waist, a cut velvet overgown, and a three-foot train. Her hat had black feathers that looked like horns. Anna eyed the gown appreciatively but frowned at the hat.

Monique gave Anna a scornful once over. "This is your detective?"

"That's her," Madam Lulu said.

Monique made a face. "*Mon Dieu*! She can't come in like that. My girls are courtesans! She looks like a licentious clown."

Anna took off the cape, displaying the slippery red costume that hit just above her knees. Monique groaned.

Madam Lulu clicked her tongue. "Yeah. I was gonna ask if she could borrow somethin'."

Monique gave a big, French sigh of disgust. Anna was too distracted to be insulted. She looked past Monique into the parlor where a group of men—men she knew—played cards. An unjustly beautiful woman, in an evening gown that could almost be from the House of Doucet, smoothly lit a man's cigar.

The burning stick rested between familiar lips, beautiful lips that she had wanted to kiss. The lips belonged to Edgar Wright.

Anna squinted in confusion, not trusting her eyes. It took a moment to believe them. Her fiancé, *her* Edgar, was welcoming the attentions of a whore in front of Mayor Smucker and a parlor full of her father's business associates. Edgar was betraying her. In public.

The unjustly beautiful woman made a quip stolen from Oscar Wilde, and the men surrounding her laughed. She laid a hand on Edgar's shoulder, put her lips to his ear, and whispered. He smiled and whispered back.

Anna saw red. She forgot about murder, forgot about her cover, and shoved past Monique.

Monique barked, "Stop!"

Anna flew through the elegant parlor like a cardinal protecting her nest. She spooked the elegant woman and landed before Edgar, hands on hips. Edgar gave the pretty little misfit an amused, indulgent smile. "Well, hello there."

Anna's lip curled up. "Hello, Edgar."

Though he hadn't known the painted face, he knew the voice. Anna and Edgar locked eyes. He spoke the words slowly. "My God."

Anna cocked her arm and punched him in the eye. What she lacked in technique, she made up for with temper. The blow knocked the cigar from his lips and onto the rug, spraying the fancy whore with ash. The mayor and the businessmen burst into laughter, as if the little tart's jealous rage and Edgar's predicament was somehow charming.

In the doorway, Monique put fingers to her temples. She hissed at Madam Lulu. "*Mon Dieu*! You bring me a romantic fool who strikes my customers?"

"Yeah. That didn't work out," Madam Lulu said.

Anna bolted for the foyer, past Monique, and out the door. Anger and the enormity of it swallowed her. She could never marry a man who slept with brothel girls, but that point was moot. Not even Heathcliff would espouse his Cathy if he'd found her in a brothel dressed like a whore. They had each crossed a line and could never go back. There would be no wedding. She would never forgive Edgar for betraying her. Never.

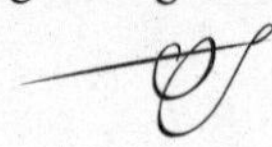

Monique called to Anna, who was flying across the back lawn. "You stupid girl! He comes for business. Only business!" Monique spewed a string of sharp words in French.

Madam Lulu put hands on hips and whined in a Parisian accent. "*Mon dieu*!" She picked up her skirts and ran after Anna. "Hey princess! Wait for me!"

Anna flew through back yards and alleys. On the street, her outfit would get her vagged. She slowed to a walk as she approached Canary Cottage, hyperventilating from the shock. The backyard had an outhouse, and a tatty lawn with lots of brown spots. A rainbow of colorful drawers fluttered on a clothesline in the moonlight. Anna held onto the metal laundry pole and leaned a hand on her knee, gulping empty, shallow breaths. Madam Lulu skid into the yard like a hippo on roller skates. "I'm guessing the wedding's off."

Anna gasped. "My whole life is off."

"Oh. You think he's gonna tell all the society people you was in the brothel and they'll kick you out of their little club?"

Anna shook her head vigorously. "No. He's too much of a gentleman. And besides, it wouldn't reflect well on him."

"What then?" Madam Lulu asked. "Those other men didn't see you. They saw a feisty little whore with a crush on one of her customers. It ain't the first time."

"It isn't only that," Anna said. "Father and Edgar are business partners. Without Edgar, our bank is in trouble. And father owes Edgar a tremendous lot of money. He can't pay it back. No one's going to marry me now—not with a scandalous elopement, a broken engagement, and no fortune."

Madam Lulu looked her up and down. "Oh, I don't know. You got other assets."

"I'll die father's prisoner in some poor house! Or, worse yet . . ." Anna's words came out like a sob. "I'll have to become a nun!"

Madam Lulu grunted. "I never thought Edgar Wright was good for Anna Holmes or Anna Blanc."

"I used to think Edgar was very good for me. I thought he was a good man." Anna looked up and searched Madam Lulu's eyes. "Could Monique be telling the truth? Could it be that he was only there for business?"

Madam Lulu shrugged. "Lots of business is conducted in brothels."

Anna put her head in her hands and moaned. "You mean, he's innocent?" She looked up quickly, eyes wide. "Does my father go to the Poodle Dog?"

"Like I said, lots of business is conducted in brothels."

Anna squeaked in distress. She wondered if she knew anything at all about the world. "I'm such a fool. I've ruined my life. I risked my cover. If only I'd been more measured."

Madam Lulu reached into her cleavage for a cigar and chewed the end off. She lit it. "Princess, you ruined this life. You'll find another one."

Anna's lower lip trembled. "My old life was boring, but this will be worse. We'll have to sell the house and live in a shack that I'll likely have to build myself. I won't be allowed to leave our shanty. Old friends will bring me charity hams and gossip about how I couldn't keep a man."

Madam Lulu drew in a long breath from the cigar and let the smoke slip between a gap in her front teeth. "I heard you had something going with Joe Singer."

Anna's head snapped up. She looked at Madam Lulu for a long second. A madam was an excellent confessor when no priest was at hand, perhaps better than a priest, as they held to the same code of secrecy, assigned no penance, and were less likely to judge. Anna sighed with her whole body. "I like him intensely. But I doubt he'll ever speak to me again."

Madam Lulu chuckled. "Hmm. What'd ya do?"

Anna's voice went squeaky and high. She wrung a handful of her silky gown. "I killed Eve. It's my fault she's dead."

"You screwed her good, but I wouldn't go that far."

Madam Lulu took out a second cigar, bit off the end and lit it. She handed it to Anna, who mindlessly inhaled and coughed.

"He used to kiss me when we were working undercover. It was part of the job, but I could tell he didn't mind."

Madam Lulu raised one eyebrow. "I thought it was the other way around."

Anna fumbled her cigar and it rolled into the grass. She flushed. "What do you mean?"

Madam Lulu picked up the cigar, snuffing it out on the metal pole. "I thought you kissed him and you didn't mind."

Anna searched Madam Lulu's face with suspicious eyes. "How would you know that?"

"I know everything."

"Well, you're wrong. It was he that kissed me. The first time, anyhow. And I showed him just how much I minded."

Madam Lulu puffed away. "Uh huh." She handed Anna the snuffed out cigar. Anna stuck it down her cleavage.

"I suppose that the second time, *I* kissed him. Very thoroughly." She sighed. "And the third time. We were extremely thorough. I only ever kissed him for police purposes, you understand."

"Uh huh." Madam Lulu leaned against the pole.

"But by the third time I was lost—hopelessly liking him intensely." Anna straightened. "But one can't trust passion. Luckily, I knew better than to let feelings rule my heart."

Madam Lulu blew out a big cloud of smoke. "That's stupid."

Anna frowned.

The women's conversation floated through the cut-out moon on the outhouse door. The occupant, relieving himself of his whiskey, heard every word. Detective Snow, his head still throbbing, finally placed Anna's voice and strained to make sense of it. Matron Holmes was at Canary Cottage confiding in Madam Lulu about screwing Joe Singer.

Matron Holmes was married—the LAPD required it. She was also engaged to a man named Edgar Wright and went by the name of Anna Blanc.

He peeked through the moon and caught a glimpse of Anna in her little red gown. She was the whore he was trying to screw when he got bashed on the head. She was three people having love affairs with three different men and selling her body on the side.

What a crazy, floozy bitch. She'd done a good job of keeping it a secret. He rubbed the bump on his head and sniggered. He'd be happy to spread the word.

Chapter 40

Madam Lulu took a drooping Anna by the arm and steered her from the laundry pole, through the smoky kitchen of Canary Cottage, and over to the bar. She settled Anna on a barstool amidst a group of drinking, whooping, laughing men. "Why don't you get somebody to buy you a drink?"

Anna nodded. A drink was exactly what she needed. She tentatively raised her eyes to the nearest man. In an instant, his wallet was out and she had a shot glass in her hand. Anna slammed the shot. He smiled and bought her another. And another. A different man stepped in. Unlike Big Cindy, Anna drank the whiskey men bought for her. Men bought Anna more drinks. She began to supersede Big Cindy as Canary Cottage's champion B-girl. Madam Lulu made the bartender switch Anna's drinks to colored water.

Anna didn't notice. She grieved for Edgar, a man she'd depended on and liked—a man she had planned to love someday. At the same time, she wondered whether liking Joe intensely was the same as being in love with him. If she were in love with Joe, then her tragedy doubled, because neither he nor Edgar could possibly forgive her.

The lights went out, leaving the room and Anna's soul in darkness. The heavy curtains blocked any moonlight. The crowd whooped and bellowed. Amidst the party sounds, a door slammed open, hitting the wall with a *bang*. There was the sound of shuffling feet. Light flooded the room. The fine officers of Central Station stood in their olive drab uniforms and black helmets, blocking the doors, hands on billy clubs.

A sergeant shouted, "You're all under arrest!"

Anna did what any levelheaded girl would do in her situation. She screamed.

Snow and the other cops who had been patrons that night changed sides, arresting girls they'd just loved for three minutes and men who'd bought them drinks.

The man from Anna's parish charged the bar. "Oh God! Oh God! Oh God!" Anna dove off her stool to get out of the way. He grabbed a bottle by the neck and smashed it against the wall. Glass shards sprayed the room. His eyes flitted around in desperation. He brandished his weapon at no one and ran upstairs.

Tilly, the photographer from the march, waded in against the flow of cops dragging men and girls to paddy wagons. He snapped pictures as fast as he could change film.

Anna bounced around the chaos like a hard-hit billiard ball, dizzy from drink. She sought refuge on her knees under a table. Glass and whiskey sprinkled the floor beneath her fingers and her pinky began to bleed. She looked up to see Officer Snow leering at her. "Good evening, Matron Holmes. Or is it Miss Blanc?"

The name "Blanc" pricked the ears of Tilly, who was being jostled nearby. He watched Snow yank Anna up by one arm.

Snow bent down and ran his veiny hand along Anna's exposed leg. "I'm glad to see you found another job."

"You rat! You cad! You cad rat!" she cried. Tilly turned his full attention to the scuffle between girl and cop. Anna ground the heel of her cheap shoe into Snow's fleshy foot and shoved him back. He let go of her momentarily. She scuttled off. Snow regained his balance and charged after her like an angry bull.

Anna drew her gun, set her stance wide, and pointed it at Snow.

"Miss Blanc?" Tilly shouted, on the off chance that pigs fly.

Anna looked on reflex. Tilly grinned behind a camera flash that made her see stars. Anna whirled on him and growled. She shot at his camera and the flash exploded. The bullet pierced the heart of the plaster of Paris Venus standing behind him. The goddess toppled to the floor. Tilly dropped the camera and it *thunked* to the ground. The eyes in his long, pockmarked face expanded in fear, and he raised his hands.

Wolf appeared and reached around from behind Anna, easily disarming her. "You shouldn't play with guns, pumpkin. You could hurt someone." He pocketed her beloved gun.

Anna stared at Wolf, panting. Her wild, false hair stuck to her damp skin. Wolf took her by her arm and steered her to the paddy wagon. He patted her bottom as she ducked inside.

Anna peered through the bars at Wolf, who went about his business, negotiating the mayhem, as if he didn't recognize her.

Snow approached Wolf, his teeth set in a gleeful smile. "You just arrested Matron Holmes."

Wolf's face contracted. "That girl? That little blond cherry? That can't be Matron Holmes."

Snow gave a lascivious snort. "I felt her with my own hands."

Wolf winced. "Well, go unarrest her!"

A junior patrolman tugged frantically on Wolf's arm. "There's a crazy man upstairs! He's waiving a broken bottle at everybody and smashing up Lulu's furniture."

"I'll get him." Wolf waded back into the fray, leaving Snow where he stood.

Reluctantly, Snow lumbered toward the paddy wagon to liberate Anna.

Tilly poked Snow's arm, jabbing until he stopped. "Hey! I'm with the paper. Is that Anna Blanc?"

Snow flashed a gargoyle grin. "Yeah, that's one of her names."

Tilly scribbled in a notebook. "One of her names?"

"She's been working as a police matron under the name of Anna Holmes."

Tilly shook his head. "What in the devil is she doing here?"

Snow made a noise between a grunt and a chuckle. "She fancies herself some kind of detective. She thinks whores are being murdered, but she's crazy. Whores aren't being murdered. They're committing suicide."

Tilly wrote faster. "Why does she think whores are being murdered?"

"Cause she's a stupid bitch."

"That's very interesting. And your name?"

"Detective Amos Snow."

Wolf came hurtling backward through an upstairs window, flailing in a waterfall of tinkling glass, and landed flat on his back on the lawn. He lay among the shards, unmoving. Snow rushed over and pried back one of Wolf's eyelids. He saw white. "Ambulance!"

The paddy wagon pulled out with a lurch. Men and girls were packed in like fish, scrooched up on benches and the black metal floor, panting their liquor breath into the close quarters. The men smelled sharp and foul and some trembled. From rage or fear, Anna couldn't tell.

Squished near the front, Charlene pushed down her cuticles. Madam Lulu looked bored. "I need to find a better counterfeiter."

Big Cindy began to tell Anna how sheep were sheered on her grandpa's farm up north in Mendocino. Anna sat half listening with her numb mind while the faces in the wagon spun in circles. Big Cindy hugged Anna from behind and pulled her close. "So when he's sitting up on his bottom, you snuggle 'em right against you, so you can get his tummy." Big Cindy released Anna. "And that's that."

Anna thought she might puke and screwed up her face. Big Cindy dug in her skirt pocket and handed Anna a flask of whiskey. "Oh, You're gonna suffer in the morning. You better have this with your biscuits." Anna sniffed it and it burned.

The caravan came to a screeching halt in front of Central Station. The cops herded the prisoners up the steps of the station for booking. The first time Anna had been arrested, butterflies of excitement had fluttered inside her, overwhelming any fear of punishment by her father. Now, she felt only dread. She wobbled on her heels, her dimpled knees bare for anyone to see, occasionally steadying herself on a nearby prisoner.

The prisoners lined up for booking, men and women alike. Big Cindy reached the front of the line and gave her name to Mr. Melvin. He spoke to his ledger. "That's one hundred dollars."

She ducked down and put her nose near his. "But Mr. Melvin, I didn't wallop any of your officers. I'm just here to get vagged."

Mr. Melvin blushed. "I know, Biggy. That's the fee for vagrancy tonight."

Big Cindy shook her head. "The mayor must be real mad. Heard he got caught trying to spend Lulu's smash at the Poodle Dog." She left the counter to be taken to the cells with the other girls until their fines could be paid.

Mr. Melvin cited the men for vagrancy, too, but only fined them twenty-five dollars and released them on the spot, if they could pay. Madam Lulu paid two hundred dollars for violation of the blind pig laws and vanished into the night without looking back.

Anna had the disheartening thought that she could have gotten the names of the men from Mr. Melvin without going into the brothels. She wouldn't have seen Edgar. She wouldn't now be under arrest. She would marry Edgar this Saturday, fall in love, and start a new life, albeit a dull one.

When Anna took her turn, she gave the name, "Aimee Amour."

When he heard her voice, a shadow flitted across Mr. Melvin's averted eyes. "One moment."

He stood and walked over to a brass peg on the wall, lifted down his coat, and returned to the desk. Without meeting her gaze, he handed it to her.

Anna tied the coat around her waist, tugging the sleeves tight. She pressed his hand. "Thank you, Mr. Melvin."

Officer Dodds, a patrolman that Anna knew, hustled her back into the paddy wagon with the other girls and drove them to the jail. He looked bored, and when he put her in the cell he didn't bother to frisk her or take her flask.

The cell's commode had not been emptied. The floor was sticky, and the hard, rough bench left splinters in her thighs. Big Cindy peeled a shard of wood from the bench and used it to scratch her name into the grey plaster wall. She handed it off and other girls followed suit.

Big Cindy smiled at Anna. "We always do it. I guess you wouldn't want to."

Somewhere down the corridor, a man shouted, "Wicked whores!" Anna's spine stiffened. She knew that vitriolic voice. He'd said something similar to Anna when she'd gone to his lecture. She set her chin in defiance and stood, took Cook's paring knife from her garter, and carved in big, deep, swoopy letters, "Aimee Amour."

The coroner shouted again, and it occurred to Anna that his voice came from one of the other cells. Her heart beat faster. He'd been jerked up. Joe Singer had arrested him sometime after Anna had spooned Joe in the dressing room.

Chapter 41

Chief Singer banged on Joe's apartment door. Joe opened in his nightshirt, squinting and tugging on his ear. The chief shoved him back into the house, a gale force wind, scaring his cat and nearly knocking him over. "You wanna tell me why Edgar Wright's leaving town? Why he's withdrawing his support and his money from Blanc National? No explanation. No warning. That bank is gonna fail!"

"Huh?" Joe asked, rubbing his eyes, which were very red. The knuckles on his left hand were swollen and bruised.

He shoved Joe again. "The wedding's off! I can't be sure, but I'm gonna wager it has something to do with you taking off his fiancée's drawers."

Joe's heart pounded sixteenth note triplets. "I didn't . . ."

His father cut him off. "Snow told me all about it. She's down at the station now. You see, there's been a brothel raid and she's been vagged. How much you got in your piggy bank 'cause I just talked to her daddy. He claims he doesn't have a daughter, and I can't imagine Edgar Wright's gonna pay her fine."

Joe squeezed his eyes. "Miss Blanc was at the brothels?" He slipped into his denim trousers and out of his nightshirt in one quick motion. He dug under his mattress and pulled out a wad of cash fastened with a money clip. He crammed the whole thing in his pocket.

"Yeah," the chief growled. "She thought she was investigating a murderer. Now she's in the cells. And I can't help but think you've got something to do with it!"

Joe threw on a shirt and fell onto the bench, pushing his feet into socks and shoes. The chief took a hat from the table and shoved it into his hands. "Go get your sweetheart, Joe!"

Joe sped along the inky streets, shirt untucked, his untied boots pounding the rocky asphalt, his shoelaces trailing through mud and horse shit. He flew up the station steps and through the doors, panting. The station was quiet. Everyone had been booked and was either at home or stewing in a cell. Joe charged over to Mr. Melvin, who held his lunch pail and hat. "Where's Miss Holmes?" he demanded.

Mr. Melvin cleared his throat. "Matron Holmes doesn't work here anymore. There is a remarkably similar girl, a Miss Aimee Amour, who's down at the jail."

Joe wiped sweat from his forehead with his sleeve. "I want to pay the fine for Aimee Amour, then."

Mr. Melvin coughed. "It's three hundred dollars."

Joe screwed up his face. "Three hundred? Isn't it normally fifty?"

"Tonight, it's one hundred. But the chief set Miss Amour's fine higher than the other girls." Mr. Melvin pushed the button that opened the cash register. "He said he wanted it to hurt."

Joe swore as he dug in his pockets for his money clip. He slapped it down in front of Mr. Melvin, dug in his other pocket for a beat up leather wallet, and emptied it onto the polished counter. It contained a few ratty bills. A few tarnished quarters, dimes, and pennies rolled in circles until they collided and collapsed. He counted the pile. "Here's fifty. I can give you two hundred and thirty tomorrow when the bank opens. More next time I get paid. But, that's all I got."

Mr. Melvin reached under the desk and produced Anna's gun. "It belongs to Miss Amour." He slipped a crisp twenty out of his pocket and added it to the pile. Joe looked at him gratefully. "I'll pay you back." He scooped up the gun, grabbed his uniform coat from the rack, and pounded out the door. He careened through the jail entrance, skidding on the wooden floor. "Let me in!"

The jailer raised his droopy eyelids. "Hey Joe, what's the big hurry?"

"I'll tell you later. Come on!" Joe banged on the bolted door to the cells.

The jailer unlocked the door and Joe hurtled through. He peered into every cell looking for Anna. The girls had settled down for the night, lying together on bunks, propped up against walls, trying to sleep. He looked from face to face. Finally, he called out, "Sherlock, where are you?"

Anna and Big Cindy curled around each other like two lap dogs, sharing Mr. Melvin's coat. Anna waited for her father to come like a storm cloud, to take her home and rain on her, to strike her with his lightening. It wouldn't be gentle Edgar this time. Anna didn't want to see either man, with their inevitable horror at her behavior, their lack of understanding. She wanted Joe Singer—to have him forgive her and share in her grief over Eve, to hold her and sing her songs, to kiss her and other things.

Joe Singer wouldn't come. Anna had caused the death of a woman he had cared about, maybe even loved. She held Big Cindy a little tighter and said a silent prayer to St. Leonard, patron saint of prisoners, that she would survive the lightning strike without too many bruises.

Anna heard Joe's voice echoing in the corridor, as if summoned by the saint. The miracle spread through her body like love. She looked up. "Officer Singer?" Maybe he hadn't heard about Eve and had come to bring her bread and water. She spread Mr. Melvin's coat across Big Cindy and padded to the door, grasping the bars with both hands. Her palms were dirty red from rust and blood. She wiped them on her legs. She could smell the whiskey on her own breath.

Joe peered uncertainly at Anna. She peered uncertainly back. She had wanted to know what Joe Singer would think of her going undercover in the brothels—whether he'd shun her, mock her foolishness, or admire her bravery. Looking at him now, he simply seemed worried. At least, Anna hoped that wasn't pity in his eyes.

Joe unlocked the cell, took her gently by the arm. "Sherlock, I know who you are and I still don't recognize you." His eyes went straight to her neckline, then down to her knees. "Good Lord." He draped his coat over her shoulders.

A terrible thought came to Anna. Joe wasn't visiting. He was bailing her out. "My father's not coming?"

"No." Joe slipped his arm through hers and guided her down the hall.

She glanced up, full of dread. "Why didn't they call him?"

"They did. He's . . . not coming."

"Why not?" In her heart she already knew.

Joe stopped and put his hands on Anna's arms. He gazed into her eyes. "Anna, he says he doesn't have a daughter." He held his breath and watched her crumble.

Her eyes blurred. "I see."

Anna felt like a tightrope walker, far, far off the ground and falling, and whose safety net had been taken away. She looked at Joe, her eyes raw and transparent. "I saw Edgar in the brothel. It's done between us. He only goes for business. But that's no excuse. There's no excuse for a man to be in a brothel."

"So you would never marry a man who goes to brothels, no matter the reason?"

"No."

Joe nodded. He held her up, kept her moving toward the door. Anna knew his friendship and comfort was temporary. He would despise her once he found out about Eve.

When they were alone in the mild night, he wrapped his arm around her and guided her toward the horse smells of the stables behind the station, where they had fought crime together in the straw that lovely, lovely afternoon. She pressed her eyes shut and felt him, inhaled the yummy scent of him and the tack and the hay, so she would remember. He would never kiss her again.

Joe sat Anna down on a hay bale. The baling wire poked her leg. She hardly noticed, though it ripped her dress and made her bleed. She took out her flask, unscrewed the cap, and swigged.

She watched Joe lead the black mare out of its stall and saddle it up. "Where are you taking me?"

"Home."

Joe lifted Anna onto the mounting block. Her shoes clunked on the wood. Straw dangled from her tattered stockings. She stuck the flask down her cleavage and grasped the horn, sticking the toes of one foot in the stirrup. Joe boosted her onto the horse. "You're gonna have to ride like a man." Her foot slipped, and she fell like a lump across the saddle. She felt a breeze on her behind through the gap in her two-piece drawers.

Joe tugged her skirt down. "Sweet Jesus." He helped her scooch her bottom around and straddle the horse. Her white legs glowed above her garters in the lamplight. He lifted the coat from her shoulders, spread it across her thighs, and swung up in front of her. Anna leaned against him and put her arms low around his waist, linking her fingers over his soft denim trousers.

Flushed and bemused, he twisted to see her. "You sure you can you hold on?"

"Yes." She clung to him. "But I can't go home. I won't go home."

"You gotta sleep somewhere. You got a friend or somethin'?"

"Clara. But, she can't see me like this. She'd disown me too, and she's all I have. I want to sleep with you."

Joe closed his eyes and grimaced. He waited a long time to answer, and Anna was afraid he'd say no. But where else could he take her? No reputable hotel would accept her.

He sighed resignedly. "OK. It's almost morning anyway." He made a clicking sound and the horse began to walk.

Anna hugged him and laid her cheek against his back. "Thank you, and thank you for arresting the coroner." She kissed his limp cotton shirt. "He didn't do it, you know."

"He's an accessory. He knew it was happening."

Anna swayed to one side, then another, leaning her chest against Joe. "Of course. He's protecting the killer." She yawned. "But I don't know why."

"I questioned him 'til he was punch-drunk and purple, Sherlock. He doesn't know who the killer is."

"Why would he protect someone he doesn't know?"

"Have you ever thought it might not be a person he's protecting but the act itself?"

"Jupiter. I think that's worse." Anna pulled out her flask and swigged.

An owl glided down from a palm tree and snatched a rat from the gutter without making a sound. The rodent dangled from its talons. Owls made it look so simple.

Anna took another swig.

"Go easy, Sherlock. You're already fallin' off the horse. Though, I have to say, you make as much sense drunk as sober."

"Benzene gives me courage." Anna took a big, burning swallow. She made a face. "I need lots of courage."

"I could use some courage."

Anna handed him the flask. Joe took it and stuck it in his boot. "Mighty kind."

Anna scowled, but was distracted by another thought. "You didn't arrest Snow?"

"Snow was off chasing a bicycle. Anyway, he can't spell 'was.'"

Anna squeezed Joe and smiled into his shirt. Joe shook his head. "Snow isn't smart; he doesn't think for himself. If the coroner says it's a suicide, he's gonna believe it. I doubt he even noticed that girls were being killed."

"How did I convince you that the murders were real?"

"I said I would follow the coroner, didn't I?"

Anna let go of Joe Singer.

She slid away from his body. She had assumed that, just this once, Joe had broken his promise, but no. He knew about Eve. Joe reached around and grabbed her before she toppled. "Hold on!"

She stared at the hand steadying her, perplexed. His rescue made no sense. His kindness made no sense. He couldn't know about Eve. She must have kept him too long in the dressing room, and he missed seeing the body. Someone told him about the girl and didn't tell him it was Eve.

Satisfied with her deduction, Anna scooted forward on the rough wool blanket and wrapped her arms around Joe's belly. She closed her eyes, pressed her lips to his shirt, and let them linger, savoring him. The axe would certainly fall, but not yet.

Joe was talking. "Everything happened like you said. The girl wore a wedding veil. She only wore one shoe, but it was too small and her toes were broken. There was a sixpence . . ."

"But you didn't see the girl. You couldn't have."

"I didn't see the coroner's wagon. You sent me to the cribs. They found the girl in Echo Park. I saw her in the morgue, with Wolf."

Anna's body went rigid, like a dead girl's.

He squeezed the arm around his waist. "Sherlock? You OK?"

Her words caught in her throat. "Why did you come for me, then, if you knew Eve was dead?"

His voice lifted in surprise. "You knew?"

"It's all my fault," she said. "Are you taking me off to shoot me? Because you can. I won't mind."

"Not on account of Eve, Sherlock. You didn't do it. Maybe for the stunt you pulled in the dressing room."

Anna fell silent. She laid her cheek against him and let the rhythm of the horse rock her, its hoofs cloppity clopping on the pavement. She knew then that she didn't like Joe Singer intensely. She loved him desperately.

When they reached Joe's apartment house, a thin line of sunshine glowed on the mountaintops. Anna's limbs hung like weights designed to foil her balance. Joe dismounted with a thump onto the dewy cement. She reached out, slid sideways into his arms, and smiled at him. He smiled faintly, propped her on his hip, and draped the horse's lead around a post.

The street was empty, save for a sprinkling cart, spraying water to settle the dust on the street, and a lone newsboy. The boy called out, "Hey Joe!" and tossed him a paper. Joe caught it in one hand. On the cover, in black ink, Anna held Snow at gunpoint. She looked surprised. Bold letters spilled across the page. "Socialite caught in brothel raid."

"Sherlock, I'm afraid your secret's out," he said.

Anna made a despairing sound. "But I shot his camera. I thought the picture was dead!"

Anna's arrest was now public property. Heartbreak overlaid heartbreak. In her mind, she said goodbye to Clara.

Joe guided Anna into his basement apartment, trying not to think of Edgar Wright's grand mansion on the hill. He kicked his nightshirt behind the door and blew out a breath. "Welcome to paradise."

The apartment held a sink, a homemade bench and table, and an upright piano that looked ready for the dump. Two cats slept curled up on a blanket on the floor. Oranges moldered in a bowl with fruit flies.

"It's very nice," she said.

Joe gave Anna an ironic half-moon smile. "Sit here." He took her around the waist and lifted her onto the table. She leaned against the wall. Her nose ran. Her kohl ran. Her chin was cut, her knees were skinned, her wig hung like a shaggy little dog. He sighed and shook his head. "Sherlock, you look like hell in its underwear."

She snorted.

He dipped a towel in cold water and gently washed her face. "You look terrible for you, which is still better than anybody else."

Joe smiled at her but felt leaden. Anna was in a pickle that made her unmasking at Boyle Heights seem like a cakewalk. He gently lifted off her wig and unpinned her hair. It tumbled down, past her shoulders in a messy mass, the way she would wear it to bed. He remembered Anna in her nightdress, all ruffles and lace. What would she sleep in now? His nightshirt? He closed his eyes and imagined himself in bed with her wearing no nightshirt, which he shouldn't imagine because she wasn't his girl.

Joe allowed himself to run his hands through Anna's hair once, on the pretense of arranging it. It slipped through his fingers like water, perfuming the room with her flower scent.

He smoothed Anna's hair and let it lie. "There. Now you look like a girl and not a Pekinese. A beautiful girl. A gorgeous girl." His mouth quirked. "In her underwear."

Anna's eyes shone, wet and gray like the ocean, her lashes butterfly wings. Her lips parted with an unreleased sob. He pulled his coat tight around her. "Don't you dare cry, Sherlock. You're the bravest man on the force."

She took his hand and laced her baby soft fingers through his calloused ones. She smelled like roses and whiskey. He wanted to hold her and ease her pain, but he knew better. They'd be back on the dressing room floor, with no Miss Baumgartner to chase him out of the store. She wouldn't remember it in the morning and she didn't love him. She wasn't going to stay.

Joe reclaimed his hand and used it to pick up the cloth. He dabbed at the cut on her chin, careful not to drip on her dress. Anna breathed slow and heavy, watching him. His eyes drifted to hers.

"Kiss me," she whispered.

He looked away and kept dabbing. "You'd regret it."

"I wouldn't."

Joe strode to the sink and wrung out the cloth. "You should find somebody you love."

When he turned, she stood right behind him, smiling up at him through whiskey tears. "I love *you*. Like a Juliet. I do. So kiss me."

Anna lifted on tiptoes and tried to kiss him. Joe stepped back against the sink. "You just lost the man you love."

"No. I planned to love Edgar. Maybe I could have, but I never had the chance because of you. It was always you. I just didn't know it."

She took his hands, first one, then the other, and placed them on her waist, gazing up at him from beneath heavy lashes. "You make me feel so dizzy, I forget to breathe. Why?"

Joe sighed and looked away. "Anna, you're bent."

She shook her head vehemently. "No. And I'm not fighting crime. I'm yours now, truly." She held him with a fierce tenderness. "Forever."

Joe clenched his jaw and stared up at a stain on the ceiling. Anna didn't love him. He loved her, and she'd always wanted Edgar Wright. So why did she kiss Joe like she desired not only justice but him? Had he ever been in the running? That is, when she wasn't friendless, homeless, destitute, broken-hearted, and drunk. While Anna pressed her body against him, his mind raced through every one of her romantic ambushes in the name of the law, hoping for some sign that he was more than just a means to an end.

Anna pulled at his shirttails and slid her hands onto the skin of his back. "I love you." She breathed her sweet, spiked breath onto his lips.

Joe held on, stiff and sweating. He thought of Anna smiling shyly at his rhododendron bush in Boyle Heights, trying to hold his hand in the morgue when Snow was no longer looking. His heartbeat quickened. He thought of how her gray eyes had followed him around the station, even when they weren't speaking, and how she looked at him when he held her, like now—like she was falling, and wanting to fall. Wanting him to fall.

Anna's eyebrows drew together in distress and she searched his eyes. "Aren't you going to make love to me?" She demanded. "Tell me I'm honey sweet!"

Joe shook. His heart, which he had hardened against her, was starting to crack. He opened his mouth to protest, but Anna silenced him with a kiss. Her kiss burned with all the intensity of a life in flames and all the passion required to overcome it—her desperation, his mistrust, her notoriety, their poverty, a fifth of whiskey, and a dumpy apartment with a single bed.

Joe fell.

He believed her. She loved him. They were going to have some pretty babies and lots of fun making them. He hoped to God there was a school for wives.

Joe swept Anna up like a bride and carried her into his bedroom, his heart sounding like a timpani. "You're honey sweet."

Chapter 42

Anna lay draped over Joe's arms like a sheaf of offertory grain, the soft, bare skin of her thighs one layer of fabric away from the skin of his arms. She didn't care. She wanted no fabric between them. She wanted Joe to do whatever men liked to do to girls they loved. And why not? She was ruined already, and he was delicious. She let her head fall back.

He dropped her down onto his soft mattress and the unmade sheets that smelled of his deliciousness. She closed her eyes, because the world was spinning, and waited for the mattress to sink under his weight, waited to feel his body next to hers, waited for the sound of him removing his clothes so that she could open her eyes and find out what was underneath his Arrow shirt suit.

Instead, she heard the door click shut, and then silence. Anna opened her eyes to darkness. "Joe?"

"Good night, Sherlock." He was on the wrong side of the door.

Anna tried to sit up to protest. There was a rushing in her head, a haze of stars, and she fell back onto the bed. Anna slept.

Anna awoke in Joe's bed, holding Joe's pillow, her heart beating love, her head pounding like someone had squished it. Sticks of light from the basement windows poked her sore eyes. She flinched. By the time her father opened his newspaper, Anna would be the most notorious woman on the West Coast. She could abide it because Joe Singer loved her. It wasn't just that he looked better than the Arrow Collar Man, that he sang her songs, that his kisses made her nether parts shout hallelujah, or that she had nowhere else to go. He was the best man she knew, and the only man she had ever truly loved. She'd always heard that men would spoon any girl, anytime, even scrawny, cross-eyed ones with carbuncles. Even convicts, like Anna. But Joe Singer was too noble to take advantage of her in her vulnerable state, though she had wanted him to, and they were in love.

Anna dragged herself up from the bed and into the one room that served as parlor, dining room, and kitchen, dirt from the floor sticking to her bare feet. "Joe?" The place was too small for him to hide. His coat was on the gritty floor where she had dropped it, but the man himself was gone. It was already late afternoon and her tongue had grown fur. She had a keen desire to water it. She walked to the sink and poured herself a glass of cold water. Joe's toothbrush lay on the counter. She dipped it in salt and used it.

Anna's gun lay on the table next to a note, which read, "Sherlock, I've got to work, maybe very late. Stay here and wait for me. I love you." Anna's heart fluttered, and she smiled despite her headache. Then she noticed the fateful issue of the *LA Herald* lying on the table. She lowered her ill body onto the bench and studied her image. It stared back in distress, blonde, barelegged. She took a deep breath and read. Tilly had written the article. It said that socialite Anna Blanc, a renegade police matron, had gone undercover in the brothels to catch a killer. That much was true. It reported that Anna was closing in on the killer. Anna groaned. Tilly was a cad rat and a fool. Now the killer would come after her.

The article went on to quote Snow. "Anna Blanc is delusional. There are no murders. There is no killer." An anonymous man claimed to have had relations with Anna for five hundred dollars. The worst possible line came next: "When asked if this were true, Miss Blanc replied, 'I have done and will do anything necessary to save these girls.'"

Anna threw down the paper. "Lies, lies, lies." She ripped it into tiny pieces and threw them hard into the air. They fluttered to the sticky floor.

Her previous life seemed so flimsy and unreal—the life of pink balls and tennis games. Her life at the station, stalking criminals and spooning Joe—that felt real. She had lost her job, but she still had Joe.

Anna waited in Joe's apartment for five long minutes before she became desperately bored. She considered her options. She could wait for Joe and die of ennui or go back to Canary Cottage and hunt the killer. She decided on the latter course.

Anna's whore outfit wouldn't do for daytime, and she needed a disguise. She rifled through Joe's armoire, perusing all of his delicious smelling clothes, including his lowers. She donned his best suit and an Arrow shirt collar. She rolled her petticoats up around her middle to make her belly seem big and her bosoms less conspicuous. She clipped on an old pair of Joe's suspenders, and rolled up the trouser legs just short enough to cover her stockings and high heeled shoes. The suit hung off her like the skin of a Chinese dog, and she didn't care. She hid her hair under a derby and hoped that if she kept her face to the pavement she could make it to Canary Cottage without anyone recognizing her as a woman, or worse yet as Anna Blanc.

Anna turned out all of Joe's pockets and searched among the dust bunnies under the bed, gleaning pennies for the trolley. She took all his change, her notebook, her holstered pistol, and Cook's paring knife strapped to her garter. She stepped out into a colder world.

That night at Canary Cottage, men spilled out onto the street like seeping tar ready to ignite. As far as the eye could see, cars lined both sides of the street, some double parked. Brand new customers, howling and bent, came hoping to see the socialite turned detective turned prostitute. Men called out, "Anna! Arrest me, Anna!"

Anna watched from a window in a large, second-story closet under the stairs. She thought she saw Theo Breedlove, and it made her feel sick. The space was dark and smelled of moldy things. When men pounded up the stairs with girls, the door rattled.

Anna sat on the rough plank floor and reviewed her list of suspects, trying to remember if she'd seen any of them at mass. When she found a Catholic, she crossed him out. She crossed out Edgar.

Anna still wore Joe's suit, though there were plenty of tasteless frocks to choose from in the brothel. Amidst all these horrid men, his clothes reminded her of what a man could be.

The door to her hiding place swung open. Anna's rod popped up. Big Cindy stared down the barrel like an owl, her lips pursed in a kiss of surprise. Anna lowered the pistol. "Hi."

Big Cindy grinned and slipped in. Charlene followed with a cynical smile and closed the door. "Damn you're good for business."

"Too good." Big Cindy wiped her brow. "It's hell's kitchen out there." They plunked themselves down.

Charlene stretched, chandelier earrings grazing her shoulders. "There's a rumor you do things in bed that even whores haven't heard of, and you're good at it."

Anna's eyes got big. "Oh, cock. Like what?"

Charlene smirked. "Don't you got an imagination?"

Big Cindy batted away the idea. "Never mind them stupid men." She unwound Anna's silky hair, running her fingers through it. "Lulu says you're in love." Big Cindy squeezed Anna's shoulders and giggled.

Charlene fumbled in her pocket for a cigarette, lit up, and leaned against the wall. She raised her eyebrows cynically. "I was in love once. Married, even." She blew out smoke. "Now my daughter's boarding in the country and I'm here."

"Oh be quiet you hearse driver." Big Cindy hugged Anna from behind. "I know life seems as black as Hades. But sweetie, we know what you're made of. And not all husbands run around on their women."

Charlene guffawed. "Just every married man I've ever known." The smoke curled up to the ceiling and down around the walls, seeking an outlet. It burned Anna's throat. She took a gulp of whiskey, and it stung like acid. Like Charlene's words. Anna went back to studying her list.

The lights went out. The crowd whooped. A man's footsteps pounded up the stairs. Anna heard him pass right outside the closet—

three, four, five heavy strides. A door opened and shut nearby. The lights went on again.

Anna closed her eyes and rubbed her forehead. "Every man in town is here tooting his horn. Why does this one hide?"

"He's a Baptist?" Big Cindy guessed.

"Or he's the killer," Anna said.

Charlene plucked at a piece of lint on her garter, her drawers cinched tight on her thighs. "Lulu doesn't think so."

"If he's here, he's a suspect!" Anna's eyes bored into Charlene with an authority born of sacrifice. "Describe him."

Charlene threw up her hands. "I don't know! I didn't go with him. Did you Biggy?"

Big Cindy tied Anna's hair in a knot on the top of her head and stuck hairpins in it. "No." She topped it with Joe's derby.

Anna eyed Charlene. "I only heard one set of footsteps."

"Lulu will send somebody," Charlene said.

Anna stood, bending her neck so as not to bump her hat on the ceiling. "I'm going."

Big Cindy's owl-eyes widened. "Are you crazy?"

"I've lost my reputation. I may as well go down with honor—of a sort." Anna palmed her gun.

Charlene leaned back and yawned. "She won't do it. She'd go two steps and get tackled."

Anna smirked. "If you read the papers, you know I'll stop at nothing."

Charlene threw back her head and laughed. Anna flung opened the closet, took five giant strides on the sticky floor, and slipped through the nearest door. She heard Big Cindy cry, "Aimee! No!"

CHAPTER 43

The room was dark and close, with the smell of burning tobacco. She saw him peering through a window overlooking the grand salon, one strip of his body illuminated by a beam of light that Anna had let in through the door. Startled, he turned and raised his arm to cover his face. "This room is occupied!"

His voice sounded angry and falsely deep. Still, she recognized it. Anna's heart leapt and she smiled into the dark.

Joe Singer had come to catch the killer.

"Get out!" screeched a feminine voice that she did not recognize. A beam of light fell across the bed and lit a lock of blonde hair, a pair of small red lips. Even in the dark, Anna could tell the whore was not pretty.

Anna's hands fell limp at her side. Her gun clattered to the hardwood. She knew then that all men were liars, that love was just an illusion, and that it would have been better for her if she had never been born. Despair rose in her throat. "You . . . you . . . pig!"

Joe Singer's voice broke. "Oh, Lord."

Anna bolted. She pushed past Charlene and Big Cindy, who were hovering in the hall. She hurtled down the stairs, shoes clacking on every third step.

Joe charged after her. "Sherlock! Stop! I can explain!"

Anna touched the tile and lunged past some men from the force. She bolted past Wolf, whose arm hung in a sling, and shoved her way through the crowd, running toward the kitchen.

Joe hit the bottom step calling, "Sherlock!" The cops' heads followed Joe as he pushed out the front door, headed in the wrong direction. Wolf sighed. "Someone arrest Joe."

Anna streaked into the kitchen, past a smoking oven and out the back, through the empty lot where Peaches Payton's body had been picked apart by vultures. Cats trailed after her, waving their tails in the air, hoping for food. She left them behind, cutting across to the sidewalk. Prickly burrs stuck to her stockings and she trailed a stalk of anise. She kicked off her heels.

Joe fought his way through the crowd, pushing out the gate that jingled with cowbells. He saw his suit heading east down New High Street and followed at a gallop. "Sherlock!"

Anna ran fast. Joe's hat jumped from her head and rolled into the gutter, and her hair came undone. She splashed through garbage and muck that smelled like a privy and stained her tattered stockings. Her feet were raw from the pavement. Footsteps rang out behind her.

Joe was gaining. She heard him call, "Anna! Sweetheart! It's not safe." Anna didn't fear the red-light district, with its rough saloons and pleasure houses. She feared Joe Singer. He had slain her.

Up ahead, a man was watching Anna, her gait and hair betraying her gender. He began hulking in her direction. His bearing exuded hostility. Anna despaired. It was Scylla or Charybdis, the known reprobate or the unknown hulk.

She didn't think twice. Her small, cut feet slapped the pavement toward the shadowy stranger. As she neared him, she lowered her head and tried to dodge around him, but he caught her up, squeezing her around the waist with tree branch arms. Anna shrieked and thrashed, bashing his shins with her heels, and getting smelly muck all over his very nice sack coat and contrasting trousers.

"Anna!" he said. "Anna! It's me. Edgar." Stubble peppered his well-made jaw, and his eye had swelled purple from where she had punched him the night before. A new welt rose on his cheek, probably from her elbow. "Anna! It's okay. Anna. You're safe." She stopped struggling and went limp in his arms.

Joe bore down on Edgar like a freight train, his hair flopping, flinging sweat. "Sherlock! I'm coming!"

Anna threw herself against Edgar's chest. His arms clamped protectively around her. Joe reached them and stumbled to a stop. His uncertain eyes flitted between Anna and Edgar. "Sherlock?"

Anna buried her face in Edgar's armpit. Edgar boomed, "You did this to her! You did!"

Joe ignored him. "Anna, look at me. Sweetheart. It isn't what you think!"

"And what would you have her think, Singer? That she's a detective? So you can dress her up like a whore? I can't imagine what you had planned for her in the red-light district tonight!"

Joe pointed at Edgar. "You, shut up."

Edgar bared his teeth. "She was innocent! And you lured her with lies, because you wanted her. You ruined her!"

Joe pleaded, "Anna. You gotta let me explain."

"Stay away from me you . . . you lowly dog! I hate you!" Anna buried her face again. She could hear Joe standing there, breathing like a beast. She felt him watching, but she didn't look.

"Go away, Singer! Before I kill you! This is the last time I say it. Stay away from my fiancée!"

Anna began to tremble. She couldn't stop. She shook and shook while Edgar stroked her hair. "It's all right, Anna. Shhh. It's all right."

Anna didn't hear Joe anymore. She turned her head to liberate one eye and looked down the alley.

Sirens wailed and a cop car pulled up behind Joe. Wolf ran into view with Captain Wells.

"Let's go," Edgar said. He guided her quickly to the curb, where a black truck waited. Ugly red-light women laughed and blew kisses to Anna from their stalls.

Salt tears stung Anna's lips. Edgar coaxed her onto the rough leather seat, holding her hand, which was slick with their sweat. He set the crank and climbed behind the wheel. As he pulled away from the curb, he glanced back and laughed bitterly. "Joe Singer is getting arrested. That should make you feel better, darling. I know I do."

Anna didn't look. Her face wrinkled up like a cabbage. She made a sound—something between a laugh and the bark of a dying seal.

Edgar slid his hand down her back, nudging her forward. "Put your head between your knees and breathe. You're going to be all right. You're safe now."

Anna did as she was told, still trying to catch her breath, trying to calm her shaking self. But she wasn't safe. She was irreparably damaged and not at all sure she wanted to be in a world where Joe Singer was not good.

Edgar steered the truck down Commercial Street, heading east, out of town. Anna wiped under her eyes and blew her nose on Joe's suit sleeve. "You were at the brothels again . . . for business?"

"No. I came to find you. I looked everywhere for you—the police station, the Breedloves', the Orphans' Asylum, the church, the club. Then I heard a rumor you were at Canary Cottage," he said. "But it's bedlam. Cars and horses everywhere. Crowds blocking the street. This was the closest I could park."

Anna sat up straight. "Edgar, didn't you see the paper?"

"I saw the article."

She laid her palms on her hot cheeks. "But everyone in the country is going to know that Anna Blanc was arrested for vagrancy in a downtown brothel."

"It's . . . unfortunate."

Anna's face flashed. "Unfortunate? It's ruinous! I can never be in society again. What on earth are you going to do with me?"

"Take you home with me. Marry you, if you want."

Anna blinked at him, eyes wet, and wondered again if she knew anything at all about the world. "I don't understand. How could you still want me?"

He took his gaze from the road and fixed her with it. "I guess I'm mad for you, Anna. I can't help myself."

He *was* mad. Mad like Heathcliff. Crazed by a Wuthering Heights love that transcended death and betrayal. Yes, he had neglected her, but only to win her hand. Now he was banishing himself for her sake. Anna felt a tenderness for Edgar that she'd never felt before.

Still, she would trade this good man's love to have Joe Singer back. Not the real man, the profligate liar, but the imaginary one that she had loved and now knew had never existed. The thought of him sent her weeping again and it made her feel guilty.

"Don't cry, Anna. We'll start over. We'll go to Europe and live privately." He took her hand and squeezed it. "Or go to Buenos Aires. It's very civilized."

Anna nodded. She didn't care where they went, as long as it was far away from Los Angeles.

Edgar sped down Commercial Street, heading out of town, toward Pasadena, where so many of the East Coast rich had settled. Tall buildings gave way to single stories. Buildings were fewer, then rare. They passed an ostrich farm and groves and groves of oranges. Edgar took a private lane. It was lonely and dark and Anna coughed on the dust. It ended at a large house, a Gothic Revival, nestled among acres of fragrant citrus. There was something solemn about its pointy roof, like a church. A trellis hung with blood-red roses.

Anna put her hand on the truck's window. Her breath fogged the glass. "This is your farm?"

"One of them." He shrugged. "But I'll sell it. Anyway, it's a good place to hide out until we make some plans." The lights in the house sputtered and went dark, every room at once. Anna gasped. Edgar squeezed her hand. "It's just the electric plant, darling. It shuts off at midnight." He got out and opened the truck's door for Anna.

Anna nodded and took his arm, limping onto the gravel drive, nursing her battered feet, the hem of Joe's trousers dragging. Edgar swept her into his arms and carried her through the arch of roses and up the veranda steps.

At the threshold, she braced her hand against the doorframe. "This isn't proper. We're . . . alone."

He smiled contemptuously. "A funny thing for you to say, but if you want I can sleep in another room."

Anna swallowed. She'd thrown propriety out the window when she started working for the LAPD. She'd virtually cast herself as a prostitute by going to the brothel. She deserved his bitter sarcasm. "I . . . I'll do what you want."

"Good."

She let her hand drop and Edgar carried her inside, setting her down on the soft carpet in the foyer.

"You never asked me what I did in the brothel," she said. "Don't you want to know?"

"My love, I don't think I could bear it."

The house was elegant and empty. In the foyer, lit by the moon, she saw a coat rack and a table. Edgar struck a match and lit an oil lamp. The smoke smudged the ruffled blue globe. It smelled like sulfur and cast shadows across the walls. Edgar hung up his hat. His voice sounded tight. "Is that Joe Singer's suit you're wearing?"

Anna nodded. "I borrowed it. For a disguise."

"Take it off!" He took a coat from the rack and thrust it at her.

She scooted into the dark parlor, away from his eyes. He followed with the oil lamp and watched her. Anna slipped out of the jacket and unclipped the suspenders, illuminated by flickering lamp light. Blushing, she removed the notebook from her pocket, and stepped out of the trousers. Her petticoats were bunched around her waist. She quickly unfurled them, smoothing them down over her drawers. Edgar's eyes skimmed her lingerie coolly, as if imagining whose eyes had been there before. She turned her back, peeled the shirt off over her head, and put on the coat.

With a sudden violence, Edgar snatched up Joe's clothes and stuffed them in the fireplace, dousing them with kerosene from the lamp. He lit a match and the clothes caught with a *poof.* The scent of burning wool invaded the room.

The violence of it made Anna tremble. She could hear mice in the walls. "Where are the servants?"

"I sent them away this morning. I thought you'd like privacy."

"I do."

He poured two brandies from a decanter and turned up the lamp, brightening the room. Several Franz Bischoff paintings of the Coast hung on the floral-papered wall. Anna loved plein-air. She hadn't known that he liked plein-air. There was a Persian carpet, a geometric Tiffany lamp from New York, and a talking machine with a stack of records. She limped over to the stack and flipped through the heavy disks—"A Bird in a Gilded Cage," "Un Bel Di Madama Butterfly." Edgar came up from behind and reached around her, raising goose bumps on her skin. He selected a record, turning the crank, and set it spinning round and round. He smirked as the machine warbled, "I Can't Tell You Why I Love You, But I Do."

Anna's cheeks flushed again. "I should warn you, the killer might come for me." Saying it made it seem true. Fear crawled up her back. She shivered.

"I'll always protect you, Anna. Haven't I proven that?" He put his hands on her shoulders and drew her to his chest. He didn't sound afraid. Anna leaned against him, sipping her brandy, and wondered if he even believed there was a killer, or if, like Snow, he simply thought she was crazy.

Anna was suddenly conscious of her dirty feet and the muck she was tramping on the carpet. She looked down at her bare filthy legs. Edgar followed her gaze. "Would you like it if I ran you a bath?" he asked.

Anna nodded. Edgar disappeared into the kitchen. She perched on the edge of the settee. The song finished and the record ran out. She picked up a book from the end table. It was a copy of *Wuthering Heights*.

Chapter 44

Anna soaked in a claw foot tub. Only her head and battered feet rose above the tepid brew. Edgar had sprinkled rose petals to make it smell nice and put almond oil in the water. He had lit beeswax candles all along the marble-topped vanity. He had given her sweet sherry in a cut crystal glass, which she had downed in one shot, and cake and cut oranges, which remained untouched. The candles cast shadows on walls that were papered with hand-painted birds nesting in wisteria.

Edgar knocked. Instinctively, Anna's arms flew up to cover her breasts and her knees bent up to her chest. "Yes?"

The door creaked open a crack and Edgar's arm appeared, holding a little knit pad with a picture of a chicken. He set the pad down and retreated, coming back with a large kettle of boiled water, wrapped in a towel to conserve its heat. "In case you want to warm up." He left the kettle sitting on the chicken. The door closed and she heard him rustling around in the bedroom.

"Thank you," she called.

The evening was balmy, so Anna left the kettle steaming on the tile. Edgar was being extra kind. He wanted to sleep in her room that night. But, for once, she wasn't dreaming about the mysteries of married love or trying to picture what Edgar looked like under his bathing suit. If Louis Taylor had made her suspect of passion, Joe Singer had discredited it forever.

Instead, she imagined Eve, a shimmering spirit with branding eyes, haunting Anna because her debt went unpaid. Anna tried to force the image out of her mind, but she felt Eve's cold presence, and the ghosts of all the girls who had never been avenged. Would Joe solve the crimes without Anna? Now that she knew Joe visited brothels, it was unclear which side of the law he was on. He himself was a suspect. The very thought sucked strength from her body and she choked back a sob.

Anna climbed from the tub, collected her notebook, and slid back into the tepid water. The rose petals swirled like snow. She read over the list of Protestant patrons from Canary Cottage, and the notes she had taken on each from their brief conversations. She had never seen Joe Singer at mass, so she added his name to the end of the list. She bit her trembling lip. He was a pig, but surely her former lover could not be a murderer, and if he was a murderer, she'd rather be his victim than live with the knowledge. She scratched his name out. Then she wrote it again. Then she scratched it out a second time. The pencil tore the wet paper. Anna growled in frustration. In addition to his other crimes, Joe Singer interfered with her deductive reasoning. She had to forget about her deceitful lover and concentrate on the clues. She crossed her cut feet on the edge of the tub.

Anna looked at the remaining names and tapped the pencil on her lower lip. The killer would need to be rich to afford the Poodle Dog, or a big fish who received services on the house. Or he could be the son of a big fish . . . Anna slipped down in the bath and put her head underwater, hoping she would drown. She held her breath until she saw twinkling stars and surfaced gasping. She wrote "rich or powerful" at the top of the page and crossed off Douglas Doogan, the patrolmen, and any men with bad clothes.

Anna ran a dripping finger down the list. Her suspects had been whittled down to three men—the mayor, Louis Taylor, and M. M. Martinez. Her pulse quickened.

Madam Lulu said the murders had started seven months ago, late in January, and that she was aware of no murders prior to that time. This made sense from Anna's counts of suspicious deaths in the police files. Twice, a girl in the cribs had been beaten to death by a boyfriend or the maquereau for whom she worked, but those deaths weren't passed off as suicides.

Like all beginners, criminals must start simple. Wolf had said so.

A person doesn't simply wake up one morning and, after coffee and kippers, lure a prostitute out of a brothel, dress her up like a bride, and fake her suicide. A beginner might, say, crack a girl's skull with a rock and leave her where she fell, in a puddle of bloody brains.

According to Monique, the first murder had had all the same elements as the last three. The first brothel victim should have died simply, but she hadn't. Anna could only assume that she was not the first victim. The New High Street Suicide Faker had not begun on New High Street. He knew seven different ways to kill. He killed in one place and staged the suicide in another. The wedding symbols told a complicated story, and he felt confident enough to leave them as his signature.

Maybe, like the Boyle Heights Rape Fiend, the New High Street Suicide Faker had been killing brothel girls for years, somewhere else. In another neighborhood? Maybe he'd killed brothel girls in another city and had to flee because the police suspected him. There were several men on the list who'd come to LA recently. She crossed off longtime residents.

Anna scanned her notebook. She put the pencil back in her mouth and chewed. She chewed and chewed until the paint peeled and the wood splintered.

There was no one left on her list.

Edgar called through the door in his round, upper-class accent. Anna jumped. There was something harsh in his voice—an angry urgency. "Are you all right? You're taking an eternity."

She heard his forehead rubbing on the door, his hair making friction sounds. She had left him alone too long, and he was no doubt stewing on the image of Anna in the brothel.

The bath chilled her now. She had forgotten the hot water. Anna stood up and wrapped herself in the warm towel that had covered the kettle. "Just a minute." She looked down at the little pile of underthings on the floor next to her holster, the mucky shredded stockings, the garter tangled with her knife, a pair of garish new red drawers that she had borrowed from Big Cindy because Anna had no clean ones. Anna wilted. At home, wrapped in tissue paper and lavender, her tasteful, silky robes de nuit languished with the rest of her trousseau. Garish red, secondhand drawers were not what she had planned to wear on her wedding night.

She pressed her mouth against the door. "I have no clothes. Not a stitch."

Now she detected a smile in his voice. "I have something. Just wait a minute."

His footsteps receded and a wardrobe creaked. In a moment, Edgar's hand poked through the door holding her wedding gown on a hanger—the one she'd ordered for Saturday. His arm was draped in the silk sleeve of an oriental robe. The fabric shone, lovely and blue, embroidered with lotus flowers.

Anna took the gown from his hand and his sleeve disappeared. When he closed the door, Anna dropped her towel down the laundry chute and put on the corset, drawers, and gown. Her hair dripped on her silk dress, leaving long rivers of gray. She twisted the strands up into a plain bun without looking in the mirror. She knew she looked bad for Anna Blanc, but Edgar had no Princess Pat or walnut stain—not even a hairbrush. There was nothing she could do, so why wallow in it. She sat on the cold porcelain commode with the lid down and chewed her lips for color.

This felt all wrong. She didn't want to be deflowered. Not so soon after falling in love with Joe Singer and being thrown violently out of love by his inconstancy and whoring. Edgar didn't seem to know how to be. One minute, he was as sweet as Hershey's chocolate, and the next minute as bitter as the cooking kind, which looks the same but packs a nasty surprise. She couldn't blame him for being different now. She could only be grateful. He had done so much for her and, unlike Joe Singer, he only went to brothels for business. So tonight she would let him have his way. It was the least she could do.

Edgar knocked again. "Don't be nervous, darling. I know . . . It's all right if . . . you're not a maiden. I'm resigned to it."

Anna frowned. Surely Edgar didn't believe the libelous paper or the dirty rumors. Did he think that she was lying about her brief, unconsummated marriage to Louis Taylor? Or, worse yet, that she had given herself to Joe? Of course she *had* given herself to Joe, but he hadn't taken her and so it didn't count. She lifted her chin in indignation. Edgar was the one who wasn't a maiden.

"I am," she said indignantly.

Edgar sighed into the door. "I know you did things . . . for a reason. Your intentions were good. Someday, you can explain, and I'll be ready to hear it. What I mean is, I've thought a lot about it, and I love you regardless." The heel of his hand made a thump on the wood. "Anna, you are my Gomer."

Anna's lungs stopped. She braced herself against the wall, lest she slip off the commode. He had lied to her.

Edgar wasn't Catholic.

Not only that, her fiancé was certainly the killer. The man she cared for and planned to love once her heart mended, the man who would shelter her and buy her pretty things, the charming, very presentable man who liked plein-air—he was a killer. And there was a distinct possibility that she was about to die. Though she had nothing left to live for, Anna didn't want to die. Not yet.

Anna squeezed her eyes shut and puffed her mouth out like a blowfish. Edgar didn't seem like a killer, with his curls and his sometimes shy smile. But if she had learned anything from this series of tragic debacles, it was to rely on her head and not her heart. And so she concentrated.

The answer came to her. She would hold him at gunpoint, tie him up, and call the authorities. It was as simple as that. She scrambled across the rug to her holster and picked it up. It swung from her hand empty. She had dropped her gun at Canary Cottage while fleeing from Joe—one more reason to be angry with her former lover. She hitched up her wedding gown and slipped on her garters, fastened Cook's paring knife onto her leg. As a second thought, she unbuttoned her dress and removed her corset for the sake of agility. She would try to run for the trees, but if Edgar caught her she would have to fight.

Edgar voice was darkly insistent. "Let me in, darling, or I'll simply get the key."

Anna picked up the kettle of boiled water using the little knit pad with the picture of a chicken, which she slipped from underneath. She lifted the lid and hot steam assaulted her face. The key turned in the lock with a click. The door opened and Edgar stood in the doorway in an elegant *chinoiserie robe de chamber* and matching slippers, his brow furrowed, his bruised shins bare, his eyes glittering. She hesitated. He looked spanking fine in Chinese silk. The black eye she had given him made him look more interesting, more adventurous. He smelled nice, too—like silk and petunias.

Edgar moved towards her. "Anna?"

Anna was momentarily paralyzed by the absurdity that a man so beautiful could be a killer. He reached out one smooth, manicured hand. "Anna?"

Edgar's touch galvanized her. She splashed the steaming kettle in his face and slipped past him into his bedroom, her bare feet skidding across the carpet.

He screamed, "Are you mad?"

He was quick, charging after her as she flew for the bedroom door. She put her hand on the knob to swing the door open, but he was already upon her, forcing it shut with his full weight and trapping her between his outstretched arms. He shook his head like a wet dog, spraying her face. His face glowed as if sunburned. "Anna! What's wrong with you? That hurt!"

She cowered beneath him, moon-eyed, her teeth chattering, her heart beating like a hummingbird's wings. He simply stared at her, red and furious. Air from each of his hard breaths pelted her cheek. He didn't move. They stood there and the clock ticked. Gradually, his breath softened and slowed. She watched his rage melt into confusion, then concern, and finally understanding. The deep furrows on his brow were like ripples in water. His voice was flat. "You aren't well, Anna. It's all right. I'll call a doctor."

He grabbed her firmly by the wrist and steered her down the stairs into the hall. She let herself be taken. He was leading her closer to the door.

Edgar sat her in a hard oak chair in the corner near a hall table with a telephone, and blocked her in with his long, lean body. "Stay." He shoved his palm out, gave her a stern look, and turned his back to her to pick up the telephone. The room was perfectly quiet. She heard the telephone click.

Anna sat stiffly in the chair and hoped. A doctor might be her salvation. When they were alone, she could tell him that Edgar was a vicious, insatiable killer who preyed upon prostitutes, like Jack the Ripper. She ground her teeth. It would do no good. Edgar would tell the doctor that she was insane. Isn't that why he was making the call? Because he thought she was mad? Isn't that what the newspaper printed—that she was delusional? The doctor wouldn't listen to Anna. He would give her pills and lock her up in the giggle-giggle ward of the bat house. He would throw away the key and she would roam the halls forever in a shapeless hospital gown with no corset and no drawers.

The white lotus flowers on Edgar's silk robe stretched innocently across his broad back, in perfect contrast to his dark curls. Anna's eyebrows rose together in a little teepee of consternation. He looked so handsome in that robe—nothing like a killer. But that kind of thinking had been her downfall when she failed to stop the Boyle Heights Rape Fiend. She vowed not to make that mistake twice—not to flinch because of beauty. Her very life depended on it.

In one swift motion, she picked up the chair and conked him on the head with it. There was a loud crack as wood splintered. He stumbled backward, losing his balance, clutching the telephone receiver. Anna shoved him, and they went down together. His body broke her fall, and his head smashed hard on the tile. The receiver clattered to the floor, the wire no longer attached to the telephone.

The blow left Edgar stunned. Anna gulped air, face down, spread eagle across the silky lotus flowers on his chest. She slithered off him and crawled on her belly toward the door, her diaphragm seizing. She dug beneath her skirts and fumbled to unhitch the paring knife from the stiff lace garter.

Anna scrambled to her knees and twisted around in time to see him at his full, glorious height, descending upon her. "Anna!"

She had a flicker of time to raise the knife before he could grab her arm. Despite her good intentions, instead of aiming for his heart she closed her eyes.

He screamed. Anna landed flat on her back with Edgar on top of her. The weight of his body forced the blade in deep. But Anna had missed. The knife found its sheath not in his heart but in his arm.

Edgar rolled over onto his back, taking her with him as she clung to the slick handle of the knife. The cutter slipped from the wound with a sucking sound and a spray of bright, warm blood. He rolled her off and climbed on top of her like a lover, pinning her. He was dripping hot blood onto her face, the metallic salt of it flooding her tongue. "Anna, stop!" His eyelids were spread wide, his irises dark drops in a pool of white. He would surely kill her now.

Anna kneed him in his secret man parts, not hard, but that was the nice thing about secret man parts—they were man's Achilles heel. She had learned that from Douglas Doogan and Joe Singer.

It felled him like a redwood. His face paled and he curled into a ball, wheezing. His eyes were open but unfocused. Blood spread across his robe, wet and dark, turning the lotus flowers scarlet. His mouth went slack. His lids fluttered closed. He didn't move. She kneed him hard in the groin again, but he did not stir. His body remained still, splayed out under the blue robe. She lowered her ear to his full, unkissed, white lips. His breath went in and out almost imperceptibly. Anna panted like an overheated poodle. She wiped the back of her hand across her brow, flinging sweat onto the floral wallpaper.

Anna clambered to her feet and looked around. Her heart beat in her ears. She didn't want to kill him. She would tie him up until the police could come. Slowly, she moved toward the dark kitchen to fetch twine, never turning her back on him. She would grab the twine and tress him like a roasting chicken. If he struggled, she'd conk him on the head. Anna walked backward, assuring herself that whatever might be in the kitchen could not compete for the attention she must give the fallen villain. Edgar remained still. Though she knew she was alone with him, she didn't feel alone. She felt a heavy presence, imagined cold breath, as if any second a dark creature—the demon that drove his evil deeds—would rise up and swallow her.

Anna made it to the kitchen pantry. She could no longer see Edgar. She quickly rifled through the cupboards in the dark, feeling for the tiny rope. She moved on to drawers full of sundries—wooden spoons, nutcrackers, matches, and an ice pick that pricked her finger. No twine.

Then it dawned on Anna that she was wasting time. Of course Edgar's cook had no twine. He didn't like chicken. She would find something else. She felt lightheaded and leaned her palms onto the chopping block where Edgar had sliced the cake. It was grainy with crumbs. Through the window, in the moonlight, she could see the barn. Maybe she could find rope there.

Something warm and living gently grazed Anna's fingers. Anna screamed and swatted at it. A tail disappeared behind the cake. She fell against the door, breathing heavily. It was just a mouse. She wondered that Edgar didn't have a cat to catch mice, and then she remembered that he was afraid of cats. The murderer, Edgar Wright, did not like headcheese, he did not eat chicken, and he was afraid of cats.

Anna knew then that she had stabbed the wrong man. Edgar couldn't be the killer. He couldn't have left Peaches Payton dead in a field teaming with feral cats. The place had tens of cats and their kittens. Furry, lousy cats that the brothel girls fed and that were not afraid of people. Cats that came up to be stroked whenever any human—innocent or killer—stepped into the field.

Anna ran to her fallen lover and skidded onto her knees beside him. She watched for the rise and fall of his chest. She could hear the faint whistle of his breath, weak and irregular. She tore a strip from her petticoats and bound the wound, leaning on it until the bleeding stopped. "Edgar, I'm sorry." She showered his white, unconscious face with kisses.

But if Edgar wasn't the killer, who was? Anna's mind spun like a merry-go-round, dizzyingly, settling nowhere.

She heard the front door open and close, and stiffened. Was Edgar expecting someone? Surely not. He had dismissed the servants so Anna could have privacy, and whoever it was had not knocked. She skittered out of sight, wrapping herself in the heavy chintz curtains.

Joe Singer appeared on the threshold looking fierce, his dimples flattened by a grimace, his shirt stained with sweat. His hair swept up and out like the mane of a lion who rode a motorcycle while wearing too much brilliantine. Anna's breath caught. Had he changed his mind? Had he followed them here to reclaim her for himself? It was a romantic gesture. She choked on a sob. But she wouldn't have him, no matter that she had just stabbed her groom, and she was alone in the world.

She watched him move into the parlor and turn around. His shirttails were untucked. He called out, "Anna! Anna!"

She steeled her heart. He couldn't hold a candle to her Edgar, standing there in his denim trousers. True, he was not afraid of cats. He was very brave and owned two. But he slept with brothel girls, while Edgar only went for business. As the son of the chief of police, Joe probably got as many beautiful girls as he wanted for free. He probably went twice a day. Likely three times.

Anna could feel a volcano erupting inside her. Every muscle in her body clenched so tight she trembled. Sweat dripped into her wild, bulging eyes. Joe Singer was a reprobate, why not a murderer? He had arrived in LA just before the murders started. His uncle was British and probably had buckets of sixpence. Not once had she seen him in mass. Worst of all, he had made her hysterical with desire, just to muddle her head so she couldn't solve the murders. Then, he rejected her in favor of a prostitute—an ugly one. Anna watched Joe through narrowed slits. He had said that he loved her, and he had never loved her. And he was standing in the doorway holding *her* rod.

Joe had not seen Anna. Quiet as a hawk, she circled behind him. He scanned the room and saw Edgar lying in a shining puddle of blood. He looked around. "Anna!" Silence. "Aaannaaa!" He tucked the gun into the back of his trousers and crouched before Edgar.

Edgar's blood was thickening on the knife in Anna's hand. She stole behind Joe in her bare, raw feet. She could wield her knife better if she didn't have to see his dimpled face. Anna slipped the wet blade against his throat. Joe's lids lowered and he stiffened. She put her lips to his ear. "If you move, I'll kill you. I'll probably kill you anyway." She could smell his deliciousness and feel the prickly stubble on his neck. She wanted to rake her teeth across it, but instead she said, "It was you all along. That's why you wouldn't investigate the murders."

Joe was balanced tightly on his toes and fingertips. He relaxed a bit when he heard her voice. Anna sensed it and bristled. How dare he think she wasn't dangerous? She deliberately stepped on his finger.

Joe tensed up again. "Ow."

She pushed harder on the knife. With one hand, she groped in his trousers for her gun and flung it, sending it spinning across the floor. It slid through the door into the dining room, making a clattering sound.

Joe's voice squeezed from beneath the knife. "Sherlock, Edgar Wright and I can't both be the murderer."

"That's right." She arched one eyebrow. "But he's afraid of cats, although I didn't realize it until after I stabbed him."

Joe swallowed. She let the knife follow his Adam's apple slightly up, then slightly down.

"Anna, you're not making any sense."

"Oh, no? He wants me! He's marrying me and taking me to Buenos Aires!" She ran the sharp blade across his stubble leaving a trail of hairless, agitated skin. She nicked him.

Joe winced as a trickle of blood ran down his neck—his blood mingled with Edgar's. "The clock is ticking, Sherlock. He's bleeding, and you know I didn't kill those girls. You're just mad about the prostitute."

"Hah!" Anna tugged on his mane, cocking back his neck, and met his angry, upside down eyes. They stared at each other, his grim, beautiful lips turned up in a cynical smile. He said she knew he didn't do it. But why? Because she'd loved him? Because her heart told her so? Her heart said he didn't sleep with prostitutes, and he most certainly did. But was Joe Singer a killer? What had she missed? Her hand shook.

"Anna, your lover boy's gonna bleed to death. Who you gonna run away with then? You say he's innocent. Let me take him to the hospital."

Anna's mind raced, rolling through their history, looking for an insight that would show her what to do. What had Joe said in Boyle Heights? He was neither for prostitution nor against it. It just was.

Anna's hand dropped. "You're too blasé about prostitution to get worked up enough to kill a girl."

Joe took the knife from her limp fingers. "Thank you." Anna went and leaned her forehead against the wall, while Joe got to his feet. When he saw her wedding dress, he narrowed his eyes. "You certainly are eager to marry Wright."

Anna's voice quivered. "As if you cared. I hoped you were in jail."

"The jailer let me escape so I could save you. And I'm gonna pay for it later."

"Good."

Joe chuckled mirthlessly. He picked Edgar up by the armpits, squatted, and heaved the big man over his shoulder, grunting with the effort. One of Edgar's blue silk slippers tumbled to the ground. Joe headed for the door. Anna followed Joe outside and down the porch steps to Edgar's truck, each step a needle on her sore soles.

The rims of two tires rested on the ground in puddles of rubber, not having survived the rocky road. Anna stomped her scraped foot and wiped a nervous tear. "Biscuits! Biscuits!"

Lulu's poison-green motorcycle sat in the drive. Anna's stomach clenched. Joe knew the madam well enough that she would let him borrow her motorcycle. He was a whoremonger. Joe hauled Edgar over and slid him carefully into the sidecar. Edgar slumped forward. Joe took off his coat and cushioned Edgar's head. He sounded pragmatic and so cool. "I'd like to take you Sherlock, but there isn't room. Find your gun. Lock up and hide. I'll come back for you."

Anna scrunched up her face and suppressed a sob, her shattered heart breaking all over again. He was a Beelzebub, but still, she wished he cared. She didn't want him to know, so she squatted down and gave Edgar's white lips a lingering kiss. Joe turned as pale as Edgar. He swung a leg over the seat and stood hard on one pedal. The motorcycle lurched forward. He pedaled off, becoming a shadow. Halfway down the drive, the motor caught and they were gone.

Anna was alone.

She went inside and locked the door. The lamp had gone out, leaving the parlor in darkness. She reached for it. It was slick with overspills of oil, and hot from burning. She jostled it, listening for the swish of liquid, but there was nothing. She would have to look for the oil jug, but first she would lock up. She locked the kitchen door and began to circle the house, downstairs, then upstairs, checking each window, one by one.

Who knew she had left with Edgar? The whole city by now. The red-light girls, the officers, the men in the street all saw her get into his truck. They would spread the word. If Joe could find her, the murderer could. Good. She wanted to trap the murderer. Now all she'd have to do was wait for him to come to kill her.

But who was she waiting for?

Her mind raced. She'd been wrong about Edgar. The killer might be a longtime resident. If the New High Street Suicide Faker had been active in LA prior to January, the victims were not brothel girls. He must have seduced and killed ordinary women. He had to seduce them, or they wouldn't make good Gomers for the Prophet of Doom.

If the early victims had been decent women, the coroner would never have covered for their killer. He would have reported a rash of murders thinly veiled as suicides, and Wolf would have investigated. But Wolf hadn't investigated. Why not? Because the murders weren't thinly veiled. They must have been thickly veiled.

The murderer skillfully hid his crimes prior to January, and now he hid them poorly. Why? Had he become careless or cocky? Did he want people to know he murdered the city's Gomers? It must be a terrible secret to keep. Possibly he felt proud of his crimes.

But he wasn't afraid to get caught. Did he suddenly feel immune to justice? And what made a man immune to justice in LA?

Money.

Then there was the sudden switch from ordinary women to parlor girls. They were beautiful, except for Joe's whore, and easier to obtain. They didn't have to be seduced. One only had to pay.

Anna knew who the murderer was.

If the murders had started one month earlier, she would have discounted him as a suspect. Money was the key.

Outside the window, a man stood on the porch steps. She'd been lost in reverie and hadn't heard a motor. Where was her gun? She'd forgotten to find it. It lay somewhere on the floor in the dining room. But the house doors were locked. If he cared to break one down, it would take time. Time enough for her to find the gun?

Anna flew to the stairs and down into the shadowed parlor. She scanned the room for her pistol, but the floor, with its rugs and furniture, was blanketed in darkness.

She heard the front doorknob rattle. Anna fell to her knees and crawled, frantically running her hands along the waxed parquet. Her heart pounded in her ears, rapid and irregular. There was a violent *bang*, as a man threw his weight against the door, then silence. *Bang. Bang.* Anna groped faster, as the banging continued, breathing like frightened prey, rivulets of sweat dripping down her face, her back, between her breasts. No gun.

With a *crack*, the door gave. Anna kept searching. She heard rustling in the foyer and then she saw him, a shadow sauntering into the parlor holding a bottle and one shoe. "Good evening, Anna."

She rose to her feet. "I was expecting you."

The man leaned casually against the wall. "Were you? How did you know?"

"You married Miss Curlew just before the first Poodle Girl died. You never set foot in a parlor house before January. You never had the coin. The parlor girls were out of reach, but the prostitutes in the crib were too ugly. So you killed ordinary girls. You were very clever at hiding it. But once you had the money, you weren't afraid to get caught. In fact, you wanted someone to know."

"Bravo. Go on."

"The LAPD's corrupt. If you came under suspicion, you thought you could bribe your way out of it. But you wanted the world to know that someone was cleaning up the town. I suspect you were disappointed when the coroner covered up your crimes."

"He did that? For me? How kind. I had come to the conclusion that the police were stupid. Anything else?"

"The police are stupid. But, yes. There's more. The day we eloped, I lost my shoe. I found it again on Peaches Payton's foot. You had gone back for it. The woman they found on the tracks that night—did you kill her, too?"

"You're good."

"I am. Then there was your British ancestry, your general lack of courtesy, and the rumors about your mother's affairs. She's the original Gomer."

He moved toward her. "You're a bit of floozy yourself, Aimee Amour."

Anna limped backward and began to mount the stairs one at a time, fumbling for each step with her stubbed toes and the pads of her scraped feet. He floated closer, his Cheshire cat grin reflecting the moonlight.

"You think you're Hosea, Prophet of Doom, saving the souls of loose women. But you're the Gomer, Louis. You slept with Miss Curlew, and no one would do that without getting paid."

"You bitch." A flame had caught in his eyes, and for the first time he had the look of a murderer. He kept coming, slowly, deliberately, placing each foot like a panther.

She reached the dark hallway at the top of the stairs. She turned her back on Louis and fled into Edgar's bedroom. She tried the window. If she jumped, and landed in the roses, she might survive the fall. She heaved at it, rattled it, but it was stuck with paint. Outside, she saw a future in the rows and rows of citrus trees. She jammed the nails of both hands into the cracks and pulled until her nails bent backward. She could feel the orange-scented air leaking through the gap, but the window wouldn't give.

Louis kept coming. Anna moved across to the bed, grabbed a goose-down pillow and, like a knight, held out her feather shield.

Louis laughed. "Look at you. You ran straight for the bed. But of course you would. I hear you slept with the police chief's son." He licked his lips.

"You're the whore, Louis. A prostitute. A floozy."

Louis growled and unbuttoned his coat. A trickle of sweat dripped down Anna's temple. Louis stalked her, his skin glistening, his eyes black and burning. She threw the pillow at his head and scuttled backward on the mattress like a crab. It missed. He looked amused. "How about Edgar Wright? You sure showed him."

"He loves me, and . . . and so does Joe Singer. If you touch a hair on my head, they'll settle their differences and kill you together." That was a lie, but she'd completely run out of ideas. She was flat against the oak headboard with nowhere else to go.

"From what I just saw, I don't think either man loves you anymore. No, they'll be relieved when you throw yourself in front of a train," he said. "No one will be surprised after what's happened. Everyone thinks you belong in the giggle-giggle ward. Especially Edgar."

"You're the lunatic." Anna dodged sideways.

"No!" Louis Taylor lunged and grabbed her ankles, yanking her flat onto her back. Red finger marks bloomed where his hands squeezed her. She tried to twist away, thrashing in her skirts, but he jammed his knee into her belly, forcing the wind out of her lungs. She gulped air, wheezing like punctured bellows, unable to catch her breath.

He relaxed the pressure a bit and looked at her with something like tenderness. It made her skin crawl.

"I'm not doing this to hurt you, Anna. I've always liked you. You'll die my faithful bride. Anna, you'll go to heaven."

She scoffed. "Does your wife know you're a murderous bigamist?"

His eyes went half-lidded. He jammed his knee deep into her diaphragm, forcing out her breath, sending out bolts of white-hot pain. Louis lowered his reddening face until their noses were touching and their lashes entangled. Anna clamped her trembling lips closed. Her eyes wondered at his demented ones. It was all very clear now. He was as mad as a March hare.

He put a hand around Anna's throat, leaning his fingers into the mattress, so that her breathing tapered to a faint rasp. With his other hand, he snatched a handkerchief from his pocket and reached for the bottle. He unscrewed it, tipping it onto the handkerchief one-handed. The liquid spread, wetting his fingers and turning the linen gray. Chloroform.

He was going to drug her, play groom with her. He would kill her and leave her body on the tracks and the papers would say that she had committed suicide. She would not be buried in a gown by Vionnet of the House of Doucet. Her gory, dripping pieces would be buried in the potter's field alongside the murdered brothel girls and others who had truly committed suicide. No one would mourn her. Everyone would tut tut because Anna Blanc had gone to hell. She would have descended from gold to silver to bronze to a slimy blob of damned rotten flesh. And she had thought her reputation could not get any worse.

Anna tried to wriggle free, but he pushed his knee deeper into her diaphragm, until she stopped breathing altogether. She struggled ineffectually, beating her hands on his back, and when she thought she would lose consciousness he eased off. She gasped, gulping air. Louis laughed. He brought the handkerchief with the chloroform down toward her face. Anna grabbed his arm, yanked it down to her mouth, and bit him, drawing blood. When he recoiled, she grabbed the chloroform bottle from the nightstand and smacked him over the head. The bottle shattered. Chloroform ran down his hair and dripped onto her face. Before she could spit, she blacked out.

Chapter 45

Someone was ringing a bell. It woke Anna. She lay supine on Edgar's slippery sheets and couldn't seem to complete a thought. She felt like a fishing weight. Each beat of her heart sent a painful rush of blood to her head. Her mouth tasted like cotton and Louis Taylor. She tried to suck saliva to spit him out, but couldn't. Her limbs were buzzing with sleep. She tried to wake them up, but they patently ignored her.

Ding. There was the bell again. She smelled kerosene burning, thick and heady, and saw the shadows of a lamp flickering on the ceiling. With effort, she was able to lift her chin. Louis Taylor sat beside her, his face flaring in shadow. He looked like a malignant spirit, one of the fallen angels who seduced the daughters of men. He held a little bell. "Do you remember the campañas at the Mission Inn?"

Anna didn't answer. She still wore her wedding gown, and on one foot she wore Eve's red shoe, which fit Anna loosely. She whimpered.

"You almost killed yourself with that chloroform, and you gave me a nasty headache," Louis said. There was a dark stain on one shoulder of his undershirt and a lump from a bandage. His eyes were dilated to black.

Anna cleared her throat, her voice raspy and raw. "Joe is coming back for me, and he's going to kill you."

Louis checked his pocket watch. "We have time. The nearest receiving hospital is twenty miles, and I siphoned most of the gas." He smiled.

Anna's stomach turned. Was Edgar stranded on a country lane, wounded and far from help? Would she ever see him alive again? How far could Joe carry him? Her dear, sweet Edgar—her savior, whom she had stabbed, clubbed with a chair, and bludgeoned between the legs, simply because he knew the Minor Prophets. Simply because he had loved her like Heathcliff, with a love that transcended betrayal. Would it now transcend death? And whose death? His or hers? Anna said a silent prayer to Philomena, patron saint of lost causes.

Louis gave a lift to his groomed eyebrows that she once would have thought debonair. "Would you like champagne?" He didn't wait for a reply but stood and crossed the room out of sight. Anna worked on her fingers, running her thumbs across their tingling tips. She made a fist with her left hand. She could move her arms a little, though they were cold with pins and needles. Both legs were numb. How long would it be before she could feel them again? She needed time so she could fully wake up and fight.

Louis was coming back with two bubbling flutes. She lay still. He sat beside her and lifted her hand, cradling it in his own. He turned her hand and drew a slow figure eight on her bare palm. She shivered in utter repulsion. He smoldered at her. Then he slapped her. Her cheek stung like a sunburn rubbed with sand. Adrenalin shot through her body and her eyes watered. She found she could wiggle her toes. "How are you going to kill me?" She flexed first one foot and then the other.

"Do you have a preference?"

He put Anna's champagne glass to her lips and tipped it. She swished the drink in her mouth and then spit out the bubbly pink, blood-wine mixture. It burbled over her lower lip and dribbled down her chin. Louis winced and wiped her face.

"I prefer that you don't kill me," she said. "But, if you insist, don't slit my throat. It's ugly."

"All right. But it's not as if you're going to have a wake. I'm throwing your dead body in front of a train."

She tensed her calves and released. "Oh please don't. That's even worse. And not fire. Burning is the most painful death."

"All right, no train, not fire. That leaves . . . what?"

"Carbon monoxide poisoning, natural gas . . . You could throw me off a cliff. A high one, please." She commanded her thighs to contract and they obeyed her.

"I'm not prepared for that," he said. "And we're running out of time." He smiled. "Strangling is quick." He ran a finger down her cheek and along her jaw. He put his hands around her throat. She gritted her teeth.

He laughed and moved his hands to graze her collarbone. "Not yet, my queen."

Anna found she could move her arms a little, though they still felt like they belonged to someone else. She lifted her right arm a discreet inch and let it drop. Her legs had no strength. Once more, she scanned the vicinity for a weapon. There was nothing on the table now but the oil lamp and a large jug of kerosene that Louis must have used to refill it.

Louis sat back in his chair and sighed. "Anticipation is half the pleasure."

Anna flung out her rag doll arm and knocked over the kerosene. It chugged out of the bottle, running across the tablecloth and down Louis's shirt, filling the room with its heady odor. It poured onto his lap and down onto the carpet. He jumped to his feet. "You've ruined my trousers!"

Anna closed her clumsy fingers over the tablecloth and yanked. The lamp tipped and tumbled, rolling to the edge of the table. The globe smashed onto the floor. For a moment, the flame reflected off the shards, sending a hundred tiny lights dancing on the ceiling. Then, the burning wick touched the wet cloth. The fabric caught and the table exploded into flame. Across the spreading fire, Louis looked at Anna with saucer eyes. His trousers caught. He dropped onto the floor and rolled, a marshmallow on fire. Flames crawled across the saturated carpet. The bed curtains caught. The feather tick caught. Maybe Anna would die by fire after all, but she would not die alone. She would take Louis Taylor with her. She slithered off the bed and rolled onto the floor, her legs jelly. Tiny black feathers flew on drafts around the room. She inhaled one and coughed, pushing it out of her mouth with her tongue. She dragged herself toward the stairs, away from the spreading flames.

Chapter 46

Anna lay in the dirt and crunchy leaves beneath Edgar's orange trees, a half resurrected phoenix, hiding from the firemen and reporters who would inevitably come, drawn by the smoke. Her face was black. Her thighs and forearms stung, scraped from crawling on her belly through a flaming house and onto the gravel drive. Her smoky hair fell down her back in a frizzy mess. Her wedding dress was black with soot, with several large holes in the back where falling cinders had burned all the way through her drawers. No doubt her bottom was as black as any bottom at the Octoroon.

Anna heard a motor and saw Joe Singer ride up on Lulu's motorcycle with the sidecar empty. He held his head and yelled, but his words were lost in the *whoosh* of the flames. His face contorted in anguish. He bolted to the water trough and jumped in, wetting his hair and clothes. Anna stood. What was he doing? He charged back to the porch. He must think she was in the house. She hoped the wanton cur felt guilty.

Joe leapt onto the porch holding his wet shirt over his mouth, peering into the parlor. Smoke streamed from the windows. He doubled over, coughing. He would be hurt if he stayed on the porch. Anna stood and called to him, "I'm here! Here I am!" Her words were lost in the roar of the fire.

Anna said a silent prayer to Saint Rose of Lima, patron saint of the vain, that no firemen or reporters would arrive because of the smoke and see her ebony face or her bare, blackened bottom now visible through the holes in her wedding dress. She picked her way across the rocky drive in her tender bare feet and wobbly legs. She felt the breeze on her derrière and the jiggle-jiggle of her body as she hopped along without a corset.

Anna gave a cry of horror as Joe dropped to his knees and crawled inside the burning house. The faithless Beelzebub had trounced her heart, yet there he was, risking his life to save her. She couldn't sort it out. She began to run on the sharp gravel, suddenly covered in sweat, her heart pounding. "Joe!"

Anna watched as the roof of the veranda caught fire. She stumbled to a stop at the porch. If she went inside after him, she would likely burn to death, and burning was the most painful way to die. There would be no grave for Anna Blanc in the potter's field. Her ashes would be mingled with those of Louis Taylor's, and they would blow into the orchard, fertilize the oranges, and be eaten by the people of Los Angeles. She might save Joe, but more likely, he would become orange juice too. If she didn't go inside and tell him to stop looking for her, he would be orange juice for certain.

Joe Singer would die for her. She would live on to tell the world his heroic story. She would write a book about his glorious sacrifice. It was a rather stupid thing to do, to crawl into a burning building, but she wouldn't say that in the book. Nor would she mention the prostitute.

A beam crashed from the upper floor, crushing half the porch into cinders. Anna screamed, and then screamed his name over and over. There was no decision to be made now. Joe Singer, the hero and the profligate, was certainly doomed if he wasn't dead already.

And so, Anna did what any girl would do in her situation. She dodged around the flaming beam, dropped to her knees, and slithered head first into the burning death trap.

The stairs were obscured by a mushroom of black smoke. One wouldn't know that the sun had risen. She saw her gun on the floor and thought how useful it would have been to have had it earlier. She would not have had to light Louis Taylor on fire and spoil Edgar's farm. She crawled closer to the blaze. Though she was breathing, there was very little air. She breathed faster, coughing and breathing, her cheeks and eyes burning. The Franz Bischoff painting of the coast was burning, the cypress trees curling into the cliffs.

Beneath the plein-air masterpiece, she saw Joe's feet on a thick Persian rug. They weren't burned, but they were no longer crawling.

Anna crawled faster and grabbed him by his boots. She tucked her skirts into her drawers. Like a burro pulling a yoke, she turned her back to him, put his legs across her shoulders and hauled him feet first and face down out across the parlor floor. The rug dragged along under him. He began to kick. Anna held tight. She pulled him into the foyer, over the bumpy threshold, and out of the house. She hopped off the edge of the burning porch and dragged him after her. He fell three feet into the rose bushes on his magic carpet, his face swinging down with a thud. Anna fell forward on the gravel drive onto her scraped and bloody knees. She stood and grabbed the rug, tugging with both hands, pulling him out of the thorns and away from the house toward the trees.

The top floor came down in an explosion of heat, smoke, and cinders. It shot out a blast of hot air and sparks that singed Anna's eyebrows and hair, leaving pieces short or missing altogether. She pulled harder, faster, her bare, skinless soles caked with gravel. She was thrown forward by another blast. A wheel from Lulu's motorcycle, folded in two like a taco, flew over her and penetrated a tree in front of them. She kept moving.

And then the ground was soft. She stepped on a squishy, moldy orange. They were in the orchard. The air was cleaner and she could breathe. She rolled Joe onto his back and loosened his collar. She undid the buttons on his shirt, then the buttons on his undershirt, just to be sure. His bare chest rose up, and went down, up and down. She laid her cheek on his belly and sobbed. She sobbed until she slept.

"Holy . . . Holy drawers," a male voice said.

It roused Anna from sleep. She lay across Joe Singer. She thought she'd heard him praying—a very good sign. She opened her eyes to the morning light and saw the boots. Twelve shiny ones. Anna tilted back her sleepy, sooty face and let her eyes follow the boots to their occupants and the speaker of the words. Not a man looked at her face. The volunteer fire brigade and two reporters were staring down through the large holes in her wedding dress and the big holes in her drawers, at her bare, black bottom.

One snapped a picture.

Chapter 47

When Mr. Blanc opened his paper the next morning, Anna's bottom was on the front page, accompanied by the true story of her adventures in the brothel—that is to say, Anna's version of the story as explained to a very romantic cop from Pasadena, as he explained it to a *Los Angeles Herald* reporter over the phone. The article told about the dead and missing girls, how no one at the LAPD believed her, how Eve's death had driven her to the brothels to hunt for her killer, how she had solved the crime on her own, slain Louis Taylor, and saved Joe Singer from a fiery death, then selflessly saved him again by being his blanket when he was in shock. She left out the part about stabbing Edgar, as it didn't reflect well on her detection abilities, and he might not want the world to know that he had lost a fight to a girl.

Mr. Blanc didn't read the article, but the rest of Los Angeles did. Though some readers said Anna's behavior represented a terrible breach of decorum, many women in Los Angeles felt a certain pride on her behalf. Most men framed the picture of Anna's bottom and hid it from their wives. Everyone had an opinion and everyone was talking about her.

Anna missed the article. When the papers hit the newsstands, she was driving her yellow convertible through the mustard gold hills of California, heading for the spiritualist colony at Summerland, looking like a fairy that had fallen into a campfire. She congratulated herself on having had the foresight to take two dollars from Joe's pocket. Now she had money for Coca-Cola and gas. She had also stolen Joe's shoes, which fit her bandaged feet like canoes. He didn't need them, as he was horizontal and unconscious.

Madam Lulu and Charlene had delivered Anna's car to the Pasadena police station, bearing the news that the crowd had re-gathered at Canary Cottage, making it impossible for Anna to return. Anna didn't think Edgar would receive her after she'd tried to kill him. For a brief moment, she considered calling on the Breedloves. Of all the people in the world that Anna had loved, Clara was the only one that Anna was sure had truly loved her back. But Clara had surely dropped her. Clara would never approve of her stabbing Edgar, because Clara was not that kind of girl.

Anna took a swig of Coca-Cola and wished it were brandy. Without Clara, Anna's life could never be more than half worth living. They had been a two-woman sorority united against the Miss Curlews of the world—partners in subverting every cruel repression under Anna's dictator father. When Anna had needed books, whiskey, or an alibi, Clara had provided. When Clara had to visit her spiritualist aunt's haunted house, Anna had been there, brandishing her crucifix.

But now, other than some very nice prostitutes, Anna was friendless and utterly alone.

When the second article about Anna appeared in the paper, which featured Joe's side of the story, she was smashing a window at Clara's dead aunt's empty beach house. Unlike people, ghosts didn't care about tattered reputations, ruined fortunes, and mistakes one might make with a paring knife.

The house was full of furniture covered in sheets. There was an organ, a sonorous grandfather clock, and framed photographs of the aunt with ghostly images of transparent dead people hovering around her. There was a windowless room for séances, stairs and doors leading absolutely nowhere, and a library of spooky books—*The Salem Seer* and *Eusapia Palladino and Her Phenomena*. It was deliciously creepy, but not somewhere one would choose to sleep alone. She would have felt very safe with a policeman in her bed—one that could sing her to sleep with lullabies. She bit her lip and banished the thought.

Anna hadn't eaten in two days. Her stomach panged and she headed for the kitchen. The cupboards brimmed with crackers, pickles, canned peaches, jars of peanut butter and, to Anna's delight, several tins of kippers. Anna stuffed a salty dill pickle into her mouth and bit it like an enormous cigar. She opened a can of fish, slipped an oily creature into her mouth, and chewed it with the pickle. She moaned with pleasure. Three giant cucumbers and ten kippers later, she was satisfied.

Anna was too tired to see ghosts. Only Joe Singer appeared in her dreams, and in them he had left her for Helmut Melvin. She cried and cried in her sleep. Anna slept all night, all the next day, and into the following evening.

She awoke to the sound of footsteps on the stairs and sat up in bed. The door creaked open. A dark figure stood there, barely visible on the threshold. Anna rubbed her bleary eyes. Maybe Louis Taylor had come to apologize.

She reached for her crucifix and held it high. "Be gone, oh restless spirit!"

The ghost giggled.

Anna's arm dropped. "Clara? What are you doing here?"

"Oh, Dearest! When we saw your picture in the paper, we searched everywhere for you. Theo's been combing the brothels since the raid. But of course you'd come here."

"That's why Theo was at Canary Cottage." Anna blew out a long breath. She looked sideways at Clara. "You're talking to me? Looking for me? Are you here to tell me we can never speak again?"

"Oh, Dearest." Clara's face flushed and scrunched up. She came and sat next to Anna, wiping tear after tear off her rosy cheeks. "I've been a terrible friend." She sniffed. "I should love you no matter what your career is or who's seen your bottom, and I do. I think you're heroic." She kissed Anna's stunned face. "Forgive me?"

Anna slipped her arms around Clara's waist and squeezed her tight. "You're good."

"You're famous now."

"Infamous." Anna laughed and put her head on Clara's shoulder. "So is Enid Curlew."

Clara and Anna spent the next week wading at the beach and digging through the aunt's drawers for incriminating personal items, while Clara's maid packed old knickknacks in boxes. In the evenings, they ate canned fish and pickles and watched the sun set from the porch. They drank every drop of the dead aunt's whiskey.

Clara told Anna all that had happened in her absence. A girl from the club had a bun in the oven. Clara's sister-in-law had learned a new card game. Miss Curlew-Taylor had gone into hiding. Anna told Clara about her adventures in the brothels, what it felt like to kill a man, and what Joe Singer could do with his tongue. She told her that she never really knew Edgar until the end, how he had never once kissed her, but how she loved him for all he had done and would think of him whenever she smelled petunias.

The next morning, Anna drove Clara and her maid to the train station in Santa Barbara. Theo was expecting them home. Anna planned to stay at the beach house until she had eaten every last cracker and pickle, at which time she would have nothing to eat and would have to return to Los Angeles. Hopefully, by then people would have forgotten her.

As soon as Clara's train was puffing its way down the coast, Anna went to the post office. She sent a letter to Edgar, begging his forgiveness for thinking he was a murderer and for all the rest, and saying how lucky it was that he looked so splendid in his chinoiserie robe and matching slippers, because otherwise she would have left her eyes open when she stabbed him and wouldn't have missed. She said she was very sorry, but she could not marry him, but asked if she could call on him when she returned to LA. Edgar did not reply.

Late one afternoon, Anna padded up the steps from the beach, all salty and rosy in one of the dead aunt's swimsuits. She wore it without stockings, exhibiting her bare, sun-kissed shins for anyone to see. But the houses on the bluff were empty. There was no one to see, just the purple islands in the distance and the oilrigs adorning the ocean like tarnished silver filigree.

She reached the crest of the yellow hill, cooled by the ocean breeze on wet wool, the tired sun warming her legs, and heard a man singing.

> She'll spoon you for a collar.
> She's a menace with a paring knife.
> Her bottom's black and famous
> and she'll burn a man alive.

Joe Singer sat on the dead aunt's porch railing, holding a burlap sack, his face pink in spots from where the scabs had been after she dragged him across the driveway on his face. Still, he looked good enough to eat and Anna tingled. She had to steel herself.

Joe stopped singing. He looked down at her shins and let out a low, scandalized whistle. "I could arrest you for that, Miss Blanc."

She tossed her singed, uneven hair. "Do you wear stockings when you swim, Officer Singer? I guess not. And you're out of your jurisdiction. I can do anything I want. I could swim naked . . ." Anna mentally kicked herself.

"I'd like to see you try." He gave her his "mocking Anna" smile.

Anna glowered at him. She didn't have to be nice. She owed him nothing for his misguided heroism. She had saved him, not the other way around. She crossed her arms over her chest. "Why have you come? Shouldn't you be with your brothel girl? She was ugly by the way."

Joe chuckled bitterly. "Shouldn't you be with Edgar Wright?"

She lifted her chin. "I would be, but . . ."

"Oh, that's right. You stabbed him." He smirked. "You know, Anna, I'm glad you think I sleep with prostitutes, because if you didn't, the next time you needed something you'd be giving me your Juliet line, and I'd probably fall for it."

Anna's eyes flared. "Are you trying to deny you sleep with brothel girls? I caught you red-handed!"

"Did you?"

"Yes!"

His stare was cold. She had to look away. "Why did you come here bothering me?"

"It's nothing personal. I'm supposed to track you down. Captain Wells wants you back."

Anna's face lit up like Chinese New Year. "Really?"

Joe tossed her the burlap bag. She caught it in her hand, reached into the sack, and pulled out a wad of red fabric—Peaches' whoring outfit. She had left it on the floor in Joe's apartment, along with Lulu's blonde wig.

"I don't suppose you're gonna return my best suit," he said.

His suit was now ash, and Anna was glad. She ignored the comment and held up the dress. It, too, was ruined, the filmy fabric torn diagonally up the back in two frayed pieces. She gave him a puzzled look.

"I commandeered it and Melvin ripped it. On behalf of the LAPD, I apologize." He mocked her with a deferential incline of his head. "Captain Wells said he'd give you two new matron's uniforms in compensation, since you go through them so fast, if you'll come back."

Anna blinked at the tattered dress. "Mr. Melvin ripped it? You did a sting? You . . ."

She glanced up at Joe and held her breath. Joe looked away, as aloof as the real Arrow Collar Man. "Big Cindy said the doggy wig was Lulu's so Melvin left it on the bed."

Anna's mind whirred. What had she seen that night in the Mystery Man's shadowy room? A lock of blonde hair. The outline of a body in a dress. A tiny rouged mouth . . .

Anna let out an anguished cry. Joe Singer hadn't been with a prostitute. He'd been undercover, helping her solve the case. That ugly girl had been baby-mouthed Mr. Melvin. Anna grabbed the porch rail to steady herself, reeling under the weight of her mistake. Hadn't she known it in her heart? Joe wasn't a Beelzebub. No. He was an angel. She could have loved him all along. But now he looked like a wrathful angel—the kind that carried swords and didn't accept apologies.

Anna's brows drew together in an anguished appeal. "I'm sorry! I couldn't have known."

He smiled a crooked, vinegar smile and heaved himself to his feet. "Don't be, Sherlock. You would've run off anyway, the first time Edgar Wright whistled. This way it was a little easier on my ego." He swept up the bag and took the porch steps two at a time.

"Oh, please. Don't go yet."

Joe turned and waited, his lids lowered. There was something flickering beneath the hostility, some tiny light, and though Anna couldn't name it, it made her hope. She smiled with all her sugar sweetness, desperate to hold his attention but fearing she could not and that she never really had. "We should … It would be swell if we could … debrief about the case."

A shadow passed over Joe's face, and the tiny light extinguished. He let loose a joyless guffaw. "The case." He pivoted and sauntered down the drive.

Anna's voice broke. "I'll see you at the station, then?"

He called back over his shoulder. "Nope. I'll be patrolling the streets of San Diego."

This news shook Anna like an earthquake, and a panicky feeling rose in her chest. All she wanted in the world was to be in those indignant arms, kissing those lovely, smirking lips, and other things. And to fight crime. But Joe Singer was leaving her.

She had to stop him. Anna scrambled after Joe and grabbed his sleeve. "What do you mean you're leaving Central Station? I need you! You're the only man I've ever loved."

He removed her hand from his coat. "You said that before, Anna. Right before you eloped with somebody else. Where were you going? Buenos Aires?"

"But you were sleeping with Mr. Melvin! And you didn't want me!"

Joe threw up his hands. "Of course I wanted you! Every man in LA wants you. So don't worry, Sherlock. Just wait a minute and something better will come along."

Anna's cheeks burned like they'd been slapped. "If you loved me, you had a funny way of showing it. You could have told me you were going to the brothel!"

"Tell you I was in the brothel? Hah! You said you could never marry a man who went to a brothel for *any* reason."

"Yes, I definitely wouldn't! Sometimes! But other times . . ."

"Like when he's Edgar Wright? Well Anna, I have a confession. Every day for four months Lulu's pianist gave me lessons on her Steinway. And I don't regret it! How do you like that? Well, my father didn't. But I never slept with any of the girls." Joe continued walking, leaving Anna stunned in the drive.

"I don't care!"

Joe didn't stop. Her eyes welled with tears. "Fine! Just . . . just go. I hope you get eaten by a great white shark. And don't you ever try to tell me what to do!" Anna lifted her skirt and defiantly showed off her shins. "Officer Singer! Look!" Joe didn't look. She lifted her skirt above her knees. "Officer Singer!" He kept on walking.

Anna was both desperate to hold him and determined not to be ignored. If he got away now, she might lose him forever. She must act decisively and confess later. Anna struggled with the buttons on her swimsuit and stripped out of it. She chased after Joe and threw it at his head. It landed with a *splat*, like a wet nightcap.

Joe spun sharply. He saw her standing in the yard in wet underwear, and his eyes widened. His head snapped to the house next door and back to Anna. "No!"

"You can't boss me!" She sprinted for the cliff, peeling her corset cover over her head, her wet petticoats sticking to her legs. Joe bolted after her, scooping up her sandy, dripping clothes and tucking them under his arm. "Damn it, Anna! You have neighbors!"

"Yes! A whole family of spinsters. They'll drop dead from shock, and I don't care!" Anna shed a soggy petticoat. She pattered down the steps that led from the grassy bluff to the beach below in her remaining petticoat, the color of her skin visible through the wet white fabric. She raced to the bottom, across the shifting sand and toward the water, spooking a baby elephant seal. It loped off barking.

Joe caught up to Anna at the water and yanked her by the corset strings. "Put your clothes on!" He grabbed her arm and wrestled it through the sleeve of her corset cover, while Anna used her other hand to pull her last petticoat down to her knees.

He reached down to pull up her petticoat, while Anna unhooked the front of her corset. When he went to fix her corset, Anna untied her drawers. Joe tackled her and she landed on her bottom. He pushed her flat on the wet sand and straddled her, pinning her wrists. He breathed peppermint breath onto her face and shouted. "What do you want from me, Sherlock? How do I get you to stop torturing me?"

Anna let loose a string of teary hiccups. "Write me a nicer song! One where I'm not a homicidal vamp. Say I spooned you for love. Not for a collar."

He shook his head. "Then give me some material, Sherlock. You gotta stop breaking my sorry heart!"

"Don't go to San Diego! I'll spoon you for love. I'll make love and kiss you and . . . and give you material."

Joe's eyes dropped to her unhooked corset and the wet cotton clinging haphazardly to her hips. He closed his eyes and inhaled. "Oh, Lord." He searched Anna's face. "Don't lie to me."

"I'm not!" She bit her lip. "Well, I lied about the spinsters. There's nobody for miles, except fish and . . ."

Joe kissed her.

Acknowledgments

I would like to thank my husband, Jonathan, for his unfailing support.

Many thanks to Neil Blair and Zoe King at the Blair Partnership (TBP) for being extraordinary agents and fighting my fight. I'd especially like to thank Liz Bonsor of TBP for discovering my work and tracking me down on LinkedIn. Your confidence in my novel, your suggestions, and your support made all the difference.

I'd also like to thank everyone at Seventh Street Books (SSB) for being so good at what they do—Dan Mayer for his gentle, insightful edits, Jill Maxick for patiently enduring my wacky efforts to promote the book, Nicole Sommer-Lecht for her amazing cover design, Sheila Stewart for diligently checking the facts, Cheryl Quimba for publicizing the book, and my fellow SSB authors for their advice.

Without my writer's group, the Denver Writer's Workshop, there would be no novel. A special thanks to members Ethan Elliot, Gary Patterson, Mary Villalba, Dave Durkee, Karen Smith, Jamie Gordon, Jenny Peterson, Heather Bell, and Brock Wood. They taught me how to write. Thanks also to everyone who reviewed the manuscript and encouraged me—David Weiss, Stephanie Manuzak, Christa Jorgensen Shorey, Joe Weber, Cassi Clark, Livia Harper, and especially Susan Ludes and LA historian AnneMarie Kooistra. Thanks to authors Quincy Allen and M. H. Boroson for your advice and support.

Thanks to my sisters, Erin, Lisa, and Kristi, and my mother, Sandy, for cheering me on.

Lastly, I'd like to thank my readers for taking a chance on a new author. If you liked this book, please spread the word. Tell a friend. Post on Facebook. Write a review. It's the number one way readers find new authors.

About the Author

Jennifer Kincheloe is a research scientist turned writer of historical mysteries, formerly on the research faculty at UCLA. She grew up running wild on the beaches of Southern California. She now lives in Denver, Colorado, with her husband and two children. *The Secret Life of Anna Blanc* is her first novel.

COUNTY LIBRARY
TILLAMOOK, ORE.
DISCARD